PRAISE FOR KATHLEEN KENT'S

THE DIME

NOMINATED FOR THE EDGAR AWARD FOR BEST NOVEL

NAMED ONE OF THE BEST BOOKS OF THE YEAR BY THE *DALLAS OBSERVER, BOOKRIOT*

"One of the most breathless, inventive, and—be forewarned—violent suspense plots I've read in a long time."
—Maureen Corrigan, *Fresh Air* (NPR)

"Kathleen Kent finds the noir side of Dallas...Betty Rhyzyk is an engaging twist on traditional tropes. Sure, she has to deal with soul-corroding police matters...but she also brings freshness and new energy to the role...There's no shortage of Pine Curtain gothic in this landscape of mangy dogs, religious nuts, and violent meth-heads."
—Doug J. Swanson, *Dallas Morning News*

"Exciting...Grisly but likable."
—Tom Nolan, *Wall Street Journal*

"Smart, gritty, and populated by a rogue's gallery of unforgettable characters, *The Dime* is relentless. As it races full bore its way toward a climax that's truly creepy, the best you can do is hang on—and it's a hell of a ride."
—Kelly Braffet, author of *Save Yourself*

"Kent is an effective storyteller and an acute social observer, with a sharp eye for Texas-size absurdities."
—Rob Latham, *Los Angeles Review of Books*

"Terrific...Kent's ability to avoid predictable outcomes and keep the reader on edge bodes well for future installments in this series." —Lloyd Sachs, *Chicago Tribune*

"The broader appeal is Kent's offbeat humor, which pulls up reins just before it takes the story off a cliff."
—Marilyn Stasio, *New York Times Book Review*

"I loved *The Dime*. Betty is my hero. Smart, determined, and so unique. The writing is as smooth as Texas spring water, and the story grabs you by the throat and drags you happily through a briar patch of surprise and excitement and leaves you exhausted under the Dallas skyline. More please!" —Joe R. Lansdale, author of *Jackrabbit Smile*

"Only a fan blowing in the right direction could flip the pages of this lightning-paced tale any faster. It may be her crime fiction debut, but Kathleen Kent writes with the hard-boiled confidence of a veteran...Betty is buff, brave, and believable. She is a terrific, fully realized addition to her genre." —Maureen McCarthy, *Minneapolis Star-Tribune*

"Gritty and gripping, explosive and emotional, Kathleen Kent's *The Dime* grabs you from its opening scene and never lets go. Kent tears off the glossy facade of Dallas to show us a dark underbelly of crime. A great start of an exciting new series."
—Jeff Abbott, author of *The First Order*

"As hard to forget as Kent's main character is, the breakout star is the city of Dallas."
—Rachel Williams, *Dallas Observer*

"Kent knows her craft. *The Dime*'s tight plotting and masterful suspense is no surprise."
—Ginni Beam, *D Magazine*

"Violent, sexy, and completely absorbing. Kent's detective is Sam Spade reincarnated—as a brilliant, modern woman...The mystery succeeds as both whodunit and as a deeper character-driven novel. Kent neatly balances the tough talk and high body count of a traditional hard-boiled detective novel, reminiscent of Raymond Chandler and Dashiell Hammett, with the modern strength of this complex, flawed, and interesting woman...Every layer of this novel strikes the right note."
—*Kirkus Reviews*

"Outstanding...Kent never sacrifices robust characters, or biting humor, during scenes of brutal violence, which, though disturbing, are essential to the rich plot."
—*Publishers Weekly*

"Kent explodes into the crime genre with a detective who has all the qualities that'll make her stand out from the crowd...Kent's brilliant, sometimes gentle and humorous observations humanize and set this book apart."
—Barbara Clark, *BookPage*

"This fast-paced, adrenaline-producing suspense novel will appeal to Karin Slaughter fans."
—Sharon Mensing, *Library Journal*

"Betty is a terrific character...A worthy addition to the ranks of strong female detectives."

—Jane Murphy, *Booklist*

"Kent has written a brilliant detective with hard edges and heart while striking the perfect balance of humor, violence, action, and procedural." —Jamie Canaves, *BookRiot*

"In *The Dime,* Kathleen Kent introduces an exciting new force in the crime-thriller world: Detective Betty Rhyzyk. You probably can't pronounce her last name, but she doesn't give a shit; she'd more likely roundhouse kick you in the ear for your stupidity. Betty comes from a long line of battle-hardened NYC cops, but when she dives into the criminal world of Dallas, Texas, Betty quickly realizes that she ain't in Brooklyn anymore. The tension escalates to a shattering, shocking conclusion that will take Betty to the very edge of what she can endure, physically and psychologically. Kent masterfully draws upon the rich tapestry of neo-noir Dallas, a city of grit, glitter, and guns, that hasn't had its proper treatment in contemporary crime fiction. Until now." —Matthew Bondurant, author of *The Wettest Country in the World*

THE DIME

ALSO BY KATHLEEN KENT

The Outcasts
The Traitor's Wife
The Heretic's Daughter

THE
DIME

KATHLEEN
KENT

MULHOLLAND
BOOKS

Little, Brown and Company
New York Boston London

Copyright © 2017 by Kathleen Kent

Hachette Book Group supports the right to free expression and the value of copyright. The purpose of copyright is to encourage writers and artists to produce the creative works that enrich our culture.

The scanning, uploading, and distribution of this book without permission is a theft of the author's intellectual property. If you would like permission to use material from the book (other than for review purposes), please contact permissions@hbgusa.com. Thank you for your support of the author's rights.

Mulholland Books / Little, Brown and Company
Hachette Book Group
1290 Avenue of the Americas, New York, NY 10104
mulhollandbooks.com

Originally published in hardcover by Mulholland Books, February 2017
First Mulholland Books mass market edition, January 2019

The publisher is not responsible for websites (or their content) that are not owned by the publisher.

ISBN 978-0-316-48928-7
LCCN 2015956806

10 9 8 7 6 5 4 3 2 1

OPM

Printed in the United States of America

For Jim

A patient woman can roast an ox with a lantern.

—Chinese proverb

THE DIME

1

From my position in the hallway—on my ass, head pressed against the door frame, legs drawn up with my gun held two-handed against my sternum—I try to recall the layout of the room: three sets of bunk beds, four corpses sprawled across bloodied sheets, my partner, shot three times, lying motionless next to the nearest bunk, and, somewhere in there, one lunatic, a screaming infant in one hand and a semiautomatic pistol in the other. The last time I sneaked a look around the open doorway, he fired at me, the bullet knocking a crater in the wall opposite. He followed up by threatening to shoot the baby and then himself.

I've been a cop for five months, one week, and nine and a half hours.

It was the crying baby that brought us to the apartment in the first place. Dispatch had gotten a call from the super of a three-story residential building on Norman Avenue of four shots fired inside one of the top-floor apartments. My partner, an older, more experienced Brooklyn cop named Ted O'Hanlon, and I were only minutes away.

The stairway was narrow up to the second floor, and several neighbors, mostly thick-waisted women and some small kids, were milling around, more curious than frightened. Ted had told everyone to clear the hallway, to stay inside their apartments, and we climbed cautiously to the third floor, hands on our service pistols.

We could hear the baby crying as soon as we reached the landing. It was a healthy, steady cry that made me think no one was holding it. The super had let us know that the place opposite the possible shooter's apartment was empty, so no chance of a neighbor stumbling out at the wrong time.

Approaching the apartment, we saw that the door was open a small crack, and as we drew our weapons, Ted called out, "NYPD. Hello? Everybody okay?"

Ted had approached the door slowly, on point, and he palmed it open with his left hand.

"Jesus," he'd said.

I was right behind him, and, being taller than him by several inches—at five eleven, I'm taller than a lot of the men in my squad—I got a good look inside. A pristine, almost sterile living room with the three bunk beds set against three separate walls. Written in orange spray paint above each top bunk and again in giant letters on the gray-ing linoleum covering the floor was the word *Uplifted*. Crude, childlike drawings of winged stick figures were painted onto the struts of the beds. Pale sunlight, spilling in from the rear kitchen window, made everything in the room appear hazy and indistinct. There was no movement, no sound except for the baby wailing.

There were four people in the first two sets of bunks,

two females and two male youths, all dressed alike in dark blue sweat suits, their arms neatly crossed over their chests, all shot in the head. There was a larger figure completely covered with a gory blanket on the lower bed of the third bunk. Next to the bulky shape was the baby, red-faced and squalling.

My partner motioned to me to stay in the doorway and instructed me to call Dispatch for backup and medical. Then Ted, a man who had once jumped into the icy waters of Newton Creek in a January snowstorm to save a stray dog, turned his attention to the baby.

And then I remembered the super had said he'd heard four shots, not five. My mouth opened to warn him when the bulky figure under the blanket reared up and fired three rounds at Ted, hitting him squarely in his torso.

Instinctively, I threw myself to the floor and scrabbled into the safety of the hallway as he fired in my direction. I waited for him to rush me, but instead he started pacing frantically, ranting in the kind of fiery, talking-in-tongues nonsense of manic televangelists— *"Bara oona beresh peka, beresh ontaba oona"*—interspersed with tuneless, agitated humming.

A few months of street patrol, giving out parking tickets and chasing kids pilfering oranges from a neighborhood fruit stand, did not prepare me for this. Backup was on its way, but much too slowly.

Benny, I think now. *What do I do?*

My uncle, a decorated homicide cop, mentor, and father figure who'd seen just about everything there was to see on the streets of Brooklyn, had never, to my knowledge, said anything about a gun-wielding, baby-slinging, murdering cult guy.

But just like that, I hear Benny's voice in my head

telling me, *Betty, chaos in crazy people has its own pattern. You've got to break the pattern. Jam up the works.*

Some of his wisdom, remembered through the thick fog of fear.

The guy is chanting again. "Ready for uplift, ready for uplift…" His voice rising to a hysterical pitch. "The angel says be ready for uplift…"

I try to think about all the clues in the room. The drawings, the word *Uplifted* scrawled on the walls, what the victims are wearing. They're in sweat suits, but the shooter's got on a Mets jersey.

At the top of my lungs, I scream out, *"Fuck the Yankees."*

There is a pause in the squeaking of his shoes.

"That's right," I yell. "You heard me. Fuck the Yankees."

Even over the baby's shrill crying, I can sense him listening, straining to hear what I'll say next.

"That guy Clemens," I say. "Can you believe what he did? Slinging the bat like that at Mike? Did you see that game three months ago when he beaned Mike in the head?"

I'm soaking every word with as much disdain and outrage as I can summon, hoping to God, or whatever power is watching over the subway series the entire country is watching, that it's enough to distract this lunatic. I hear sirens approaching Norman Avenue. There'll be more officers here within four minutes, but that may be three minutes too late.

"He shouldn't have done that," the guy says sadly, like he's just lost his childhood pet.

"Right?" I say. "Hey, did you watch the whole game yesterday?"

It sounds like he's repositioning the baby, shushing it gently, as though he hasn't just been threatening to shoot it in the head. "Yeah," he says. "They oughtta do something about that guy Clemens."

"What did you say?" I call out. "I can't hear you so well over the baby crying."

I ease myself to a standing position, sliding up the door frame, taking deep breaths to quiet my shaking hands. The sirens are louder now, and I'm afraid the piercing sounds will only hasten the impending violence.

He yells, "They oughtta do something about Clemens! He's dangerous."

"He's a thug!" I yell back. And then, softly, "Too bad the Mets lost that one. The Mets can be such losers."

"What?" the guy calls out. "What'd you say?"

"Hey," I say, my cheek pressed hard against the door frame. "I really want to talk to you about the game. But, honestly, I can't hear what you're saying over the baby crying. You think you could set the baby down, just for a sec, so we can have a conversation?"

The guy's humming dangerously again, and it sounds like the responding officers, and probably the medical units, have arrived at the front of the building.

"Come on," I plead. "Just for a minute. Christ, all this crying's giving me a headache. Did you ever meet any of the Mets in person?"

There's a long pause and then he says, "I shook Piazza's hand once."

"No shit," I say, closing my eyes. "You shook Mike's hand?"

I can hear voices coming up the stairwell. My palms are sweating so bad that I'm afraid I'll drop the gun.

"Okay," the guy says. The tone of his voice is flat, all enthusiasm for baseball gone. "I'm going to set the baby down. She's tired. I need to put her to sleep first."

I risk a glance into the room. He's bending over the squirming infant, who he's placed on the bare floor. The gun is pointed at the baby.

He's saying, "And then we can talk about the Me—"

I fire six times, a tight cluster of body shots. He crashes heavily against one of the bunk beds and falls into a sitting position, legs spread wide. He jerks a few times and then slumps forward.

I melt onto the floor across from him, my legs too weak to hold me up anymore, and watch the guy's Mets shirt turn dark with the blood leaking from his chest. I'm afraid to look at Ted, not sure I want to see him not breathing. I can't even pick up the screaming baby for fear my rubbery arms will drop her.

The hallway floods with responding officers, guns drawn, who crash into the room swearing, incredulous at the scene in the apartment.

A young cop with acne on his neck mutters at me, "Holy shit, Rhyzyk, what'd you do?"

Then the medics are hovering over me, lifting me up and out into the hallway. They put Ted onto a stretcher—miraculously, he's still alive—and take him down to a waiting ambulance. Someone picks up the baby and she mercifully stops crying.

I'm questioned by the senior officer on the scene, who passes my Mets-Yankees story down the hallway. It reaches the cops on the street before I even exit the building.

Examined once again by the medics, this time in the second ambulance waiting at the curb, I'm quizzed by a ring of disbelieving, envious policemen who missed out on all the excitement.

The EMTs assure me that the doctors will do everything

they can for Ted. He regained consciousness while in transit and was asking to see his wife, they tell me.

Sergeant Stanek shows up and looks me over in an embarrassingly concerned manner.

"So," he says, wagging a finger in my face, "I hear you took the Yankees' name in vain. I ought to suspend you without pay for that one."

He offers me a ride to the hospital where Ted's been taken. And I gratefully accept.

Someone hands me a phone and I call my uncle Benny at the Ninety-Fourth Precinct.

"Poor bastard," he says about the shooter after I finish filling him in on what happened. "He got stuck in the abyss of his own morass." There's a pause while he listens to my breathing. "You okay?" he asks.

"Yeah," I answer, but I'm not so sure I am.

"That's the thing about cults," Benny says. "They not only dig the ditch, they lie in it, cover themselves over with dirt, and then cry about how dark the world has gotten."

I can hear someone in Benny's office trying to get his attention.

"Listen," he says. "I gotta go. What you need is a good meal, a hot bath, and a few Jamesons, right?"

I smile and agree with him.

"Now, tell me, is there any place in the world you'd rather be than Brooklyn? Tell me true."

And I assure him that, no, there's no place in the world I'd rather be. "Especially now that the Yankees are winning," I say. "Clemens may be a thug, but he's our thug."

He laughs gleefully. "And, Betty," he says, "you can call me anytime. I'll be here."

2

I think that the Mexican waiter behind the breakfast counter is kidding about Fuel City. I tell him I've been in the Lone Star State for only forty-eight hours and he says that if I want to see the real Dallas — *la verdadera ciudad,* the Dallas of truck drivers, Mexican laborers, lawyers, parolees, and cops mixed elbow to elbow with white privileged gringas driving expensive SUVs — I need to drive farther south, past the city jail, the bail bondsmen, and the highway construction sites, to Riverfront Street. There I'll find the beating heart of the city.

It's eleven o'clock when I walk back to my car, and already the elevated temperature is a monster wrapped around my head, all bristling mirrored scales, sliding tongues of sweat into my ears and down my neck. I go fishing in my pocket for my car keys, thinking how foolish it was to take a to-go cup of scalding coffee.

Driving the car down the Tollway toward Stemmons Freeway, I think of summers with my folks on the Jersey

Shore, Bradley Beach or Ocean Grove, where the water was always a few degrees from stroke-inducing cold, a frigid slap against sunburned skin that made me and my brother scream in outraged delight. Buoyed in the murky waves for hours, we swam, our untamed auburn hair floating out from our heads like scarlet seaweed in the strong ocean currents. At noon we'd eat the sandwiches my mother had made—beach picnics being the only time lunch for us kids wasn't five dollars and a note—and then run back into the waves, my mother screaming, "You'll give yourself a heart attack."

Jackie and I moved into our place only yesterday, a ground-floor, two-bedroom apartment with an outer breezeway, gated and locked at both ends. The thermostat by afternoon read 112 degrees. One of the movers, an off-duty fireman used to *Fahrenheit 451* temps in a Kevlar suit, passed out just outside our door. The air-conditioning unit in our bedroom gave up the Freon ghost by four o'clock, and Jackie and I floated in our own sweat the entire night, despite the electric fans we had placed on each side of our bed.

Texas, we were cheerfully informed by the apartment manager—himself a transplant from New Orleans—was evidently the only place in the known universe, including Louisiana, that actually got hotter after the sun went down.

"Holds the sun's rays like a giant warming plate," the manager warned.

Jackie, ever sunny-side up, responded, "It beats shoveling snow."

The manager looked at her, then at me, and smiled knowingly. "She's cute," he said, and walked away laughing.

As I drive toward Fuel City, the glass skyscrapers of downtown are to my left, the sun just above the tallest buildings. Reunion Tower, looking like a giant puffball on steroids, flares the sun like a supernova. Instinctively, I slow down near Dealey Plaza and wonder what it must be like growing up in a place where every visiting outsider, upon seeing the book depository for the first time, asks, "What's it like living in the city that killed JFK?"

My thoughts keep returning to my uncle Benny, once robust and capable, spending his last days in hospice care. The man had been burly—there could be no better word to describe him. My father's younger brother, a cop with the Ninety-Fourth Precinct his whole life, never bothered by so much as a hangnail, now desiccated and diminished by lung cancer. The last surviving member of my immediate family.

My intention had been to visit him sooner, before the last stretch of his illness rendered him semiconscious. But the move from Brooklyn—selling the old house in Greenpoint, processing all the papers for my new job with the Dallas Police Department—took longer than expected, and by the time I arrived at the hospital in Florida, his place of retirement, he had begun losing the thread of awareness due to all the pain meds.

He had been sleeping when I entered the room. Someone had covered him with a thin sheet up to his chin; his face glistened with the dew of a morphine sweat. One arm lay on top of the sheet, and the IV, threaded into a prominent vein on his hand, had backed up with blood. The bag hanging overhead was flaccid, empty of fluid. Before ringing for the nurse, though, I traced one finger gently over his knuckles. He stirred and opened his eyes.

He smiled. "Betty."

I leaned over and kissed his cheek. "Benny. How're you doing?"

"As you see." He inhaled raggedly and grimaced.

I reached for the call button. "Are you in pain?"

He stopped me. "Not too bad yet. Talk to me awhile. Once they dose me, I won't know you from Eve."

He began to shiver and I found a blanket and tucked in the edges, like he was a child. I pulled up a chair at the bedside and took his hand in mine.

"You got the paperwork taken care of?" he asked.

"Yeah." I nodded. "I leave for Dallas tomorrow."

He smiled. "You gonna get a horse?"

I laughed. "The only horse I ever plan to ride is the coin-operated pony outside of Neergaard's."

"You still running?" he asked.

"Every day. Seven miles yesterday. Six this morning."

Benny stared at me for a long while. "You look good, Betty. Grown into those long legs and wild red curls of yours. Just don't expect things to be any different in Texas. You end up with the same shit on the bottom of your shoes you'd pick up on Franklin or any other street."

"I know, Ben."

"And don't take any crap from the yahoos."

My uncle privately called any cop outside of New York or Jersey a yahoo. But I hadn't been too worried about the Texas cops. That is to say, I knew I was going to get crap. My biggest challenges had come from my own family members, many of them cops, who could dish out crap with the best of them.

I bobbed my head once. "Right."

"Okay." He nodded back, done with his lecture. "How's Jackie?"

I smiled gratefully at him. He was the only one in my family who had ever mentioned her name. "She's good. We have an apartment lined up." I rolled my eyes. "But she's already house-hunting."

He wagged a finger at me. "Take my word for it, she'll be wanting rug rats next." His gaze drifted to the Saint Michael medallion hanging at my neck. "Your mom would be so happy to know you wear it. You're the third Rhyzyk woman to have that medal."

I made a face. "Yeah, but probably the first to wear tactical boots."

"Don't you believe it," he says. "In World War Two, the Germans on the eastern front used to carry cyanide pellets in case they fell into the hands of the female Polish Resistance fighters. You come from a long line of fierce *kobiety*."

Grimacing, he pressed his free hand over his chest and breathed rapidly, as though he were racing the devil.

"Christ," he said. His breathing slowed after a moment and he turned his head to me. "Look me in the eye and tell me you're happy."

"I'm happy, Benny."

"Good," he said. "That's good. You know, your dad at one time was a great cop—"

I began to nod my head in agreement, but he held up the finger again.

"But that's what helped make him such a miserable human being. No, now listen. He was my brother and I loved him more than anyone. But he was devoid of certain feelings that would have made him a better family man. Having his work be the most important thing in his life did that to him. You have a chance to find some balance."

He dropped his hand onto the bed. "Balance. Christ, listen to me. I sound like some New Age nut job."

I placed my palm on his cheek. "You are a nut job, Ben. 'Stuck in the abyss of your own morass.' Isn't that what you always used to say to me?"

He gripped my fingers tightly. His eyes were fever

bright, shards of glass in a stretched, pain-filled mask, but he smiled. Soon the nurse came to administer more pain meds, and he fell asleep. I sat with him through the night.

In between his narcotic drifting, we revisited his more memorable cases, some of which were solved (a naked dead guy in clown makeup) and some of which were never solved (a dead guy who was found in pieces scattered throughout Greenpoint and Williamsburg and Park Slope and Bed-Stuy).

We cast into the ether familiar tales of other cops and families of cops, spinning out stories that I knew would never be told again unless I decided at some point to recount them to strangers, people who were not family. There was no more family, except for Jackie. Mother, father, brother, all gone.

He asked me to promise him one last thing: That upon arriving in the wilds of Texas, I would drive somewhere that was purely Dallas, a place that was immersed in the land's history, floating in the warp of its successes, stewed in the woof of its failures, and confront the beast. Hoist up both middle fingers, he had said, and tell the sidewinding, belly-crawling, sand-blown Fates of the West that the Polish cavalry had arrived.

When I left him in the early-morning hours, he was sleeping fitfully. That was two days ago.

I turn off onto Riverfront Street and see two large, white cylindrical tanks with red and blue lettering announcing FUEL CITY WASH. The parking lot's already full, so I drive around until I find a space next to a life-size bronze statue of a buffalo that's planted in the shadow of a rusted oil derrick, before which stands a pay phone. The first pay phone I've seen since leaving New York.

The Dallas skyline behind the buffalo swells like a contained mountain range, and I can make out the red Pegasus sign, the old Mobil Oil logo, a tiny, wavering mirage on top of one of the office buildings.

The taco stand is a large convenience store and kitchen, with lines forming at several outdoor food windows as well, but I'm drawn to the back of the lot, where, standing behind some metal fences, are half a dozen longhorn steers. Beyond the steers is a concrete wall on which brightly colored balloons and beach balls have been painted around an inscription: WHERE DREAMS COME TRUE.

Next to the pen is the car wash humming like a North Korean nuclear plant; dozens of cars and trucks queue up for a rapid wash and rim polish. Most of the SUVs in line are white, the pickups red. The men and women scrubbing down the vehicles are all brown.

Leaning against the metal fence rail, I contemplate the nearest steer, wondering at the strength that keeps his head up under the weight of his sweeping horns.

My mind wanders to Jackie, who's in our new apartment, unpacking. I told her this morning that I needed to do something for Uncle Benny. I had gotten the call from the hospice nurse that he had passed away during the night, transitioning peacefully out of his narcotic slumbers and into death. But I had cried angry, guilty tears that he had gone alone, without family, after so much suffering. Thinking on it now, I'm amazed that he lasted the forty-eight hours.

I stare at the huge, spotted red-and-white beast in front of me, expecting to feel derision, but instead I find dignity in his stillness—in his utter disregard for the chaos of the car wash, the determined picture takers, the shouts from the kids at the nearby picnic tables. The rheumy eyes gaze in my direction, shoulder hide twitching, the bony outgrowths as long as an elephant's tusks. He has outlasted all comers, the upward-tilting ends of his horns already a dismissal to the taco stand, the oil derrick, the vans overflowing with overfed gawkers and underweight poseurs. Even to the life-size bronze buffalo hulking in the background.

"You magnificent old bastard," I tell him.

So I turn and, in solidarity with him, hold up my two middle fingers toward the skyline.

"The Polish cavalry has arrived," I whisper.

Then I take out my phone and send one final text to Benny's old number: *Message delivered. Love you always. Betty.*

3

The setup is perfect. It should all be working, except for the woman who's just crossed into our surveillance zone, a Good Samaritan with more free time than common sense. The kind of woman who wears full makeup and a diamond tennis bracelet to walk her dog. The well-intentioned, moneyed type who would lean over the homeless guy lying on the sidewalk to feed the hungry dog next to him.

The Good Samaritan out walking her schnauzer does not notice the white surveillance van with service logos on the side panels where my partner, Seth, and I are stationed, or seem to have any awareness of another van, maroon in color with three more undercovers in it, parked across the street from the target house we've been watching: a McMansion identical to the other faux-Tudor dwellings in this part of North Dallas, all packed together in zero-lot lines, VOTE REPUBLICAN signs prominently displayed in the beds of drought-hardy geraniums like pit bulls on neighborhood-watch duty.

The five of us have been keeping vigil over this particular house for weeks, collecting hundreds of duty hours, acquiring a federal wiretap through a special FBI task force, and calling in countless favors for intel support. And this woman sprints over to the Mercedes parked in our target's driveway and starts talking to someone or something inside the car.

I hear Hoskins's voice over the radio. "The hell . . . ?"

It's surface-of-the-sun hot outside. In Brooklyn this time of year, the sun would already be softening into a gentle, sticky caress. The midday sun in Texas will burn pale, freckled skin like mine as quick as a grease cooker. No one else is on the sidewalk, and I watch the woman circling the car, cupping a hand over her eyes against the glare to peer inside.

A backseat window in the Mercedes has been left partially open and a frantic, furry nose appears through the crack. It's a small dog, maybe a poodle, panting mightily, and the woman looks toward the house questioningly. She pats the dog and coos to it, letting it stick its tongue into her water bottle. She caps the bottle and takes a few uncertain steps onto the front walkway.

Hoskins's voice on the radio to me. "Detective?" He has a panoramic view of the house from the maroon van, but anyone looking at the vehicle will see only darkly tinted, reflective glass.

"Give it a minute," I respond into the radio and look briefly at Seth, who is shaking his head.

The owner of the Mercedes—an older guy named William Bender who looks like the manager of a local supermarket chain—has just gone into his house. He's waiting for the arrival of the biggest cocaine supplier in North Texas, one Tomás "El Gitano" (Gypsy) Ruiz, a Mexican national. Ruiz grew from being a drug runner, carrying product in his school backpack on the streets of Juárez, to leaving headless bodies of people on the streets of that same city because they'd refused to work as his mules or had threatened his distribution channels.

We have the house monitored to the rafters and have been working a long time to get on tape the names of the participants, the date, and the location of a large drug deal. Not epic in Mexican-cartel terms but, in North Dallas terms, sizable—a significant amount of cocaine with a street value of over two million dollars. Bender was graduating from a successful meth-distribution business in the trailer parks and lakefront shanties of East Texas to a more expensive product. He had been caught on wire saying he wanted a better brand of client in Big D.

The woman reconsiders approaching the house and goes on her way.

Hoskins again on the radio. "Uh, Detective?"

Here it comes. It's either a dig or a bad joke.

"Yes, Hoskins?" I say.

"You disappointed you didn't get to frisk her?"

I can hear Ryan and Craddock in the background, laughing.

"I'm deeply morose. Now shut it and pretend you're working."

Hoskins, a scrawny, barely-made-it-through-community-college type, likes putting a sexual spin on everything, typical cop bustah-balls humor. But he seems to take special glee in skating on the edge of protocol with me.

My partner for a year, Seth, knows better than to laugh at Hoskins's jokes in my presence. "He does remember you're lead on this one, right?" he asks.

"Why do you think he's riding my ass so hard?" I answer.

Hoskins is the kind of guy who appears to nurture a constant seething disappointment with the world, using his cop status to settle long-standing personal scores. His favorite (and overused) mantra is "Never trust a man who won't get angry and a woman who doesn't seek revenge." Uncle Benny would have advised me never to trust a short man with a tall list of grudges. Hoskins, with more years on the force than me, expected to be lead on this case.

"I have to admit," Seth says, "the look on Hoskins's face when the sergeant picked you is something I'll savor for a long time." He smiles, scratching at the stubble on his chin and stretching his legs out.

Tanned and fit, Seth Dutton is absurdly handsome in a Scandinavian/Midwestern sort of way. At six feet, Seth is almost exactly the same height as I am. The joke in the department, or one of them, at least, has been that I'm the only woman in all of North Texas who does not get the vapors every time Seth walks into a room.

He picks up the conversation where we left off, one of the golden triangle of topics for a lot of Texas men: sports, women, and church—which is different than talking about religion. Telling someone what Dallas church you attend is similar to a Jersey local mentioning what exit he lives off.

"So, Riz, your family Yankees fans?" he asks.

I give him a sour look. "Why do all straight people assume that I follow sports?" Seth is the one person I let call me Riz, a contraction of my almost unpronounceable—at least to Texans—last name: Rhyzyk. But anybody who's had my back as much as Seth has and carries a SIG nine-millimeter gets to call me Riz.

He shrugs apologetically, and I cut him a break. "Mets fans," I say.

"What self-respecting New Yorkers root for the Mets?"

"What can I say? And my family's not from New York. They're from Brooklyn." I shift in my seat, pulling aside the long mass of hair that always seems to have its own core of animation—the hair that my mother jokingly called hussy red—and rub the muscles in my neck. I've promised myself to cut it a thousand times, because at work it can be a liability. But a stubborn vanity always takes hold and I let it grow. Maybe it's my personal war cry, a Polish Amazon with her ruddy helmet or an Eastern European Boudicca raised from the dead with her head on fire. I rake the hair off my neck with my fingers and tie it up with a rubber band.

My mind wanders back to the dog in the Mercedes. It's pretty cruel leaving a dog in a car in this heat, but its owner, who knows full well that his cocaine is going to end up being sold to kids in a high school not a mile away, can't be expected to be a PETA supporter.

"Actually," I say, "I'm the Yankees fan. It was the best way to get under my dad's skin. My dad was a Dodgers fan and stuck with the Mets even after they'd broken his heart too many times."

"Loyal," Seth says.

"Stubborn," I say.

"Hey, I hear you. You gotta be dedicated to be a Cowboys fan. On paper they are the most talented team. But Jerry Jones is a control freak. And Romo can't win in a tight situation. He's a better player than Manning, but Manning always comes through in the clutch. Every time—"

I sit bolt upright. The woman out walking her dog must have changed her mind because she's returned. She marches up to the front porch, and even before Hoskins can contact me, she's knocking on the door.

"Stay put," I radio to Hoskins.

Bender opens the door, words are exchanged, and the door is slammed shut. The woman pulls out her phone and makes a call.

"Do not move," I instruct the maroon van.

We wait, observing her standing on the front lawn, hands on hips, and within four minutes a neighborhood patrol car pulls up.

"You have got to be fucking kidding me," I say to Seth.

The patrolman, in freshly creased black shirt and pants and sporting Ray-Bans wrapped tightly across his face, gets out of the squad car. The woman approaches him, gesturing to the car and then to the house. I know by the way he hangs his head, crossing his arms over his chest while listening to her, that the last thing he wants to do is get involved.

Seth asks, "Do I contact the local station? Get them to back this guy off?"

I tell him no. Contacting the locals, explaining to them the scale of our operation and the scope of the drug deal in their backyard, will complicate things. As in them initiating their own bust for the sake of making the five o'clock news.

"Come on…" I whisper, willing the patrolman to disengage and get on with his real job, ticketing moms talking on their cell phones while driving in their kids' school zones.

But the woman is insistent and the officer goes to the door of the McMansion and taps it briskly with the brass knocker. The door is opened and Bender steps out onto the porch to talk to the patrolman. The woman has stayed some distance away, reluctant to repeat the earlier confrontation.

Bender goes digging around in his pocket, all the while running a nervous strand of dialogue with the cop, and pulls out what must be his car keys. He walks out onto the lawn, toward his Mercedes, making a windmill of placating gestures. I can see Bender looking up and down the street in front of the house because he knows that Ruiz is due to arrive soon.

Seth elbows me hard just as a white Ford Expedition cruises by our van, slowing as it approaches Bender's house. There are two occupants in the vehicle, both male, but the windows are too dark for me to identify the driver. It comes abreast of the house, passing close to the squad car, and the officer, noting the reaction on Bender's face— which, even from this distance, I can see registers hair-raising alarm—turns around to look at the slowing car. The officer's gleaming bald head follows the movement of the SUV, his shades now pulled up and resting on his forehead. He takes the universal I'm-watching-you stance, legs wide apart, chin jutting out, brow furrowed importantly. The SUV regains speed, drives to the end of the street, makes a left, and disappears.

Hoskins comes over the radio, his voice strained. "Do I follow the SUV?"

My hands are throttling the console.

"Detective Rhyzyk, do I follow?"

"No," I tell Hoskins, sweat beading my forehead. "Stay put. Let's see how this plays out."

I'm hoping that our guy will bring his poodle inside, the lady will be satisfied, and the patrolman will just go away. I'm also hoping that Ruiz will circle around and, after a while, reappear. But I'm willing to bet the farm that's not going to happen. El Gitano didn't stay alive in the drug game by making second pass-bys. He and his bodyguard will be checking the rearview mirror as fast as marmosets on speed, and any vehicle that appears behind them will be suspect. It's a sorry stroke of fate that our drug dealer appeared on the scene at the same time Patrolman Good Deeds showed up.

I need to hear what's going on and I don't want the officer to know he's being taped and recorded by Dallas Narcotics, equipment provided by the FBI, so I instruct Hoskins to hang tight and motion for Seth to quietly follow me out of the far side of the van. We're both wearing shorts and T-shirts, our SIG Sauers holstered under our loose clothing, so we pretend we're typical neighborhood joggers, daring heatstroke to prove our physical prowess. I gently close the van doors, slip onto the sidewalk, and start doing a relaxed, easy jog.

As we approach the officer, who's continuing to talk with an increasingly agitated and belligerent Bender, I hear the woman apologizing profusely and repeatedly to both of them.

We run in place for a bit, at a safe distance, merely concerned citizens.

"What's going on?" Seth asks her.

The woman turns to us, her schnauzer yapping excitedly, and says, "I've made a terrible mistake. Just terrible." Her face is wet with tears and sweat, her bottom lip quivering; she's wiping her nose with the back of her hand. "I was just worried about the little dog. But this man, he's from my church."

The officer gestures to get my attention and points back the way we've come, saying, "Folks, you need not to be here right now. Everything's okay."

So Seth and I turn around and begin slowly jogging back to the van while the white Expedition that passed the house earlier appears on the street, headed our way.

I stop pretending to run and face the SUV as it passes. The window nearest me rolls down with a robotic buzz and the driver's face turns toward me briefly, the hatchet nose and almond eyes, reminiscent of a pre-Columbian mask, floating starkly within the dark interior. He has seen me and discounted me as an immediate threat, but I get the creeping sensation that some channel within him has been engaged. The same channel that sent his ancestors scurrying atop vast pyramids to hack the hearts out of their victims with stone adzes.

A semiautomatic pistol emerges from the driver-side window and a pulse of rapid fire commences. Bender does a jerky dance for an instant before falling, blood spattering like a burst balloon onto the cop standing next to him. The officer, scrabbling for his gun, is hit in the second pulse and falls backward onto the yard.

Seth and I crash into some border shrubs, yelling for the woman to get down, but she's standing on the walkway, shrieking and clutching her schnauzer to her chest in a terrified grip. The barrel of the semiautomatic does an elegant, minimal sweep, finds her, and drops her in three shots.

From the passenger side of the Expedition, automatic-rifle fire sprays Hoskins's maroon surveillance van, punching holes in the metal and shattering glass. Seth and I return fire, but the SUV is accelerating, burning rubber for a count of four before finding traction and hurtling toward the far intersection.

Seth sprints for the van, and at the same time, from a house a few doors down, a big man in briefs and a terry-cloth bathrobe flapping crazily around his torso like wings, comes pounding out onto his front driveway and begins firing his own large-caliber pistol at the retreating SUV. The gun roars massively five times, sending plugs of wiry Bermuda grass in his neighbors' yards flying upward like small demolition works.

I scream at him—"Stop firing, you asshole!"—while kneeling down next to the woman who has fallen, face-first, over her dog. She has no pulse; her blood oozes down the walk like a slow-moving stream, and the dog has gone the way of its owner.

The back of the maroon van snaps opens and the undercovers spill out: Hoskins and Craddock are okay; Ryan, the youngest team member, not so lucky, with a piece of ricocheted metal in his shoulder. Seth has called for backup and within a few minutes, the street is an anthill of local police, tactical and heli support, and other members from our Narcotics unit. The local news vans are not far behind. The FBI is the last to make an appearance.

Overhead tracking eventually picks up the white Expedition, but the house it's parked in front of turns out to be empty, the elderly owner and his Lincoln Town Car already missing.

I give my account of the events to my sergeant, Verne Taylor, who arrives on scene sweating and swearing at the activity around him as the local neighborhood shooter— mopping his face and naked chest with the edge of his robe—loudly complains to jostling reporters and fellow neighbors that "if the cops in Dallas would just carry their fuckin' guns like they're supposed to, us citizens wouldn't have to do their jobs for 'em. And now the police have taken my gun into their possession. Where's *my* goddamned protection now?"

We identify the Good Samaritan by the things in her designer fanny pack, which contains a platinum American Express card and a compact Beretta with a diamond-pavé grip. (A Valentine's Day present from her husband, as it turns out. He wanted her to stay safe while out walking the dog. Safe from what danger in this upscale neighborhood, he didn't say, but I know he never imagined that the orgy of violence of the Mexican drug wars would find its way to his peaceful, impeccably landscaped streets.)

The Good Samaritan appeared, at a distance, to be in her forties, but closer up she looks older. Her driver's license puts her at sixty-eight. There are gray roots in her blond hair, and the scars from a recent face-lift shine in angry pink ribbons behind her ears. I want very much to pat her hair back into place again—she worked so hard to hide the entropy—but of course, that would be interfering with forensics. As soon as the local cops start making fun of her boob job, her augmented breasts continuing their upward thrust even as the rest of her sags like melting ice cream onto the pavement, I walk away.

An ambulance transports Ryan to the hospital for treatment, and Seth volunteers to take Bender's dog into his care, temporarily, after it becomes evident that it will otherwise be put into a shelter.

I sit on a curb. My teeth are chattering even though the temperature has got to be in the nineties. Christ, how I wish I could call Benny.

An EMT, a large black woman with a uniform so tight it looks spray-painted on, threatens to carry me into the treatment van if I don't go there under my own steam. She takes her time checking my vitals.

She winks at me. "Us females got to stick together in this. Right, baby?"

She puts a cold pack under my neck and a blanket over my chest—"Some Sunday," she says mournfully, shaking her head—and spends fifteen minutes filling out five minutes' worth of paperwork.

My shakes subside and I try and lie quiet with my eyes

closed, but my thoughts continue to circle around the cascading events of the past hour. If Bender hadn't left his dog in the car, if the woman hadn't shown up, if Ruiz hadn't driven by when the policeman was talking to Bender. And on and on. Uncle Benny used to say that there were three kinds of coincidences that could occur during a case. The first was the happy coincidence, which could lead to every piece of evidence folding together like exquisite origami, solid and connected, forming an indisputable picture of a crime.

The second was the unhappy coincidence, where the unexpected broke the back of an operation: an important witness dying, a crucial piece of evidence disappearing, an inexperienced officer mucking about the scene of the crime, or the good intentions of civilians wreaking havoc. According to Benny, civilians could screw your case quicker than a drunken carny did a fourteen-year-old Polish virgin; witness the lady with the pocketbook schnauzer.

The third kind of coincidence, the rare, bat-shit-weird sequence of connecting circumstances that oozes into the world seemingly from an alternative universe, was so dangerous you didn't even want to think about it. The Rhyzyk cops in my family referred to that chain of happenstance as *popierdolony,* Polish for "cosmically fucked up beyond human control." Every cop who stays on the force long enough will catch one case that gives him the Cosmic Screw. Like a superstitious sailor who fears a coming storm, I reflexively touch the Saint Michael's medallion at my neck—Saint Michael is the patron saint of cops—and squeeze the thought from my mind.

I've had two great years with Dallas Narcotics, with solid buy-and-busts and good case closures, no deaths other than self-inflicted overdoses. As of today, though, my first case as lead, I've got one suspect, one civilian, and one cop all deceased. And one of my own wounded.

The medic finally clears me and tells me to go home, and I take her advice.

4

Jackie has set the table and done most of the dinner cooking by herself. Usually, we do it together, but she knows how badly the day has gone and so she gives me the opportunity to brood alone in the tiny second bedroom in our apartment we call the office. I've spoken to my sergeant twice already, and he knows, being an almost thirty-year veteran of the force, that sometimes even solid things fragment and fall apart, and judging by the events still unfolding, it doesn't look like it will get better anytime soon.

Taylor tells me on the second call that the stolen Lincoln has been found with the owner dead in the backseat, shot twice in the head. Another innocent bystander, who was unfortunate enough to be home when El Gitano rang his bell or just walked in through his unlocked door. The Lincoln was located in Oak Cliff, south of downtown Dallas, next to an abandoned auto-repair shop. The local cops were canvassing the area, but so far no one had seen nada. He tells me to try and get some sleep and he'll see me in the morning, eight o'clock, for a departmental meeting to regroup.

I disconnect from the call and feel, like a dull toothache, the vibrations from the television in the apartment next door, the volume turned up to stun, the anchor reporting the slaughter in suburban Dallas on the evening news.

Jackie has dinner on the table when I come out of the office—a totally vegetarian meal, which serves me right for leaving all the work to her.

"How're you doing?" she asks. She wraps her arms tightly around me, laying her head in the crook of my neck, her exhalations moist against my skin, a vapor of wine on her breath.

I try peeling her arms from around my waist. "I'm fine," I say.

"And the young detective that was wounded, Kevin Ryan? How's he doing?"

I kiss the top of her head and squeeze her tightly.

"Ryan will recover," I assure her.

Sitting down at the table, I stare at the pea pods and Brussels sprouts swimming like tiny brains in olive oil, trying not to let my disappointment show. But I don't want to hurt her feelings, so I spear some with my fork and wash it down quickly with wine.

Jackie watches me pretending to like the rabbit food and smiles. She says, "You'll thank me when your cholesterol registers 'human.'"

A pediatric radiologist in a large children's hospital, Jackie has, over the course of her ten years as a doctor, identified hundreds of instances of child abuse. She's an after-the-crime child advocate who is never more beautiful than when she's giving testimony in a courtroom, a witness-box Fury who uses her knowledge of forensics like a dagger. Her department sees about one suspected case per week.

I remember to ask her about her day.

"Busy," she says. "I had more than twenty files across my desk before noon. We are really short-staffed right now, so I might be working more hours. I had to scope a ten-month-old today, hydrocephalic, Gorham's disease, pericardial effusion. That was not fun…"

People overhearing our dinner conversations would think we were insensitive, given the way we describe the messy, sometimes gruesome details of our jobs. Where my stories can be heavy-handed and unimaginative—dead guy in the alley behind the Piggly Wiggly, floater in the river under the bridge—hers are elegantly Latinate (and mostly indecipherable to my layperson's ears). But I've seen the way she cradles a damaged infant, fiercely protective, like a medieval Madonna.

I watch her gleaming dark hair falling in wisps around her neck as she pushes her food artfully around the plate, waving her fork in the air like she's directing a symphony only she can hear.

When I first met her, her hair was long and she wore it in two braids hanging in front of her shoulders. She had grown up on a farm in Oregon and was the happiest person I had ever met. On our first real date, I took her to the shooting range because she seemed so confident about everything—her own intellect, her physical buoyancy, her place and purpose in the world. I couldn't think of anything else that would impress her. I wanted to be able to show her something that I could do well.

"What?" she asks me now, her head cocked, smiling. "You're looking at me funny."

I had in fact been staring at her tattoo, a red rose, like a miniature heart, edged in black, inked just under her left collarbone. She had gotten the tattoo soon after we'd seen the movie *The Rose Tattoo* together.

"I'm looking at you funny?" I ask, redirecting my gaze from the pulsing red of the rose at the tender place below her clavicle to her hazel eyes, and I'm overwhelmed with gratitude at having this lovely, intuitive, graceful creature as my partner. Whatever patience I have, I've learned from Jackie.

"That's just my face, sweetheart," I say, squeezing her hand reassuringly.

"Bad, bad day," she says, shaking her head. "It'll get better. It always does."

And for the rest of the night I believe her.

5

The next morning the undercover team is assembled at the station. Seth, Hoskins, Craddock, and Ryan, sporting a sling for his wounded shoulder, are already gathered in the task-force room. When I walk in, Ryan is being teased by Craddock about not ducking fast enough.

"Pussy magnet for sure, though," Hoskins tells him. "Playing the sympathy card works every time. Oh, sorry, Detective Rhyzyk. I didn't hear you come in. There was no hail of bullets."

"You okay, Ryan?" I ask, ignoring Hoskins. Ryan grins and gives me a thumbs-up.

"Oh, he's fine," Hoskins says. "More important, Detective, how are you? Over the shakes yet?"

I give Hoskins a warning look and walk away. Sergeant Taylor and our FBI coordinator, Carter Hayes—appearing, as usual, as though he's stepped out of an L.L. Bean catalog, wearing khakis and a button-down shirt—are conferring quietly together in a far corner of the room. Compared to the sergeant, who's broad-shouldered and densely muscled, Hayes looks like a man who's spent a lifetime behind a desk, which is most likely the case. Until a few years ago, the sergeant was still competing in amateur rodeo events, one of the few black competitors in his division.

Hoskins has shadowed me and is pointedly studying my feet. "I like your Five-Elevens, Detective." He says it sarcastically, referring to my nine-inch leather tactical boots. They're worn by SWAT team members, and I don't belong to that rarefied paramilitary group. But on the days I'm not undercover I like to wear them just for a little bit of beak-twisting for the boys on the team. My version of army boots.

I sigh, because if I don't respond now, he'll never shut up. "Why, thank you, Bob. I'd let you borrow them, but your feet are a little too dainty."

Everyone but Hoskins laughs, and karmic balance is restored.

I find a seat next to Seth. "How's Bender's pup?" I whisper to him, and he gives me a stricken look that tells me he's already in love. I shake my head. "You are so freakin' gone, Seth."

Taylor starts the meeting by saying, "The bad news is that, for the time being, we've lost track of Ruiz. The good news is that his boss, Alberto Carrillo Fuentes, has just been arrested by the Mexican authorities."

There are surprised exclamations around the room, and Taylor watches us take it in. Fuentes is the head of the Nuevo Juárez cartel, which is second only to the Sinaloa cartel and a huge player in the trafficking of narcotics across the border from Mexico into the United States. His curious nickname—all of the dealers and their enforcers have their own—is Betty la Fea. Ugly Betty.

Which, of course, Hoskins has to repeat several times for my benefit.

With millions in bribes, thousands of enforcers—some of them ex-military, known as La Línea, some of them gang members, like the Barrio Azteca—and hundreds of corpses lining the streets of Juárez and border towns, Fuentes operated for years with total impunity. His arrest will lead to a vacuum of power that his men and the soldiers of the Sinaloa federation will be fighting over with increased violence. I'm guessing that the Sinaloa cartel paid more money to the Mexicans than the Juáreznitos did. That Fuentes was arrested and not assassinated offers opportunities for exorbitant bribes to be paid to the Federales by both cartels.

What this means for El Gitano, left out in the cold, is yet to be seen.

Taylor turns the floor over to Hayes. "Because the Lincoln was found in Oak Cliff, I think it's safe to say that Ruiz may be headed south toward the border. He has most likely heard about his boss by now, but we don't know yet where this will blow him. Then again, he could be uncertain about his position in Juárez and may still be in the Dallas area. We do know that even under the best of circumstances, and by *best* I mean business as usual, Ruiz is completely capable and willing to commit murder, as we witnessed firsthand yesterday. He's canny. We now know"—and here he looks at us—"he made at least one of our surveillance vans. As bad as it was, we're lucky the fallout wasn't much, much worse."

"What's this 'we' stuff, *kemosabe*," Seth mutters to me.

Hayes continues. "There are several leads in the metroplex that you will be following. Sergeant Taylor will go over these with you now. However, until we sort out the mess from yesterday, your intel resources as a team will be limited. No more wires or surveillance materials until further notice. Just eyeballs and balls here. Detective Rhyzyk not to be excluded."

There is a brief eruption of laughter and the sergeant holds up his left hand to speak. What makes Hayes's statement funnier in that moment is that in Taylor's right hand is a red rubber ball, one of several that he keeps in his desk, which he's been squeezing tightly during Hayes's talk. A running joke in the department is "What's big and red and takes no prisoners? The sergeant's balls."

Taylor's physical therapist told him, following his most recent minor cardiac event, that channeling his tension into the ball instead of his internal organs—or his fellow law enforcement officers—will help prevent the Big One.

The bang-up yesterday has hit him hard, though. Civilians being killed does not a happy department make.

"Yesterday," Taylor says, "an officer was shot and killed making a simple house call. He left home that morning, probably thinking that he only had a few tickets to write before dinnertime, kissed his wife and two kids good-bye, and went to work. And now we're going to get to work too.

"We will split into two teams. Detectives Hoskins and Craddock will follow up with some of Ruiz's old customers and contacts. Sorry, Ryan, you're on desk for a day or two. Detectives Rhyzyk and Dutton will be making a visit to Ruiz's sometime girlfriend, a pross working out of a North Dallas salon. It's a stretch, but until we get a sighting or some snitch feedback, we're going fishing."

He ends the meeting but crooks a finger at Seth and me.

Taylor says, "Red and Riot, in my office, please."

The sergeant calling us by our nicknames is like a parent using a child's first and middle names. Never a good sign.

"You couldn't have foreseen the woman appearing," Taylor tells me, "but as lead on the case, the person responsible for your team, you should have been better prepared for the possibility that our dealer would think that Bender was talking to the cops about him and was, therefore, a threat."

"Yes, sir," I say. He's right; I should have anticipated that scenario. I spent last night imagining what could have happened to Ryan if the ricocheted metal had gouged his neck and not his shoulder.

"Three people were killed on scene, another kidnapped and shot dead. One of ours was wounded." Taylor looks at me for a long ten seconds, and I take the full weight of his gaze. No defensive body posturing, no excuses.

Taylor then asks us, "Did Ruiz make either of you?" He points to my head. "After all, you can hardly miss that hair. He certainly was able to recognize the maroon van across the street for a surveillance vehicle."

In almost every case while working undercover, I wore a wig. And a few times, in those instances, I'd been mistaken for a high-end tranny: tall, lean, muscular, attitude to spare. Once, while I was arresting a drug dealer who was wearing an evening gown, the transgender beauty had stared with admiration at my neck. "Damn, honey," she'd drawled. "I want the name of the surgeon that got your Adam's apple so small."

"Ruiz saw me," I say. When the dealer looked at me during his drive-by, I knew he'd file my image behind those Mayan orbs. "But if he thought we were cops he would've been shooting at us as well."

Taylor makes a noise with his bottom lip against his teeth. "I don't know whether I would take that as reassurance or not." He glares at Seth. "What do you have to say?"

"No. Didn't make me." Seth shakes his head. "Just a guy out for a jog."

A casual observer might take Seth's dismissive attitude as showboating, but he came by his nickname, Riot, honestly. A few years ago, shortly after he made detective, he found himself alone during a confrontation in an East Dallas biker bar, a raunchy, tin-shack hellhole named the Road Kill. Seth, working undercover, had gone there to make an arrest, expecting the potential arrestee to arrive there alone as well. The biker, though, showed up with five of his buddies, Los Homeboys, the psychopaths who eat Hells Angels for breakfast. Seth arrested the dealer, and the other Homeboys were so impressed with his cool that they went ahead and let him cuff the biker and put him in the car before they removed Seth forcibly from the driver's seat, freed their friend, and torched the vehicle. They broke three of his ribs and his jaw but let him go with a warning to never come back. He was picked up, staggering along the highway, by a passing patrol car as a potential drunk and taken to the hospital. Hence the nickname Riot, as in "one riot, one Ranger."

Ten minutes after our meeting with the sergeant, Seth and I are walking out of the station house. We'll be driving north a few miles to the Blue Heaven reflexology salon to see if we can find and question Ruiz's occasional girl-friend Lana Yu. To exit the building, though, I have to walk by Craddock and Hoskins. Craddock, always with a bag of artery-clogging fast food on his desk, is an avid hunter, spending most of his nonessential pay on a taxidermist for his trophy mounts and on ammo to kill his next round of hapless deer or doves or whatever. He is the embodiment of the kind of country cop Uncle Benny would have called a yahoo.

He fans the air against an invisible wall of heat as I pass and yells, "Uh, Dee-tective Betty, how was your meeting with the sergeant? By the way, I think your hair is on fire."

"How's that spelled, Craddock?" I ask. "F-A-H-R?"

A capable detective, he'd be tolerable if not for Hoskins always goading him into being an asshole. "By the way, Craddock," I add, "you've got mayonnaise on your chin."

I dial Jackie's number and she picks up on the second ring.

"I'm fine," I assure her right away. "Just tell me something good. Rough start to the day."

She lowers her voice an octave and whispers, "I'm going to make you wear your boots to bed tonight."

I bark out a laugh, drawing looks from the guys in the hallway. "That's exactly what I needed to hear."

I put my phone back in my pocket and wait for Seth to pick me up in the garage. He soon pulls up driving a new Dodge, and as we exit, we pass the battered maroon surveillance van, its Homeboy Pool Company logo on the side panel blown out by AK-47 rounds. The company name was the squad's little inside joke about the motorcycle club that almost killed Seth.

"I guess we'll need to come up with a more convincing banner," Seth tells me.

We drive north for twenty minutes to Richardson, a community of two-story brick houses in upper-middle-class enclaves, similar to the neighborhood where we were yesterday. But the devil is in the details, and there are differences in the population if you're alert to them. Driving on the street that shares real estate with the Blue Heaven massage parlor, you might see a few Asian kids playing in front of a nearby house with little blond-haired Caucasian kids, toys and sports nets littering the lawn. The prostitutes and their families live close to the salon and watch out for one another's kids during off-hours. Eventually, when election season approaches, the neighbors having figured out there's prostitution in the 'hood, Vice will move in and make some arrests, but until then Blue Heaven will keep thriving.

Seth looks over at me a couple of times, waiting for me to speak, and when I don't, he says, "Riz, you didn't know it was going to go sideways."

I make a noncommittal noise and continue to stare broodingly out of the window. "Stop trying to make me feel better. I've gotten worse ass-drubbings from my grandmother."

"She the one that was the nun?" Seth asks, and I have to smile.

"Guess what?" he asks.

"I don't know. What? You finally got laid."

He looks at me, flashing the perfect set of teeth that always get him laid. "I'm thinking about keeping Bender's dog. No, now don't make that face. For starters, poodles are the smartest breed of dog in the world."

I sigh and gaze out the window again. It's killing me how hopeful he's looking.

"And second, they don't shed," he adds.

"And third," I say, "you're a cop. In Texas. A Texas cop. Isn't there some kind of rule in the Texas Man's Handbook that says you're not allowed to own a poodle? Actually, I should be encouraging you. It would get Hoskins off my back for a change."

"No allergens on the skin," he persists. "I Googled it. Even people with allergies can keep poodles—"

"Oh, for fuck's sake," I say, laughing. "Would you just shut up about the dog already?"

"You know, you should get a dog," he says, nodding sagely. "A little Scottie, maybe. It might humanize you." He turns into the mini-mall lot and parks in the handicapped space right in front of the salon. A handwritten banner in the window promises *Reflexology for total relaxsashion.*

Seth turns off the car and we sit there for a few minutes watching the male customers on parade, some in shorts, beach shirts, and flip-flops, a couple in business attire, walking in and out of the front door. One man in a Cowboys T-shirt parks as far away from the storefront as possible and takes a meandering route to the massage parlor, as though the snakelike path will throw off any casual observer—for example, a neighbor shopping at the adjacent Dollar Store. You can almost hear him whistling the I'm-just-out-for-a-casual-stroll tune.

My partner has been staring at the handicapped sign, the white stick figure in the wheelchair painted on a blue background underneath the words BLUE HEAVEN CUSTOMERS ONLY, and says, "Well, that's a twisted scenario I don't want to keep in my head."

When we walk into the salon, a customer is just leaving. He's mindlessly humming to himself, regarding his shoes in a happy, fogged sort of way, and he looks up, alarmed, as he passes me in the doorway.

I smile at him aggressively, hoping I resemble his wife.

"Aren't you late for work?" I mutter to him as he exits the building, blinking into the shattering light.

Seth follows close behind me, and the receptionist sitting at the desk glances up from her magazine, frowning. The walls of the salon are a strained attempt at Tiffany blue, the furniture prefab, scratched and gouged from frequent, and often hasty, relocations.

"We're closing now," she says automatically. Even though it's not even the lunch hour, this is the standard response when a nonmale or possible undercover wanders in. She's Chinese with a long, thin face, somewhere between thirty and fifty. Setting the magazine down, she says a little louder, "We can't take any more appointments today. You'll have to come back tomorrow."

"Lana Yu," I say, showing her my badge. "I'd like to talk to her."

Her frown deepens. "She's not here."

"Where is she?" I ask.

The receptionist has reached under the desk to press the silent alarm, and soon a man, slender, wearing a plaid jacket, appears from somewhere in the back. Despite his willowy shape, he takes a military at-ease stance, hands clasped in front of his pelvis, legs spread slightly apart. His cheekbones are high and prominent, his hair short and spiky. The guy's the salon's watchdog and probably a deserter from the Chinese army, and from the spring in his step I'm sure he can goose-step with the best of them.

"What can I do for you?" he asks politely but with eyes on Seth.

"We'd like to talk to Lana Yu," I say. He sees my badge on the desk but shakes his head, looking appropriately apologetic. "She's not here."

"Where can I find her?"

"I don't know."

"Are you the manager, Mr. ...?"

"Just Tony. And yes."

"All right, Just Tony, I'd like to see your state license to practice massage therapy, please. Oh, and I'd like to see your carry permit also."

He looks briefly surprised, but then he smiles and pulls out a battered wallet from his front pocket and hands me his carry permit. Being the salon's enforcer, he wouldn't be without a gun nestled snugly behind his plaid jacket. The massage license appears to be harder to find, though, and as the receptionist makes a show of rustling papers around, Tony is tapping his wallet against his chest, indicating that he's willing to pay us to go away. There will be no state license, of course; it's easier to pull up tent stakes and move on if class B demeanor charges get too troublesome and costly.

Seth reaches out his left hand as though he's going to take the wallet. As Tony extends his arm, Seth grabs Tony's wrist with one hand and snaps the cuffs on with the other. With a twisting movement he has Tony pressed against the desk, both hands now secured behind him, the gun, a compact Glock, lifted from Tony's waistband.

At that moment, a man walks in from the street, and in the process of taking out his own wallet to pay for some realignment, his eyes adjust to the dark and he sees the arrest tableau going on, four pairs of eyes staring at him in various stages of agitation.

He pulls up short and, without missing a beat, drawls, "Is this the Pegasus Title Company?"

"No!" Seth and I yell at him at the same time, and I give him the get-lost head twitch. The customer rapidly shuffles backward, apologizes, and disappears through the door.

"Why did you cuff me?" Tony demands, twisting his head around. "I've done nothing wrong."

I have to bend down to get closer to Tony's face. "I felt threatened." I study his permit and then tell him, "Okay, here's the deal. Either you find Lana for us or we'll be here all day and your customer base is going to dry up. If you know what I mean."

A few of the salon women have emerged from their cubicles in the back and are now standing in the hallway, close to the front desk, all eyes on their handler.

Tony's eyes tell me that he'd be thrilled to see me face-down in a water tower, but he says, "I'll give you her address. She'll be sleeping."

"Oh, goody." I signal Seth to uncuff Tony. "I get to wake Sleeping Beauty. Now, if I find out you've called Lana before we get there, I'm coming back here with a warrant and I will shut you down."

I take the address from Tony, and as we get back into the car, Seth tells me, "Riz, this is just so Texas. Plenty of paper making it legal to shoot someone, but not a permit in sight to legally rub one down."

The address, as it turns out, is not next to the salon but three miles away in a more upscale neighborhood. This time I drive while Seth checks in with Craddock and Hoskins. So far, they have no leads.

Lana's house is in a gated community and I show my badge to the uniformed guard in the miniature Versailles that serves as the security station. After I warn him he is not to alert the homeowner, he opens the heavy iron gate—incoming cars to the right, outgoing cars to the left—and we drive through the meandering streets looking for Lana's place. Upon finding the address, we do an alley drive-by at the back of her house to peer through the sliding iron gate barring the rear entrance. There is only a dark blue BMW convertible parked outside in the rear driveway. We see a two-car garage, but the door is closed, so we can't tell if another vehicle is hidden there.

After parking in front of the house at the end of a cul-de-sac, Seth does a quick look-see over the high wooden privacy fence to Lana's backyard, then hoists himself atop the frame quietly, in one fluid movement. He shakes his head, seeing nothing threatening, and hops down again. We step onto the front porch, Seth standing off to one side, his hand on his firearm. I lean on the doorbell and hear the slapping sound of bare feet coming across the foyer. The door opens a crack, revealing half of a young woman's face. I hold up my badge, and the eye stares at me, but there's no movement, either to open the door farther or close it completely. She's wearing only a long T-shirt, her face smudged with last night's makeup.

"Yeah?" she says.

"Lana Yu?" I edge to the side to get a better look at her. The woman blinks sleepily, yawning extravagantly.

"Yeah?" she says again, irritated.

"Are you alone?"

"What's this about?" She opens the door a bit wider and steps out onto the porch. "I'm sleeping." She frowns, but then catches sight of Seth and startles. She has waist-length jet hair, one long section streaked with scarlet, a rounded, slightly pocked face, but a body that only a twenty-something with a home gym can maintain.

"Tomas Ruiz. You seen him lately?" I ask.

She's expressionless, but one expertly tattooed brow inches up a bit. "No," she says defensively.

"Can we come in?" I ask.

"No. You can't come in." She crosses her arms, barring the door. "You have a warrant?" she asks, but the volume of her voice has edged upward a notch. Too loud for it to have been meant for just us. I hear a rear door closing softly and the jarring sounds of scraping metal. The back gate is opening.

"Back gate!" I yell to Seth, and he barges past Lana and sprints down the hallway toward the back of the house. For an instant I consider bolting after Seth, but then I think I should get our car—

"Get the car!" Seth roars from somewhere inside the house, and I run for the Dodge parked out front. I can still hear Lana screaming for Seth to get out of her house as I start the car, put it in drive, and race to the end of the street. Ahead, I see the Beemer slam out of the alley, knocking over an industrial-size trash can, and speed toward what can only be the main enclave exit next to the guard station. I stop the car long enough for Seth, legging it from the rear of the house, to throw himself into the passenger seat. The heavy exit gates at the guard station will open automatically, but slowly, and I'm confident that we'll be able to catch up to the driver before he can get away. Seth calls for backup, and I'm praying that none of the neighborhood kids decide to dash into the street as we take sliding turns around stop signs and CHILDREN PLAYING warnings, following the Beemer as it grinds over some of the corner yards.

The car is now approaching the guard station, the gates already opening as I make the last turn a block away. Before the gates can open completely, though, with less than six feet of air between the panels, the Beemer's engine guns and the body of the car rams through the narrow opening, its side mirrors tearing loose, wide swaths of paint planed raggedly from both sides of the car, with a shower of sparks from metal scraping metal. It flies onto the main street, makes a right-hand turn, and slides dangerously into traffic. The metal exit gates are now stuck, frozen in their partially open state, and the space is not large enough for our Dodge to pass through. With some yelling and wild gesturing from us, the panicked guard opens the entrance's side gate, but by the time we turn right onto the street, the getaway car is lost from sight.

Local neighborhood patrol search commences after Seth puts in a call to Dispatch saying the driver is probably Ruiz, but overhead heli support comes late to the party because of a hostage situation at a nearby Walmart. When you've got only two helicopters in a city as large as Dallas, overhead surveillance can't be counted on.

"Goddamn it," I yell repeatedly, driving fruitlessly back and forth through neighborhood streets. How hard can it be to find a hundred-grand-plus car that looks as though it's been run through a meat grinder?

My personal phone in my left pocket rings. I dig it out, but I'm too agitated to talk while driving and so I throw it to Seth to answer.

"Hey, hi, Jackie," he says, trying to talk over my swearing. "Yeah, everything's okay. We're just a little bit busy right now. No...no lunch yet. Okay. Sure, I'll tell her. Bye." He hangs up and hands the phone back to me.

"Well, what'd she say?"

"Jackie says if you come home later smelling like Whataburger, you're in deep shit."

Then Taylor calls my work phone in my right pocket

and I pull over to answer. He informs me that, if what he's hearing about Ruiz disappearing again is true, I'm in deep shit and might as well not come back to the station.

"Go and talk to Ms. Yu," he says. "Maybe you can redeem yourself by getting her to tell us something we don't already know."

We leave the local patrols to continue their search, and Seth and I drive back to Lana's. After we pass through the guard station again, I get out of the car and pick up one of the Beemer's side mirrors that had been sheared off by the gate. When Lana answers her door this time, she's dressed in expensive jeans and a T-shirt that reads COWGIRLS RIDE HARD. She tells us for the second time that we can't come in. She smirks in a way that makes me want to hard-slap the back of her head.

I toss her the mangled mirror. "This is what's left of your car. We didn't catch your boyfriend today but, just so you understand, when we do catch him, I'm going to personally let him know that you were the one to give him up because you were trying to beat charges for solicitation and aiding a federal fugitive. So that cracked image you see in the mirror is nothing compared to what your face will look like when his friends get finished with you."

She tries to close the door, but my nine-inch reinforced tactical boot is in the way. In another minute, my fingers may be through the door frame as well, ready to tear her diamond-stud earring through one downy little earlobe.

"You know what Ruiz's bodyguard's nickname is?" I ask her. "El Guiso. It means 'the Stew.' He likes to burn his victims alive in a metal pot." I throw my card onto the floor at her feet. "Think about it, Lana. If you change your mind, my number's on the card."

She slams the door, but not before I've seen the blood drain from her little scabby face.

Seth drives to the station and I call Jackie from the passenger seat.

"Hey, babe, I'm alive, but I may be home late. And, yes, I got your message about the burger place." My stomach is still churning, but perversely, a dripping-fat burger is exactly what I'm craving.

I hear her listening to my agitated breathing. "Betty," she says, "you really need a run tonight—"

"Yep," I say sharply, cutting her off. I know what I need, I just don't want her telling me. After today I should go on a twelve-mile run to lower my blood pressure.

"I may be working late at the hospital as well," she tells me with a bit of frost in her voice.

"Okay, well, see you back at the apartment." I disconnect, jam the phone into my pocket.

Seth gives me a censuring look. "She is so going to dump you."

"Right, Mr. Expert in Love," I say defensively. I know I'm an ungrateful wretch, being so impatient with her. If not for Jackie, my idea of emotional self-help would be half a bottle of Jameson. I'd be living out of a suitcase, all my T-shirts would be black, and I'd still be buying underwear in the boys' section of Target.

After a moment of concern, I ask Seth, "Flowers, you think?"

"Yeah." Seth nods. "Chocolate's not going to do it for you this time."

The balance of the day is spent doing paperwork and

making calls to other cops and any informant who will talk
to me. Hoskins and Craddock return early evening with no
helpful information from Ruiz's known contacts. By the
time Taylor leaves, he is not wishing any of us a good
night.

I send Ryan home for the evening, although he doesn't
go without a protest, and the remaining four of us sit there
kicking around possibilities for leads, trying to pull on the
connecting strings without unraveling the whole sweater.
All our informants, all the snitches we've cultivated for
drug information in the past, are sorted through and re-
viewed. Ruiz is a major player, never doing a deal under
a million dollars. He was a close lieutenant to his boss,
but Fuentes is in a Mexican jail, and whatever chance Ruiz
would have had to grab a piece of the cartel territory as
a capo evaporates dramatically by the hour. Ruiz is in El
Norte with one bodyguard, away from the action to the
south.

He will have to be very careful whom he approaches
for help in Dallas because any practiced snitch, meaning
just about every heavy drug user or drug dealer who's got
a record, will know that information about him will bring
them repayment in drugs from the eager Sinaloa cartel and
a reduced sentence from us.

On the whiteboard with a black marker I draw a large
circle representing the city of Dallas and print Bender's
name in the circle. Below the circle, about twelve inches
down, I draw a wavy line, representing the border between
Texas and Mexico. Beneath the line, on the Mexican side, I
print *Juárez cartel* and *Alberto Carrillo Fuentes, aka Ugly
Betty.* I draw an arrow from Mexico to Dallas and write
Tomás "El Gitano" Ruiz and *El Guiso,* his bodyguard, on
top of that. I print *Lana Yu* next to Ruiz's name. I take a

red marker and cross out Bender's name, then take a green marker and cross out Fuentes's name, to show that he's alive but out of action.

With a blue marker I start putting sequential numbers where Ruiz has been seen the last few days, the number *1* in El Paso, *2* in Dallas proper, *3* in Oak Cliff, *4* back in Dallas.

I point to Lana's name with the blue marker. "We need to keep an eye on Lana's movements. Even though that particular haven's been blown, Ruiz may try to contact her again. So I'm putting Ryan on that tomorrow. Easy duty to follow her and she doesn't know his face. Hoskins and Craddock—"

Hoskins sighs loudly as though he's disappointed. "Detective, you never actually got eyes on Ruiz driving that car. You're assuming it was our guy. What if it was just a spooked john?"

"If it was a john, he would have stayed hidden in Lana's house," Seth says. "He wouldn't have taken her car and destroyed it driving through a thick metal security gate trying to get away from us."

Craddock, who's been noisily fishing around in a bag of fries left over from lunch, gathers up a few cold crumbs, pops them into his mouth, and says, "Let's assume it was Ruiz. We've lost the car. As far as we know he's headed back west on I-20 toward Juárez in another stolen vehicle." Typical of Texas-speak, Craddock pronounces it "*vee*-hi-cle."

"Not necessarily," I tell him. "We don't know that he can go back to Juárez right now because we don't know who's filled the vacuum of power left by Fuentes. The Mexican officials may be waiting for him as well. Or La Línea, or even factions from Barrio Azteca along the Texas corridor."

On the Mexican side is La Línea, the Line, a well-equipped and well-trained group of urban street fighters for the Juárez cartel. Brutal and efficient, these former policemen had sent an unmistakable message to competitors a few years ago by killing sixteen teenagers at a high-school party and then another nineteen in a rehab hospital nearby.

Across the border to the north were the Texas enforcers, the Barrio Azteca, formed in the jails of El Paso in the 1980s. Some DEA figures had put the current number of gang membership at over eight thousand in states from New Mexico to Massachusetts. These are the guys who would not only kill you but also dismember you and package you up for your mother's birthday celebration.

"I think Ruiz is long gone," Hoskins says. "All this jumping through hoops in Dallas proper is just a waste of time."

I turn away from him like I'm studying the board, but it's to hide my irritation. I could make a stinging comeback about his knowing all about wasting time, but ignoring him will piss him off more.

"Highway patrol will be looking for Ruiz along the southwest corridor," I say. "But I have a feeling he's still in Dallas."

Seth sits in his chair, one leg jiggling up and down with restlessness. "The cocaine has got to be somewhere close by. The kilos were not in either of the abandoned cars, and he can't carry that much around in a suitcase."

"Seth's right," I agree. "I'm not satisfied with the initial search we did of Bender's house, so I'll want another one conducted. I'll be getting a search warrant tomorrow for Lana's house as well."

I set the marker down and face Hoskins. What I want to tell him is that it's hard for me to take seriously a man who's three inches shorter than I am, who wears his shirt collars a size too big for his neck, and who thinks that because he's inside his car, people can't see him picking his nose.

"Detective Hoskins," I say, "tomorrow you and Craddock will be searching through Bender's house again, attic to floorboards."

"I hope the son of a bitch has crept back across the border," Craddock says. "Then it's not our problem."

"If he is here," Hoskins says, "which I doubt, then I hope we do catch him. Five minutes in a cell with us, and the good taxpayers of Dallas will only have to foot the bill for a ventilator for a few months."

"I understand why you'd feel that way," I tell him, trying to imagine what Ruiz would do to Hoskins left alone in a room with him for five minutes. "But we have to find him first. Seth and I will be in contact tomorrow with the Feds through Hayes, border patrol, and local police in El Paso. Ruiz has got to emerge somewhere soon, hopefully without inflicting more carnage. Any more thoughts before we wrap up for the night?"

"Yeah," Hoskins says, standing up and stretching. "I need a drink. I'd ask you to come with us, Detective Rhyzyk, but you wouldn't like my choice of bars."

I know I should be going to the gym or running a few miles, but I decide the only exercises I want to be doing for the next few hours are eight-ounce curls with my partner.

"Coming with us?" Craddock asks Seth.

"You serious?" Seth says. "Riz here knows all the best places to find women."

"Yeah," Craddock says, cackling. "Just not women who'd want our asses..." His voice trails off and Hoskins gives him an evil look.

I wait until the two amigos gather up their things and walk out of the room. "What was that about?" I ask Seth.

"Come on, you don't know?" he asks.

"I have no idea."

Seth begins to laugh. "I can't believe you still don't know. Oh, this is so good." Seth throws his head back and howls, wiping his eyes with the back of his hand. "Hoskins's wife left him months ago. For a woman."

6

Once a week, Seth and I visit a bar within the greater Dallas metro area. The rules are simple: Two hours minimum stay, two drinks each, maximum, and no bar can be revisited. So every Monday, we each write down the name of a bar on a piece of notepaper, fold it up, and drop it into an empty wide-mouthed jelly jar. We alternate who pulls out that week's selection. We've made some interesting choices.

We've been to biker bars, gay bars, and stripper bars; visited Asian karaoke palaces, Mexican wedding halls, Russian vodka dens, and Lebanese hookah stalls. And, of course, a country-dancing bar where Seth threatened to tell everyone in the place I was a Democrat if I didn't let the bouncer—a three-hundred-pound lineman from some red-dirt college—teach me the Texas two-step.

Tonight, I pull out of the jar the name I'd written down, and I begin my own victory howling. It's a bar called Slugger Anne's, and Seth will get in only because I know the owner and will insist. He will most assuredly be the only man on the premises.

We drive there in separate cars. It's a small place downtown, quiet and discreet, no real sign at the door, with worn, comfortable booths and a long bar that's always full in the latter part of the evening. It looks like a million other neighborhood Texas bars, except there are no handbag hooks above the foot rail and no men's room with urinals in the back. The walls are lined with vintage black-and-white photos of cowgirls, and behind the bar are two large paintings: one of Annie Oakley, and one of Calamity Jane.

I know the owner and chief bartender, Dottie, well. She had some drug problems in the past, went clean, and opened the place. She will, at times, pass on to me useful information about drug-dealing around her bar. Wearing her usual uniform of a sleeveless Western-style shirt and low-slung jeans, she waves at us exuberantly when we walk in, one bare, muscular arm raised in greeting, displaying a lush patch of underarm hair, like a nesting hedgehog, in one pit.

"Hey, girl," Dottie crows. "That your new bitch?"

"How's it hangin', Dottie? And, no, that's my work partner, so be nice." I pat the air in front of Seth, letting him know that Dottie's full of rude bluster and not to get hot under the collar about it.

We find a booth and order two shots of Jameson on the rocks from a young woman dressed in shorts, cowboy boots, and a tight Slugger Anne's T-shirt. She greets us with the ubiquitous Texas salute: "Hi, y'all."

She's not wearing a bra and I catch Seth staring.

"What?" I say to him after she walks away, the two globes of her rear end swaying suggestively. "You were expecting plaid flannel shirts?"

When the drinks are delivered, Seth gets to make the toast because I picked the place. The last two rules are that the toast can never be the same as a previous one, and we can never refer to a current case. Well, almost never. Have to have some free space sometime, somewhere.

Seth raises his glass and says, "Here's to not having to hide your true self."

I tilt my head back, surprised, but I drink to the toast.

"That's an interesting one," I say. "What's it supposed to mean exactly?"

"Well, for you, it means you're always having to hide the fact that you're a damn Yankee."

"Okay, I'll go along with that. What're you hiding?"

"That I'm secretly in love with lesbians." He smiles and looks for the cute waitress in the shorts.

"Don't even go there."

He crunches some ice between his teeth and says, "I envy you."

"Me? Why?"

"Because your place in the world seems so secure."

"Oh, right. A woman working as an undercover cop with a bunch of testosterone-driven males. Right now, I'm not feeling so secure with the way this case is going."

"You have a live-in girlfriend, a kick-ass partner, a community."

"Well, I do have the first two, that's for sure. I'd be barely human without Jackie. And my partner . . . well, I guess he's not a total ass-wipe. But a community? You say it as though being a lesbian is like being in a garden club. Like we all have a secret handshake and a special clubhouse."

"You always knew what you wanted to do?" he asks.

"Didn't you?"

"Nope. Being a cop was something I fell into. Not good

enough for a football scholarship, so I worked driving a forklift to pay my way through junior college. At twenty I signed up with the force. It was either that or the Marines." He pauses to sip at his Jameson.

Seth makes slightly slurpy sounds when he's drinking something, like a kid savoring his chocolate milk. His head hangs thoughtfully over his glass and I can easily imagine him in high school, a star on the field and in the school halls, his physical prowess and his Olympian good looks holding him aloft. Until, that is, the time that his class-mates — the ones wealthy enough to get into good colleges or athletically talented enough to get sports scholarships — went on with their lives, smugly satisfied that Seth Dutton would have to work in a warehouse even to finish a two-year college.

He raises his head and gives me the grin that, if I lusted after men, would have had me grappling with him in one of the bathroom stalls.

"Let's see how well you know your partner," he says. "If I had stayed in college, guess what I would have ma-jored in?"

I start to say something dismissive like "Girls" or "Ani-mal husbandry," but he's so earnest about the question that I bite off the remark. "I don't know."

"Environmental studies." He glances around with a guilty look, as though he's just told me that he wanted to major in dressmaking.

"No shit? Okay, well, that deserves another toast." We toast to the environment.

He rests both arms on the table, then puts his hands down in his lap, twisting slightly away from the bar where Dottie is eyeing him in a critical way. I try to suppress a laugh at his discomfort.

"Not so easy being in a sexually hostile environment, is it, Riot?" I say.

He wags a finger at me. "You love being a cop, don't you?" He says it like it's a declaration and not a question.

"Man, there is not a word for how much I love being a cop. Don't you?"

"Sometimes."

"My grandfathers on both sides were cops. My father was a cop. My father's brother was a cop..."

I come within a hairbreadth of adding my own sibling to that litany. My older brother, Andrew, who was my father's pride and joy. But I catch myself before my lips can form the words. Andrew had been a cop as well, but his career had ended badly. A drug bust, a lab explosion in a tenement, lots of charred bodies from both sides—cops and dealers—my brother's suicide soon after with a drunken, solitary swim in the Atlantic Ocean in February. Following that, my father's alcohol-sodden decline into bitterness and regret that he was left with only a daughter to carry on the Polish pride.

Seth is studying me quizzically. I take a drink, swallow, inhale. "It kind of figured I'd go into the force. Although I had to work to convince one person."

"Your mother?"

"My father. He took it as a personal affront that I wanted to go through the academy. He did his best to make me drop out."

"But you didn't."

I give him a tight grin and raise my glass. "First in my graduating class." I finish the drink and signal to the waitress for two more.

"Is it harder being a female on the force in Brooklyn or here?"

"Much, much harder up north."

"Really?"

"What, you don't believe me? Oh, now you're all disappointed that Texas cops aren't as hard-assed as Brooklyn cops? Those guys, man. Let me tell you, they were old school. Three generations of pounding concrete, fighting slum wars, and resisting bribes from gangs and the Cosa Nostra grafted onto their genes. All you guys had to fight were some cattle rustlers and a few Native Americans on horseback."

"Was there a moment you knew you were in with them?"

"Police academy. Defensive tactics. The trainer puts me in a choke hold. I don't have to tell you that's a no-go anymore."

"What happened?"

"He was behind me, had his big ol' meatpacking arm around my throat, squeezing. And I was starting to go black around the edges. It made me mad, because I knew that he knew it was not proper training. Just as I was about to lose it, I went limp for a second and bent forward, which brought him forward as well. We were only a few feet in front of the wall, so I pushed off the floor with my legs—I mean, I gave it everything I had—and sent us flying back against the plywood so hard it knocked the urinal loose on the other side. The trainer's head hit the wall so hard, he got a concussion. He admitted to me later that he'd been put up to it. Never would say by who. But after that, they pretty much left me alone. Well, mostly."

"You think it was your dad who told him to do that?" Seth asks.

I shrug.

Seth folds his arms across the table and leans in as

though he's confiding something dangerous. "So, Riz, what did you give up to be such a great cop?"

"What do you mean?" I say, but in my head I'm remembering Benny talking about my dad starting out as a good cop but ending up a lousy human being.

"You don't get to be good at this job without letting something slide. So…what're you giving up?"

"Absolutely nothing," I say, rattling the ice in my glass like a tambourine.

He gives me a doubtful look but raises his glass to meet mine. "What's Polish for 'screw 'em'?"

"*Pierdol sie.* Actually, it means 'go fuck yourself.'"

"That's good enough for me. *Pierdol sie.*"

When we leave, the bar is crowded with patrons and I get a few appreciative looks as I walk by. The whiskeys have made me feel both heavy-limbed and buoyant, careless. One long-legged girl wrapped in black leather smiles at me and tells me that she likes my boots. I imagine kissing her, without preamble, without even a hello. But that would have been the pre-Jackie, unreformed Betty.

Outside, the humidity folds around Seth and me like wet blankets, and we say our good-byes in between slapping away the mosquitoes swarming around the outdoor lights.

"You'll remember to bring Jackie flowers, right?" Seth reminds me. "To make up for being such an asshole earlier today."

I smile, pleased with myself. "Already in the car."

Seth checks his messages and begins grinning. "Just got my date for the night."

I watch him loping off to his car. "You mean *hookup,*" I yell after him. The smallest particle of jealousy raises its oily little head, but I bat it down. The days of impersonal, vengeful sex are over. Meeting Jackie changed all that.

My work phone rings and I pull it out of my pocket. It's not a number I recognize, but I answer it anyway.

A breathless voice says, "Hey, I need to talk to...I need to..." Then the line cuts off. It was a female, but the voice sounded high and reedy, almost like a kid's. I call back but get only an automated message restating the number. I put the phone in my pocket and forget about the call.

7

Jackie and I stand on the sidewalk outside a small, two-bedroom house in East Dallas, waiting for the real estate agent to arrive. It's early morning, and we're perched in the shade, the air syrupy with jasmine. There are old-growth trees lining the streets of this neighborhood, which is within walking distance of White Rock Lake. One enormous branch of an old red oak in the front yard stretches over the roof of the house, and I pass the time thinking about what one good ice storm could do, imagining that branch crashing down through the slate shingles, tearing through the drywall, crushing us in our bed as we sleep...

I catch Jackie watching me out of the corner of her eye, and I give her a grin.

She pats me on the arm and says, "Fingers off the cynical scale, right? And stop checking your watch every thirty seconds. This will take only twenty minutes."

I nod, and she goes happily back to studying the front of the house. We've been two years in an apartment and

Jackie is eager for a bigger nest. She thinks the stress of my job may be getting to me and that a house and a yard and a two-car garage, along with larger water and electricity bills, will help ease the pressure.

She also thinks I may be ready to snuff the neighbor upstairs.

Finally, the real estate agent pulls up in front of the house in a white Lexus. She gets out, cradling her cell phone between her neck and her ear, struggling to gather up her notes, coffee, and keys. In their ads, Dallas real estate agents—their expertly Photoshopped head shots appearing next to the featured houses—all seem to have variations on the same rigid, immobilized visage, probably acquired from the same cadre of surgeons: graduates of the Wind Tunnel School of Medicine. Seth once told me that there were more churches per capita in Dallas than in any other city in the United States and more plastic surgeons doing faces and boobs here than in LA. Where he got the latter bit of information, I didn't want to ask.

But this agent looks like a perky suburban mom, which is probably what she is, wearing a brightly colored suit and sandals, the kind with heels and unforgiving straps across the instep and ankle.

"Hi," the agent calls to us; she walks over energetically and shakes hands with Jackie, who has done all the legwork checking out the neighborhood.

She turns to me and shakes my hand. "Hi. I'm Donna Mitchell. My, but you're a tall one," she says cheerfully.

"Hi, Donna." I find I'm smiling in response to her eagerness to be likable. "I'm Betty. And, yes, I am tall."

She turns and leads us briskly toward the front door. "So nice to meet you. What gorgeous red hair you have. My daughter is tall too. Basketball player for Baylor. You are so toned. You must work out all the time..." She keeps the banter going all the way to the porch.

"I think you're going to like this little house, Jackie." Donna retrieves the key from the key box, opens the door, and leads us into the foyer, all the while telling us about when the house was built, the square footage, how long ago the bathrooms were retiled.

Jackie explores the house with Donna, asking questions, making lists of what would be needed in time and money to make the house move-in ready.

I think of our apartment and how good, how easy life has been, even with the infuriating neighbors. This house is staged, furnished with items that look uncomfortably new, a bit of a Western flair in the details—a leather couch with metal studs and a large landscape with a farmhouse and bluebonnets. I stare at the painting, remembering the row house in Brooklyn where I grew up. The place was dark morning, noon, and night, the windows small and facing south. Ever present was the vaporous fug of tarry smoke from my mother's cigarettes, which she kept lit in the ashtray whenever she was home. The music she played in the afternoons as soon as she got home from work at the local OTB. She listened to it all: jazz, Latin, rock, Top 40. A few hours of peace before my father came home from working with Brooklyn's Finest, ready to pop the first beer of the night, turning off the music, turning on the tube. The tension groaned outward from his core self like an oil spill, engulfing everything and everyone in its path, until the overflow caught fire, scorching my mother, me, and my brother, in that order.

Abruptly, Donna has found her way back to me. She tells me she's giving Jackie "some space."

She asks me, "You two been friends long?"

"Mostly," I say, laughing, but it's a laugh-fest of one because Donna is looking puzzled. "Actually," I clarify, "we're partners."

"Oh, you're a doctor too?"

"No." I pause. "I'm a police detective."

Jackie has wandered back into the living room and is examining the hardwood floors, following the course of the conversation. Now Donna is looking back and forth between Jackie and me.

"Oh," Donna says, still confused.

I point to Jackie. "We're buying the house together."

"Okay," Donna says, but she does not look like it's okay. A little crease in her brow is threatening to break through the Botox. "Roommates?"

"You can say that," I tell her.

There's a long pause and Jackie and I exchange looks. I know that Jackie told Donna that she was not single.

Donna says, "I'm not sure I follow you. Jackie, I thought you said you were married."

Jackie walks to where I'm standing, and, reaching down, clasps my hand tightly in hers. She brings my fingers up to her lips and kisses them. "I said I was part of a couple."

Donna stares at Jackie with the same fascinated yet slightly repulsed look people get while watching a reality show about intestinal parasites. Something that's exotic and potentially fatal, like amoebic dysentery. Thinking about my family has summoned forth a defensive meanness. I feel like a Saracen facing a swarm of Crusaders.

"We will be married," I say to Donna, looking down at

the still life that is her face. "As soon as gargoyles like you will let us."

Donna breaks her hostile staring, her mouth open, and right then, she needs to make a phone call. She walks rapidly away and into the kitchen.

Jackie purses her lips, but a smile is tugging at the corners of her mouth. "That was a bit harsh, Betty."

I shrug. "Maybe. But you know what that holier-than-thou gaze does to me. Especially when it's directed at you."

"I know," she says, stroking the length of my arm with her fingers. "It's just not going to get any easier with you becoming contentious with the real estate agents."

"Is that what I was being, contentious? I thought I was just being a bitch."

She bites down on a laugh. "Anyway, I'm not sure I even like the house."

"Oh, really?" I say, putting on my tragic face. "I love it. Especially the horseshoe wine rack."

Jackie suppresses a smile as Donna walks back into the living room, apologizing for having to get to another appointment that she just now remembered. We're hurried back out onto the sidewalk so Donna can leave. Jackie and I stand on the walkway, holding hands, waving good-bye as we listen to Donna's fast-retreating, clacking footsteps.

Before I leave for work, Jackie turns and kisses me. She says, "Don't think this means we're not looking at more houses."

I brush a strand of hair from her eyes. "Sure. But I get to pick the next agent."

8

I get the call on my way to the station. It's Hoskins, his voice sounding tight with stress. "Detective, you need to get yourself to Bender's house now. We walked in on one female body and a guy hiding in the laundry closet, so freaked out he can hardly talk. Homicide's on its way."

Through the phone, I can hear the sounds of wailing sirens and a male voice, maybe Craddock's, announcing that he's Dallas Police.

There are some rustling noises, as though Hoskins is moving the phone closer to his mouth. "From what I can tell, the female may be Lana Yu."

The short hairs on the back of my neck begin to rise. "What do you mean, from what you can tell?"

"I think I recognize her from the photo during the briefing yesterday, but I can't be sure. No one's touched the body yet. Just get over here as quick as you can, okay?"

I call Seth, who picks up on the first ring, and let him know about the body. He tells me he can make it to the house in ten minutes. The Tollway is jammed for morning rush hour, and because of construction feeding three lanes into one, it takes me a full twenty minutes to make it to Bender's place. Texans may be polite pedestrians, but put them in cars and it's every man for himself.

By the time I arrive, there are two EMT vehicles and six local patrol cars. Several of the officers are already putting yellow crime scene tape in front of the house; others are searching around the yard, trying to ignore the frightened but curious neighbors who have started to gather in the streets for the second time in as many days. My partner's car is parked on the curb, the driver-side door open, a sign of Seth's rush to get into the house. The Forensics team is there, suiting up.

The fat shooter who had the large-caliber pistol is standing on the civilian side of the tape. He's out of his robe, wearing baggy shorts and a T-shirt designed by Omar the Tentmaker. He nods at me like a demented puppet, holding up two thumbs, and says, "Yeah, great job there, Officer. Y'all keep up the good work."

As I walk into the house, he calls after me, "I still don't have my fuckin' gun back."

A patrolman immediately hands me some shoe covers, which I slip on over my boots, and two pairs of latex gloves. He throws a disapproving look at my hair, certain in its untamed state to be shedding all over the evidence, so I wind it up at the nape of my neck and jab in a few bobby pins to hold it in place.

Four Homicide detectives are already on the premises, one of whom I know. Marshall Maclin is standing in the office just off the main hallway, but he motions for me to stay in the foyer while he finishes talking to one of his colleagues. In his late thirties, Maclin is the kind of male cop who walks into a room ego-first, casting testosterone into the air like confetti, taking for granted that he is universally liked by men and sought after by women. When I was a kid, an aunt from some faraway Midwestern city, one who obviously didn't know me, sent me a Barbie doll. To my brother, she gifted a GI Joe. Within five minutes my Barbie had beaten the crap out of Joe, tied him up, and stripped him down. I remember being disappointed to discover that the soldier, laid bare, was curiously neotenic in appearance, slick, smooth, and ill-defined.

Despite Maclin's bulging physique under his suit jacket, I have the sensation that naked, he would appear like that GI Joe, with no unique ridges or even impressive bits of protruding anatomy, just manufactured plastic, block-headed and dense.

Maclin's and my paths have crossed professionally a few times before, too few for him to have known that he shouldn't ask me out on a date. When I declined his dinner invitation, he teasingly asked, "Too shy?" To which I had responded, "No, too dyke." He maintained his sense of humor about the incident, though, at least enough to stay cordial.

"Hey, Betty," he says, walking into the foyer and holding out his hand.

"Hey, Marsh." I take his hand and give him what I hope is a painful squeeze, just as a reminder that I am immune to his pheromones.

He motions me into the office and introduces me to his partner, Bernard Tate, an East Coast transplant like myself. Compact, with the oft-broken nose of an amateur boxer, he shakes my hand in the bone-crushing manner of a self-conscious man in the presence of a much taller woman.

"Is my partner here?" I ask Maclin.

"Yeah, he's here. He's in the kitchen with Hoskins and Craddock. They're waiting for you."

Tate, not wanting to appear to be straining to look up at me, stares into my collarbone and says, "You've had an interesting start to the Ruiz case, Detective. Certainly keeping us busy." He pronounces *start* as "staht" and it's refreshing to hear a monosyllabic word stay that way. Southerners always seem to add extra syllables to the simplest of words.

"What's going on?" I ask him.

"Your detectives showed up about forty minutes ago. Said they were searching the house on the Ruiz case."

"That's right. I sent them here to look for drug money."

"They walked in on a body in the kitchen," Maclin says. "Female, early twenties, Asian. Hoskins said she might be a prostitute with known connections to Ruiz."

I watch the Forensics crew, suited and carrying their evidence kits and cameras, filing by in the hallway.

"Lana Yu," I say. "Ruiz's girlfriend. Hoskins also said there was a potential witness?"

Maclin says, "Well, the guy's alive, but he won't be much of a witness. He tells us he stayed hidden in the laundry closet the whole time the victim was being murdered."

"Nice. Will I be able to talk to him?"

Maclin looks at Tate, who nods. "Sure," Maclin says, "after he finishes giving his statement to us. Although that may take a while. The guy's a total basket case. If the victim is Lana Yu, you'll be helping by giving us a positive ID on the body."

"Sure. Whatever I can do to assist."

"Okay," Maclin adds, "but I just want to give you a heads-up: the body's still a bit of a mess."

I follow Tate and Maclin down the hall, passing a large

formal dining room to the left and a sitting room to the right. It's a big house with tall, vaulted ceilings in the entryway and wrought-iron banisters on the curved stairway to the second floor. The production and sale of meth has been very, very good to Bender.

When Uncle Benny worked homicide in Brooklyn, the first cops to a murder scene spoke in code to prepare later-arriving law enforcement for the level of carnage. They used cuts of meat to describe the crime site: *Round* meant there was no obvious external violence, little or no blood, perhaps a death by poison or a discreet puncture wound to the back of the head by an ice pick. *Sirloin* was a single bullet wound, usually a small amount of blood; *rib*, a knife wound with a bit more blood; *chuck*, multiple shots or stab wounds with lots of red. Of course, occasionally there would be *ground*, reserved for the most violent, rage-filled deaths, often the result of domestic violence, and with that designation you knew to forget eating for the rest of the day. I know how much my fellow Texas law enforcement officers value euphemisms, so Maclin's telling me that the body was "a bit of a mess" suggests that it's bad.

Seth is standing in the arched doorway and he turns and gives me a terse nod.

"Where's Hoskins and Craddock?" I ask him.

He takes a breath and points into the kitchen. I follow behind Maclin, putting on the two pairs of latex gloves, and walk into the room, large enough to service a restaurant. I stop to take in the scene.

All the tiles, marble, and cabinetry are white or off-white with expensive copper pots in pristine condition hanging above the enormous stove. The bottles in the spice rack have matching labels, and a bowl of perfectly arranged oranges sits on an island counter next to a repro Remington sculpture: a cowboy forever catching air between his backside and his mount. The door to the nearby laundry closet is open, probably the place where the witness had hidden.

The kitchen, like the house I had walked through earlier with Jackie, looks staged, never used. But in the middle of the floor, beyond the island counter, is the supine body of a female, fully clothed, dried blood over her face and pooling around her head in a viscous, rusty pond. Her throat has been cut.

I'm keenly aware that all the live people in the room— my guys, the local patrolman guarding the door, the Homicide detectives, even the Forensics techs—have stopped what they're doing to look at me. Waiting to see if I'm going to lose it: my breakfast, my cool, my sanity. You can't work Narcotics and not see bodies. But witnessing death by overdose is different than staring at a body whose features have been savaged by the hand of man.

I ask Maclin if I can move in closer and he tells me yes. Mindful not to step in the blood spatters on the floor, I rest one gloved hand on the island counter and lean down to the body. The woman's mouth and eyes are slightly open, her black hair matted close to her head at her temples but strangely bristling and choppy at the crown. There's no mouth gag, so there would have been a lot of screaming. At least until her windpipe was opened up. There are livid bruises on both upper arms from being restrained by rough hands or maybe from a pair of knees anchoring her to the floor. She's young, petite, and Asian, wearing a stained T-shirt that reads COWGIRLS RIDE HARD.

"Yes," I say to Maclin. "It's Lana Yu."

I track my gaze back to her face and imagine I can see

defiance in the pull of her lips baring strong, frequently whitened teeth and in the half-mast droop of her eyelids.

One of the Forensics guys moves in and with a probing tool carefully lifts a section of her hair away from the side of her face. Her left ear has been severed.

I look at him questioningly and he says, "The right ear is missing too."

There is a guilty tug of memory from yesterday: my desire to rip the diamond stud from her earlobe when she was being a smart-ass. There's no way to know yet whether the removals had been pre- or postmortem.

I back away from the body as another Forensics team member moves in to photograph Lana's remains. I turn toward Maclin, meaning to ask him if the house has been searched in its entirety yet, when the skin on my arms begins a slow creeping crawl, and I pull out my phone and hit redial on the last incoming call from the previous night. There is a pause and then the muffled sounds of a cell phone ringing begins somewhere behind me. I turn toward the xylophone chirp and realize that it's coming from Lana.

The Forensics photographer bends down and tugs a cell phone from the front pocket of her expensive jeans.

"She tried to call me last night," I tell Maclin.

"What time?" he asks.

I check the time stamp on my phone. "About nine thirty. I didn't know it was Lana. A woman started talking and then the call cut off. I tried calling back but got no answer."

"Well," Tate says, motioning to the "bit of a mess" on the floor. "That gives us a possible start time to all this."

My team and I follow Maclin and Tate back into the dining room, and we stand around the formal table.

Craddock, his face pale and shiny with sweat, looks close to hurling his breakfast, and I have to wonder if this self-proclaimed hunting enthusiast has the stomach to skin and eviscerate his kills. He points to one of his own ears and asks, "What was that for?"

"Trophy of some kind, maybe," Maclin offers.

"Maybe," Tate answers. "Or sending a signal to someone. Your guy Ruiz like to take body parts?" he asks me.

"Not that I know of. If Ruiz had wanted to send a message, he would have removed her whole head. Think the murderer could be our witness?"

Tate shrugs his shoulders, says, "Doubt it. No evidence of blood on him."

He leaves to check on the progress of the interview so I can question the witness, and the rest of us continue to stand together in the dining room, our heads bowed, brooding silently on what lies in the kitchen. Something nags at me about Lana's appearance, apart from the obvious, but I can't quite put my finger on it.

Maclin is studying me. "What is it?"

"I'm not sure," I say. "Looking at Lana—her clothes are the same as when I saw her yesterday, but something's different about her."

Hoskins mutters, "You mean like both of her ears being gone?"

Seth opens his mouth to say something to Hoskins, but I hold up a hand.

"It'll come to me," I say. "Maybe the witness can help us out."

One of the Forensics team members walks into the dining room holding up a key and the card that I had thrown at Lana the day before. "We found these in the victim's pocket," he tells Maclin. "The key works the back-door lock."

Maclin asks me, "Did Lana Yu know Bender?"

"I wasn't aware of it. But both Bender and Lana knew Ruiz."

Tate appears at the doorway and signals to me, says that the witness has refused to give any information and is asking for a lawyer.

"I don't know what you'll learn from him," Tate tells me. "But you can give it a try."

I follow him into a sitting room and find the witness sitting in a large armchair, pointedly ignoring a plainclothes detective, wearing a plaid jacket. The oversize chair has made the man seem even more diminutive, the colors of his jacket garish against the subtle silk upholstery. Seeing me, he looks ready to bolt.

"Hello, Tony," I say. "Your witness there," I tell Tate, "is the owner and manager of a massage parlor called Blue Heaven. My partner and I paid him a visit yesterday. Lana Yu was one of his prostitutes."

Tony takes a deep breath, pulling his posture up straighter, and gives me a familiar hateful glare. But behind the glare is a fear that must have blossomed like a toadstool in the black of the laundry closet as he listened to Lana being murdered. I have to admire the little bastard for trying to puff himself up to a more dignified height. There are a lot of unanswered questions—why he was in Bender's house with Lana, how she came to have a key, who the killer was—but I know just by looking at him that he's not going to give me anything.

"No," I tell Tate. "He won't talk to me. I can send you whatever I have on file. But you'll probably get more on him from Vice."

Maclin walks with Seth and me to the front door, tells me he'll send me any progress notes on Lana's murder. I tell him that's fine but that, wherever it won't interfere with the murder investigation, Hoskins and Craddock need to stay and continue looking for any cash left hidden in the house for our case against Ruiz. Maclin takes my elbow and steers me out the door, away from Seth. His grip is light but insistent.

He walks me onto the lawn, pulling a dark face at the news reporters who have gathered, yet again, to comment on another neighborhood murder.

One male reporter leans into the crime tape and shouts at me, "Hey, Red! Yeah, you, the tall one. What's going on in there?"

Maclin motions for the guy to step back and says, none too quietly, "Fucking reporters."

I stare down at the hand resting on my elbow. What I first perceived as a friendly touch now feels predatory. "Well, Marsh, they've got their jobs to do. Just like us."

Maclin drops his hand. "You really kept it together back there," he says, smiling. It's a TV smile, like he's got Vaseline on his teeth so his lips won't stick to them.

I don't feel like smiling back, but I do. Keeping it friendly. "I'm sure you'll be telling all the men the same thing."

"That's not what I meant, Betty. I've seen cops twenty years on the force lose their lunches to a body in that kind of shape. Your guy Craddock, for instance, looks about to faint."

I glance back at the front porch, where Seth is making an arms-wide what-gives gesture.

"So did you pull me out onto the lawn to tell me that you're impressed with my cool"—I look at my watch to hide my annoyance—"or to insult members of my team?"

He's right, I did keep my composure. Not because I didn't feel shock over a violent death, especially the murder of a young woman, but because I've had so much practice in hiding it.

Maclin asks, "You been to a rodeo yet?" For the first time I notice that he has TV hair as well, cut to perfection at some sports-clip salon where he can watch on a big screen as the pigskin cowboys grind each other into the turf.

I blink a few times and exhale with exaggerated patience. "Wow, actually, I have not. You're not asking me out again, are you?"

"Everybody in the rodeo has their function," he says as though he didn't hear my last question. "You've got your wranglers, your emcees, your clowns. They've got these cowboys called pickup men. They ride in the rough stock events, rescuing bronc riders from the horses after they've made their time. They don't make a successful rescue, the cowboy gets bucked off his horse and sometimes he gets trampled."

"Okay, I get it," I tell him, understanding that he's marking his territory, and we've gone from a friendly, comrade-in-arms chat to a pissing contest. The time-honored dance between departments. Doesn't matter that we're all DPD. The department that makes the collar is the department that gets the glory, the news coverage, the political support, the funding, the promotions.

"I get it," I repeat. "Sometimes you get the bull, sometimes the bull gets you. Are you warning me about something specific, Maclin, or are you giving me some arcane Texas wisdom?"

"I'm telling you," he says, "that the rescue men now are Homicide, and at a murder scene, we've got precedence over a thwarted-drug-deal search. What's your body count now, Betty? Four? No, actually, it's five as of today."

"So no more we're-all-in-this-together bullshit." I signal

for Seth to join us and as soon as he's in earshot I say to Maclin, "My partner is now going to call FBI liaison Carter Hayes to request his operatives here on scene. Our little drug sting has federal support."

Seth pulls out his phone and makes the call.

"You know," I tell Maclin, who's no longer smiling, "we didn't have rodeos where I grew up. But we did have the circus, and if I learned one thing as a kid, just a girl, sitting on the bleachers with my uncle eating my cotton candy, it's that the guys with the biggest whips control the biggest cats. And the FBI has very big whips. Good luck, Detective. Nice seeing you again."

Seth walks with me to my car and I glance over my shoulder once and see Maclin standing on the front porch with his hands jammed into both pockets, watching me, no friendly wave good-bye.

"I want the three of you to stick close to Maclin's team," I tell Seth. "Lana was there for one reason: to find Bender's money. I don't really care right now how or where she got a key or why she was there with Tony. I think Ruiz sent her there to search the place, hoping it would not be under close scrutiny, knowing that if it was, she'd be the one caught."

Tate has joined Maclin on the porch and now they're both watching us.

"Like waiting blackbirds at a picnic," Seth says.

"I know Ruiz is a psychopath and all," I say, "but this doesn't feel like one of his. He leaves bodies on the streets to scare off competition or in retaliation. He had easy control of Lana. If he meant to kill her, he would have taken her into the woods. He wouldn't have been so..."

"Obvious?" Seth offers.

Lana wasn't bound or gagged. Someone would have had

to sit on her chest and arms to do what he did, up close and personal. It would have been loud and bloody. The cartel shoots its victims in the back of the skull and then, when there's no more struggle, cuts off the offending head.

"No," I say. "He wouldn't have been so messy. As soon as Hayes's people show up, I want that house torn apart. And better call Ryan and tell him he doesn't need to be watching Lana's place anymore."

The persistent news reporter has edged closer to Seth and me, trying to hear our conversation. The guy's head is shaved clean, but he sports a full, bushy beard and wears plaid shorts, black socks, and white sneakers. It's the kind of forced hipster look that makes me want to tie him to a chair, shave the pubic hair from his face, and glue it to his shiny pate.

He yells, "Come on, Red, tell me something I don't already know."

"Okay," I yell back, getting into my car. "You're a douche bag."

9

The mechanical bull on which I'm sitting seems to be emblematic of my life right now. No head, no tail, no real forward momentum, just a lot of twisting, circular motion controlled and manipulated by an unseen hand, like the hidden wizard in the tale of Oz; the intent and construction are all designed to unseat the hapless victim in the most uncomfortable and undignified way.

The bull ride I am about to take is due to a lost bet with Jackie that I could get her grandmother Rodean to talk to me within the first fifteen minutes of our arriving here at Babcock's Barbecue—a huge, barnlike building with old farm tools, like implements of torture, nailed to the walls—for the old woman's eightieth-birthday celebration. It cannot be overstated how much the women in Jackie's family hate me. In their minds, if I hadn't corrupted her, she'd be happily married to Bud or Stew or Billy Ray, have two kids, and be an accepted part of her community, not an outcast living with her lesbian "friend."

Jackie's mom, Anne Walden Nesbitt, had grown up in Texas before moving to Oregon with her husband to raise a family. After Anne became a widow, she moved back to Dallas to be with her parents. A few years ago, Anne was diagnosed with a heart condition—an ailment that she insisted was liable to result in her death at any moment— which is one of the reasons why Jackie and I moved to Texas, so that Jackie could help take care of her mom in her final years. Her mother's symptoms seem to include rapid heartbeat and dizziness, headaches, the onset of chronic complaining, and a rabid strain of xenophobia and bigotry. Jackie worries that her mother has only a few years left. I believe the woman will outlive all of us.

The Walden family female who hates me the least, Jackie's older sister, Susan, gives me a weak nod from the table and goes back to trying to coax her surly fifteen-year-old son away from his iPhone.

Susan's husband, Neal, and her grandfather Terence are at the long bar drinking beer and watching sports TV. From time to time they look in my direction, grimacing the way they might after discovering that a possum had crawled up into the engine of their John Deere tractor and murmuring tight-lipped opinions about me under their breath.

There are some technical difficulties with the bull, the operator informs me. Sit tight, he says. It's hard to look natural sitting astride a barrel with a saddle, so I slump over my work phone, my feet dragging the ground, looking for more text updates on the Ruiz case. Two hours after the Feds showed up at Bender's house they found the cash behind a false wall in the attic. About eight hundred thousand dollars, along with four pistols, two semiautomatic rifles, and enough meth to light up a small town for weeks.

The mechanical bull gives a lurch, and my hand instinctively reaches for my Saint Michael's medal—a superstitious hiccup to ward off bad luck, and a gesture that seemed to start the instant my mother fastened it around my neck.

The bull mechanic gives me the signal that the ride is about to begin. (When asked earlier how much of a ride I wanted, I had glared at him and hissed, "Disney slow. Mess with me and I'm coming for you.")

The bull starts a sedate, gentle bucking motion, easing to the left and then to the right, and I begin to loosen the death grip on the pommel. It makes a full circle, bucks a few more times, and stops just as I see Jackie capturing the scene with her phone camera.

Jackie stumbles over the injury mat toward me, laughing. She kisses me in a gloriously unself-conscious way, yanks at my hair, and says, "Now you have to be nice to me, or I post this to the DPD site. This is fun, right?"

"Oh yeah," I say. "Lots of funsies here."

Looking over Jackie's shoulder I can see the senior-most Walden watching us from the bar, his mouth downturned and sour. Last family gathering, I had to sit through Terence's angry tirade about "hom'sexiality" leading to bestiality.

Jackie punches me playfully on the arm to get my attention. "Betty, you promised you'd be friendly."

Despite all her advanced, first-world medical training, she still believes in the power of positive, intentional thinking. That's why she's in the business of bringing the human body back to health, and I'm in the business of picking up the pieces after scumbags have torn it apart.

We all sit together at one long picnic-style table, already crowded with buckets of coleslaw and potato salad, watching platters of scorched meat being presented by several waitresses at once.

I become aware that everyone is staring at me staring at the ribs, and it's an uncanny reminder of the earlier scrutiny by the cops in Bender's kitchen. The viscous brown sauce coating the ribs resembles too closely the dried blood congealing at Lana's throat, and I have to tamp down a momentary gag reflex.

"Well, g'won," Jackie's grandfather prompts impatiently. "It's not gonna bite ya."

Jackie's nephew Lonny has set down his iPhone, and, tired of waiting, he mutters, "Fuck this," and reaches for a rib. He gets knuckle-rapped on the head by both his parents, and then we're all wading into the meat. The caramelized flesh sets my mouth to burning almost immediately and I down, much too quickly, my beer. Soon we have built pyramids of stained paper napkins, and the food and the beer begin to put a thaw in the general conversation.

I've been placed at the far end of the table with Jackie's great-uncle James Earle Walden, a Vietnam War vet who has struggled with alcoholism his entire life. He sits next to me with a prop of club soda beside his plate, white-knuckling his way through another family gathering. He smells of decades of nicotine, seeping through every pore, his overly long hair slicked back with combed-through layers of drugstore hair gel. His hands shake as he brings a rib up to his mouth, splashing comets of grease onto his shirt. But there is a quiet, wounded-bear quality about him, and his efforts to appear normal, to make polite conversation while trying to mask with cautious smiles the ruined state of his teeth, make me want to hold him and weep. He is, other than Jackie, my favorite of the clan.

Grandma's carrot cake is served, alight with a battery of birthday candles, and James makes it through two bites before excusing himself from the table. I take two bites more than he does and follow him out of the restaurant. I find him on the front steps, smoking and slipping something silver and flasklike into his pants pocket.

"Hey, hold on a minute," I say. "Mind if I join you?"

He hands me the flask and I drink deeply of some liquid that tastes like what I can only describe as paint thinner added to whiskey.

He takes the flask from me and toasts: "Here's to the unclaimed."

His voice is gravelly, like stones inside a cement mixer.

"That's us," I say. "The undesirables. It's amazing they let us sit at the family table."

"Except for Jackie, they're all assholes. Even more than most people," he says cheerfully.

"Jackie's certainly been my guardian angel."

"You're lucky on that score," he says. "But I think you're equally Jackie's angel. She told me that when you two first got together in New York, a crazy woman at a fruit stand tried to rob her, and you chased her away with your umbrella." He regards the flask thoughtfully. "I'm pretty sure my guardian angel drinks."

I laugh. "The woman was just a street crazy, but I thought she was threatening Jackie."

"It's a natural trait for you, protecting the ones you love." He takes another drink, dribbling a bit of dark liquid onto his already stained shirt. A group of people leaving the restaurant give us a wide berth while moving down the stairs.

"Some people have to be taught to do the right thing," James says, throwing a gawking kid the stink eye. He exhales a cloud of smoke sharply through his teeth and hands the flask back to me. "What are you working on now?"

"Big drug case," I say. "But things are not going well. People have been killed."

"That happens when you deal with bad people. You close to catching the bastards?"

"I don't know. Something happened today. Really shook me up." I tell him about Lana's murder.

"Nam vets used to take ears from dead Vietcong. They were proof of kills. Some of the guys who stayed in-country too long kept them as trophies. So maybe the killer is a vet?"

"I don't think so. But it just doesn't feel like our boy. He has no problem wasting people, but it's not his MO. At least, not one we've seen before."

James takes back the whiskey and pats me on the knee. "You know the last thing a murder victim prays for before lights-out? A smart cop. You're a smart cop. You'll figure it out." He drains the flask and shakes the empty container dejectedly. "Did you know I was an MP? I was in Saigon during the last days. Sunsets like bloody ribbons across the sky, from the fires in the jungles. The stench of smoke and gasoline together to this day makes me puke."

My heart rate accelerates and I look at him, startled. "The red streak," I tell him. I remember Lana's ragged, blood-matted hair as she lay on the kitchen floor. "When I first saw Lana, she had a bright red streak in her hair. But today it was missing. Somebody did a rough job cutting it off. I only just realized it."

"You think it's another trophy?"

"There would be no other reason to take a piece of her hair. Removing it wouldn't hide her identity."

"Well," he says, using the railing to pull himself painfully to his feet. "My training sergeant used to say that anything added to a crime scene was a clue. Anything missing was a direction." He looks at the restaurant door and then at me. "Will you take my good-byes back inside? I think it's time for me to go home, and your telling them I've left will soften their disappointment at your returning."

"Thank you, James. I owe you one."

He rubs a hand over his mouth and scratches his chest. "Invite me to dinner sometime."

I nod. "Absolutely. You okay to drive?"

"What time is it?"

"About eight."

"As long as it's before nine, I'm good." He gives me a pat on the arm and I watch him shambling toward his car, an old Crown Vic, and then I return to the table, where no one but Jackie seemed to notice I was gone.

As soon as we get home, I put on my sneakers and go running along the jogging trails close to our apartment. I run for half a mile before I thrash my way into some bushes and relieve myself of the burden of the barbecue extravaganza I had eaten earlier. I thought the ribs had burned going down, but it's nothing compared to what comes back up. All the toxic energy of the evening, all the hate and fear, all that fire.

I wipe my mouth and continue the course for another four miles, squeezing Tabasco sauce and bad juju from my pores. We've had a tough start to the case. But we now have Bender's money and weapons and some of his meth. I try to believe that Lana's will be the last civilian death before we have to deal with Ruiz.

The Saint Michael's medal knocks rhythmically, comfortingly, against my sternum as I quicken my pace, offering the possibility that maybe higher forces are already handling El Gitano. I hear Benny's voice, as I often do while settling into the vacant mental space that a long run gives.

Betty, he tells me. *None of them know what you're worth. They'll always start you in the outfield. But that's why God gave you those long legs. So you could run the bastards down.*

When I get back to the apartment, Jackie is waiting for me under clean linen sheets.

10

I stand staring at the whiteboard in the station's task-force room, and then I take up a red marker, cross out Lana's name. I informed the team earlier about Lana's hair being cut, the red-dyed section removed, and got only puzzled looks from the men.

I called Maclin to tell him about realizing the hair was missing, and he'd thanked me by sharing the crime scene photos.

Ryan has been studying the board and the photos as though they are ancient texts to be translated. There's a constant furrow to Ryan's brow that makes him appear earnest and contemplative. Surprisingly, Ryan has never seen a dead body, even though he's been on patrol in Dallas for five years — plenty of insensible drunks and passed-out junkies, but never a victim of a violent homicide.

Having gotten his shield only a few months ago — fast-forwarded in his career by being consistently the best marksman in the department — he hasn't yet absorbed what

Uncle Benny used to tell me were the hardest lessons in detective work: how to tolerate frustration, fight boredom, resist apathy, and inure oneself to the evil that men do.

I also suspect that I scare the shit out of him.

"Ryan," I bark, startling him. "Where's Ruiz?"

"Umm," he says, his color rising. Adjusting his shoulder sling and cracking the knuckles on both hands, he offers, "Mexico?"

Craddock snorts. "Good guess. I guess we can all leave early today." He peels back the wrapper on an oversize Texas Moon Pie, a chocolate-and-marshmallow-stuffed cookie, and takes a mouthful.

"No reports of Ruiz in El Paso," Seth tells us. "Or in any of the other usual crossings. Both Homicide and FBI are running fingerprints from Bender's house, but it's going to take more time to get IDs. Path reports on the body will take longer. All Forensics will say is that Lana's throat was cut with a large, very sharp knife, and it looks like the killer sat on her chest and arms to do it. The witness, Tony Ha, is saying nothing; he's totally lawyered up. He's been pretty much ruled out as the murder suspect, though."

"As tiny as Lana was," Hoskins says, "she could have beaten the bejeezus out of Ha if she'd wanted to."

"Maybe Ruiz is dead too, lying in a ditch or in the desert somewhere," Craddock says. "It's just plain creepy how quiet it is on this guy's whereabouts. No one on the streets of Dallas has seen or heard from him."

I try returning my focus to the whiteboard, wondering if our attention to Lana's murder is pulling us away from Ruiz or leading us closer to finding him. Last night I had a nightmare, prompted by the thundering footsteps of the Russian woman upstairs. Believing that I was awake and certain that someone was making pounding noises in the bathroom, in my dream I had disentangled my legs from the sheets and walked cautiously to the door. After pausing to listen to the sounds of someone knocking erratically on the baseboard, I opened the door to witness Lana lying on the floor, bleeding profusely from the upper body. The gaping slash in her throat opened like a ventriloquist's dummy, and a voice came from the wound, saying, "What is taking you so fucking long?"

"Maybe she just cut her hair," Hoskins adds now. "Women do that, you know."

"Not usually by a butcher," I say.

"It signifies something." Ryan says this so softly that I almost miss it.

"What did you say?" I ask.

Ryan clears his throat, gesturing at a photo with a close-up of Lana's contorted, bloody face. "The missing red hair means something."

James Earle had said last night that things missing from a crime scene give direction. "Okay. Go on," I prompt.

"He could have taken the hair from anywhere on her head, but he took only the dyed part. So maybe she broke some code or taboo or something by dyeing her hair, and the killer removed it."

"That's good, Ryan," I say. "You just got yourself a project for the next hour. I want you to do some research on whether any of the cartel enforcers in the recent past have taken these kinds of trophies, locks of hair or body parts."

"Oh, great," Hoskins says, standing from his chair, restless and obviously irritated. "More tail-chasing."

When the team disperses I sit with Seth and stare at the board. "What's this feel like to you, Riot?"

"What it doesn't feel like is Mexican cartel," he says.

"It's weird. Sadistic. This does not seem like the work of Ruiz. Possibly Asian-gang retaliation?"

"You still got any gang connections?"

"As my Lamesa grandma used to say, 'Hell, yeah.'" He tells me to hold tight for a few minutes, he has an idea. He leaves the room to make a call and I go searching for Hoskins.

Things have been strained between us ever since the Bender shooting. Hoskins takes every opportunity to bait me, to nip at my heels, testing my patience. I could put the hammer down on him, but I need his cooperation. My mother used to have a saying that, spoken in Polish, ran on like the Gettysburg Address. The gist of it is this: Tough beef twice boiled is as soft as an egg. Or, as Jackie would advise, kill him with kindness.

I find Hoskins hunched over his desk, frowning in concentration at his phone, which he's maneuvering like a hovercraft to better catch the light so he can read his texts.

"Detective Hoskins," I say.

Hoskins looks up at me in a way that tells me he's bracing for a rebuke or a reprimand and he's already mentally forming his comeback, telling me how miserably I'm managing the Ruiz case. Itching to say how even finding Bender's hidden cache of money does not make up for all the trouble of sorting through the bodies and missed arrests.

"You know, Detective, I think the way you handled yourself yesterday at the crime scene was really admirable."

He regards me with a surprised, wide-eyed expression, as though I've slammed a crowbar down on his head. It is absolutely the last thing he had expected to come out of my mouth.

"Seth tells me you stood your ground at the Bender

house, shadowing Homicide until we showed up. I just wanted to say good work, Bob."

Sometimes a kind word is more effective than a crowbar. At that moment Seth signals to me and I walk away repressing a grin, knowing that Hoskins will spend the rest of the morning trying to figure out what exactly I meant by my little speech of support.

We drive in Seth's car south on the Tollway, and he tells me we're going to Little Korea, a place known locally for massage parlors and small industrial office complexes housing various legit and nonlegit businesses. There is also a mah-jongg parlor and social club nestled among the office buildings that, Seth informs me, is a front for the gangs responsible for most of the Asian sex- and drug-trafficking trade in Dallas.

"You heard of Operation Flaming Dragon?" he asks me.

I nod. "Yeah, of course."

Operation Flaming Dragon was the largest sex-trade bust Texas had ever seen. Dozens of massage parlors in and around Dallas had been shut down following a two-year undercover operation, supported by local police, a special Vice task force, and the FBI. The arrested were women, most of them Chinese, who had been lured into the sex trade, along with some of their handlers. The bosses at the top, however—many of them working from the East and West Coasts—remained untouched. Blue Heaven, where Lana had worked, was a satellite operation that was lucky enough to have escaped being shuttered.

"My buddy Brant was one of the undercovers on that operation. He's aware of the Lana Yu case, and I told him we needed some inside help to determine if her murder was in any way connected to the Asian-gang activity. He told me one of his contacts owes him a favor."

The mah-jongg parlor is a one-story, windowless stucco building with a small plaque by the door inscribed with Chinese pictographs.

He parks his car in a spot close to the entrance and turns off the motor.

"They're still going to be a tad resentful about the most recent arrests, so we need to be eyes wide open. You okay with me taking the lead on the questioning in there?" he asks.

"Absolutely," I tell him. "But, Riot, you know we're edging into a Homicide investigation."

"Yeah, I know," he says, showing teeth and slipping on his sunglasses. "Ain't it fun?"

We walk through the unlocked door without knocking and pass through a narrow foyer into a large, dimly lit open room with pool tables on one side and card and mah-jongg tables on the other. A long bar lines the far wall, covered with neon beer signs. The only people in the place are four old ladies playing mah-jongg and languidly smoking.

They pause in their game and look at us briefly but then pointedly ignore us and resume expertly slinging their tiles against the green felt.

Almost immediately a young teenager with a black helmet of carefully coiffed hair enters the hall from a back room.

"I'm here to see Mei," Seth tells him, bringing out his badge.

The guy signals to me to show my badge as well and then motions for us to follow him into the back. The room we enter is paneled with fake wood and smells of decades of nicotine and mold. In an expensive leather office chair sits a Chinese man, perhaps in his thirties, wearing tight jeans, a pearl-snap Western shirt, and pricey Nocona boots, which are propped up on the desk. Singer K. D. Lang, piped in through high-end Bose speakers, is singing about constant cravings.

Eyes closed, head nodding to the music, he pretends we're not in the room until the song stops. Then he opens his eyes and smiles, but with his mouth only.

"We need to talk to Mei," Seth tells him. "I think you were notified we were coming."

"Mei's not here."

"And you are...?" Seth asks.

"I'm Mr. Lee," he says, lighting a cigarette.

Without being asked, Seth and I sit on the two chairs facing the desk. Lee quickly pulls his legs off the desk and opens a drawer just wide enough to put his hand inside.

"I like your coat, Detective," Lee says, referring to Seth's aged denim jacket. "You a real cowboy?" He giggles and grinds his teeth as though he's leveled a deadly insult.

My partner gives the grin he saves for careless, posturing perps who mistake his good looks for dim-wittedness, not realizing that a shiny package can hide something that can both tell time in a calm and relentless way and explode, taking most of your face along with it.

Without looking away from Lee, he says, "Riz, I want you to take out your gun, and if this fucker removes his hand from the drawer holding a weapon, I want you to shoot him in the head."

I unholster my gun, rest it in the crook of one elbow. And just to make the point more indelible, I stand up. All five foot eleven of me. Lee has to refocus his gaze on my partner or risk a neck sprain.

Seth puts both elbows on the desk. "Now, where is Mei?"

The door opens and I turn on my heel defensively, but

it's only one of the old ladies shuffling in, cigarette in hand. Seth, who has not taken his eyes off Lee, says, "I want to talk to Mei. I'm not leaving here until I speak to him."

The old lady has moved behind Lee's chair and says something to him in Mandarin or Cantonese and he answers her. She calmly stubs out her cigarette in an ashtray on the desk and then, without warning, begins to viciously strike the back of his head. Lee ducks, folding both arms over his ears to protect himself from the flurry of blows. She continues slapping him with surprising vigor, using both hands, until she has driven him from his expensive chair and sent him out of the room accompanied by a stream of insults.

She then sits in Lee's chair and tells us, "I am Mei."

"You know who sent us?" Seth asks her, doing his best to mask his surprise.

"Yes, I know," she answers. "The Vice detective told me."

She deliberately closes the drawer Lee had opened, and I holster my gun.

"You know we're in Narcotics, not Vice, right?" I ask.

She flicks her eyes briefly toward me and says, "My other grandson is in prison on a drug charge. If you can help him, then I can perhaps help you."

"We'll do what we can," Seth says.

She nods once, motioning for me to sit. "What can I do for you?" she asks.

"You know about Lana Yu?" Seth asks. "The one who was murdered yesterday?"

Mei takes her time lighting another cigarette as though carefully considering the question. Finally she says, "I watch the news, Detective."

"Then you know how she was murdered."

Mei cocks her head to the side and exhales a long stream of yellow smoke. "Someone cut her throat."

"That's right. We're pursuing a Mexican drug dealer she was involved with, but it doesn't feel like a cartel murder."

"And you want to know if the killer could be Chinese."

"We just want to rule out any uninterested parties."

She studies the long column of ash on the end of her cigarette. "To look here is to look in the wrong place. You say the killer is not Mexican. Your murderer is not Chinese either. He's . . . something else."

She folds her hands on top of the desk—just a demure little grandma in an oversize chair—and turns her attention to me. "This man is a destroyer of women. He cut off her ears, is that right?" She studies my red hair. "And also a piece of her hair."

"Did Tony Ha tell you that?" I ask. The ears and the hair being taken had been kept from the press.

Mei takes a small piece of hard candy from a glass bowl next to the ashtray, slowly unwraps the paper, and puts it in her mouth.

"Detective, I know everything that happens in my family and in my community," she tells me. "But I have no idea who killed Lana."

She extends the candy bowl to me. "But maybe you don't want to know either."

As we're driving back to the station, Sergeant Taylor calls to say that a highway patrolman in Weatherford, a town about sixty miles southwest of Dallas, just found Lana's battered and abandoned BMW. With a body in the trunk.

11

Seth and I drive the sixty miles to the rural farm road just south of Weatherford where the Beemer has been found. Within fifteen minutes of leaving Dallas, we see the flat terrain begin to roll into gentle hills; the sunburned grass lining the highways is yellow and spiked. We pass tiny houses, double-wide trailers, and a few car lots the size of small cities flying enormous Texas flags in the suffocating heat—at the same level as the American flag, because as any true Texan will tell you, Texas is a republic, not merely a state—on poles the height of cell towers.

But mostly it's just miles and miles of nothing but miles and miles. There is literally one cloud in the whole damn, never-ending sky.

Before leaving the station, I called the Weatherford Sheriff's Office and was put through to their Detective Peavy, lead criminal investigator with the CID unit. He confirmed that a battered BMW with Lana's plates attached had been found abandoned on a dirt road just outside the city limits. And that there was indeed a dead body in the trunk of the car. I filled Peavy in on our investigation with Ruiz and on Lana's murder.

It's been ten minutes of silence in the car with Seth. My stomach is in rebellion, and I'm wondering if one last stubborn bit of scorched meat from Babcock's is yet clinging to my insides like Ripley's nesting alien. Seth has been stealing looks at me from the driver's seat, trying to gauge my mood since my last uttered phrase, which was "Doesn't it ever fucking rain here?"

"Hey, Riz, I've decided to keep Bender's dog," he says. "What do you think of my calling her Delilah?" He does a right-hand pass on a car doing at least eighty in the left lane.

I glance at the speedometer. "You know you're doing ninety, right?" I drive fast, but Seth drives like he's perpetually on the Autobahn.

"Yeah. So what do you think of the name?" He takes his eyes off the road an unnervingly long time to look at me. When I don't answer, he glides back into the left lane but eases up on the gas pedal a bit.

"I think, Seth, that if you're going to keep a poodle, you need to give it a stronger name. Like Spike, or Tornado."

Grinning, he winks at me. "I've already taught her to sit and roll over."

I mutter something obscene about all females rolling over for Seth and he says, "What was that?"

"I said the dog already knew how to sit. Christ, you're going all queer on me. Delilah was Samson's undoing, remember?"

Seth gets quiet for a bit and then says, "How about Rita?"

"It's better than Delilah," I say. "Although Riot and Rita sounds like a country band."

"Riz?" he says.

"Yeah?"

"No matter how this goes, I've got your back."

"I know," I say. If I'm thankful for anything this day, it's my poodle-toting partner.

I notice that the one cloud in the sky has elongated into the shape of a celestial pointing finger.

We turn off the highway onto the dirt road and, after a few miles, see Lana's BMW with several squad cars and a local EMT van parked behind it. Parker County Forensics is still working the scene; a body bag's on a stretcher. We introduce ourselves to Peavy, a tall, broad-chested cop about forty-five, wearing boots and a straw Stetson. He tells us first thing that it was supposed to be his day off.

"It never fails," he says. "First time in a month we find a body, and my partner, who is supposed to cover for me, is having emergency back surgery. He fell off the roof this morning moving his dish."

He continues the running monologue with his own home-maintenance injuries. There've been a few.

When we're ready, Peavy unzips the body bag, and inside is an older, corpulent man, bound wrists and ankles, shot twice in the head. The corpse has been a corpse for maybe a few hours, and Peavy tells us he thinks the guy had been placed in the trunk soon after the shooting. Seeing a body so recently separated from life is always a jolt.

I look at the man's slightly purpled eyelids, the black and gray lashes like the bristles of an artist's brush, the lips as relaxed as a Buddha's smile, and can readily imagine what the man would have been like animated.

The body is wearing a gray uniform with shiny brass buttons.

"That some kind of a band uniform?" Seth asks.

"No," Peavy answers. "It's a Civil War uniform."

"Civil War," I repeat, unsure I've heard him right.

"See those patches and the sash?" he asks, pointing to the dead man's shoulders and midsection.

I blink a couple of times. "And ... ?"

"A Confederate reenactor," Peavy offers, trying to clarify.

"Reenactor," I echo, having no idea what he's talking about. My first thought is that he's an extra from a movie set.

"It's a group that gets together and stages Civil War battles. Uniforms, armaments, sometimes small cavalry units. Even cannons. They do it a lot around here."

I look at Seth and he shrugs.

"They do drug deals too?" I ask Peavy.

"Not that I know of. It's not that kind of group."

I detect a note of defensiveness creeping into the investigator's voice, but I ask, "Then what was he doing in the trunk of a car we suspect was being driven by a large-scale drug dealer?"

Peavy shakes his head. "I have no idea. But it looks like whoever was driving ran out of gas. The keys are in the ignition. Maybe the driver took off on foot? Got picked up?" He shrugs. Ruiz is not his problem, but the body is.

He looks around as though to point out the obvious. It's dusk, we're ten miles away from Weatherford, and it's going to be dark soon. One of the local cops who's been murmuring into his car radio comes running with the news that the wife of one of the reenactors called in because she's not heard from her husband in over twenty-four hours.

Peavy tells us that the reenactors do military exercises on several hundred acres of private undeveloped land nearby that's used for deer hunting in season. It's somewhat hilly and full of dense brush, boggy after it rains, criss-crossed with small streams. Cell phone reception is poor to nonexistent.

"They leave their cell phones in their cars and are allowed only one call a day, at noon," he tells us. "The parking area is on higher ground, where the reception is better. The wife says that some of the other women have called her and they've not heard from their husbands either."

"How many men in the group?" I ask.

The patrolman shrugs. "About fourteen. Give or take."

I point to the corpse. "Was he part of that group?"

He nods. "Probably so."

"Could they be lost?" Seth asks.

Peavy shakes his head. "Not likely. They've all grown up hunting around here."

The ball of light to the west is well below the horizon, flaming the lone cloud to a deep magenta.

Peavy asks us, "Do you want to trail us to the encampment? See if the men know the victim or have seen Ruiz?"

It's unlikely that El Gitano has headed back toward the costume party, but it's worth a look.

Peavy traces on a map the farm-to-market road that leads to a gate entrance to the deer lease, beyond which, somewhere, is the reenactors' encampment. We drive caravan-style: a Weatherford patrol car, Peavy, then us. We trail behind for several miles through a curtain of dust kicked up from the dirt road. After fifteen minutes or so, I see through the headlights a high deer fence stretching into the darkness on either side of the road and a tall gate straddling it. The cop stops at the gate, opens it, and signals for Seth to close it after we've passed through.

The road just beyond the gate forks, and the two cars in front of us veer to the left in the direction of the base camp. While Seth gets out of the car to wrestle the gate closed, I glance to the right and see in the distance a faint, solitary light bobbing its way toward us. It's not a flashlight beam. It's yellowish and winking, more like a candle flame. It starts swinging crazily as though someone's trying to signal us.

When Seth gets back into the car, I point to the right. "Do you see that?"

Squinting through the windshield, he puts the car into gear, turns to the right, and drives slowly toward whoever is signaling us. He puts the headlights on high and within a few minutes a boy of about twelve jogs into the blue, columned beams carrying a lantern and panting like he's been running for miles. He's dressed like an extra in a Western movie, with high-water pants, linen collarless shirt, and a thumb-buster revolver shoved under a broad leather belt.

When he sees us get out of the car, he drops the lantern in the road, puts his hands on his knees. He points back up the road and gasps. "Help...please...they're trying to kill us."

"What's your name, son?" Seth asks him, hand on his own gun.

"Kyle Parsons," he says.

"We're Dallas Police, Kyle. Get in the car," I tell him, and he scrambles into the backseat. I get in next to him, but not until I make him give me his pappy's pistol. It weighs a ton. He must have to grasp it with both hands to hold it aloft.

"Who's trying to kill you?" I ask.

"The Mexicans."

I catch Seth's eye as he gets in the car. The kid looks terrified. "What Mexicans, Kyle?"

"I don't know. Just Mexicans. They've been shooting at us." His eyes tear up. "It's all my fault."

From the front seat Seth hands him a bottle of water and Kyle drinks half of it without pausing. "What are you doing out here alone?" Seth asks.

Kyle gestures in a westward direction and says, through choking breaths, "There's a group of us camping over by the stream. I'm with my dad and uncle."

"Better call Peavy," I tell Seth. We're not on the local police's radio band so he tries calling him on his cell phone. No signal.

"Okay, Kyle," I say, putting my hand on his shoulder. "Take a deep breath and tell us what's going on."

"I took a bucket down to the stream to get water for our horses—"

"What time?"

"This morning. On the other side of the stream, at the base of a tree, I saw a big red bag. I crossed the stream and looked in the bag and...there was a lot of money in it."

"How much money?" I ask.

"I don't know. A lot."

"Okay, then what happened?"

"I took the bag, but I forgot the bucket at the stream. I hid the money in the old barn. I figured finders keepers. Right?" He looks to me for validation, but I just motion him to go on.

"When I got back to the camp, my sergeant, Mr. Billings, yelled at me for leaving the bucket behind. Mr. Billings went to get it. But he never came back. We heard shots by the stream and we all ran to see what was going on.

"That's when we saw the Mexicans. Five of them. There were some cars parked up on the far side of the stream and these guys started firing at us. One of them had an automatic rifle, but we returned fire with our muskets."

Muskets. They returned assault-weapon fire with Civil War muskets. My mouth must be hanging open in disbelief because Kyle says, "It's all we had. We couldn't call anyone…" He begins to cry.

I have to ask him the next question. "Was your sergeant, Mr. Billings, a heavyset man in a gray uniform? Blue sash around his middle?"

He nods and wipes his nose with his sleeve. "Is he okay?"

Kyle sees the look on my face and covers his eyes with both arms.

"We shot one of them," he says with surprising anger. "But two of ours went down at the river trying to make it to the fort. I think they're dead too."

"The fort?" Seth asks. He's still trying to reach Peavy on the cell.

"It's just an old house in front of the barn. We use it for our maneuvers. There were eleven of us barricaded at the house all day." He looks at me, eyes filled with tears, snot mixed with dirt running down his upper lip. "They kept yelling at us, telling us what they were going to do to us when we ran out of ammunition. They said we had their money and a big package of drugs. But I swear there were no drugs in the bag. Just money. I would have given it back if I could've. When it turned dark, the others told me to go and try to get help. I snuck out and made my way to the road."

While he's talking, I'm doing the math. If there were five dealers to begin with and one got shot and one drove Lana's car away, that leaves three armed, pissed-off dealers working to get their money and drugs back.

And maybe we've just stumbled onto the place where Ruiz has hidden his stash of cocaine. The main highway through Weatherford, I-20, runs southwest directly to El Paso.

I peer through the rear window at the road stretching back into the darkness and wonder when the hell Peavy's going to realize we're not behind him and come investigate.

It dawns on me that Kyle's lantern was a beacon not only for us but also for the drug dealers.

"Kyle, when did you light the lantern?" I ask the boy, and then I see headlights approaching in the distance; it's Peavy coming back to check on us.

At the same moment, the front of our car is sprayed with gunfire, explosively shattering the windshield inward, pellets of safety glass hitting like BB pellets.

I throw myself down over Kyle, unholstering my gun, and I hear Seth swearing from the front seat. It sounds like two shooters with semi pistols and they're moving clockwise around the car. The front passenger-seat window shatters as well, the bullets punching holes in the metal frame. I reach over Kyle, open the back door away from the shooters, and shove him out onto the road. Seth opens his door and falls out, gun drawn.

"Goddamn it, they shot me!" he yells angrily.

I return fire over the hood but only briefly, as the shooters are spraying the length of the car with a closer-range assault.

Behind me, the headlights of Peavy's car have come to a stop, and I hear the distinctive ping of bullets hitting the vehicle's frame. Then the headlights begin to rapidly retreat, "advancing to the rear," as Uncle Benny used to say. Peavy can't see who he's shooting at and takes the sensible course. I would have done the same thing.

The assailants are firing at us again and I feel Kyle's hand tugging mine.

"We're about to lose our heads, partner!" I yell at Seth. "We gotta do something—"

Kyle yanks hard enough to pull my arm out of its socket. "Come on, come on." He points to the woods opposite the road.

"Can you move?" I call to Seth.

"Oh, shit," he moans, but he manages to stagger up and the three of us run blindly into the underbrush. The ground slopes into a shallow gully, and we fall, tripping over thorny ground cover. It's thick and it's dark, but the assailants have heard our progress, and they're shooting in our direction. They've taken up a defensive position behind our car. We return their fire, but they're relentless. They can't see us well in the thicket, but eventually a bullet will find its mark.

Kyle is tugging at me again. He says he can find his way back to the barn and we can take cover there. If, that is, the dealers haven't already overrun it.

We have a choice. We can wait for Peavy's backup, which will take no less than twenty, thirty minutes, or we can advance to the rear also. Now I'm wishing I'd let Kyle keep his thumb-buster.

"How bad are you hit?" I ask Seth.

He takes my hand and guides it to the wound at his side. My hand comes away wet with blood.

"Are you in a lot of pain?" I whisper.

"Well." He pants. "It hurts worse than a pulled tooth."

"How far to the barn?" I grab at Kyle's sleeve and he looks at me, his eyes huge in his head.

He says, "Ten minutes, if we run like hell."

"I can make it," Seth says.

We plunge deeper into the trees, Kyle's white shirt showing a blur of pale in front of us, and soon we're running a narrow, cleared footpath. The evening is sweltering, with a groundswell of dampness that smells like burned oatmeal. There's no breeze and the mosquitoes are swarming. I feel them boring into every bit of exposed flesh.

We keep moving at a steady pace for about five minutes, until Seth's legs buckle and he collapses, breathing hard, onto the ground.

I crouch down, looking back up the path, and in the distance I see an occasional sweep of a flashlight through the trees.

"Shit," I whisper.

I hear Benny's voice in my head telling me to get up. Now.

"Get the fuck up, Seth," I say, and I haul my partner roughly to his feet. I don't have to tell him that these guys won't give a rat's ass that we're cops.

"We're close," Kyle whispers, and we keep moving, Seth's arm draped around my neck.

Another few minutes and we come upon a clearing and the hulking form of what must be the barn on a slight rise about thirty yards away. There is no light coming from the barn, no sound. We could stay crouched where we are, but the path leads to us and we're too exposed.

"Keep moving?" I ask Seth.

He takes both my arms and pulls himself up. "We can't stay here."

Hunched over, we stagger for the barn across the exposed clearing and hear gunfire coming from behind us, the dull thunk of bullets throwing dirt clods around our feet. I see the barn door but have no idea if it's unlocked or what's on the inside, and I'm thinking we're better off running for the far side of the building.

A rifle is fired over our heads. It's coming from high up, like the shooter's on the roof. We cringe and throw ourselves flat, but from the blackness of the open loft door, a man's wavering voice calls out to us. "You all better run faster."

Then whoever's in the barn begins firing off a large pistol, with earsplitting, echoing rounds. It's aimed at our attackers behind us, and we scrabble up again, yank at the barn door, and throw ourselves inside. Kyle bolts the doors and we sit, blind and gasping.

For a moment there's total silence. I can't hear our defender up in the loft and so with my gun still drawn I call out, "Hey...hello? Dallas Police!"

"Move toward my voice," the man says. "Toward the ladder. It's safer up here."

We feel our way to the ladder, our eyes adjusting to the dark, and I see the silhouette of a figure in a long coat standing in the shadows above me.

"Come on," the man calls to us. "The boy knows me."

Telling Kyle to go first up the ladder, I holster my gun and crawl up behind Seth, who has to make his way slowly and one-armed.

The man helps Kyle onto the loft and says, "Hey, boy. Good to see you're alive." He hoists Seth off the ladder and reaches down a hand for me. I can see now that he's an older man, in his eighties at least, gaunt and wearing a gray uniform with a lot of medals pinned to his chest.

He's also wearing a sword.

"My," the man says, guiding me up, "aren't you—"

Finding my footing, stepping onto the loft, I finish the sentence for him. "Yeah, I know. I'm tall."

Kyle says, "General, these two are the police."

The man gives me the once-over. "Uh-huh, right..." he says doubtfully. Then he extends his hand to shake mine. "I'm General Stuart Lyndon Haskell, Company E, Fourth Texas Infantry, Hood's Confederate Brigade."

"Of course you are," I say. I can just make out Benny's laughter barreling across the void.

A forceful rattling at the barred door we've just entered through causes the general to draw his pistol and fire wildly through the wood. The explosion is deafening but the rattling stops.

From outside the door the word *putos* is screamed in retreat.

"We're safe here," the general says. "Unless they decide to burn us out. You've entered through the back door. The front door is over yonder. Through that door, a few hundred feet away, is the fort that's been under attack all day. It's about time you showed up."

"You've been here all day?" I ask.

The general has taken off his sash and he balls it up, presses it to Seth's bloody abdomen. "Yes, that is what I just said. Until now they didn't know I was here. I figured the best offense was a good defense." He hands Seth a canteen. "Good thing they didn't think to check the back door earlier."

"How many reenactors are in the fort?"

"Close to a dozen," he says. "A few are wounded, I think. They've been pinned down a good while now. Outgunned."

"How many attackers?" Seth asks.

"Three. It was down to one man watching the house with an automatic rifle." He turns to me and sniffs. "Until you led the other two back here again."

"How do you know all this?"

"I'm old, ma'am, I'm not deaf. Those Mexicans have been making enough noise all day to wake the dead."

"You know what they're looking for?" I ask.

The general gets up and, from under a pile of hay, pulls out a large red duffel bag. "I believe this is what they're looking for," he says.

"This is all my fault," Kyle whispers.

The general and I agree with him at the same time.

"There'll be more police here soon," I tell him. "We just have to sit tight."

"We're going to burn you out if you don't come out now!" the voice from outside yells. There is a pause and then: "You have one minute!"

I look at Seth and he shakes his head. He's in pain and bleeding heavily. It's been nearly twenty minutes; Pcavy's police should be at the encampment soon. The question is, will it be within the one minute we have left before the Mexican barbecue?

The general hands Kyle his small sidearm, another cap-and-ball job, and says, "I'm thinking we have one Mexican at the front and another one at the back of the barn now. I don't think we can make a run for it."

The old man leans in and pats me sympathetically on the arm. "And, my dear," he says, "I wasn't going to remark on how tall you are, only how lovely you are. I've always been partial to redheads."

"Fuck it!" the voice outside yells. "We're just going to burn you out!"

"Well, we can't sit here and be burned alive. There's

only one thing for it," the general says, straightening up. He walks to the hayloft door at the front of the barn and pitches his large pistol to the ground. He yells, "I'm unarmed now!"

"What are you doing?" I shout. "Get down!"

"Yeah, fucker," the voice outside roars, "but you've got cops with you, and they're armed."

"I have what you want!" the general shouts. He turns to me and winks. "Ever heard of Stonewall Jackson?" he stage-whispers.

"What?" I say. Stonewall Jackson? We're trapped with a lunatic.

"Harpers Ferry?" he asks gleefully.

Even though I order the general to move away from the open hayloft, he stands fully exposed to our attackers outside, one hand resting on a tall, bulky object, some long-abandoned farm implement covered with a canvas cloth. He opens the red duffel bag, pulls out a stack of cash. "You burn us," he tells the men outside, "you burn the money too."

"How 'bout I just shoot you and come up and get the money. Or burn down the house over there, now we know you've got it!"

"Then my officer friends will have to shoot you." There is silence outside the barn and the general continues. "I'll make a deal with you. Give me your word you'll leave and I'll throw down your money."

"Listen," I whisper fiercely, "you throw that money down and we've lost our bargaining chip. They'll set fire to the barn quicker than you can say Gettysburg."

The general looks at me, the bag hugged to his chest, his face set, and I know I've lost all control or even influence on the outcome.

"We are so fucked," I tell Seth.

I crawl frantically to the open loft, dare a quick glance outward, and yell down to our assailants, "Take the deal! Weatherford Police are on their way!"

That brings laughter, but it's a tense laughter because they know it's only a matter of time before reinforcements come.

"Fucking country-ass Weatherford Police. Shut up, bitch! Okay, throw down the money and we'll leave."

Without hesitation, the general heaves the bag with all the cash down into the clearing in front of the barn.

There are a few seconds of quiet and then I yell for the general to get down out of the line of fire because I know they're going to start shooting at him. I crawl as quickly as I can away from the open loft, imagining we're going to have to run for it, hoping the dealers won't pick us off as we escape from a burning barn.

But the general yanks the canvas off the bulky object, and I see that it's not a farm implement as I had first thought. It's a cannon, the barrel pointing downward. And he's holding in one hand a long string lanyard attached to the barrel. He alerts me that one of the Mexicans is approaching the duffel bag, gun drawn.

With his other hand, the general quietly unsheathes his sword, and I distinctly hear him say, "When it's war, draw the sword and throw away the scabbard!" He bounces on the balls of his feet a few times, satisfied. "I've always wanted to say that," he muses.

He turns to us and, in an aside, says, "Cover your ears."

He gives the lanyard a good yank and a shattering, echoing boom erupts, the explosive recoil sending the cannon careening backward. It plummets over the edge of the loft and crashes to the floor of the barn.

The general ducks, and the shooter with the assault rifle begins spraying the loft with bullets, sending wood planks, metal fragments, and smoking strands of hay in all directions around our heads. Then the assailant's fire is drawn away from the barn and I realize there are now other shooters in the woods. A lot of them. It's the Weatherford reinforcements. Less than five minutes later, the firing comes to an abrupt end, and from the cover of darkness, Peavy calls our names.

12

As it turns out, the Weatherford Police have come to our aid with most of their on-duty force—eight squad cars, four highway patrolmen, a few unmarked detectives' cars, and two ambulances—as well as half a dozen off-duty police wearing dove-hunting camos and carrying 12-gauge shotguns who had picked up Peavy's radio calls and decided to come and join the battle.

To say there is overkill from department-issued weaponry would be an understatement.

What's left of the south-of-the-border incursion are two bullet-riddled drug dealers at the barn; one dead at the stream, shot earlier by the reenactors; and a fourth casualty, hit by the general's cannon, who has to be bagged in pieces. Evidently, a six-pound cannonball will do that. This last assailant turns out to be Ruiz's bodyguard El Guiso, aka the Stew. Seth and two wounded reenactors are taken immediately by ambulance to the Weatherford hospital. As Kyle had feared, two more from his group are found dead in the water. Additionally, one costumed reveler, an overweight smoker, suffers chest pains and is taken by a patrolman for treatment.

To the best of my ability, I confirm that none of the four attackers is Ruiz, but a brief search of the barn uncovers a large quantity of cocaine. As soon as I get a cell signal, I call Taylor and let him know that we have recovered the drugs and a significant amount of cash. Ruiz is still missing, but he's been stripped of everything: money, drugs, and men.

After seeing Kyle safely reunited with his father and uncle, I catch a ride to the hospital with a local policeman.

The general agrees to be checked out by medical staff only if he can ride with me in the back of the squad car, and, during the half-hour drive, lights flashing and siren blaring, he explains to me about Harpers Ferry.

"It was one of Stonewall Jackson's most brilliant Civil War engagements," the general hollers over the siren. "A tactical victory ensured by cannons hauled over mountain ranges, some of them during the dead of night, so that they could be fired at Union troops from high ground. It was an impossible maneuver, but the stars aligned, and disaster for his troops was averted."

The general then pats me on the knee and tells me again how taken he is with redheads. "And," he adds, waggling his brows, "I don't mind dating a woman who's taller than me."

When we get to the hospital, the surgeon assures me that my partner should make a full recovery.

I find the general a blanket and a chair in the hallway and call Jackie on my cell, which, to my great relief, has a strong signal.

She picks up on the first ring, her voice breathless with

worry. "Your sergeant just called," she says. "How are you doing? Truthfully, Betty."

I wander down the hallway looking for a quiet place and duck into an open supply closet. "Truthfully, I'm exhausted. Shaken up. Scared as shit for about an hour. I need a shower and a few Jamesons. But I'm not injured."

"And Seth?" she asks.

"He's having surgery. He'll be okay. I'm going to stay the night here, though."

"Do you need me to be there?"

I smile because I imagine that she is already getting dressed, ready to drive down and take over the entire hospital wing.

"No," I tell her. "You sleep. As soon as it's light, if Seth's doing well, I'm coming home."

"Did you get Ruiz?" she asks.

"No. But we got everything else. There's nothing left he can do." I press my forehead against the cool tiles in the alcove, closing my eyes. I open them again, though, when my brain tries replaying the image of the general's cannonball wrapped in intestines.

"I love you, Jackie," I say. "I'll see you in a few hours."

13

From the shadows I watch Jackie's form slipping through the water like a selkie. She does five laps in an easy breaststroke, arms sweeping out evenly at every attack, neatly tucking and rolling her body below the surface so that her feet can push off the tiles at each end.

She pulls herself out of the pool in one effortless movement, her supporting triceps lean and sharp, walks to my chair parked under an umbrella, and purposely stands close, dripping cold water down onto my T-shirt. I make a playful grab at her, but she jerks away, laughing. She picks up a towel, wraps it around her waist, and sits in the chair next to me.

"You shouldn't sit so close," I tell her. "I look like a mushroom next to you."

I'm not the only pale-skinned person at the pool, but I seem to be the only sensible one. It's midday, the sun sparking off the water in blinding flashes. There are several women rafting their babies on floaties at the shallow end, and the women's shoulders and arms are all burned to a bright flamingo pink.

Jackie has the kind of skin that turns golden at the mere hint of sun. Now, at the early part of September, she is like some Mediterranean goddess who took a wrong turn at Greenland and ended up in a Viking settlement.

"Why don't you come in?" she asks, toweling her hair.

"I have a better idea." I trace a finger briefly over her thigh. "Why don't you come back to the apartment with me for a nap." I air-quote "for a nap" and she laughs again and shakes her wet hair at me like a young water spaniel.

"It's too nice to go inside right now," she says.

The heat has diminished over the past few days, the evenings less humid. North Texas manages to produce a dozen perfect days a year, and today seems to be one of them.

I hear laughter from across the pool. Not joyous, carefree hilarity, but derisive, nasty, high-school-boy giggling. One of our Russian neighbors, an acne-faced teenager named Sergei who has the high cheekbones and cruel mouth of a Chechen rebel in training, is sitting with two of his creepy friends. They've been watching Jackie, making comments to one another in furtive exchanges. I've seen Sergei and company around the apartment complex late at night, hovering between parked cars (no doubt trying to figure out how to steal them), smoking acrid-smelling weed, flicking the lit ends away with practiced carelessness.

Jackie catches my scowl and follows my gaze across the pool to where the three are sitting. The two friends duck their chins, grinning, but Sergei looks at me defiantly, holding my stare.

"Little pricks," I mutter.

"Poor things," Jackie says, unfazed. "Just think how

miserable it must be to have to whack off all the time just to be able to finish an entire sentence." She reclines the lounge chair and lies down on her back. "I talked to Seth's surgeon earlier," she says. "He's sending me all the charts. Your partner's making good progress."

Seth spent two days and nights in the hospital in Weatherford and I drove him home upon his release. The bullet that struck him had nicked his right kidney but no other major organs or arteries. On the drive back, loopy from all the pain meds, a thick bandage around his middle, he had insisted that we stop at a Dairy Queen, where he finished not only his large chocolate-dipped cone but mine as well. By the time I got him to his apartment, his shirt was covered with chocolate, like a four-year-old's. He was told he'd be on medical leave for at least a month, although he insisted that he'd be back to work in two weeks. It's been five days since the shooting and he is already driving me crazy with phone calls, looking for updates in the Ruiz case.

The Dallas and Weatherford press had made a very big deal about the shoot-out—one news channel using the lead-in banner "A Second Chance for the Confederacy?"—and announced that a manhunt was continuing for cartel member Tomas "El Gitano" Ruiz. Most of my on-air appearances, captured at the hospital where Seth was being treated, involved me swatting away microphones and glaring into lenses.

The general, however, seemed to hover in the background of every shot, waving to the cameras, willing to speak to any interested reporter.

Jackie reaches over and gently scratches the back of my hand with one nail. "Hey," she says. "Want to go out for dinner tonight?"

"Better yet," I say, "let's do takeout from that Korean place and then spend the rest of the evening causing a domestic disturbance."

The three boys, their swim trunks comically low on their skinny hips, shuffle past us, scraping their flip-flops against the concrete. Sergei makes piggy snorts, his hand covering his mouth, as though we won't know whose hole is producing the noise.

"Speaking of domestic disturbances..." I say, burning the back of Sergei's shaggy head with my eyes.

Late last night, Sergei, or maybe his brother, had been making a racket bouncing a basketball right above our bedroom. I banged on the walls, but the bouncing got louder. Taking a few deep breaths and determined to keep it friendly, I walked upstairs, knocked on the door, and politely asked the boys' mother, Nadia, to tell whichever son was making the noise to desist.

"Hey, I saw you on TV," Nadia had told me, her eyes round with surprised recognition. "In hospital, with the crazy old costume guy." She looked me up and down. Her initial antagonism had been replaced by an appreciative interest. "I didn't know you were cop."

"Yes, I am a cop," I said.

"Your partner gonna get well?" she asked.

"He'll be fine. Thanks for asking."

"Okay. I make Sergei quit."

"Okay, thank you."

I started to turn away, but she stepped out into the hallway, motioning for me to stay.

"You know manager?" she asked.

"Yes," I said. Jackie and I were the super's two favorite tenants. Having a doctor and a cop in one apartment was pure gold for Jimmy—emergency CPR services for heart-attack victims, ejection of noisy, disruptive kids (like Nadia's son) from the parking lot—and anytime we needed maintenance, he usually fixed whatever was broken on the spot.

"Tell him we have rats in wall, please," Nadia said. "One is dead and it stinks. He needs to do something. You get Jimmy to take out dead animal, I make sure the noise stops."

I had noticed the faint but distinctive tang of something rotting wafting from Nadia's apartment but had thought it was old garbage. The heat was impressive enough to accelerate any decomposition process, and a dead animal would make itself known pretty quickly.

Her request seemed reasonable so I dialed Jimmy's number on my cell phone and left a message for him to check Nadia's apartment, as a personal favor to me, for an expired rodent.

Nadia thanked me and, true to her word, ensured that there were no more practice games upstairs for the rest of the evening, although I could hear her admonishing the boys in rapid-fire Russian.

After the encounter with Sergei at the pool today, however, I'm not sure how long the quiet will last.

Jackie and I spend the next few hours by the pool reading and talking. The women finally harvest their dripping, squirming children from the water like they're pulling up fishing nets filled with krill, and soon we're alone. The sun has moved behind the building and I float on my back in the pool, eyes closed, and feel Jackie's wake as she swims past me until I stand in the water up to my chin and embrace her. She wraps her legs around my waist and kisses me, weaving her fingers into my hair.

The Ruiz case has all but ended. Let someone else in some other flyblown Texas town catch the missing dealer. My partner will heal; Jackie and I will get on with our lives. Tomorrow we'll look at another house. And tonight... Korean food and early to bed.

At four I bring out wine in two paper cups and we sit and watch the sun turn the clouds purple. Once the sky starts to darken, Jackie goes in for a shower and I leave to pick up two spicy Korean dinners.

At the restaurant, one of the few in our neighborhood open on a Sunday, I tell the waitress to slip some pork into my order, and we laugh like conspirators. Ha-ha! Crazy vegetarians.

When I get back to the apartment, Jackie's in bed. I set the food on the counter and join her.

14

I wake in the morning with the back of Jackie's head nestled under my chin, her whole sleeping body neatly tucked into the resting curve of my own. The skin on her forearm is cool and dark against the sheet and I run my fingers down the length of it to her wrist, play with the stack of beaded bracelets I gave her, one for every year we have been together. Each bracelet has three hundred and sixty-five tiny wooden beads, smooth as beach sand—the days of our lives on eight circlets of gold, a secret Braille of desire, of trust, of love, of gratitude. It's Monday, and we both need to be at work early, but I allow myself another few moments of entanglement.

When the woman starts screaming, it's muffled, but it sounds as though it's coming from above, and I'm instantly annoyed that the Russians' TV has been turned up so high, so early. But the voice immediately gets louder, more desperate, the pitch soaring upward to an almost operatic range. I hear a door slam open, and the voice is now in the public breezeway right over us. The woman is yelling in Russian, *"Oobistva! Oobistva!"* You can't be raised in a Polish community in Brooklyn without learning some Russian, including the word for "murder." *"Oobistva!"* she screams again, this time in one drawn-out wail.

Jackie wakes with a start at the last and vaults out of bed and pulls on a robe; I've already thrown on a T-shirt and shorts. I run barefoot into the hallway and at the stairs see Nadia above me on the second floor, shrieking in Russian.

"Sergei!" she cries, and I run up the stairs, two risers at a time, thinking that the kid must have really screwed up to make his mother come so unglued.

Standing outside Nadia's apartment, the door wide open, I see Sergei with his arms wrapped protectively around his younger brother, Ivan. He looks up, bug-eyed, face drained of color, and when he sees me, he presses himself against the wall, and I realize he's terrified of me.

Nadia utters Russian phrases too rapidly for me to catch, but she points through the open doorway, insisting that I go inside. Jackie has come upstairs and instinctively she goes to the boys, kneels down, and calmly begins asking them questions.

I enter the apartment, but Nadia will only stand at the threshold, clutching her robe with one hand, clawing at her hair with the other. Her voice has dropped to a whisper, and it sounds like she's praying.

The rotting smell is like an ammonia fog sprayed from an industrial-size canister, and I pull the bottom of my T-shirt up over my mouth and nose. The apartment is in a friendly state of disarray, but there is a large, square shipping box on the kitchen counter, the top open and folded down. At this distance I can't see what's in it.

Nadia finally comes in, points to the box, and demands, "Look…look."

She takes a few steps back as I approach the counter. The smell is now stronger, the bottom of the cardboard box stained dark, as though something liquid has leaked through. There is a box cutter on the counter as well, probably what Nadia used to slit open the clear packing tape sealing the top.

Closer in, I begin to see the contents: a rounded, melon shape topped with thick, dark fur. No, it's coarse, black human hair, and below that the sloped beginnings of a forehead transected with scrubby, jet brows. The forehead is crimped and deeply lined, the brow prominent and masculine. At that point I quit looking. With the Saint Michael's medallion firmly in hand, I back out into the breezeway. The thought crosses my mind that we've been residing below a psychopath, and I search my memory for any suspicious visitors to Nadia's apartment—a boyfriend, a relative from the Crimea covered in prison tattoos.

Jackie moves the boys, along with Nadia, farther down the hall. I'm not ready for them to see my face, so I turn away and pull my phone out of my shorts pocket. After the bile has settled, I dial the police dispatcher, tell her who I am, and ask to be put through to the Homicide division. I provide them with as much information as I have and then I slip the phone back in my pocket. I feel a hand on my shoulder, and I startle, but it's Jackie, her eyes searching and worried.

I don't know any other way to soften the information, so I whisper into her ear that in the apartment, in a box on the kitchen counter, is a human head. She jerks backward, but I put a cautioning hand on her arm. "Just keep Nadia and the boys down the hall and calm until Homicide gets here, okay?"

She nods and goes back to stand with Nadia's little family. Five minutes later a patrolman shows up, followed by several more. The cops go into the apartment and quickly come back out again, asking me for the whys and wherefores that I can't yet give. I can tell by the expressions on their faces, though, which ones have eaten too much breakfast. Then we stand around waiting for Homicide to arrive.

From down the hall, Jackie signals for me to come over. She tells me in a low voice, "You need to talk to Sergei."

The kid has maneuvered his younger brother between us, positioning him like a shield.

"You have something to tell me, Sergei?" I ask him, trying to keep my voice calm.

The kid is deeply frightened—although I don't know how much of the surprise package he's seen—but he doesn't want to appear scared, so he presses his lips together and stares up at me with hard eyes. It's an impressive look and will hold him in good stead six months from now when he's being booked for something, most likely a B and E.

"Did you see what was in the box?" I ask him.

He nods, a barely discernible dip of the chin.

"Obviously, your mother saw it too."

The mention of his mother puts a momentary crimp in his hard-guy attitude, but the chin dips again.

"If you know something, Sergei, you need to tell me now. Before Homicide shows up."

He says, "The box was for you. I took it."

I feel the hard crawl of flesh along my spine and I think I've misheard him. "What do you mean, the box was for me?"

Sergei's eyes flick toward his mother. "A man left it at your door. A few days ago."

I want to grab him up by his *Dumb and Dumber* T-shirt because now I'm deeply frightened—some guy left a box with a head in it at my and Jackie's door—but I fold my arms instead. "What man, Sergei?"

I think I'm keeping my voice neutral, but Jackie has placed the flat of her palm against my back, reminding me that I'm not interviewing a hardened criminal.

Sergei looks at his mother again. "I don't know," he says defensively. "A deliveryman."

"Was he wearing a UPS uniform? FedEx? A postman's uniform?"

He shrugs and looks at his shoes.

"Why would you take a box left for me?" I ask him.

"Because..." Sergei meets my gaze and I realize that he took the box for no other reason than that I am the bitchy, bossy, lesbo neighbor. He pilfered it just because he's a teenage kid and the opportunity presented itself. But he hadn't opened it, which meant that maybe he had second thoughts about the theft and was contemplating returning it later.

Nadia, who has been hovering next to me, says anxiously, "He had box in his closet. That's what smelled so bad. I found it this morning and opened it without thinking. I didn't know it was for you. I didn't know..."

Nadia begins to sob hysterically, and I see Maclin and two others from his division appear at the top of the stairs.

I tell Nadia, "You and the boys stay here with Jackie, okay?" She looks at me with her wild-eyed, tear-streaked face, ready to dash away, but she agrees and I walk back to join the Homicide team.

Maclin greets me by saying, "I've never seen you in your bare feet before, Detective."

A wall of cops, all men, all eyes on me. When heading nearly naked into battle, it's best to go on the offensive.

"I'm not wearing a bra either, Maclin, but don't let that throw you."

Maclin smothers a smile and looks down the hallway. "Those the tenants?"

"Yes."

"Wow," he says, staring at Jackie. Through the filtered light of the breezeway, I see what he's seeing: the silhouette of a shapely woman with long, tanned legs wrapped in a thin silk robe. The neckline has opened, showing the red tattoo below her left collarbone, shining like a bull's-eye.

I move into his line of sight and point at the open doorway to the apartment. "What you need to be looking at is in there."

I follow him into the apartment, watch him peering at length into the box. The open door has diminished the smell only slightly.

Maclin asks me, "Did you get a close look?"

I shake my head.

"There's not a lot of him to see," he says, making a face. "Male. Maybe Hispanic. Not young, not old. Days' worth of decay, though, so it's hard to tell."

He takes a pen from his pocket and carefully lifts up the box flaps.

"Damn, Rhyzyk," he says, surprised, his eyes meeting mine. "Your name is on this box. No shipping label, though."

"You need to talk to the tenant's son Sergei," I tell him. "He says the box was delivered to me a few days ago but that he took it."

"Delivered to you?"

"Some man left it outside my door. Kid's got a thing for me, so he swiped it. Kept it in his closet."

"You're just making friends all over the place." Maclin gestures for us to step into the hallway. "No need to stand in the charnel house." Outside, he takes a few deep breaths and asks, "What did this deliveryman look like?"

"I don't know," I say. "I was just about to ask the kid."

I take Maclin down the hall and introduce him to Nadia, who shakes his hand in a formal, deferential way. He spends a little too much time introducing himself to Jackie and then turns to Nadia's elder boy.

Sergei has let go of his little brother and now stands off to one side, arms crossed, trying to look bored over the lack of drama.

Maclin says, "Son, this police officer tells me that the box in your kitchen was originally delivered to her apartment. Is that right?"

Sergei mumbles something in Russian.

"In English," I say. "Exactly when? What day and what time?"

"Three days ago," he answers. "Friday, I guess. In the afternoon."

"Where were you?"

Sergei points to the stairs. "I saw him down below leaving the package."

"Did you get a good look at him?"

"Kind of. Yeah."

"What did he look like?" Maclin asks.

Sergei regards me for a few beats. Then he points to me and says, "Like her."

15

Seth lies on his couch in shorts, bare-chested except for the large bandage covering the healing bullet wound just below his right rib cage. He's eating a Popsicle, dripping orange slush onto a truly hideous crocheted blanket across his legs, one that looks to be a thousand years old. It had, in fact, been made for Seth by his grandmother as an eighteenth-birthday gift, a large Cowboys logo hot-glued onto one corner. He assures me that at one time it had been white.

He's also dribbling all over a printout of the report I created for Taylor to update the sergeant on the events surrounding the gruesome discovery on my neighbor's kitchen counter. Seth reads the report while keeping an eye on his TV, playing clips of the Cowboys' last game.

"Where's the pup?" I ask, watching Seth watching the replays, a mixture of horror and disgust on his face. I toss a stack of his dirty sweatpants and shirts off a chair and sit down.

"The lovely Shawna is taking care of Rita, and me, at the moment," he says, smiling now, one brow raised like a victory flag.

I can only imagine what "the lovely Shawna" must look like based on the women my partner's dated in the past: upscale blondes with perfect teeth who carry expensive handbags.

"Why do men do that?" I ask, pointing at his forehead. "Waggle their eyebrows around like scuzzy caterpillars when talking about getting laid?"

Seth shrugs coyly, biting off the end of his Popsicle.

"Yeah, well," I say, lifting a woman's camisole off the coffee table with the toe of one boot. "If you're fit enough to be gettin' some, then you're well enough to come back to work."

"Right? That's what I keep telling the sergeant." Seth holds out his Popsicle. "Want one? I'd offer you a beer, but I'm out." He grins, palming away some of the sticky residue on his naked chest. "I can give you an Oxy, though."

He does a pretend narco-nod, mouth slack, eyes rolling back in his head, chin drooping onto his chest.

"No, thanks," I say. "And if you get too used to those pain meds, I'm going to kick your scrawny ass all over Dallas."

He laughs and hands the report back to me.

"My being on leave certainly hasn't curtailed the excitement factor for you. Or your neighbors," he says. "Shit, Riz. Someone got to the scumbag. Well, part of him, at least."

The head in the box turned out to be Ruiz's. Delivered to my door like an early Christmas present. He was identified by dental records provided by the Mexican authorities. Evidently, despite all of the Gypsy's other character flaws, he took excellent care of his teeth. The mystery everyone was working to solve, besides where we might find the rest of the body—which could be ID'd, in part, by a large jaguar tattooed on the back of his left calf—was who Sergei's deliveryman was.

The description Sergei gave was of a man over six feet tall, Caucasian, muscular in build, with bright red hair—in Sergei's words, "Yeah, man, a fuckin' ginger. With freckles and shit"—dressed in khaki pants and shirt, wearing a black ball cap with no insignia.

Forensics had provided the following: The rate of decay showed that death had occurred about four days before the head's discovery. Which meant that Ruiz had been dead twenty-four hours before his head was delivered to my apartment. It had been severed from the torso cleanly (and, hopefully for the victim, postmortem) by a very sharp knife. There were, however, no bullet holes to the back of the head and no skull trauma, so, as there was no complete body to autopsy, no clear cause of death could be ascertained. Like with Lana, both ears had been removed.

The box was a plain, generic cardboard box, sixteen by twelve by twelve inches, thoughtfully lined with plastic wrap to catch most if not all of the leaking liquids. The box was addressed, in neat block letters with a medium black ballpoint pen, to me.

Another interesting bit of forensics that Maclin shared with me was the confirmation that a section of Lana's hair had been cut off just above the scalp. The bit of hair below the cut was dyed a bright scarlet.

"There's one more thing," I tell Seth. "In one of Lana's hands they found a few strands of human hair, follicles intact. So she did put up a struggle. Tests show that the hair's human, and red. Not dyed red like Lana's missing hair, but a natural red."

"Like the delivery guy's," he says, eyes coming to rest on my hair. "Or yours. That's interesting."

"Maclin told me that his partner, Tate, threw a fit getting the news, thinking that I had somehow polluted the crime scene. But I gave a sample and it wasn't a match. Of course, there's no way to know right now if the crime scene hair came from a male, but it had to come from someone strong enough to hold Lana down while slitting her throat.

"The description of our delivery guy makes him big enough to do the job. He certainly does not match the typical cartel enforcer, though. Not unless the Irish mafia is moving into the Texas drug trade."

Finished with the Popsicle, Seth places the stick on the coffee table and wipes his hands on the blanket. "So, following the timeline," he begins, marking the days off on his fingers, "Ruiz, driving Lana's car, is in Weatherford, a week ago today. The car is found and there's the Mexican standoff with the boys in gray. Then for a few days Ruiz is missing, unaccounted for. Ruiz is killed on or about last Thursday; his head is delivered to you in the box on Friday. Sergei steals the box that day and it sits in his nice, warm closet ripening for three days. On Monday morning, Sergei's mom finds the package and El Gitano is unveiled. Did the kid ID any photos?"

"No positive ID," I say, remembering Sergei's running commentary on the mug shots, looking to get a rise out of us by conjecturing at length on the crimes each prospect had committed. I make a face. "How does a fourteen-year-old know so much about sheep shagging?"

"Internet," Seth answers readily. He shifts on the sofa to

find a more comfortable position and then stares thought-fully out the window while I check my text messages.

I really don't like hovering over Jackie, but she keeps forgetting to check in and it's making me worried, which is tipping me into being irritable and testy. Sleep has been in short supply, and the dark hours have been spent nervously imagining scenarios of Jackie being stalked by a maniacal carrottop in the hospital's underground parking garage.

I decide it's time to go, but I hear Seth muttering something.

"What?" I ask, looking up from my phone.

"You said Irish mafia before. These murders don't feel like Mexican cartel. But who's crazy enough, or connected enough, to kill and mangle a big-time dealer's girlfriend and the dealer and then put his head in a box and leave it at a cop's door? And what's the message? 'Back off'? A Wes Craven–style thank-you for getting rid of the competition?"

"Whoever he is, he's still walking around somewhere. Taylor's got some extra patrolmen near our apartment for a few days just in case."

"We found a lot of meth crystal in Bender's house," he says.

"And…"

"And despite Bender's wanting a higher class of customer with cocaine, he had his fingers in the meth business for years, and it made him a boatload of money. The Mexican cartel has been looking for ways to get into that trade for a long time. Maybe Bender's old associates didn't like his new partners."

"See, this is why I miss you, Dutton. It just so happens I've got Ryan running a check on North Texas meth dealers matching the description of our delivery guy."

Seth nods, satisfied. "I'm so ready to be off this sofa. I need to be back at work."

I stand up and stretch, returning the phone to my pocket. "Give it some time. I don't want you splitting your stitches all over the car."

"Craddock tells me they're making you pair up with Ryan while I'm out," Seth says. "Poor guy."

The front door opens and a lithe young woman in gym clothes enters the foyer carrying Seth's poodle.

She calls out, "Hey, sugar buns, I'm back."

The girl walks into the living room but startles when she sees me standing next to the couch. The workout gear she's wearing is the kind of cheap stuff you'd pick up in a teen shop even though she's well past her high-school years. The heavy eye makeup, only partially covering the fading remnants of a black eye, and synthetic hair extensions scream a decade of bad choices and elusive luck.

She puts a hand on one hip; her brows come together with displeasure.

"Hey," Seth says. "This is my work partner, Detective Riz."

I give her a friendly nod.

Immediately, her posture relaxes. The relief of something not being what it looks like is palpable. She exhales, and smiles. The lovely Shawna gives a wave before taking the dog into the kitchen.

I grin at Seth and whisper, "You're not just rescuing pups these days, are you?"

I bend down, kiss him fondly on the forehead. "Just don't forget who got you that extra-large DQ, sugar buns."

Seth snorts. "And you just be careful, partner. Don't be accepting any more mystery packages."

16

Talking heads. Two of them. Lana's and Ruiz's severed heads on my kitchen counter, their mouths opening and closing like large bass. But there're no sounds coming from the rubbery blue lips. Their eyes are closed, which somehow makes the dream worse. In the fogged reasoning of my sleeping state, I think that if I could see their eyes, I'd know what they were trying to tell me. I hear Uncle Benny's voice asking me if I'm done Reaping the Grim. Then he tells me to wake up.

I come to full awareness sitting upright in bed, sour sweat misting my arms and legs, breathing like a collapsed marathoner. Jackie stirs and turns over but continues sleeping.

The nightstand clock reads 4:38 a.m. There's no use trying to get back to sleep, so I get out of bed, my heart hammering, and put on my running shoes. After slipping my iPod with headphones into my arm holster, I take my

SIG nine out of the bedside drawer and walk quietly into
the living room to look through the peephole at the front
door. I unlock both locks and ease the door open for a quick
scan of the breezeway. It's empty, no one on the stairs, no
sounds coming from any of my neighbors. I return the gun
to the drawer, watching Jackie breathing deeply and peacefully beneath the sheets.

After softly closing and locking the door behind me,
I walk out onto the street. The sky overhead is a dark,
translucent blue, the moon half full, a few of the brightest stars still showing. The evening patrol cars assigned
by Sergeant Taylor—one parked in front of the apartment, one at the rear entry of the building—would have
left at four. Jackie and I have two more days of taxpayer-
paid protection and then we're on our own, the rationale
being that if the deliveryman was going to return, he
would do it within the first week of leaving the box at
our door.

The air is actually cool, and I debate returning to the
apartment for a sweatshirt, but I decide the chill will help
quicken my pace. Walking briskly for a couple of minutes,
I tie my hair up off my neck with a band and begin the music feed through the iPod. First, the Breeders and Veruca
Salt to warm up. Then I quicken my pace with the group
Go Betty Go, and finally pound into a steady, loping stride
with Metric.

*All the gold and the guns and the girls could never get
you off...*

I halt for an instant before choosing the path into the
park next to the local community college. I've never hesi-
tated taking the park route before—although I usually run
it in full daylight—and so I veer onto the path precisely
because of the electric frisson of fear that has caused me to

reach for the Saint Michael's medallion tucked snugly beneath my already-damp-with-sweat T-shirt.

I know a lot of cops and civilians, including the Texas state governor, who run with their pistols clipped to their waistbands. But if I'm running where I think I might need a gun, then I'm probably going to be in trouble before I can unclip it and fire, and I need to pick a different route. Runner muggings and assaults often come from behind; an arm around the throat, a blow to the head, and down you go. If someone thinks taking on an almost-six-foot-tall blazing harpy with legs like steel-belted radials who's clocking on average seven-minute miles is a good idea, he's certainly welcome to try.

It's two miles to the college, three miles around it, two miles back to the apartment. An easy run. If I keep up my current rhythm, I'll be home about the time Jackie wakes up.

The chorus of the Metric song fades out and I'm running under large oak trees lining the path, the shadows blackening to bottomless pools along the college track. A new song begins, "Outlaw" by the Sounds, and I have to smile. Jackie put together the playlist for me for my running time. She knows me so well.

It's an hour to sunrise, and yet there's already a brightening in the air, only Venus left glowing in the proximity of the moon. The hangover from the dream is fading, but Benny's voice is clear: *Are you done Reaping the Grim?*

It was an expression he had coined during his time as a sergeant in the Homicide division of the Ninety-Fourth Precinct, Brooklyn. The meaning was that, unless you were a psychopath, there were consequences to witnessing the effects of bloody violence, and in order to stay sane, a human being had to expel the outrage of unnatural death or the horror would turn cancerous, eating its host. It didn't matter if the exhalation of poisonous thoughts was in the form of perverted jokes (the sicker the better), angry ranting, or confused, despondent wailing. The point was to get it out.

My uncle's form of cop therapy occurred at Donovan's, a Brooklyn bar over a century old, perpetually murky and cavernous. A collective of off-duty cops from several precincts standing on shaved cedar below a begrimed tin roof, half-empty Jameson bottles lining the mahogany bar, a thick bank of cigarette smoke engulfing everything, served as comrades to the beleaguered and witnesses to the ritual. Irish, Polish, Italian, it didn't matter.

Benny would stand toe-to-toe in front of the traumatized officer fresh from a murder scene. The victim's body was perhaps yet warm, just a short, but irreparable, distance from being someone's father or husband or son, the corpse pulpy and distended by a stabbing or a bludgeoning or a shooting. Benny would clasp both hands firmly behind the officer's neck, pull him so close that their foreheads were touching, and ask, demand, "Are you ready to reap some grim?"

The brotherhood around them like a wall would chant, "Sick it up, sick it up," until the troubled officer could begin the healing. Sometimes the officer screamed while describing the crime scene, pumping his fists in futile anger, a string of obscenities flowing unchecked. The verbal expulsions were like a mop and a pail of ammonia water, cleaning the gore off the kitchen tiles.

Occasionally, the besieged man would abandon all pride and weep like a baby. Once, a cop balled up his fist and gave Benny an uppercut to the jaw, knocking him senseless to the floor.

The worst for most of them was the homicide of a female, usually the result of a "domestic dispute," a euphemism for some twisted perv's crushing the life out of the woman who'd likely given birth to his children.

Reaping the Grim in Donovan's tavern was the stuff of cop legends. A secret club where only the most trusted were included, and you had to be asked to join—didn't matter how many years you had put into the force. Afterward, there was no lingering shame, no calling out, and no repeating what had gone on while Benny worked his magic. Ever.

Although it was never documented, it was a widely held belief that Benny's cops had the lowest rate of burnout, the least amount of sick days, the fewest number of suicides and domestic incidences of any precinct in a fifty-mile radius.

There were never any women at these sessions. I wouldn't have heard about them, even after I joined the force, if Benny hadn't described them to me. Benny always said that the officers you had to worry about were the ones who pretended the carnage didn't bother them. Like my father, who stuffed down every recoiling reflex and wounded thought as an exercise in strength, sealing the canister of rage with more and more alcohol until he ended up reenacting the very things he worked to contain. No surprise that my father died of cancer of the gut.

Of course, Benny died of cancer too. But it was honestly gotten, smoking a pack of Winstons a day for thirty years. His gut, and his conscience, stayed clear to the day he died.

Soon after I joined the force, he counseled me to find my own way to expunge the dark chaos. Running like my life depended on it became my reaping, where all the spiked thoughts growing in my head could be cut down to a manageable size.

The ending song on the iPod is another pounding, fast-paced anthem, and I hit the last quarter-mile stretch before leaving the park.

The lane of sheltering trees ends and the looping path becomes brighter. On the grassy lawn of the campus ahead is a grayish sphere, a weathered soccer ball, perhaps. But it's the wrong color and texture; it's mottled and banded—fleshy, even. The size of a small head.

"Jesus…" I pitch and roll away from the path, crab-crawl on the ground to get some distance between myself and the object, my eyes jerking from side to side, looking for any movement from another human form along the lawn. I know I don't have my gun, but I instinctively reach for it anyway, my breath high and whistling through my windpipe. I press my belly farther onto the grass, trying to tamp down the panic.

The rounded shape has begun to quiver as in a high wind, but there's absolutely no breeze, and I stop breathing entirely.

A pointed snout and ears rear up from the leathery mound, along with a long, scaly tail, and the creature shuffles away from me like a miniature primordial tank.

"A fucking armadillo?" I yell. "You've got to be fucking kidding me…"

I roll over onto my back and howl with laughter until my pulse stops racing. Anyone seeing an armadillo for the first time, especially a city-bred Yankee, will have two immediate reactions: revulsion, and disbelief that something alive and well during the dinosaur age is still trotting around suburban lawns. Looking, under the right circumstances, like a warty, bald head.

After brushing the grass off the seat of my shorts, and grateful no one was around to witness the embarrassing exhibition, I continue my run back to the apartment.

I have to stop twice more—bent, hands on knees—to cackle hysterically over what an ass I can be.

17

The night-light shines in the breezeway, dispelling any lingering shadows in the hall and around the door, and I lean against the wall, kicking off my running shoes. I open both locks with my two keys and slip into the apartment, listening for the sounds of Jackie stirring. All is quiet, so I decide to take a shower first before turning on the grinder for the coffeemaker.

I peel off wet clothes on the way to the bathroom, smiling, thinking how Jackie will laugh when I recount my armadillo adventure.

Or maybe not. Maybe my running through a darkened campus, alone, will not be thought of as humorous, so I decide that for now I'll just tell Seth and fill Jackie in later, when we've had more time and distance from the last mortal remains of El Gitano.

I turn on the water, let it run until it's hot and steaming, and then step into the stall.

The Ruiz case is closed for the time being. Ryan and I

will be meeting with the sergeant first thing about a new drug operation: finding a cheese-heroin dealer to several North Texas high schools, *cheese* being a blend of black-tar Mexican heroin and over-the-counter cold medication popular with teens. Two seventeen-year-old students died last week, the overdoses immediately following an early school dismissal. Both students were champion wrestlers headed for full scholarships at Harvard. Nothing like a couple of deceased Caucasian star athletes to get City Hall's attention.

Ryan has such a baby face that I can easily imagine Taylor embedding him undercover in the school as the new senior transfer from some Texas hamlet like Nacogdoches. Or, as Seth calls it, Nack-a-Nowhere.

I hear the outer bathroom door opening and I tense reflexively, soapy hair falling in dense waves, blanketing my face. "Hello?" I call out, trying to clear the shampoo from my eyes.

Jackie's muffled voice answers, "Good morning."

The shower door is steamed, and I swipe at the glass with my fingers, making out the marine-blue smudge of Jackie's robe. I open the shower and she's standing there smiling, but in a puzzled way.

"What's this?" she asks, holding up something long and flowing in her right hand.

"It was on the bed," she adds.

It stirs in her hand in a snakelike fashion, flexing subtly in contrary motion between the inrushing cooler air of the bedroom and the heavier, heated air of the shower. About six inches long and scarlet, it first looks to be a ribbon from a party package. But it is the missing section of hair cut from Lana's scalp. It had not been on the bed when I got up an hour ago to go running.

I stand in the shower for an instant, and then bound toward her, drenched and scattering shampoo foam. It startles her, and her mouth opens with a burst of surprised air until I place my palm against her lips, silencing any further noise. Her eyes are wide with alarm, but I shake my head, cautioning her to stay silent.

My bedside table is just outside the bathroom door and I reach for it, ease the top drawer open, pull out the SIG Sauer. I rack the slide quietly, the metal slipping in my wet hands. I'm hoping the running shower will mask the metallic click, and I motion for Jackie to stay where she is. There is no one that I can see in the bedroom, the bed in disarray from where Jackie has thrown back the covers. My eyes focus immediately on the bed frame, high enough off the ground to allow someone of reasonable size to hide underneath.

After taking a few steadying breaths, I throw myself down on my side, arms extended, and sweep the gun along the space. There is nothing there, and I quickly stand, my naked ribs and thigh stinging from rug burn. The bedroom door is partially closed and I slip behind it, look through the space at the hinged side for any movement coming from the living room.

I step around the door and walk softly across the large, open space of the living room to the opposite side, where the office is, leaving splatters of water in my wake, my bare skin goosefleshed from the air-conditioning blowing through the vents above my head. Listening for any sounds in the office, I crouch down, grab the door handle, twist it, and propel the door open with as much force as I can manage. There is no one in the room, and before I can talk myself out of it, I make a run for the closet, yank the sliding door open, and sweep the gun inside the small space. The closet is empty.

The gun lowered to my thigh, I pad shivering back into the living room and check to make sure I'd locked the door upon returning. I know that both locks were secure when I returned from my run because I used my keys to get in. Someone had to have had keys to gain access to the apartment while I was gone.

Jackie is standing in the bathroom, breathing shallowly, holding on to the section of hair. Through her eyes, I must look as though I've morphed into some dangerous, aquatic nymph. I'm fully naked; my hair, speckled with drying shampoo as with sea foam, sticks to my face and upper body in untamed, stringy clumps; the length of my right side glows an angry red from the dive to the floor.

"What the hell is going on, Betty?" She's whispering, as though afraid to hear the sound of her own voice.

"Jackie, put that back on the bed," I tell her. "Exactly as you found it."

She sets it on my side of the bed, coiling it around like it's a serpent.

"What is it?" she asks.

"Baby, I need you to be very calm right now." I set the gun on the bedside table. "It's a piece of hair from a murder victim."

"What?" She wraps her arms around herself, following me into the bathroom. "Did you put it on the bed?"

She can tell from my face that I did not.

The water has been running the whole time and I step into the stall, frantically rinse off the remainder of shampoo crusting my scalp and skin.

I get out of the shower, wrap myself in a towel. "The girl who was murdered at the Benson house, Lana Yu, had a piece of her hair cut off and taken from the scene."

"You mean like a trophy or something?" Jackie asks.

"I don't know. The missing hair was dyed a bright scarlet. That information was withheld from the press."

"Oh my God," she whispers, sagging against the bathroom cabinets, her knees buckling. "Someone was in our apartment. While I was sleeping."

"Both locks were locked when I got back from running."

"Who would have a key? Is it the killer?" she asks. Her eyes, searching my face, have begun filling with tears.

I've put on a shirt and a pair of pants, and I'm tugging on a boot, but I drop it to the floor and pull Jackie to me. The flesh beneath her neck is exposed by the robe falling away from one shoulder. I kiss the pulsating hollow above the collarbone where the rose tattoo lies, hugging her tightly, as much for my own comfort as for hers. I've got the shakes bad; the muscles at my temples are clenched to stop my chattering teeth.

"I don't know," I tell her. "But first things first: We get some cops here, and the locksmith. Then I ream the super for being so careless with the master key. We'll figure this out."

As soon as I mention Jimmy the super, though, I realize he would never willingly give up a copy of a tenant's key, especially ours.

18

Sergeant Taylor sits in a chair in the task room, his heavy-lidded eyes gazing at me in a wary fashion, the way a bull terrier might watch a person who's stepped on its tail one too many times. There is a milky film at the corners of his mouth from the antacid tablets he's been chewing. He peels back the paper wrapper on the roll and pops two more onto his tongue like candies from a Pez dispenser.

In the room with us are the usual suspects, Craddock, Hoskins, and Ryan, as well as Maclin and his partner, Tate, from Homicide. The sergeant has just informed the group that Forensics has confirmed a match of the hair segment left on my bed to the dyed hair on Lana Yu's scalp. It's been several hours since the home invasion, and Taylor has spent a good part of the morning in his office hunched over his phone, head in hands, talking to his department chiefs.

I stare at the whiteboard, where the red lines indicating deceased are multiplying like stripes in a candy-cane factory. El Gitano's name has been crossed out, along with eleven others': Bender, the patrolman, the Good Samaritan with the schnauzer, the kidnap victim in the Lincoln Town Car, Lana, Ruiz's bodyguard, and the three Mexican dealers and two reenactors killed at the camp.

What Taylor has not said is that he's under enormous pressure from the department to shut tight the Ruiz case. What started out as a straightforward drug investigation has morphed into a murder case to be handled by Homicide. The FBI has withdrawn all support, moving on to another high-profile Mexican supplier.

"Detective... Detective," Taylor says, and I realize that he's speaking to me. "You look very unhappy at this moment. You have something you want to say before we let Homicide get on with their day and we get on with ours?"

"There's a connection between Ruiz and my home invasion," I tell him.

"Okay," he responds. "But there were no drugs involved. The hank of hair is related to the Lana Yu murder investigation. Your home invasion is now linked to that case as well. Let Detective Maclin and his partner connect all the dots."

"But it wasn't their homes that were broken into. Or yours, with all due respect, Sergeant. I'm really pissed off about this."

"I know it," Taylor says, holding his hands out in a placating way. "That's why it's better that Maclin and his department take over."

"Look," I say, "I'm not ready to let the Ruiz case go. Not yet." I struggle to keep my breathing even. I swallow, relaxing my throat muscles so that my voice stays out of the flying-monkey-squawk-box range. "There is a connection between Bender, Ruiz, Lana, the delivery guy, and now my apartment. And it has everything to do with drugs. We just haven't found the link yet."

"That's why we're going to offer every assistance to Detectives Maclin and Tate. But, Betty," Taylor says, holding me with his gaze, "you need to let them spend their time and their resources solving this. We have two teenagers dead from Mexican heroin. Last night, four more kids were brought into North Dallas hospitals comatose, most likely from the same stuff."

"And I will begin working with the team on that right away. But, with respect, Sergeant, with just a little bit of digging—"

"Has anyone noticed the body count?" Taylor asks sharply. He stands and points to the whiteboard. "I count twelve since this benighted case started, including the poor costumed bastards in Weatherford. You don't seem to be hearing me this morning, Detective Rhyzyk. The Ruiz drug case is closed. It is now the Ruiz-Yu murder case, and it's been passed on to the proper department. We," he says forcefully, using his finger like a metronome, gesturing back and forth between us, "are not murder investigators."

The gathered cops are all looking at either their shoes or, under their brows, me.

"It's been a dirty business, Sergeant," Maclin says. "Detective Rhyzyk is certainly not the first lead on a case to stack the bodies. But she didn't start the war."

Taylor sits back down. "I don't mind the scumbags dying, Mac; it's the citizens being killed that are of concern to me. And now we've got a newcomer, possibly our delivery guy but possibly not, leaving a section of hair from a murder victim in a police officer's home."

Not to mention Ruiz's head, Hoskins mouths to Craddock.

There is a dangerous moment when Craddock begins to smile, but I glare at him and the smile disappears, and he busies himself by pulling a bag of corn nuts out of his shirt pocket.

I then look at Maclin, whose profile is turned toward me like a Byronic portrait. His comment that I couldn't be blamed entirely for the mounting carnage feels like support from a fellow officer. Almost. Except that I know his murder investigation is still wide open. For some as-yet-unknown reason, I seem to be of interest to the perpetrator, who keeps leaving gruesome or provocative offerings at my apartment like some demented Christmas elf. Maclin is thinking that by staying close to me, he'll stay close to the killer.

"Right," Taylor says, "if there's nothing else, this meeting is closed. I'll let the team know who's taking lead on the high-school investigation. And, Detective Rhyzyk, you need to find someplace safe for a while until we find out who's leaving body parts at your apartment. I'm telling you this not as your sergeant, but as your friend."

Maclin follows me out of the meeting room and into the break room. He signals Tate to go on and stands against the door frame, arms crossed.

"You okay?" he asks.

"Great," I answer, crossing my arms as well.

Ryan starts to walk in, coffee cup in hand, sees the two of us standing like guardians to the underworld, and ducks away again. Maclin belongs to the 1 percent of humanity who don't look corpselike under fluorescent lighting, since he spends two hours every day at the gym pinking his skin to Aryan perfection.

"You know we'll do everything to find out who's stalking you."

"I'm sure you will, Marsh."

"Jimmy Aubrey, the super at your building, says all of his keys are accounted for. Nothing missing, nothing stolen."

"And . . . ?"

"And you're certain all your keys are accounted for?"

I nod curtly. "Jackie's too. We're not missing any keys."

"Weird. And yet someone watched you leave your building at five in the morning, gained access to your apartment, and left some of Lana's hair."

"On my bed, without waking Jackie," I add. The apartment locks had been changed by nine o'clock that morning, replaced with top-of-the-line, expensive cylinders, but I was working on Jackie to stay at her mother's place until I felt we were safe again. No surprise that she was reluctant. I had already decided that I'd rather camp out in the middle of the Chiapas Mexican rain forest than have a sleepover at Anne Walden Nesbitt's house. I could stay at Seth's. He'd already called twice to get updates and offered his place to me and Jackie, but his apartment is tiny and messy, with a constant parade of women playing nursemaid. Not conducive to a restful night's sleep.

"Homicide's dusting every inch of the apartment for prints," he says. "Searching outside, too, for shoe impressions. Problem is, that complex is really busy."

"Sounds like you don't have much to work with. But I'm sure you'll figure it out."

"What would you do differently?" he asks.

I want to repeat to him an old Polish proverb that Benny used to say when he was done with something: "Not my circus, not my monkeys." But what I say is "Well, for one, I would have asked Jimmy if he'd had any unexpected delivery- or repairmen to the office lately. Someone who might have been left alone, even for a few minutes, who could have copied the keys. There are phone apps that can scan a key to be copied in a few seconds. But I'm not a murder investigator, so what do I know."

"What else?"

I just smile at him. "Let's not kid ourselves that this is a partnership. Of any kind."

"Too bad," he says. He moves toward me, but with palms open, as though he's showing harmless intent. He reaches around me for the coffeemaker and pours himself a cup while standing close enough for me to smell the starch in his shirt, like he's a point guard in a basketball game. His hair is artfully tousled, carefully gelled, fingered into layered perfection.

He sniffs theatrically at the air above my head. "Detective, did you change your shampoo? It's like a fruit orchard..."

I stiffen, remembering the peach-shampoo residue in my hair as well as my vulnerability being naked and afraid in my own home only a few hours earlier. "Is this one of your interrogation techniques," I ask him, "or is this you being charming?"

He takes a sip of coffee and smiles, his face a few inches from mine. "Wow, Betty, remind me never to invite you to any of my poker games. You could break a cement trowel off your face right now."

"Is there a problem here?" a voice from the doorway asks.

It's Hoskins, his neck reddening beneath his too-large shirt collar, forehead bulbous and shiny, his coffee cup clenched in one hand. He glares at Maclin with a heat he usually reserves for failed border raids. I think at first he's irritated that the coffeemaker is being hogged. Then I realize that Hoskins is angry because he thinks I'm being harassed and bullied. He's being protective—of me.

Hoskins, a good five inches shorter than his Homicide counterpart, moves purposefully into the room. "Excuse me," he says loudly to Maclin, crowding him out of the way. "Some of us here actually have work to do." He takes his time filling his cup from the carafe, adding powdered creamer, methodically stirring the liquid. He sips loudly from the cup, on which is printed COFFEE, BECAUSE CRACK ISN'T ALLOWED AT WORK.

"Detective," Hoskins says to me, "when you're ready…" And he strides out of the break room, casting one last warning look over his shoulder.

I step around Maclin, grinning, and follow Hoskins through the door.

Hoskins, Craddock, and I gather at Ryan's desk. Following my directive, Ryan's been quietly running system matches on meth dealers resembling the description of our delivery guy: tall, muscular build, red-haired, pale skin, about twenty-five to thirty-five years of age.

I look around to make sure Taylor is in his office and then tell Ryan, "All right, you've got five minutes."

"No matches yet," he tells us. "But I did do a deeper background check on Bender's family, and some interesting things popped up." To my questioning look he adds, "I figured if Lana Yu's murder was not cartel-related, maybe it was something more personal."

"Show me," I say.

Ryan begins rustling nervously through some files next to the computer screen as though he's been asked unexpectedly to hand in a homework assignment, and I think how perfect he'll be working undercover at the high school. With his pressed jeans and collared polo shirt, he'd be every student counselor's wet dream. Also, his arm's still in the sling, and the injury to his shoulder causes him to move more cautiously, more tentatively, giving him a vulnerable air. The teenage girls will be on him like white on rice.

He opens a slender folder and pulls out a photograph. "There are no remaining blood relatives. Bender's parents and sister passed away. However, he was married briefly to a woman named Evangeline Roy. After five years of marriage, they divorced, in 1997. A few months after the divorce, Evangeline Roy was arrested for the manufacture and sale of meth."

Ryan hands a photo to me. Taken at the Smith County jail, it's a color mug shot of an attractive but disheveled woman with the vacant eyes of a person firmly in the grip of a stone-cold addiction. And her hair is a bright coppery red.

"Guess who posted bail for her?" Ryan asks.

"Bender?" I ask.

"Right. No jail time was given, mandated six-week rehab stay. I did a search for her last known address and found it just outside of Tyler. The house where she was living burned down in a meth lab explosion in 2003. They found three corpses, burned to a crisp, but no positive ID could be made due to the condition of the bodies. No fingers, no teeth. Skulls bashed in, either from falling timbers or intentional blunt force trauma. From that time, Evangeline Roy does not show up in a jail, hospital, or DMV database in Texas. Officially, she is presumed dead. But the

Smith County Sheriff's Office has doubts because of the suspicious nature of the burn site."

"Did she have any children?" I ask.

"Two sons born of a previous marriage, Tommy and Curtis Roy, who were both teenagers at the time Evangeline married Bender. But I can't find anything in the system for the Roy brothers either."

"So what now?" Craddock asks me. "There were no prints on the box containing Ruiz's head. And Homicide will likely not find any prints at your apartment either. But somebody must have seen this delivery guy around. He's big and redheaded—"

"And slick," Hoskins adds. "For a big guy, he sure gets in and out of places unnoticed, without leaving a trail."

"Any photos of the Roy sons?" I ask.

"No," Ryan says. "But the two boys were in custodial care while Evangeline Roy was in jail and rehab. I've asked for photos of them from CPS."

Hoskins is studying the photo. "You got any family in East Texas, Detective?" He points to the woman. "I can see some resemblance. The keen gaze, the intelligent face."

"Very funny," I tell Hoskins, grabbing for the photo. "Good work, Ryan. Let me know when you get photos of the kids. Also, check on biker-gang affiliation with the Roy family. Where there's meth being produced in Texas, there're bikers around to distribute it. We've got to start working on the cheese problem at the high school, like now. So all this," I say, indicating the file, "needs to be done in the dead zone. Okay?"

Everyone nods in agreement.

"Okay," Craddock says. He slaps his hands to his knees, stands, and begins sauntering back to his desk. "I'm ready for lunch now, y'all," he says, rubbing his sizable belly.

"First Mac and now cheese. All this talk of food is making me damn hungry."

Before I break away to my own desk, I pull Hoskins aside and say, teasingly, "Thanks, Bob, for coming to my aid back there in the break room. I had no idea you had such tender feelings for me."

"Oh, for Christ's sake, don't get all weepy on me," he says, walking off while fanning the air aggressively with his arms, like he's chasing away mosquitoes. "Last thing we need is a sexual-harassment suit, sucking up resources and wasting valuable man-hours, because a male police officer's intent was misunderstood..."

He keeps talking all the way down the hall, then he takes a hard left and disappears into the men's room.

19

I sit in an unmarked car parked just across from the main entrance of St. Borromeo High—one of the largest, most expensive private institutions in the state—during afternoon carpool, waiting for Ryan to be enrolled into the senior honors program. The school will let him sit in on a few classes every day so that he can blend in by walking the halls and acting like every other student: trying to get laid, harassing the weak, submitting to the strong, and, hopefully, scoring some cheese. The dealers will not be showing up in the schoolyard, so Ryan will have to get himself invited to a few parties.

The archdiocese has been aware of the drug problem for some time but had hoped that ramping up the religious instruction and sponsoring more Just Say No programs after school would do the trick. Now, two of their brightest students and champion wrestlers are going in the ground.

The students are dressed in their regimented uniforms but will most certainly be stripping down to their Ralph

Lauren polos and pastel shorts once they get home. For twelve years I went to a Catholic school in Brooklyn that had its share of rich kids, so I recognize the look of aggressive entitlement from the boys and the hostile, raking glances from the girls. The same confidently self-aware girls I'd seen in Dallas upscale malls who wore painted masks of disdain and disappointment. Females who never for a moment doubted that some camera, somewhere, was capturing their every studied move.

In high school my nickname had been Thelma, partly because I resembled the tall, flame-haired Geena Davis in the movie *Thelma and Louise,* but also because there had been the titillating sophomoric buzz that the two heroines in the movie had the hots for each other, which explained why they were always running away from their men. The fact that they had had the shit beaten out of them, had been intimidated and raped by their men, was evidently not enough of a reason to run screaming for the hills. Or, in Thelma and Louise's case, the canyons.

In my classmates' minds, the nickname was all the more appropriate because of my intense and obvious crush on my gorgeous history teacher, Talis Apreya, the name itself like a lover's whisper. She had made the fatal mistake of simply being kind to me, sensing that behind my obnoxious posturing was a self-conscious, insecure young woman struggling to find a tolerable place inside the bleak walls of adolescence. She was terminated within her first year of teaching.

Rousing myself from daydreaming, I take my phone out of my pocket to call Seth. I get no answer. Ryan's perfect for this job, but his undercover field experience is limited and his conversation is confined to sports and updates on his fiancée, a young woman he met while they were on a mission trip to Guatemala and the only girl he has ever kissed.

Perversely, I'm torn between wanting to mother and protect Ryan and wanting to take him to a truck drivers' strip club in Little Korea, get him piss-drunk, and pair him with a cross-dresser I know stage-named Sally Balzzac.

A small group of protesters from a nearby Baptist church have gathered a block from the school property and are marching with homemade picket signs reading IDOLS ARE NOT PLEASING TO THE LORD and DO YOU TRUST YOUR KIDS TO THEIR PRIESTS?

I wonder if it's just a coincidence that these good Protestants have singled out this school, as Saint Charles Borromeo, nephew to a Medici pope, made it his life's work to rid the world of the godless reformers of the sixteenth century by tying them to stakes and burning them alive.

I begin to dial Jackie's number but am startled by a twenty-something woman sticking her head through the open passenger-side window.

"Hi," she says, pronouncing it "hah." She looks painfully hopeful and purpose-driven and is wearing braces on already perfect teeth. "I don't mean to intrude, but are you one of the parents at this school?"

"No," I say. "I'm just waiting on a friend—"

"Did you know there are pedophiles teaching there? We're a group of concerned parents trying to protect innocent children."

Certainly by *children,* she can't be referring to the venal little tech junkies I've just watched swarming out of the halls of St. Borromeo. "Ah, I can't really talk right now," I say, holding up my phone. "I'm kind of in the middle of something. But I get it." I give her a thumbs-up. "Just say nope to the pope."

Her disappointed gaze falls on my Saint Michael's medal. "Oh, you're Catholic."

"Only when it comes to burning Protestants," I say. I give her a fixed stare until she backs away from the car and rejoins her group on the other side of the street.

I reach Jackie on the phone and she tells me that her mother is happy for us to stay at her house until we can move back into our apartment. But I can tell that *happy* is probably not the emotion that Anne is feeling right now.

"Baby, this might be an opportunity for Mom to get to know you better," she says, her voice sounding plaintive.

When I walked Jackie to her car that morning, she looked younger than her thirty-five years, and vulnerable.

"I don't know, Jackie," I say. "Seth's invited me to stay at his house. Maybe it would be less of a hassle for you to spend a few days alone with your mom."

There is a pause, a subtle intake of air.

"Come stay at the house, Betty, please," she begs.

Jackie's a respected doctor, but she's no different than the rest of us, reduced to a quivering, insecure puddle when faced with disapproval from Mom or Dad.

"Why don't I come for dinner and see how it goes," I say.

"Great, thanks, babe," she says, exhaling, obviously relieved.

"Can I bring anything?" I offer, trying to lighten the mood. "Beer? Wine? Valium?"

"Don't worry," she says. She laughs, but it's a dry, strained laugh. "I got the sedatives covered. One each for us, and two for Mom. I'm going to put them in her afternoon gingersnaps. Oh, and just so you know, I'm getting a gun."

"Okay," I say after a few seconds. "If it makes you feel

safer." She got her license within six months of moving to Dallas but had never before felt the need to buy a pistol. She always said that one armed and dangerous person in the house was enough. That she wants a gun now tells me how much she has been shaken by the intruder. "We can go buy one over the weekend," I assure her.

"That's all right. I'll just take one of Mom's. You know she still has Dad's arsenal in her closet. I think she may even have his assault rifle. Typical Texan."

"Right," I say. "Typical Texan."

"I love you, Betty."

She hangs up before I can respond, and I try calling Seth again. I need to talk to my partner to stop the hamster wheel in my mind, which keeps returning to the question of how someone gained access to my apartment. Craddock interviewed Jimmy again only a few hours ago, asking him if he had had any repairmen or deliverymen at the complex who could have taken a quick photo of the master keys. Jimmy swore up and down that the keys were never out of his sight, that all the maintenance crew and service individuals were known to him.

Seth finally answers and I tell him about the Roy family and the possible gang affiliation due to the meth connection. He tells me he'll do some checking on his own.

I watch Ryan walk out of the front entrance of the school and across the lawn toward the car, carrying a jacket and tie that he'd bought at the school's uniform shop. He gets into the car grim-faced. A few hours at St. Borromeo and he's already hooked up with a junior named ShaeLynn who invited him to a party next Tuesday night that will be, in her words, "a kick-ass fiesta, for real."

The party is in one of the high-rises near the arts district downtown. A building, no doubt, with killer views of the

Bank of America Tower, with its acid-green neon outlines, or the Crescent, which looks like a child's glass stacking cubes. And it would be in an apartment where the parents were gone, the concierge turning a blind eye to the wealthy tenants' inebriated offspring.

"That's good news, right, Ryan?" I ask.

"Man, these girls. She grabbed my ass in the hallway. What if I have to kiss her?"

"Or, worse, you may have to go down on her."

"What am I going to tell my fiancée?" he asks, throwing the jacket into the backseat. "I thought only Vice cops got into these types of situations."

"You've got me at a disadvantage there, Detective Ryan. What do male cops usually tell their wives and fiancées? Hey, you know who'd know a hell of a lot more than I do?"

I look at him, and after a few beats, we both say at the same time, "Hoskins."

On our way back to headquarters Jackie texts me, asking if I can go by the apartment to pick up a few more items of clothing.

Dropping Ryan off at the station, I tell him I have an errand to run but will be back before six. It's four thirty and the rush-hour traffic southbound on Interstate 75 has already begun. The sun is low and blinding through the passenger-side window and, as usual, Dallasites have begun their assault-with-a-deadly-vehicle exodus, ignoring proper lane-changing techniques.

"Just put on your goddamned blinkers once in a while," I yell at a Dodge Ram, a V-8-powered Death Star of a truck with a Confederate flag sticker on its rear bumper, which muscles itself into my lane without signaling.

At a traffic light a few blocks from the apartment, I pull out my cell phone and hit auto-dial for Jackie's great-uncle James Earle. Not so long ago, I would have been calling Benny to get some experienced perspective. Drug-dealer retaliations usually stick to a script, a bloody but predictable series of shootings, maimings, and beheadings. Two in the back of the head—Los Zetas. Two in the front of the head, one in the groin—Aryan Brotherhood. The be-heading of El Gitano might have been Mexican cartel, but there were no bullet holes in his skull, and the whole hair thing felt off-script and unpredictable. James had been an MP, not regular police but a cop nonetheless, and he had had his share of unraveling the kinks of a killer's mind.

James picks up on the fifth ring. "All okay?" he asks, his voice rumbling like a squeezebox at a Polish dance.

"Hey, James. It's Betty."

"I know it's you. That's why I picked up."

"Can you talk for a minute?"

"Wait, first let me take my truffle butter off the stovetop before it burns. Of course I can talk to you."

He coughs raggedly a few times, and then I tell him about the home invasion, Lana's missing hair being left on the bed, and Jimmy's insistence that no keys were taken or copied.

He asks almost immediately, "Was the hair left on your side of the bed or Jackie's?"

"My side," I say.

"Then the message was meant for you. To get your attention."

There was the familiar sensation in the pit of my stom-ach of a settling truth. But I ask, "How do you know that for certain?"

"Because a killer takes a body souvenir for only two rea-sons. To remind him of the kill, or to send a message."

I hear the crackling sound of a cigarette being lit, followed by a deep, satisfied inhalation. Then he says, "In 'seventy-one I was with the Eighth MP Brigade in Long Binh. We had half a dozen girls working out of the local massage parlors who'd turned up strangled, their middle fingers sheared off. Whoever was killing the girls left the fingers outside the stockade. Little pointing fingers in the dirt. Turns out it was an active-duty soldier. He was pissed at his CO for putting him in the brig for roughing up a Viet prossie. The guy wanted to get his CO's attention. It did the trick. Does the killer have your attention now?"

"Fully," I tell him.

There is the pop and fizz of a carbonated-beverage can being opened. "Don't worry," he assures me. "It's a Dr Pepper, not a Shiner Bock." He takes a drink, belches quietly, and says, "You say that the door was locked, both locks, top and bottom, when you came back?"

"I had to unlock both the knob and dead-bolt locks."

He has taken another deep drag of the cigarette, but he blows the smoke out abruptly, almost impatiently. "You've got to know that locks are more of a psychological barrier than a physical one. Any lock can be picked. I got pretty good at picking them myself. Yet one more skill I learned in the U.S. Army. Never knew when you'd have to sneak up and arrest some mean, drunken armed serviceman."

I pull up in front of my apartment, park a few yards from the breezeway gate. I cut the motor and watch familiar and unfamiliar tenants going in and out of the portal, most of them to walk their dogs. The complex is large enough so that not every guest or delivery person is going to be recognizable to every tenant.

It's late afternoon and Forensics would have packed it in long ago. Jimmy the super has locked up with the new ASSA pick-proof cylinders, although James Earle has reiterated what I already know: with enough time and skill and the right tools, any lock can be breached.

"Here's the thing that's bothering me, though," he says.

"What's that?" I check my watch, realizing I've spent too much time just sitting and shooting the breeze with James Earle. I need to get back to the station.

"If the guy gained access to your apartment to leave Lana's hair," James says, "why did he bother locking the door again when he left? He could have just unbolted the door and walked out."

A prickling at the base of my neck and a surge of adrenaline brings back a memory of hiding in a basement closet with my brother, his face invisible to me but the sound of his voice reassuring. "He'll never find us here," my brother is whispering to me—"he" being our father. And my brother is right. The closet's next to the spare refrigerator where the beer is kept, the location too obvious for the now raging man upstairs, turning over furniture, to bother checking.

"You carry your service piece at all times, right?" James asks.

"I will from now on," I tell him.

"Okay, then. Stay alert," he warns, and after I assure him that I'll be vigilant, I end the call.

Putting the phone back in my pocket, I get out of the car and walk through the gate into the breezeway. I pull the new keys out of my pocket and stop in front of my apartment door. It's wide open.

There's a blank hole in my mind where an immediate impulse to act should be, but then I jerk the SIG out of my holster and press myself against the wall, away from the gaping space between the door and the frame. I can feel the cold air of the AC vent in the apartment blowing past my cheek, and, irrationally, I think how high our electric bill is going to be this month.

I do a quick look-see, eyes scanning between the gap, and call out, "Jackie?"

There's no answer, no noise coming from inside.

Maybe the super or the Homicide unit decided to check on the apartment again. An alternative explanation is trying to break through the growing fear, but I push it away.

"Hello," I yell. "Jimmy?"

I look up and down the breezeway, but there is no one in sight. A dizzying thought occurs to me: Maybe Jackie decided to come get her things herself and ran into trouble. I see nothing in the living room but furniture, some of the walls and cabinetry dark with smudges from Homicide's fingerprinting dust. The door to the master bedroom is fully open and there is no movement there either.

After checking the kitchen and main bedroom, calling out Jackie's name several more times, I move cautiously into the office, gun-first. The door is open, the room empty. But in the closet ceiling there is a three-by-three open square of blackness that leads to a narrow crawl space where the AC repair work is done. The panel that's usually there has been dislodged and moved into the crawl space. It was in place when I left earlier today.

I grab a small tactical flashlight from one of the shelves and shine the beam up into the space, which has a head clearance of several feet, illuminating the wires and ductwork, blanketed with dust. Jackie and I have heard rats and mice sometimes scurrying through the area, and in the two years we've lived in the apartment, Jimmy has squeezed himself up there half a dozen times to lay traps and poison. There is no sound now coming from the crawlway.

I pull a stepladder under the opening and shine the light farther up, the beam capturing only floating particles of dust and insulation. My heart rate has accelerated to the point where I have to move or risk my legs giving out. Bracing my gun hand over my left hand holding the flashlight, I creep as soundlessly as I can up the ladder, doing a twisting, one-eighty sweep with the flashlight once my head clears the ceiling.

There is nothing in the crawl space, but along the rough planking there is a wide swath rubbed clean of dust where something large has lain. Homicide could have opened it to search there, but the detectives wouldn't have hoisted themselves completely into the space unless they'd seen something of interest.

The ladder had not been set under the opening when I walked into the closet. Without it, a person would have to be tall enough and strong enough to pull himself up into the crawl space. Difficult, but not impossible.

A sense of how and when our home invader operated expands in my head like a night-growing fungus.

I begin to step down the ladder and a sound behind me makes me startle. There is the touch of a furtive hand along my leg, and I gyrate wildly, stumbling down the ladder. I manage to keep the gun extended along with the blinding flashlight beam and I look down the barrel sights into the face of a figure standing in the office.

"Don't you move, motherfucker!" I scream and realize immediately that the blinking, cringing form in front of me is not a man, but a boy: Sergei, the Russian kid.

"What the fuck, Sergei," I say, lowering the gun away from his torso. My heart is a berserker inside my chest.

I drop the flashlight to the floor, holster the SIG, and grab him by the arm. "What are you doing in my apartment?" I yell into his face. I gesture above my head. "Were you the one up in the crawl space?"

"No...no..." he sputters. He's trying to pull away from me, but I clamp down harder on his arm and give it a good shake.

"I saw door open," he says. "I was just in hallway."

His fright has resurrected the Russian in him, and he's dropping articles of speech like a son of a bitch.

I let go of him and move back a few steps.

"Jesus, Sergei, you almost got shot." I push the hair away from my face, mainly to steady my hands against my skull.

He starts rubbing his arm, and he must be recovered enough to remember his grammar, and his surliness, because he says, "The door was open. I heard your voice, okay?"

"Did the other cops leave the door open when they left?"

"No. I mean, they left about two o'clock. But they closed and locked the door. I was upstairs in my apartment getting some shit for my mom, so I saw them go."

Getting the rest of his stash and snooping, more like. He and his family went to stay with friends after the head in the box was found, and his mother hasn't been back since. "Have you been upstairs in your apartment all afternoon?" I ask him.

"Yeah, mostly. I came down around four and the door was open again. I thought the cops had come back, you know? So I went out for a little while. I just got back and saw the door was still open." He sniffs a few times, taking a wounded tough-guy stance. "I heard you inside, yo."

"Did you see or hear anyone else in the apartment from the time the cops left until a few minutes ago when you heard me here?"

"No."

"You're sure?"

"Yeah, I'm sure," he says forcefully.

I pull out my phone and call Maclin, who puts me on hold for a few minutes and then confirms what I already suspected: his team searched the apartment thoroughly and left at two thirty, and they had not checked the crawl space because the hatch looked undisturbed.

"Mac," I say. "I think whoever left the hair on the bed was in the apartment the whole time, even when your guys were here." He's not saying anything, but I can hear him breathing over the phone. "I think he was waiting in the crawl space until everybody left, then opened the hatch, unlocked the door, and just walked out."

He tells me he'll have some officers over to my place within ten minutes and to stay put. My legs have become too heavy to support the rest of me and I sink down onto the couch.

This is one bold motherfucker. A guy who sneaks into a cop's apartment by picking two locks and then hides patiently in an overhead crawl space while Homicide detectives and a Forensics team check every square inch of the premises. Almost every square inch.

The phone ringing snaps me to attention. It's Ryan calling to ask where the hell I am. He tells me that he's received the photos of Evangeline Roy's two sons. They're black-and-white case photos, but there is a physical description of the boys. Both have red hair. I tell him what's going on at the apartment and that I'll call him back.

Immediately following, Jackie calls to say that we'll need to pick up dinner. Anne doesn't feel well enough to cook tonight. Apparently, the invasion of the lesbians has left her incapacitated. I don't tell Jackie about the visitor in the crawl space; I'm putting that one off indefinitely. I talk to her in monosyllables, telling her that I'm in the middle of something and have to call her later.

I have my head in my hands and see a pair of sneakered feet in my field of vision. I've all but forgotten Sergei's presence, but he's standing close to the couch, holding out a glass of water. His hand is shaking, sloshing the liquid over the edge.

"Thank you," I say, taking the glass from him and drinking.

"My mom cries all the time now," he says.

His clothes are rumpled and none too clean-looking, and I can imagine that her waking hours are distracted by the recurring nightmares she's having.

"She's scared," I tell him. "If it makes you feel any better, I'm scared too, Sergei."

"I saw something..." he starts to say, looking down at his feet. His tough-guy act has vanished. "The delivery guy that left the box had a tattoo."

I set the glass of water on the coffee table, reminding myself to keep my voice even. "A tattoo?" I ask him.

"When I was on the stairs that day, the day he left the box, I couldn't see his face too good. But he reached up to pull his hat down." He mimes with his fingers pulling the bill to a cap down lower over his brow. "There was a tattoo of wings on the back of his hand."

"What kind of wings?"

"Like an angel's wings."

"Could you draw it if I gave you some paper and a pen?" I ask him.

He nods. "The ink was blue. Bright blue," he tells me. "With something red in the middle. Like a sword, I think."

My hands are unsteady as I rifle through drawers looking for some paper and blue and red ballpoint pens. He sits cross-legged on the couch in front of the coffee table and quickly sketches a pair of up-swooping wings with a transecting sword in red. The image is surprisingly detailed, drawn with confident strokes. The kid is a good little artist.

Studying the drawing, I'm initially disappointed, though. When Sergei mentioned the wings, my first thought was that the tattoo was gang-affiliated, like a Hells Angels branding. But the Angels' trademark is a winged death's-head in profile, and what Sergei has drawn looks nothing like that. But when he adds two letters, one on either side of the wings, that might be a capital *A* and a capital *B,* the hairs on the back of my neck stand at attention. The biggest distributor of meth in East Texas is the Aryan Brotherhood of Texas, or ABT.

Maclin's team will be at the apartment any minute, so I fold the paper and put it in my pocket.

I tap Sergei on the top of his greasy, uncombed head. "Hey, can we just keep this between you and me for a bit?" I ask. "You don't need to be explaining to more cops why you're hanging around a crime scene. Just write down your phone number in case I need to get in touch with you."

"Sure," he says. He looks me full in the face, his eyes wide. "He saw me. The delivery guy."

I sit down on the couch next to him. "I thought you just said you didn't see his face fully. Why didn't you tell us earlier about this?"

He shrugs miserably and looks away, and for one awful moment I feel like giving the kid a hug.

"Did he threaten you?" I ask.

"No," he says, rubbing a finger alongside one nostril. "He smiled at me. Friendly, you know? Like a nice guy. I felt bad 'cause I took the box. I figured no way someone like that would know about what's inside. Right?"

Sergei looks at me nervously, tentatively, waiting for me to validate that perception, because a cheerful, smiling executioner can be more terrifying than a brooding, threatening one.

The ABT, more than any other group, more than law enforcement, more than local, homegrown security organizations, have kept the cartels at bay in East Texas. But not by being nice guys.

Their methods are as ruthless as their Mexican counterparts', their retaliation swift and brutal. There's not a snowball's chance in hell that their delivery guy wouldn't know what was in the box.

I think of Kostucha, the Grim Reaper. As Uncle Benny might have reminded me, Death himself, according to Polish legends, grins amiably and wears a white robe.

20

The drive to the Gas Monkey Bar 'n' Grill takes about twenty minutes from the center of town. It's a Friday night, and the parking lot is full, but it's late enough that the band has finished playing. There are twenty or more motorcycles out front, along with a few vintage cars that shine lustrously under the towering neon sign of a deranged chimp, teeth bared, tongue lolling. I find an open spot near the back of the property and wait for Seth to show up. The lot is dark and quiet, giving me a chance to gather my thoughts. I dry-swallow a couple of headache capsules to ease the tension band around my temples and lean back against the seat, closing my eyes.

A few minutes after I told Sergei to leave my apartment, Maclin's crew showed up and began searching the closet for fibers, prints, or any other residue that someone hiding in the crawl space might have left. I revealed to Maclin the events preceding my discovery of the opened hatch without telling him about Sergei and his drawing. I'd eventually share it with him, but I wanted some lead time to try to ID the delivery guy by running matches of the winged tattoo. Maclin would be pissed when he found out, but he would have done the same thing. I would simply tell him that I wanted to verify the information before we sent his team on a wild-goose chase.

While I was watching Forensics work, my phone rang. It was Seth telling me that he had tracked down a CI who had some things to say about the Roy family. I told him about Sergei's drawing and we decided to meet at eleven that night at the Gas Monkey, a restaurant and bar in West Dallas.

Jackie and I agreed to get takeout at a restaurant in Anne's neighborhood for the merry band of three—me, Jackie, and her mother—before I went out again to talk with Seth. The restaurant was packed and we had stood in line close together so we could talk without being overheard. She looked exhausted. It had been a full day at the hospital, and, unthinkingly, she'd slipped her hand into mine, leaning into my shoulder. If I'd not been so tired and on edge myself, so focused on not letting slip the latest drama in our own home, I would have noticed the hostile glares from the employees, as well as some of the customers.

When we'd made our way to the front of the line, I started giving my selection, but the zombie taking the order, an overweight young woman with the underbite of a pit bull, interrupted me. "I'm sorry," she said stiffly. "I can't serve you."

"What? Are you closed?" I had asked, surprised. The sign on the door, with the logo of a chicken waving a Texas flag, clearly stated that the restaurant was open until nine o'clock, an hour away.

She was immediately joined at the counter by an older man. His name tag read BILLY, and he stared at our intertwined hands like he was watching mating cobras.

With the full picture coming into focus, I dropped Jackie's hand and placed both of mine on top of the counter.

"How about this young lady just takes our order so we can go?" I asked. My voice was low, but my face was over the centerline of the counter.

I felt Jackie tugging on the back of my coat, but I ignored the warning.

"How about you go to another establishment?" Billy said, crossing his arms. His face flushed with anger. "We reserve the right to refuse service to anyone. For any reason."

I ignored Benny's ghost telling me to walk away from a battle I couldn't win, especially if it involved coleslaw and fried chicken.

In my mind, my immediate response to Billy had been *How about I kick your self-righteous, pimply ass across the Trinity River?*

But what I actually spat out was "Just so you know, sir, I'm a cop."

His back stiffened and he said, "Then you should know better."

"What?" I had felt in that moment that all the wiring in my brain would short-circuit and that I would either start laughing maniacally or grab Billy by his poly-ply work shirt. Of all the insults, threats, and admonishments I had ever received, that one seemed the most absurd.

I could feel Jackie moving closer to the counter, coming to stand next to me.

"Excuse me," she said, getting Billy's attention.

He turned to her, clearly expecting more abuse from an angry dyke, his eyes narrowing as though preparing to face into a battering wind.

"I'm sorry to interrupt," she said, her voice mild, the lanyard holding her doctor's credentials clattering against the counter, "but that mole, over your eye?"

"Huh?" he responded, surprised at the turn of conversation, reaching reflexively to touch his right eye.

"No," Jackie corrected. "Your left eye. Have you had that checked out? I'm a doctor at Children's Hospital. Can I just... take a closer look?"

She leaned in, frowning with concern, giving the prominent mole over Billy's left eyebrow her best professional assessment. One exhalation of air through the nostrils signaled an unfortunate diagnosis.

"That doesn't look good," she had said. "Dark, with irregular borders. Really, sir, I'd get that checked out right away. If it's cancer, it will need to be removed, and soon."

For another thirty seconds, Jackie held Billy and the entire restaurant, including Pit Bull Girl, rapt with her graphic descriptions of various treatments for late-stage malignant skin cancer.

When she finished, she slipped a pale and anxious Billy her business card, tugged on my sleeve, and left. I followed her out like a court jester trailing her queen.

Jackie stood outside the restaurant, one hand clapped over her mouth, eyes wide and disbelieving. Then she whispered, "Oh my God. What I did was so unethical."

"And *mean*," I said, laughing and impulsively hugging her. "I'm finally rubbing off on you."

Afterward, we had a rushed dinner of Chinese takeout at Anne's house, where, over duck sauce and wontons, I spent the better part of an hour convincing Jackie that she was *not* going straight to hell just because she put a little fear of God into Billy the Bigot.

The roar of a large engine rouses me, and I see Seth maneuvering his oversize truck into a parking space a few rows behind me. He climbs stiffly out of the driver's seat, a hand pressed against his middle, where he's still bandaged, and I wait for him under the lights in front of the entrance.

"You're looking better," I tell him.

He does look remarkably well, clean-shaven and without the puffy dark circles under his eyes from the pain meds.

"Excellent nursing staff," he says with an exaggerated leering grin.

"Oh, it's a staff now, is it?" I give him a friendly finger jab just above the wound. "It's good to see you vertical again, Seth."

He gestures for me to follow him away from the bright lights and onto the restaurant's deck. We stand at a railing overlooking a small artificial lake, built to give the customers eating outside more of a sense of "country" dining. The only people on the deck tonight are a few overweight urban cowboys drinking beer.

"My CI's name is Wayne Rutherford," Seth tells me.

"Of course it is," I say. "They're all named either Wayne or Delbert."

"He may not be the brightest bulb, but he's been a good CI. A fountain of information for the past few years when it comes to meth gangs. Been in and out of prison for possession. He's been a prospect with several of the OMGs but always screwed up too bad to make the cut."

OMG means Outlaw Motorcycle Gang. There are more than three hundred OMGs in the United States, some of them with only a few members, others with thousands. The Hells Angels, Bandidos, Mongols, Sons of Silence—they all traffic in drugs, extortion, and even murder for hire. The common perception among average citizens is that the bikers are Neanderthal thugs, screwing, drinking, and fighting their way through the trailer parks, bars, and back roads of hick-town America. But they have become transnational, even international, with sophisticated drug-smuggling operations across borders in Canada and Mexico and across every state line.

The OMGs call themselves the 1 percenters, meaning that 99 percent of U.S. bike clubs are composed of law-abiding citizens; the remaining 1 percent are pathologically proud, efficiently organized, and savage.

I follow Seth into the restaurant, where fewer than a dozen people are eating in booths or at tables littered with longneck beer bottles, plates of fried food, and scattered groupings of hot sauce that could take the finish right off the vintage cars parked out front. On the weekends the wait time would be close to an hour.

To the left of the entrance is the bar. Seth signals to the bartender, who directs us to a small private room off the main dining area. Inside, the only diner seated at a table is a rangy, gaunt-faced man in a blue-jean jacket eating from a plate stacked high with ribs, a jelly jar filled with soda next to the plate. His dark hair, parted in the middle, is long and falls like two curtains over his eyes. He bends his mouth toward the plate with each bite rather than raising his arms, and the bottoms of both sleeves are stained with barbecue sauce from the meat. The middle and ring fingers on his right hand are missing, giving him a permanent advantage at rock concerts when he flashes the horns.

When he sees Seth, he smiles, the thick coating of sauce on his lips and teeth making him look like a vampire.

"Hey, Riot," Wayne calls to Seth.

Seth responds by clapping him on the back and saying, "Hey, Flush. But that's 'Officer Dutton' to you."

Wayne's close-set eyes flick briefly toward me, head bobbing like a tweaker on a binge, but there's cunning there, if not intelligence.

We sit in chairs on either side of him and a waitress comes to take our order. Seth asks for two beers.

"Kind of risky, meeting us in a place like Gas Monkey, Wayne," Seth says.

"Yeah, I know," Wayne says, nodding. "But the ribs, man, are just too good."

He takes a few more bites and then leans closer to Seth. "Uh," he whispers, "can I get a beer too?"

Seth shakes his head. "Not from me. You're still on probation."

Wayne shrugs his shoulders. "Okay, I get it. You just lookin' out for a brother. Hope you don't mind I ordered already. Haven't eaten today." He says this through lips working around flesh and gristle clinging stubbornly to bone.

"No problem, Wayne," Seth says. "You want another plate of ribs?"

"Yeah, man, sure. Thanks."

While Seth signals the waitress, Wayne turns his attention to me.

"You his bitch?" he asks casually. He sucks at his fingers—what's left of them—suggestively, his eyes falling to the front of my shirt. Rather than being threatening, though, Wayne seems like a freshman trying to score points in front of an upperclassman.

I just smile pleasantly. "You break your fingers off inside your old lady's snatch?"

Wayne snorts out a laugh and turns to Seth. "I like her, man. She's got some snap."

"She's got more than snap," Seth says. "So watch yourself."

The beers are delivered and Seth takes a drink from the bottle. "I'd like you to tell my partner here what you know about the Roy family."

Wayne sets the bone he's been gnawing down on the plate and deliberately wipes at his hands like he's about to give a state address. He takes a few sips from his soda glass.

"Yeah, right, the Roys." He turns to face me, all the twitchiness gone. "Riot here tell you anything about me?"

"A little," I say.

"So you know I've been with some bikers in my time, right?"

I nod my head. "They supply your meth."

"No, see, no. That's where you're wrong," Wayne says, moving his hands for emphasis. "It's not for the crystal. I can get that anywhere. It's for the love of the clubs, see? I had a bike. I had the time and the inclination. I was a prospect in three different clubs over the past fifteen years. I just lacked the will. Just couldn't get my addiction under control. I'd get a package and a run for a client. But I'd always end up using the product. I couldn't be trusted, see? I'd let the brothers down. And they tend to cleave to the unforgiving. The only reason I'm still breathing is 'cause I went down on a drug-possession charge in East Texas. I was lucky, ended up in Angelina County Jail and not, like,

Huntsville, where I'd have had my balls cut off by one of the diamond-patch members."

Diamond-patch bikers often have the number 13 inside the patch they wear on their vests, the letter *M* being the thirteenth letter of the alphabet. *M* for *murder*.

"I was there for eighteen months. In for dealing crack. My old lady was trying to help me get off the meth, see?" He sniffs and bobs his head up and down a few times to make sure I get the nobility of this last statement.

"Anyway, she was from Lufkin and I'd been staying with her, trying to put some distance between myself and a misunderstanding with the Bandidos back in Dallas."

He shakes the hair out of his face and for the first time I can see the meth scars gouged into his cheeks like small lunar craters.

"Mostly everyone at Angelina is in for meth, and the thing is, they're all family in one way or another. All Aryan Brotherhood and shit. And here I am, a stranger in their midst."

His eyes fall on Seth's beer, and he scratches thoughtfully at the scabs flowering his neck. "All this talking's making me real thirsty."

When Seth moves the bottle farther away, Wayne settles for more of his soda.

"Once they realize that I'm in bad with the Bandidos," he says, "they're cool with me, though. They have my back. They even teach me shit. Like how to short-cook Piney Woods meth. Man, I thought I'd died and gone to heaven. You ever hear of red phosphorus dope? I can walk into any Walmart now and, for a hundred bucks, get enough product to make fifteen grams in ten minutes. A one-pot cook, man."

Large old-dope labs use professional-grade equipment

and need people with chemistry knowledge to create a purer form of product. The labs take a lot of time to set up and have to be located in open, well-ventilated areas because of the acrid fumes from the cook. The operations are put into production only once or twice a month and make a couple of hundred grams of crystal meth at a time. Shake-and-bake setups, though, can be done in bathtubs, small boats, even the trunks of cars.

Wayne laughs nervously, rubs his palms together between his two jiggling knees, as though simply talking about the meth is making him euphoric.

"We get it," Seth says. "You're a one-man operation now. Get to the Roys, please."

Wayne wipes his hands nervously across his T-shirt, a WALK FOR THE CURE rag, probably donated to some Goodwill center, and says, "People are real friendly, real open about stuff once you're accepted. They talk about everything in Angelina. Their old ladies, their small-time scores, their busts, their come-to-Jesus moments in rehab. One thing they don't talk about is the biggest supplier of meth in East Texas. Not directly. I heard about them once by accident. Came across some of the skinhead brothers in a huddle, talkin' about 'the Family.' "

He mutters the last two words in a whisper.

I ask, "You mean like the Manson Family?"

"Who?" Wayne asks.

"Charles Manson. The Manson Family." I speak the words slowly, deliberately.

Wayne shakes his head, pulling at one ear, clearly having no idea who I'm talking about. I look at Seth for a beat and then say, "Never mind. Go on."

"So," Wayne continues, "one skinhead shoves me against the wall and says, 'What'd you hear, fuckface?' I tell him, 'Nothing. I heard nothing.' And he tells me that if I ever mention anything to anyone, ever, about the Family, I'd be picking up my own eyeballs off the floor."

Wayne shows me his horns on his right hand, the hand with only his thumb and two fingers left.

"And just to prove the point, he cut off two of my fuckin' fingers quicker than I could piss myself."

He starts to shiver, although the room is warm and he's wearing a long-sleeved jacket. Seth pushes his beer in front of Wayne, and he picks up the bottle and drains it in a few swallows.

"The worst part," Wayne says miserably, "is that they flushed my fingers down the john. I wasn't a snitch, though." He looks at me and grins, showing gaps where the battery acid from the cook has rotted away his teeth. "I told the guards, when they asked me what happened, that I had gotten a paper cut from playing cards. Man, the brothers thought that was the funniest thing they had ever heard. That's how I got the nickname Full Flush. Get it? Cards? Toilet flush?"

"I get it, Wayne," I say. I push my beer in front of him too and he smiles at me like a surprised child. He drains my beer in short order.

He wipes his mouth with one sleeve. "After that, people weren't so tight with their talk. But I learned only a few things about the Family. They make good meth, almost as good as the Mexicans. But they always wear masks and regular clothes during a deal so no one knows what they look like, where they're from, or how many of them there are. But even the Aryans and the Mexicans are respectful, man. The Family pushes back hard. You kill one of them, they kill five of you."

"Anybody ever mention the Roys?" I ask.

"Sure," he says. "They were the big suppliers for a time. But they all died in a fire a while back. The woman and her two boys. From what I hear, a fire set by the Family."

He picks at his teeth and glances around the bar as though looking for someone. "The Family takes tributes, see? Body parts."

Seth looks at me with a raised eyebrow.

"What kind of body parts?" I ask.

"Whatever you got that can be hacked off."

I look at the three remaining fingers on his right hand and ask, "You think it was a member of the Family that cut your fingers off?"

"No, man," Wayne says in all seriousness. "That was just prison talkin'."

He then stares at the clean-picked ribs from the first go-round, his appetite clearly gone, and when the waitress delivers his second order, he asks her if it can be wrapped to go.

"Wayne," I say, pulling his attention from the scattered bones on his plate. "You're not afraid of talking about this here? There're a lot of bikes out front."

"You crazy?" he answers. "There're no real bikers here. Guys wearing cuts wouldn't be caught dead in this place. I mean literally dead. All the same," he says, sitting upright in his chair, dropping his hands down to his lap, "that's why I ducked into the back room. My cousin works the bar. He keeps an eye out for me." He sniffs a few times. "I've got a plan, see. Me and my old lady are starting a business. Painting house-number signs on curbs. Those Highland Park folks like for the cops to know where they're going at all times."

The waitress brings the takeout sack and Wayne stands up. "Listen, man, I gotta bounce."

Seth puts a restraining hand on his arm and he sits back down. "My partner has something to show you. A picture of a tattoo."

I pull Sergei's drawing out of my pocket, slide the plate of ribs out of the way, and place the sketch in front of Wayne. I had hoped for an immediate reaction but he studies the drawing for a minute, chewing on his lips.

Pointing to the first letter, he asks, "Is this an *A*? It's got no crossbar thing through the middle of it."

Seth points to the second letter. "That clearly looks like a *B*."

"Do you recognize the image?" I ask Wayne.

He cocks his head, impressed. "Nice work. Could be Aryan Brotherhood. But they're usually all swastikas and eagles and shit. Definitely not in my prison. You couldn't get the colored ink in Angelina."

I fold the paper and put it back in my pocket. "Thanks, Wayne. If something jogs your memory, give Riot a call, okay?"

Wayne holds out his right hand for me to shake, which I do, his forefinger and pinkie wrapping around the back of my palm in a queerly prehensile way. "Well, you take care," he tells me, breathing caustic fumes into my face. "Don't go into the woods alone, hear?"

Seth slips him a few twenties and he does the tweaker shuffle out of the restaurant, shoulders bowed, head swiveling from side to side like a dashboard dachshund. Seth pays the bill and we stand in the parking lot in front of my car.

"Poor Flush," Seth says. "He's basically a good guy. But you know what they say about addicts: A crack addict will take your stuff and leave—"

"And a meth-head will steal your stuff and spend days helping you look for it," I say.

I'm disappointed that Wayne didn't recognize the tattoo. The more I look at the first letter, the more I'm uncertain that it's an *A*. It could be a partial letter, or it could be an imperfectly formed part of the design. The whole tattoo could be just a flight of fancy to the wearer and not an affiliation with any group in particular.

"What are you thinking, Riz?" Seth asks.

"I'm thinking that this has been the longest fucking day of my life, and I need some sleep." I give Seth's arm a squeeze. "You're looking a little pale yourself, Riot. Thanks for the snitch connect."

I get into my car and drive back to Anne's house. I figure I'll change and go for a short run to shake loose the thoughts in my head. Maybe Benny will have something to say about the tattoo.

21

Except for the porch light and a second-floor hall light, Anne's house is dark when I pull into the driveway. The key is always left under the mat, even though I've begged Jackie to tell Anne to leave it in a less obvious spot.

I slip in through the front entryway, trying my best not to let the screen door squeak, and have already secured the inside lock before I notice the smell of fresh tobacco smoke coming from the direction of the living room, just off the foyer. The upstairs hall light illuminates the entryway table with its collection of framed portraits of the Nesbitts taken at holidays and family reunions. There's also one larger photo of a teenage Jackie and her dad, each holding a rifle, standing proudly in front of a six-point elk, its head propped up on a rock.

My foot hits the bottom riser on the stairs and I hear Anne's voice out of the darkness calling my name. A voice that, despite Anne's many years living in Oregon, has managed to retain the twang of a born-and-bred Texan, with the imperious muddle of compressed vowels and tight-lipped consonants.

I stand quietly, hoping I've imagined it.

"Betty," Anne says again. There is no question mark at the end.

As I feel my way into the living room, a floor light comes on and I see Anne sitting upright in her deceased husband's recliner, wearing her robe and slippers.

"Hi, Anne," I say. "Everything all right?"

She places aside the magazine that she's been holding—apparently a Braille copy, as the room had been pitch-black until a few seconds ago—and walks stiffly to where I'm standing.

She folds her arms, her pale brows drawn in a V-shaped frown. Her nostrils flare slightly and she tells me, "You smell like cigarette smoke."

"So do you," I say reflexively.

Anne is a secret smoker. According to her, she quit years ago. But under stress, she'll sneak a few out in the backyard or in the downstairs guest bathroom. Because of her heart condition, everyone, including her doctor, has lectured her ad nauseam about the dangers of smoking. But she, like a lot of smokers her age, doesn't think the surreptitious ones count.

Her frown deepens, but I've had practice waiting out hardened felons in an interrogation room, so I meet her stare.

As the silence continues, I think the next thing she'll say is that she wants me sleeping on the couch and not in the guest bedroom with Jackie. I brace for the lecture about how only bad can come from our "unhealthy lifestyle choice." How my influence on her daughter will bring

Jackie unhappiness and social disdain resulting in racking and burning at the stake.

But what she says is "My daughter is very precious to me."

I end the stare and look at my shoes.

"As she is to me, Anne," I say.

She nods, the edges of her mouth trembling and down-turned. "Just don't break her heart." She says this while walking past me, throwing off the scent of cigarette smoke and Pond's cold cream. I hear her slippers shuffling up the stairs and the sound of her bedroom door closing.

I soon follow after, finding my way to Jackie's room. Just the thought of a run now is too much. I sit as gently as I can on the edge of the bed, taking off my boots and socks and slipping out of my pants.

Jackie stirs and sits up behind me, draping her arms around my waist. She kisses the side of my neck and asks softly, "You tired, baby?"

She kneads my shoulders and I say, "Yeah."

"Everything okay?" she asks.

I think of what I'm not going to tell her about: the visitor in the crawl space, the tweaker with the stories of jail-house brutality, the encounter with her mother. Instead I say, "Everything's fine."

22

For two weeks in North Texas, once in the spring and once in the fall, the weather is about as perfect as it can be anywhere. A bit like a landlocked San Diego, only with much bigger cars. I look at the modest but well-tended homes around Anne's and think life lived in an enclave could be much worse. A lot of middle-class neighborhoods back east would have avenues about half as wide, and breaking free from a parallel-parking job on a borough street can be a bit like an outtake from *War of the Worlds,* with panicked, impatient motorists maneuvering wildly between other drivers all the while shouting obscenities. In contrast, it's superbly quiet on Anne's street.

I stand for a moment, my face turned toward the sun, breathing in the air that's for once not weighted with humidity, and I imagine what it would be like sitting on my own backyard patio, drinking coffee, Jackie in her turquoise robe idly pulling weeds from the potted plants. I remind myself that I'm long overdue to find an agent to show us some property again, an agent who's not going to turn apoplectic at the thought of a same-sex couple setting up housekeeping in the land of the free and the home of the brave.

We've spent the entire weekend at Jackie's mother's house and, remarkably, miraculously, there've been no meltdowns, arguments, or cutting judgments made. At least, not out loud. However, I'm certain I've sustained irreparable brain damage from listening to too much Fox News.

My work phone rings with Seth's number showing on the screen. "You're up early," I say, glad that the first call of the morning is from him.

"Hey, partner," he says, "want to hear something funny as shit?"

"Absolutely," I say, retrieving the car keys from my pocket. "Give me some good news."

"You know we got that football game coming up this next weekend with Homicide, right?"

Every fall, one of the most anticipated DPD sports matches is the full-contact football game between the Homicide division and the Narcotics division. The rivalry is intense, injuries abound, and the after-parties are legendary.

"Well," Seth says, laughing, "guess whose van got broken into last night, all their equipment stolen?" He pauses for effect. "Homicide's."

"No fuckin' way." I gasp. Now I'm laughing too, and it feels good to dispel the darkness of home invaders and dismembered body parts showing up in otherwise peaceful neighborhoods with some crazy-ass, reckless news. "Those guys are going to be so pissed. Do we know yet who did it?"

"Yeah, Craddock called me. A couple of stupid crackheads got arrested trying to pawn the stuff. But I have a feeling it's going to take a long time to get it processed out of our evidence room. Probably not until after the big game this weekend."

"Don't take this the wrong way, Seth," I tell him. "But I love you."

I disconnect and I've started getting into my car when my phone rings again. It's Maclin's number and at first I think he's calling to bitch about the stolen football gear. But he tells me that Tony Ha is in his office and wants to talk to me.

"Me?" I say, sliding into the driver's seat and starting the engine. "Why the change of heart?" I knew that Tony had hired a lawyer within minutes of being questioned at Bender's place following the murder of Lana Yu and also that he'd made bail.

"We've leaned on him hard, threatening to charge him with accessory to murder, but the guy's been a wall," Maclin says, his voice sounding crisp and self-assured. "All he would say was that he had been in the laundry closet. He heard nothing, he saw nothing. Then today he has something to say about Lana's murder. He came in to make a statement but insists he'll only talk if you're here. The guy looks like he's about to shit himself all over the interrogation room."

I call the sergeant and tell him I'm going to be in Maclin's office for a new statement from Tony Ha.

There's a pause, and Taylor asks, "Why do I have the feeling that this is going to further muddy the waters? If he's got new information, Mr. Ha needs to tell Homicide, not us."

"What can I say?" I tell him. "The guy won't talk to Homicide without my being there."

Taylor sighs impatiently. "Okay. Give it twenty minutes and then get back here. You need to get Ryan to the high school."

The sergeant's stress is palpable over the phone.

I crimp my lips to keep from snickering. "Did you just tell me not to be late for carpool?"

"Look," he says, with withering sharpness, "I don't know what happy gas you've been sucking on this morning, but we've got kids dying from heroin funneled through that high school. I want you back here within the hour, you got that, Detective?"

"Yes, sir," I say after he's already hung up. The happy gas that I've been sucking on all morning evaporates before I make the entrance to the Tollway.

I drive to the North Central Division, on Hillcrest and McCallum, a large, squat, pale brick building where the Homicide unit is housed.

Maclin meets me in the hallway to his office, file folders under his arm.

"Hey," I say warily, both hands resting reflexively on my hips.

"Thanks for coming in." He reaches out to take my hand anyway, shining on the smile that's supposed to make me forget that only yesterday he backed me into a corner like he was a muskrat in heat. He ducks his head in a boyish, apologetic way.

Asshole.

"Tate's waiting with Ha in an interview room," he says, dropping his hand and leading me through the warren-like hallways.

We pass several desks, and one of Maclin's colleagues, a shaved bull of a detective, calls out, "Hey, Mac. We processing male impersonators for Vice now?"

"I'm ready whenever you are," I prompt Maclin, ignoring the talking bowling ball.

Maclin opens the door to the interrogation room, which reeks of stale garlic and an overabundance of sports cologne. Tate barely gives me a nod, less than thrilled with my being called into the unit. He sniffs a few times, says in his best East Coast townie accent, "Good mawning, Detective," and goes back to whatever notes he's been scribbling on a pad on the desk. But his apparent lack of attention is not fooling me. He can stare at the paper in front of him all day long, but I know the guy sees everything.

It's Tony's ragged appearance that gives me pause. He's evidently gotten less sleep than I have; his eyes are swollen almost shut. The skin on his face is drawn tight as a drum across his cheekbones, and his lips are dry and scaly. His breathing is erratic and shallow, and he's still wearing the same plaid jacket that I'd seen him in days ago. I imagine that Maclin and Tate have been scraping him hard for whatever information he wants to impart to me.

I take a desk chair and position it closer to Tony so we're not separated by a piece of furniture. Maclin, I decide, likes to use the desk as a prop—a physical and psychological barrier between the "good" guys and the "bad," an intimidation factor. But Benny always said that, unless the interviewee was dangerous, you should remove any barriers and just talk, person to person. Maclin places the files on the desk and I sit facing Tony, waiting for him to speak.

"I have to tell you something," Tony says to me. "About Lana's killer—"

"Okay," I say quietly. "But before you start, I have some questions I need to ask you."

Tony blinks rapidly at my interruption, and I can almost hear the lids shuttering painfully over his inflamed eyeballs. Obviously, the guy is scared and needs to spit out whatever toxic secret he's been holding, but I don't want him controlling the interview. I also want to learn some details that Maclin may not have seen fit to share with me.

Tate is impatiently tap-tapping with a pencil on the desk, letting me know the clock is running.

"How did you and Lana come to have a key to Bender's house?" I ask, taking out my own small notepad. I could antagonize Tony from the get-go, wind him up with forceful questions, but I need his goodwill and that will take some finessing. Tony, like most men, will begin to balk at being word-spitted by a female, and though he may be a lowlife pimp, he imagines himself to be his own boss, the master of his own fate, the captain of his own soul, and all that crap.

"It's my understanding that Lana was Ruiz's girlfriend," I say, keeping my tone polite, deferential. "Did she know William Bender as well?"

His eyes slide to both Homicide detectives, but they give him the thousand-yard stare, and he tells me, "Lana was Mr. Bender's friend first. He introduced her to the Mexican."

I scribble something on my pad. Tate's tapping pencil is getting louder. "What were you and Lana doing in Bender's house the night she was murdered?"

Tony pauses before saying, "The Mexican told Lana there was a lot of cash in the house." He looks again at Maclin and adds, "We were promised fifty thousand each if we found the money."

There's no reaction from Maclin when the money is mentioned, so he must already know why Lana was there.

"Where was Ruiz the night that Lana was killed?" I ask.

"In some bad hotel, Lana said. I'd never met the Mexican face to face. Only on the phone."

I give him a close look but decide he's telling the truth. Tate's tapping is now like a metronome. I reach over, snatch the pencil from him, break it in two, and hand him back the pieces.

Tony smiles unpleasantly at the look of surprise on Tate's face. Lots of contempt for the good Homicide detective in that fixed countenance.

"Be careful, Officer," Tony warns him, "or she'll put the cuffs on you as well."

No doubt Tony's been treated harshly by Homicide, and that's apparently worse than being cuffed aggressively by my partner. He crosses his arms and looks away, dismissing Tate as a presence. Maclin starts to say something, but I cut him off.

"Okay," I say to Tony. "When you're ready, tell me what happened the night you and Lana went to Bender's house."

He looks unguardedly down at his hands for a few seconds, and then he yawns. But the yawn, I know, is not from being exhausted. It's nervous energy, rippling up from his neck into the muscles of his jaw, a fright reflex that many interrogators mistake for gaping apathy. Benny had clued me in to the fact that both killers and victims of a crime will sometimes fall dead asleep in an interview rather than face the horror of what they've committed or experienced.

"Lana and I drove to the house, and we sat in the car for almost an hour looking for lights inside," he begins. "When we were sure no one was there, we drove to the alley and went through the rear gate. Lana used her key on the back door into the kitchen. It was dark, and we used the light on Lana's phone to see."

He dry-swallows a few times trying to clear his throat, and I turn to Tate and say, ever so politely, "Detective, could we please get Mr. Ha some water?"

Tate gives me the you've-got-to-be-out-of-your-mind look, but, with a sigh, he unwinds himself from the desk and walks out of the room.

"Go on," I prompt Tony.

"Lana thought the cash might be in the master bedroom," he says. "She saw him put something in the safe once. He had a little book in his desk where he kept all his passwords and the combination to the safe. We were in the bedroom searching for it when we heard a noise downstairs. So...Lana went to see what it was."

"Lana went downstairs to check out the noise by herself?" I ask. I try to keep my voice neutral because I'm thinking that he was the guy who'd trained in the army. Benny once told me that if you wanted a tough job done, send a man. If you wanted an impossible job done, send a woman.

"She asked for my gun," he says, "which I gave to her."

"And what were you doing while Lana went downstairs?" I ask, thinking that he was probably testing the second-floor windows, looking for a way to crawl out.

"I stood at the top of the landing," he continues, "and watched her go down the stairs to the hallway. She called someone on her phone—"

"What time was this?" I ask.

"It was after nine o'clock."

It was me that Lana had called, at nine thirty, the night I'd been to Slugger Anne's with Seth.

Tate walks back into the room, the sound of the opening door startling Tony, and sets a small Styrofoam cup of water on the table. Tony picks up the cup and drains it in a few swallows.

He holds the Styrofoam in both hands. "I saw something come out of the shadows and take Lana. A big man. He grabbed Lana from behind and took away the gun. He saw me standing at the top of the stairs and told me he would shoot me if I didn't come down."

The two detectives' interests are now heightened, and both of them are leaning in toward the table, making notes. This part of the story is new to them.

"So you came down the stairs?" I ask.

"Yes," he says, beginning to pull nervously at the rim of the cup.

"Did you get a good look at him?"

"It was dark. He was wearing a mask. But he was a big man wearing plain, dark clothes. And a baseball cap."

"Could you see any insignia on the cap? Any logo on the shirt?"

"No."

"What kind of a mask was he wearing?"

"Like a cloth sack. It had no features. Only holes cut out for the eyes and the mouth. He ordered me to get into the laundry closet in the kitchen, and then he closed the door. He told me that if I opened it he would kill me."

"What did he do with Lana?" I ask, remembering vividly her face crusted with dried blood, the eyes partially open, the lips pulled back as though in interrupted speech.

"She was yelling, struggling with him. He threw her to the floor. I could hear their voices through the bottom slats in the door. They were close, only a few feet away. He wanted to know where the Mexican was. She kept swearing and spitting at him."

Tony looks down at his hands again and picks at already-brutalized cuticles. "She was a very stubborn girl."

"Did her attacker ever ask about the money?"

Tony shakes his head.

"For the interview record," Maclin says loudly, "Mr. Ha has signified no by shaking his head."

Maclin is making notes again, but he wanted to remind me, officially, that it's his witness making this statement.

Tony now shreds the rim of his cup, letting the pieces fall to the floor in weightless slivers. I have a renewed admiration for Lana. She had taken Tony's gun and had died struggling with her attacker, a man much larger than herself, yelling and cursing at him. My kind of woman.

Tony looks up from his Styrofoam snowmaker. "Then she started screaming. It went on for a long time. She finally told him where the Mexican was."

It's quiet in the room, Maclin and Tate waiting for me to ask the next logical question: Where did Lana say Ruiz was hiding?

I open my mouth but Tony stops me before I can speak. He stares at his feet, but he's straightened his back, as though prepping himself for something unpleasant. "I knew from the moment he started speaking to her that she was going to die." He looks up at me. "I just didn't know it would take so long. I couldn't see what he was doing, but he was humming the whole time. Like a man happy at his work. She kept screaming until he cut her throat."

Maclin opens one of the files in front of him and pulls out a crime scene photo of Lana lying on Bender's kitchen floor, the blackened pool of blood surrounding her body like a dark corona.

He says to Tony, "This is just a reminder of what you didn't see happening. While you were hiding in the closet."

Tony looks at it, his face a practiced blank. "When it was quiet," he says, "the man came to stand at the other side of the door. I thought he was going to kill me next. But he only stood there, breathing. He told me to stay until morning or he would come to my house and cut the skin off my face and feed it to his dogs. He told me also that if I said anything to the police, he would come to the Blue Heaven and cut off the ears of every one of my girls and also of their children."

I shift slightly in my chair so Tony will look at me. "So why are you telling us all this now?"

"More specifically," Tate says, jabbing a thumb in my direction, "why are you telling this to her? Did we not interview you earlier, and did you not tell us that you hid in the closet before Lana was attacked?"

"You gave us a false statement, partner," Maclin says.

Now it's Tony's turn to give Homicide the thousand-yard stare.

"Last night," Tony says to me, putting the cup down, "I woke up to him standing in my house, at my bed." His hands, now clasped between his knees, are quivering, the knuckles bloodless with tension. "My doors have good locks, but it was the same man wearing the same mask. He said I was to find you and give you something."

"He asked for me? By name?" The same fear that assaulted me when I realized someone had been hiding in my apartment crawls its way up my intestines. Maclin and Tate are studying me now.

Tony reaches into his pocket and pulls out a piece of paper. He starts to hand it to me, but Maclin gestures impatiently for him to lay it on the desk. It's notebook-size white paper, loosely folded twice, and Maclin unfolds it using the tips of two pens. When it's opened fully, it reveals a crude drawing in black ink of upswept, feathery wings transected by a sword. Similar to the image that Sergei had drawn of the tattoo on the man delivering the severed head to my door. My fingers find a choke hold on the Saint Michael's medal, the downward tension threatening to snap the silver double-linked chain.

Underneath the wings, printed in neatly formed block letters in the same black ink, is a passage from the Bible, Deuteronomy 32:41. *When I sharpen my flashing sword and my hand grasps it in judgment, I will take vengeance on my adversaries and repay those who hate me.*

Tony takes a steadying breath. "Here's what the man told me to say to you. 'Tell the redheaded detective that she can come home now.'"

Maclin walks with me through the hallways to the exit. I had stayed another ten minutes in the interview room while the two Homicide detectives tried to pry more information out of Tony. But he'd delivered his message, and, other than insisting that the man did not sound like a Mexican and that Ruiz had been hiding in some run-down, off-ramp motel before he was killed, he had no more to tell them. When I got up to leave, for the first time, Tony looked at me with something approaching sympathy.

I've got a stone-cold murderer telling me, via a cowardly little flesh peddler, that I can go home. No, actually the message was "She can *come* home now." But which home?

I veer off into the women's bathroom, which is mercifully empty, and press cold water onto my face and neck with a paper towel, my head bent over the sink. My hair hangs in damp clumps, and the eyes that greet me in the mirror are darkly smudged with exhaustion. More than anything else, I want to return to my own home, but the new ASSA locks seem merely a thin cord between us little piggies and the wolf outside the door. Tony, snug under his blankets, woke to Lana's butcher standing at his bedside delivering a note, much as he must have stood at our bed watching Jackie peacefully sleeping.

I rejoin Maclin and let him escort me out of the building. But I happen to glance at the bullish, shaved-headed officer as we pass, and he's leering at me, his tongue flattened obscenely against his lower lip, a hiccup of staccato laughter, and I decide to leave a message of my own. I check out his desk plaque for his name.

"Detective Rice," I say, stopping in front of him. From the size of him, he's very likely one of the defensive linemen for the Homicide football team. At the very least, he's going to follow the DPD game this weekend with fevered interest. I reach out and adjust the plaque, aligning it more neatly with the edge of his desk.

"You know that police van that was broken into last night?" I ask him. "The one where the Homicide team's football gear was stolen?"

The detective's grin loses a hint of its self-satisfaction, his eyes narrowing almost imperceptibly.

"Well," I say, "when you want to know where all your shit is, you guys come see me. Good luck with that game this weekend. Y'all have a good day, now."

Asshole.

23

Jackie and I do move back into our apartment, but only after we've installed a door brace and set up a surveillance security system with an alarm. I buy Jackie a nine-millimeter Beretta to keep at her bedside, and now we're truly like every other normal gun-toting couple in Texas.

We hire Jimmy the super's sister-in-law, who owns a cleaning service, to come in with two of her best workers—refugees from a struggling, waterlogged New Orleans—to erase the fingerprinting dust and the grime of cops and the Forensics team investigating every room. Maclin had ordered another extended sweep through the apartment in case, according to him, he'd missed something the first few times. I know, however, that even though the first search uncovered a few red hairs in the attic crawl space that were not mine, the additional search was in retaliation for my keeping silent after Tony's interview. It was apparent from my reaction to the drawing of the wings and sword that I'd seen the image before. When pressed by Maclin and Tate, I simply kept repeating that I had no idea what the drawing meant, which was true. But it infuriated the both of them.

Maclin had warned me, "Detective, you need to think real hard about cooperating with us regarding any information you may have related to Lana's killer."

And I had responded, "You mean the way you cooperated with us when my team was trying to conduct a drug search in Bender's house?"

The killer had left Ruiz's head at my door in a box with my name on it. He had broken into my apartment where my girlfriend was still asleep in bed, leaving a hank of hair from a dead woman, and sent me a message through Tony Ha that was, more or less, *Betty, go home.* Nothing I had heard or seen subsequent to the shooting of William Bender regarding the related players indicated that the ensuing chaos was not drug-related. I had come to believe that two groups, the Mexican cartel and some as-yet-unknown homegrown illegal drug pushers, were fighting for distribution control, the drawing with the Bible verse referring to flashing swords and vengeance only strengthening that belief. I didn't need Maclin's help, or permission, to move forward. This was a personal challenge to me.

Uncle Benny, who would occasionally lapse into Polish to express or finesse some philosophical point regarding law enforcement, used to say, "If the beard were all, the goat might preach." *Broda nie czyni filozofa.* Meaning that the brains of an operation do not lie in the symbols of power. I chose to translate it as "Just because you've got a beard and some balls doesn't mean you've got the smarts."

I soon went back to work with Ryan, who continued to pose undercover as the newly transferred high-school up-

perclassman. He went to the "kick-ass fiesta, for real"—
held in a two-story luxury condo downtown—with the St.
Borromeo girl, who stripped down to her bra and panties
within five minutes of arriving. A dozen of her classmates
had gathered for an eagerly anticipated mix of sex and
drugs, Catholic-style. Meaning that the participants could
get wasted and laid and then go to chapel the next day,
where all would be forgiven. It seems there is nothing the
Catholic Church won't forgive a person for. Except being gay.

When the arresting officers gained entrance to the
condo, the girl answering the door thought that the cops
were male strippers, there to join the party. She giggled uncontrollably when the cuffs were put on, no doubt giving
hard-ons to every male in the place.

When I walked in following the uniformed officers, one
beefy high-school jock, wearing only his designer briefs,
shouted to one of his friends, "Hey, Carlton, your mother is
here."

He fell all over himself laughing until I grabbed the
little twenty-four-karat-gold ring piercing one privileged,
rosebud nipple and let him know that the regulars at Lew
Sterrett County Jail were just salivating to make his ac-
quaintance.

The owners of the condo turned out to be the parents of
one of the arrested youths, but both were in Budapest on
business and could not be reached by phone for nearly two
days. It took only twenty minutes of my questioning the
apartment owners' son for him to give up the name of his
heroin dealer.

Of course, there will be no end to the stories of nearly
naked adolescent girls throwing themselves at police officers; they'll be told at every barbecue and late-night beer-

and-bullshit session from now until doomsday. Great fun for everyone, except Ryan, who was traumatized by the aggressive sexual tactics of his date—she had her face in his lap at the time of the arrest—and who will forever be blackmailed by his fellow officers into doing shit duty or risk having his future wife told about the nature of the bust.

Jackie's birthday was on the nineteenth of September, and we celebrated by going to the restaurant atop the Reunion Tower. We drank too much champagne and watched the Dallas streets slowly revolving below us, the suburbs stretching into the outlying flatness like an endless expanse of celestial dust, punctuated at intervals with neon-framed buildings.

For the occasion, I had paid a fortune for burgundy-red Doc Martens, which I wore with my decade-old, custom-made black leather pants and a new velvet blazer, cut tight and long, to the middle of my thighs. When Jackie saw me standing in front of a mirror pulling the length of my hair out from under the jacket collar, she clapped slowly, as though watching a curtain rising, and then kissed me and said, "You could pull all the saints down from the heavens looking the way you do."

Jackie wore a sea-green silk blouse with a snug black skirt and skyrocket heels that stretched the calves of her legs taut as a ballerina's when she walked.

At our table I gave her a box tied with a ribbon, her ninth bracelet of gold threaded with three hundred and sixty-five tiny wooden beads. It was too early for our anniversary, which is in November, but I told her I just couldn't wait. I wanted her to know how much I loved her and appreciated her being my rock during the chaos of the Ruiz investigation.

Jackie showed our waitress the bracelet, and the woman

smiled with genuine pleasure, her head tilting graciously as she examined it.

"Qué linda," she said, her dark eyes glinting in the candlelight.

At the end of the evening we stood at the elevator banks with an elderly couple. The wife was stoop-shouldered with weak eyes and a tentative smile, and her husband was solidly portly, packed into an outdated dinner jacket and Western boots. There was a brief silence, and then he leaned in, tapped me on the arm, and asked, "Know what the secret to a long, successful relationship is?"

I shook my head, bracing for the lecture, but he simply pointed to Jackie and told me, "Always let her be right."

24

On Mondays, the team meets early for breakfast at Norma's Café, a fifties-style restaurant that opened in 1956, when Eisenhower was still president and Elvis was beginning to enter the charts. The reason I know this is that Craddock, the follower of All Things Elvis, tells me every time we eat here. Every single time.

Our usual waitress, Tammy Sue, brings us coffee before we even have a chance to settle into our red vinyl seats; our sunglasses and phones are scattered over the tabletop, which is plastered with advertising stickers from local businesses.

She gives me a nod, her dyed-blond hair lacquered into immobility. "Good morning, Betty, darlin'. You keepin' these boys in line?"

She always asks this question, and my answer is always the same. "I give it my best effort, Tammy Sue."

The bridge of her nose wrinkles in solidarity with my challenges, and she says wearily, "Uh-huh."

She spins on her heel but walks away grinning, cracking her gum. There are five of us gathered: me, Craddock, Ryan, Hoskins, and Seth, who daily improves and will soon be cleared for active duty. It's six thirty on a Monday morning, and the place is half full. Not like the weekends, when the line stretches out the door and down the block. Texans, I've found, will froth at the mouth when delayed thirty seconds at a red light but will wait an hour for three fried eggs and a minute steak.

Regardless of whatever else our department is working on, it's a matter of professional pride now, and no small degree of belligerent curiosity, to find out who keeps leaving provocative and bloody clues at my door.

"I spoke to Taylor last night," I tell them. "Here's what he told me. We get one hour a day to pursue leads to identify the redheaded bastard who's been tweaking our noses. He's hoping, though, that our ghost will go back into whatever hole he crawled out of and leave me alone for a while."

We bow our heads to look over the menu selections, featuring Tex-Mex-style *migas* with four-alarm-strength chilies, knowing full well that the Mex-Mexicans will never leave the green pastures of East Texas alone. There's too much money to be made with crystal meth.

We place our orders with Tammy Sue, and while we wait for our food, I pull Sergei's drawing out of my pocket and unfold it on the table. I recount to them my interview with Tony Ha and describe the image of the wings and the sword that the killer had given him, which, except for the Bible verse, was very similar to Sergei's rendering.

While everyone passes around the piece of paper, studying the drawing, the oversize plates of food begin to arrive. Then I relay the story that Seth's CI, Wayne, told us about the Roys and the Family. I pick at my bowl of oatmeal, absentmindedly crushing the lumps with my spoon, and listen to the quiet grunts of pleasure coming from my colleagues that only high-cholesterol foods stoked with butter and bacon fat can summon forth. I'm already regretting my renewed promise to Jackie that I would watch what I ate.

Hoskins waves his fork in a circular motion around one temple. "I'll tell you what. This whole thing about 'the Family' sounds like creeper talk to me. A bugaboo to scare the civilians."

Seth wipes at his mouth with a napkin. "Yeah, I gotta agree. I think Wayne's telling the truth about what he's heard. But it does sound like trailer-trash lore. I think the Family is just a catchall term for a loose confederation of meth dealers. They're all family, when they're not trying to slit each other's throats."

Craddock reaches across my arms to grab for the syrup bottle and pours a river of it over his short stack studded with pecans. "'Scuse me," he mumbles, his mouth full of pancakes.

I abandon my spoon in the bowl. "Ryan, anything more on the Roys?"

Ryan has just speared a piece of breakfast sausage and he regards it thoughtfully. "I contacted the Smith County Sheriff's Office in East Texas, and the case is officially closed. The fire that burned down the Roys' house was attributed to arson, but whoever set the fire remains unknown. The three bodies were assumed to be Evangeline Roy and her two sons, but the detective in charge of the case at the time, Jasper Routh, was never completely convinced that it was the Roy family. He's retired now, and the new guard wants it to just lie in a file drawer. I spoke to Detective Routh at his home, though, and he tells a different story about the Family. He believes they're real, growing in number, and have their hands in just about everything, including law enforcement."

I stare at the sign above the order counter, which reads LIFE IS SHORT...START WITH DESSERT. "Anything show up in the criminal records search on the Roys out of state?"

Ryan shakes his head, pushing his plate away. "I checked in all the states you suggested and nothing shows up for anyone matching the age and description of Tommy or Curtis Roy. Military is harder to check, but I've got some lines of inquiry started."

Craddock points with his knife to a leftover sausage link on Ryan's plate and asks, "You gonna finish that?"

Ryan says no, and Craddock crowds me, reaching across once again to stab at the sausage.

"Jesus," I say, giving him a warning look. "You want to change seats, Craddock?"

He grins guiltily at me. "A boy's gotta eat, *Dee*-tective."

Seth points to the drawing, one corner now darkened with someone's dripped coffee. "So have we all agreed that these letters are *A* and *B*? If so, my vote goes to Aryan Brotherhood. That's where we should be looking."

Craddock and Hoskins nod; however, Ryan shrugs and says, "Maybe. Makes sense. But..."

He picks up the drawing and studies it intently.

Tammy Sue appears at the table and asks Seth, "More coffee, hon?" And then she proceeds to pour more coffee into all our cups, whether we want it or not.

"But what, Ryan? Spit it out," Hoskins says, pulling his jacket off the back of his chair. "Look, I hate to break up the huddle, but I've got to get my daughter to volleyball practice."

"You've got a daughter?" I ask, surprised.

"Yeah, I've got a daughter," Hoskins says defensively. He stands, getting ready to leave.

"He talks about her all the time," Craddock adds. "Just not in front of you is all."

Hoskins makes a face. "I hate to leave before the real sharing begins, but I actually have work to do this morning. You got this one, right, Tom?"

Craddock sighs and pulls his wallet out of his pants pocket. "Crap. Guess it's my turn to get the check."

Hoskins waves cheerfully and grabs a toothpick from the counter as he leaves.

"Wow," I say. "Hoskins with a daughter. That almost makes him a person. I don't know whether to be alarmed or encouraged."

Soon both Craddock and Seth say their good-byes, leaving me alone with Ryan, who's still studying the drawing.

"Better get to the station," I say, beginning to stand.

"I don't think this first letter's an *A*," he tells me. "It doesn't actually look like any English letter. More like a symbol."

I sit back down. "A symbol for what?"

"I don't know. Is the kid who drew it literate?"

"He's a Russian immigrant, but if you mean can he read and write English, then, yeah, I think so. In theory he's been going to school. Want to check it out?"

"Sure," he says, using both arms to reach around for his jacket.

I notice for the first time that the shoulder that was wounded is now moving freely. "You're out of the sling," I say, putting the drawing back into my pocket.

He nods but doesn't look cheerful about it. "You feeling okay?" I ask him.

"Yeah," he says unconvincingly. "I'm just not sure I'm cut out for undercover."

"What's going on, Ryan?" I knew he'd been taking a lot of ribbing about the bust and the half-naked high-school girl who was his "date," so I stop myself from following up the question with a provocative comment like *Having those wet dreams again?*

"It's this drug thing," he answers. "There's no end to it. It's just a big hole that gets bigger all the time. The drugs get more addictive, the cost gets cheaper. My fiancée's already talking about having a kid, and all the kids I see, doesn't matter if they're poor, wealthy, white, brown—they're all jumped up on something. Can't get through the day without self-medicating. I mean, did you see those kids at the party? Throwing prescription pills into a bowl like candy for everyone to eat. Xanax, Vicodin, Percocet. They call it skittling. Where do they get their hands on all this stuff? They've got everything going for them. Smart, rich, beautiful, educated, and they're pissing it all away to get high. And not just with pot, but with heroin. Fucking heroin…"

I watch Ryan keying himself up, speaking more and more rapidly with increasing volume until the people sitting at the table closest to us are staring at him. Swearing is something he doesn't usually do.

"Hey, Ryan," I say quietly, tapping him on the leg. "You need some time off?"

"Maybe," he says. "I just don't see me, or any of us, doing any good."

I fold my hands together on the table and lean in closer to Ryan until I'm sure he's looking me in the eyes. "You know what my uncle Benny used to say about facing a pointless task? He'd say, 'All we can do is add our light to the sum of light.'"

Ryan thinks about this for a second. Then he nods and says, "That's actually... pretty wise."

I sit back in my chair and snort. "Nah, Benny would never have said that. What he would have said was 'Get up, go to work, go home, drink some potato vodka, and kiss your fiancée.' Only he wouldn't have said *kiss,* and in your case it would probably be a Miller Lite."

Ryan smiles, ducking his head.

"If you want to stay sane, you can't look at this job as an endgame. Ever. It's a never-ending waterfall for one reason, and one reason only: People want drugs. So we don't really get to change anything," I say. "We just get to move the pieces around the board a little bit. Like a chess game being played by blind people on one side and crazy people on the other."

"So, if I'm getting this analogy," he says, "we do our jobs right and it lets the queen stand and fight a while longer."

I grind a knuckle playfully into his right deltoid. "That's right, smart boy. And every now and then, we knock a piece off the board. You're a good detective, and I want you on the team, but you've got to let me know if you're seriously thinking about leaving Narcotics."

I pull my sunglasses and phone off the table, waiting for him to look at me again.

"Still want to check out the symbol on the drawing?" I prompt.

He nods.

"Good," I say, standing. "Now get the fuck back to the station. You're late."

Tammy Sue waves as we walk out the door, scratching at her scalp with a pencil.

"Y'all go catch us some bad, y'hear?" she calls out from behind the pie counter.

25

When I walk into the station, the whole department seems to be milling around Sergeant Taylor's office. The office door is open and they all turn to look at me at the same time with the same expressions they had when I walked into Bender's house and Lana was lying in a river of her own blood on the kitchen floor: that curious blend of male copitude that exudes disappointment and disapproval and doesn't change whether I rise to emotional detachment or decline into a loss of confidence.

"Fuck me," I mutter, moving toward Taylor's door.

Hoskins and Craddock separate to give me a better view inside the office. Taylor is sitting at his desk squeezing the red tension balls like there's no tomorrow. But his sports deodorant seems to be working, keeping his shirt dry, so the situation can't be irredeemable.

"What's going on?" I ask, looking at Craddock for a clue. But he stares back at me like a morose funeral director.

"I got a call from the Harrison County Sheriff's Office in East Texas this morning," Taylor says.

The instant he starts the conversation with "I got a call from," my muscles begin to tighten as though I'm preparing for a long jump.

He finishes with "A body was found Saturday morning floating in Caddo Lake, next to Uncertain."

"Uncertain what?" I ask.

"Uncertain, Texas," he answers with strained patience. "It's the name of the town."

"You're kidding." I flick my eyes at Hoskins, sure that this is a prank.

"I'm not kidding, Detective," Taylor says. "That's the name of the town. It's right on the lake. You can look it up on a map. And in the lake, right off a camper's fishing pier, they found a body chained to a cypress tree. Want to guess who the corpse once was? Wait, I'll give you a hint: it's headless and has lots of tattoos, including an arm tattoo that reads *Juárez* and another on the back of the left leg that happens to be a jaguar."

I have a clear flash of memory. The dream of El Gitano's head, the decaying remnants of his lips moving soundlessly, trying to tell me something. I exhale slowly before speaking. "Ruiz? But it's been almost three weeks since the head was discovered. What shape's the body in?"

"That's just one of the crazy parts. It looks like someone kept the body frozen until they decided to dump it."

"Frozen?" I want to sit down but I don't want to be on my ass when everyone else in the room except the sergeant is standing.

Taylor gets up, moves to my side of the desk, and, reluctantly, almost apologetically, hands me a dozen crime scene photos. In the first one, taken from the pier, the naked body of a muscular man floats at the surface of the lake, the surrounding water so dense that the body looks horizontally transected by a pane of indigo glass. The background is thick with primal-looking cypress trees cloaked with Spanish moss, reflecting perfectly in the motionless water. Above the trees, the sky is a rich, untroubled autumnal blue.

In a closer shot, the figure looms larger and I can see that the body does not have a head. Several more photos follow, probably taken from a small boat at different angles. One end of a heavy chain encircles the torso and the other end has been wrapped once around the tree and padlocked.

The last few photos are of the body on a morgue table, prone, the neck wound puckered grotesquely around a portion of protruding spine, the jaguar tattoo showing clearly on the left calf. The right foot below the ankle is badly mangled, either through an accident or, more likely, from something nibbling at a lakeside version of a frozen dinner.

"Where's the body now?" I ask. The oatmeal I had at Norma's is reconstituting itself as mortar in my gut.

"In the ME's office in Tyler. It was Saturday when the body was found, so it took a while to process the positive ID."

Saturday. The day the DPD Narcotics squad beat the bejesus out of a ragtag, jersey-less Homicide team. Seth, Jackie, and I sat on the bleachers during the football match, enjoying the buttery light, screaming ourselves hoarse in a victorious frenzy.

"What's the other crazy part?" I ask, and in that moment of silence between my question and Sergeant Taylor's answer, I distinctly hear Benny's voice whisper in my ear, *Here comes the Cosmic Screw.*

"The sign nailed to this tree," Taylor tells me.

He hands me one last photo, a close-up of the cypress, onto which a plank has been nailed. There are two words carved into the plank: WELCOME HOME. Below the message is a simplistic line carving of curved, upswept wings and a sword with the letter *L* on one side and *V* on the other.

Hoskins is looking over my shoulder. "It's definitely a message to someone, but what in the hairy fuck does it mean?"

I can feel both Hoskins's and Taylor's eyes on me, and I know they're thinking about the message that Tony Ha imparted to me from the killer, that I could come home now.

On the plank is the familiar image of uplifted wings and the sword, but the letters are not the same as in Sergei's drawing. I turn and look for Ryan, find him standing just outside the sergeant's door. I hand him the photo, along with Sergei's drawing.

"What do you make of this?" I ask him.

Ryan looks at each image and then, taking the two pieces of paper with him, hurries to his desk. "Give me a minute to check something out."

"And look into the Deuteronomy Bible verse as well," I call after him. "See if there's a connection."

Craddock says, "The plank was nailed to the tree, which would have made some noise—"

"So would the rattling of the goddamned chains," Hoskins adds.

Craddock makes an impatient gesture for Hoskins to shut it. "Did local law enforcement question the campers at the park?"

Taylor shakes his head. "The camping area is some distance from the pier, and there were only a few campers that Friday night. They're still trying to locate those who left Saturday morning before the body was discovered. So far, no one heard anything other than swamp noises that night."

The initial queasiness has worn off, and I'm beginning to feel a surge of relief. Ruiz has been found, and in a county that does not hold Dallas. Whatever battle brought him to Uncertain, Texas, was most certainly not ours anymore. Lana's killer has not yet been found, but it's a Homicide problem now.

"This is still a Narcotics problem," Taylor says, disabusing me of that misconception. Then he directs everyone except me to clear the room and he closes the door.

"Carter Hayes and the FBI are now back in the picture," he tells me, motioning for me to sit down. He rests one meaty haunch on a corner of the desk. "You have no idea how badly I want this Ruiz case to go away. But for the past year, the Mexicans have been moving into East Texas big-time. Local law enforcement is overwhelmed with the proliferation of high-grade Mexican crystal, and by *high-grade,* I mean ninety percent pure, and the body count is growing, not only in Texas but in Louisiana and Arkansas as well.

"We're not looking at just a few pitiful trailer-trash run-ins, we're looking at five people murdered, execution-style, four of them Mexican nationals, over the past few months within fifty miles of Tyler. One of those killed was a four-year-old girl. A bullet passed through her father's torso and into her skull. Some people behind the Pine Curtain are making it their business to clarify their territory."

He rubs his eye with the knuckles of one hand, the buttons on his short-sleeved dress shirt straining, pulled taut across his expanding waist. For the first time, I notice how much gray is hiding within the black wiry brush of his hair.

Behind him, on the wall, is a dusty championship plaque from the Bill Pickett Rodeo and a decades-old photograph of a much younger and leaner Taylor riding a bronc, his hat firmly in place, his dark face set to a determined dominance of the wild animal beneath him.

Taylor follows my gaze to the photo. "You know," he tells me, "I've seen that look on your face before."

He stretches a hand across his left pectoral muscle, massaging the flesh. "There aren't many black men riding rodeo. That knowledge encouraged me not to fall on my face."

"Yeah," I say, "I experience something similar every day when I walk to my desk."

"I hit thirty years' service next spring. And then I'm off to Louisiana with the wife. Do a little riding, a little fishing, play with my grandkids. It's going to leave a hole in this department." He watches me closely and grins, wagging a finger. "Ah, see, there's that look again."

"What look?" I ask, knowing full well that, for the briefest, untempered moment, my competitive self has broken through the visage of neutrality like an orca through thin ice.

"Red, I understand you better than you think I do. But you know that old saying, 'Be careful what you wish for'?"

"Careful?" I say. "Where's the fun in that?"

He smiles briefly at me, but then stands up from the desk and moves back to sit in his chair, the relaxed camaraderie gone. "You've been requested by Hayes and the Harrison County Sheriff's Office to make a run out to Caddo Lake to see if there's anything of significance they might have missed, either with the body at the morgue or at the discovery site. It would be a favor to Hayes for you to talk to the drug task force out there as well. Share with them our knowledge of Ruiz's contacts. But, of course, you can say no."

"What would you like me to do?" I ask.

He palms one of the red tension balls. "Make my life easier," he says.

His complexion has an ashen cast to it, and he's rubbing the left side of his chest. He sees me watching him and stops.

"You need anything else from me before I venture into Uncertain?" I ask, standing to go. *A call to the paramedics, perhaps?*

"Yeah. Some of your vitality." He gives me the get-lost wave. "You're taking Hoskins, by the way. Call me when you get there."

When I leave Taylor's office, Ryan is waiting for me. He tells me excitedly, "I don't think those letters that Sergei printed were English letters at all. I think they were Russian Cyrillic."

I follow him back to his desk and he shows me a printout of the Russian alphabet, pointing to the letter we had thought was an unfinished *A*. "It's the letter *L* in English." He points to another Russian letter, the one that looks like a *B*. "This letter is *V* in English. I think the kid got rattled and wrote in Cyrillic what were actually the letters carved into our cypress plank, *L* and *V*."

Sergei had been anxious, nervous with the knowledge that the smiling deliveryman had been leaving a severed head in a box a few feet from his family's apartment. "Makes sense," I say.

"Something else," he says. "I did a general search for

the letters *L* and *V* and got several hits for the Latin saying *Lux et veritas.* 'Light and truth.' Quite a few organizations use *veritas* in their mottoes—Harvard, Drake, the Dominican Order of the Catholic Church. But two use the exact slogan: Yale University and a small North Carolina college, Chowan, in Murfreesboro."

"I don't see our delivery guy going to Yale, do you?"

"No, but look at the insignia for the other college." I position a chair close to the computer screen, and Ryan pulls up the Chowan website, points to an enlarged image of a book nestled inside an open laurel wreath that, in a certain light, could be viewed as upswept wings. "No sword in this image," I say.

"No," he agrees. "But the slogan fits, so maybe North Carolina's a good place to start looking for one of the Roys."

I shrug. "Possibly. What about the Bible verse?"

"Here's the creepy part. The verse is commonly used to justify vengeance against one's enemies. I found a lot of evangelical-church websites quoting this verse—"

"Nice to know us Catholics don't have the monopoly on sanctified revenge."

"Then," he says, pulling up another screen, "I found this."

He clicks on a website link for OneNationOneTruth-OneRace. The darkened screen slowly brightens to reveal animated flames flickering through a backdrop of scorched buildings. Out of the flames the Deuteronomy verse appears: *When I sharpen my flashing sword and my hand grasps it in judgment, I will take vengeance on my adversaries and repay those who hate me.*

Then the message fades and is followed by several paragraphs of the usual Aryan hate rhetoric: the white man is being mongrelized by dark-skinned people, the government is coming to take away the white man's guns, Western civilization is threatened by godless academics.

Ryan scrolls through the text and at the end of the rant are two raised blue wings pierced with a red sword. The last sentence on the page: *Lux et veritas.*

The skin on my arms turns to gooseflesh. "Can you track down where this originated?"

"I'm on it," he says.

"Nice work, Ryan."

I see Hoskins walking toward the desk, coat on. It's over one hundred and eighty miles to Uncertain. Almost three hours in the car alone with Hoskins. He waves that he's ready to go whenever I am.

"I'll be out of the office the rest of the day," I tell Ryan. I point to Sergei's cell number scribbled across the bottom of his drawing. "Do me a favor and call the kid, just to be certain you're on the right track about the Russian letters. Also, check into Chowan's student records for any of the Roy family. Who knows, maybe something will show up. And one more thing," I say quietly. "Keep a close eye on the sergeant today. He's not feeling well."

I walk with Hoskins toward the garage and we pass by Booking just as two large patrolmen are bringing in a wildly agitated man wearing hunter's camouflage, a studded leather vest dangling off his shoulders. The cuffed man begins to panic, dragging his feet and skittering his legs around a row of chairs like a rhesus monkey. The chairs skate crazily across the floor and clatter together with a deafening crash, and we step out of the way as two more officers rush to help subdue the man.

He's raging and spitting, but still he manages to catch my eye. "The fuckin' Mexicans are takin' over the country!" he screams. "Can't you see that? They're gonna kill us all—"

The four officers manage to wrestle the man to the ground, securing him with zip ties around his ankles. They upend him and carry him like a sack of menacing cats feet-first through the hallway, his Old Testament beard trailing the floor.

26

Indicating how much progress we've made as colleagues, Hoskins puts up only a minor fight when I get into the driver's side of the car that we took from the department motor pool.

He glares at me at first, and then motions for me to hurry up, saying, "I'll never hear the end of it if Craddock sees I've let you behind the wheel."

I call the sheriff's office in Tyler to let them know we're driving directly to Caddo Lake and giving them an ETA. It's after ten o'clock when we merge onto I-20 headed east toward Uncertain, and within thirty minutes, we're away from suburban strip malls and the Walmarts that have parking lots with their own zip codes. The quality of light has softened further over the past week, no remnants of summer haze, and the sun casts a yellowish tinge on even the homeliest of country storefronts and grime-covered pickups. A brief rain shower has created patches of purplish clover throughout the scrubby remains of livestock hay in the surrounding fields.

We pass a faded, hand-painted sign that reads WILEY'S GUNS, FOR ALL YOUR GUN NEEDS, and Hoskins breaks away from studying the Caddo Lake crime scene photos to point out what I've already seen, which is the convenience store next to the sign, Wiley's Last Stand, the front door riddled with bullet holes. I don't bother responding when he asks if I want to turn back so he can take a picture of it for a cop-humor website.

Seeing my dismissive expression, he asks, "Is there anything about Texas you actually like?"

"I'm swimming against childhood prejudices," I say. "My uncle Benny once told me a joke that went like this: 'What's the difference between yogurt and Texas?' The answer is 'Yogurt's the one with the live culture.'"

Hoskins crosses his arms, trying not to smile. He leans back against the car door to face me. "So there's nothing you like about Texas?"

I shrug noncommittally.

"Come on," he prompts.

"Okay, the food trucks in Klyde Warren Park downtown and the margaritas at Gloria's."

"What?" Hoskins says, mock offended. "No sweet tea, no Tex-Mex, no barbecue? What about *kolaches*?"

I turn and look at him incredulously. "You're fucking kidding me, right? You're seriously going to ask a Polish girl from Brooklyn about *kolaches*?"

"Well," he says, conceding my point by nodding. "You gotta love the state fair, though."

"I'd rather swallow razor blades than eat their fried anything one more time."

Now he's really offended. "So that's it? Food trucks and sugared tequila?"

I consider his question and say, "There are some good-looking cowgirls at the Fort Worth rodeo."

Hoskins laughs out loud. "That's for damn sure." After a pause, he offers, "Bluebonnets."

"Bluebonnets what?" But his agreeing with me about the *kolaches* has moved me to cooperation. "Okay, the bluebonnets are spectacular," I say. "Now can you shut the fuck up about All Things Great in Texas and just let me drive in peace for a while?"

He smirks but goes back to studying the photo of Ruiz's body floating in the lake, frowning with concentration. I catch a glimpse of his left hand and realize he's still wearing his wedding ring. The shirt with the too-large collar is spotted on the front with some grease stains, and his pants probably haven't been dry-cleaned in a while. If I were to look closer, I'd probably find that his socks are mismatched too.

"Actually," I say, disturbing him from his reverie, "Dallas is growing on me. I even went to a play with Jackie a few weeks ago."

He takes on a pained look. "A play? Man, you are pussy-whipped."

Now it's my turn to laugh. "No, it was good. I enjoyed it."

"Yeah? My wife tried to make me go to the theater a couple of times."

"And?" I ask, for some inexplicable reason wanting to keep the conversation going.

"It was *The Lion King* or some such shit like that. Jeez, talk about swallowing razor blades."

He stares sadly out the window, and I decide to leave him alone for a while.

On the far side of Forney, though, he starts to tell me

about a girl he once dated named Forney Kate. Thankfully, before I have to listen to the story I get a call from Jackie telling me to be careful, advising me on what I should avoid eating for lunch — she reminds me how bacteria-ridden diner food is — and finally whispering that she loves me. I give an "Uh-huh, me too" response, to which Hoskins says, "Oh, for crying out loud, Detective, just tell the girl you love her."

A few hours later we drive into Marshall and at the first traffic light I check the messages on my work phone. I've gotten texts from Seth and Ryan, both telling me to be vigilant out in the hinterlands.

Hoskins reaches over and pokes me, pointing to a large billboard that reads LET US HELP YOU IN YOUR STRUGGLES. LET US PRAY AWAY THE GAY.

He watches me for a reaction and then asks, "You know about my wife, right? Twelve years of marriage and she leaves me for another woman."

"You mean *a* woman," I say. "Not *another* woman."

"Yeah, well, whatever," he says. "It could have been a dozen women, for all I know. I had her computer checked out after she left. She'd been communicating with all kinds of lesbos on Facebook." He looks at me quickly. "No offense."

The light turns green and a nanosecond later the car behind me blares its horn.

"None taken," I say, driving through the intersection, leaving the billboard behind to reflect in my rearview mirror. "I'm a proud card-carrying member."

What's bothering me is not so much that he's torn up by his wife turning out to be a lesbian but that he'd spied on her.

"You think you know somebody," he murmurs. "Twelve years and they pull a one-eighty."

He shakes his head, his lips downturned tragically, sighing the way people do when they're mystified by their own expectations.

But what I want to tell Hoskins is this: People don't just do a one-eighty. Not like that. I long to take his face gently in both my hands and then give him a vicious head butt and scream at him three decibels above ear-tolerance level that his wife didn't have a change of sexual orientation overnight. He'd spent twelve years in complete and utter denial of who she was and what she wanted.

I'm surprised he hasn't already asked me the Question: *Did you always know you were a, you know, a... lesbian?,* the word *lesbian* spoken in a hushed whisper. Or the three syllables accented carefully, as though the speaker were sitting for his or her medical boards and enunciating the word *vagina* with pained, professional detachment.

From time to time, I've been curious about having sex with men, in a squeamish, lab-experiment sort of way. But at the age of five, watching *Snow White* on television, I discovered that I didn't identify with the pale and cursed Ms. Helpless so much as with the Wicked Queen and her force-of-nature personality. And when the prince bent down to kiss Snow White, my imagination embodied me squarely as the one in the cape, the woman in my arms.

Benny was the first person I ever talked to about who I was, and that was after I'd already joined the academy. My mother suspected, sensing it through my reticence in welcoming the advances of the red-faced, overly eager boys my age. She'd never once come home to an interrupted wrestling match on the couch, the boy covering his crotch with a pillow, her daughter desperately tugging on her shirt to cover an exposed bra. And I never brought home a girl whom I was interested in, preferring covert kisses in some alleyway or deserted lot. It's not that my mother was scandalized by what she suspected; it was more that she was disappointed that her daughter would never have a family wedding or give her a grandchild.

If my father knew, he never talked about it. I was a disappointment to him too, not because I was a lesbian but because I took the place on the force that my brother had filled. After my brother killed himself, my father couldn't pretend anymore that all of the things he had done in the shadows—all the corners he had cut, all the money he had taken to look the other way, the dozens of "accidental" deaths that eradicated the street denizens in his precinct— hadn't left its crippling mark on his son. My brother died at twenty-five, the year I started the academy. And forever after, every time Phillip Andrew Rhyzyk looked into my face, he saw the fervor of a true believer, someone with the will to first do no harm and the zealotry to turn a dirty cop out of the ranks. But most of all, what he saw in my ramrod posture and challenging gaze was condemnation. Every day of his life, until the moment he shriveled up and died.

Something large and lumbering at the next light makes me slam on the brakes, and I come to a screeching halt in front of a man on horseback riding calmly across the intersection pulling, by a length of rope, an old man in a wheelchair, both legs amputated at the knees. The old man is wearing a jacket with dozens of Veterans of Foreign Wars patches. All three, the legless veteran, the young cowboy, and his horse, are blithely untroubled by the traffic around them.

"Now, see," Hoskins tells me, "you'd never get that in Brooklyn."

As the young rider clops past the front bumper of my car, he dips his chin, the brim of his hat shadowing his face more. But I can tell by the turn of his head that he's peering through the windshield, unsmiling, and the skin at my sternum where the Saint Michael's medal rests seems to warm, setting the underlying muscles to nervous quivering. The wheelchair is safely delivered to the far side of the street, and they continue on their way without a backward glance.

"Uh-oh, Detective," Hoskins laughingly warns. "Cowboy doesn't like the looks of you. Maybe you should let me do the driving now that we're in Marlboro Country."

On the far side of Marshall we take 43 North for close to a dozen miles, driving along sandy-soiled lots with small brick homes and trailer parks with junked cars abandoned out front. Near-feral dogs emerge explosively from porch overhangs or brushy cover like bottle rockets, racing out to bark savagely at our car, then wheeling about and retreating again.

Hoskins informs me that, in a few miles, we'll be turning onto County Road 2198 and into the entrance to Caddo Lake State Park, where we'll be meeting members of the Harrison County Sheriff's Office. He texts one of our contacts that we'll be there within twenty minutes.

It's midday, and only two vehicles have passed us, both pickup trucks, going in the opposite direction. The air in the car has warmed and I lift the heavy hair off my neck, cupping its mass against the back of my head. I catch Hoskins staring at me.

"What?" I ask.

"Nothing," he says immediately. "No, it's just that, your hair..." He makes a vague wagging motion toward his own head after I give him a warning look. "It's just really nice. Pretty. Oh, fuck, I don't know..." His voice trails off and he's beet-faced and squirmy.

"Pretty?" I ask, grinning with delight at his discomfort. I reach over and slap him briskly across the shoulder. "Bob, are you . . . you're not flirting with me, are you?"

"No. Fuck no," he says with a little too much emphasis, and then we're both laughing.

He catches his breath and says, "You tell anyone about this and I'll call sexual harassment on you."

"Ooh, that'd be fun," I say, wiping at my streaming eyes. "It's been a while since I was on that side of the fence."

We hit a few potholes and patches of broken asphalt, and where the road comes to a fork, a road-repair sign detours us farther east. We're closer to the state park now and the trees are denser, with fewer houses set back on dirt paths. We pass a sign for the town of Karnack.

"Home of Lady Bird Johnson," Hoskins muses. "Hell, there's another detour sign."

My personal phone rings and I dig it out of my pocket to answer. It's James Earle, but the reception is spotty, the bass tone of his voice wavering in my ear.

"Hey," he says. "Jackie just told me you're going out to Caddo Lake. What's shakin'?"

"Yeah, we're close, headed toward Karnack. Just a few more miles," I tell him. I want to fill him in on the discovery of El Gitano's body and the plank with its message nailed to the cypress tree, but I'm not sure Hoskins would appreciate my talking about the case with a civilian, even though the civilian had been an MP.

"Things are finally coming to a head, James. We're close to the belly of the beast."

In the road ahead is another sign, directing us onto an even narrower road. Hoskins studies the GPS on his phone and motions to me with hand signals which way to turn.

"Shit, more detours," I say into the phone. "Typical hick roads, right? Got to take four rights to make one left turn. Listen, James, I got to go—"

"Betty," he says, interrupting me. "You keepin' sharp, right?"

"Absolutely," I answer.

"'Cause you're in their jungle now."

"Not to worry. We should be to the lake soon. Texas DPS is just forcing us to take the scenic route."

I make a wrong turn and Hoskins looks at me, exasperated.

"James, I got to go. We're bum-fuck lost. Call you later."

I put the phone back in my pocket, turn the car around, follow the detour signs.

"Sorry," I say to Hoskins.

"That's okay," he says. "We can get to the lake once we've passed Karnack. Stay to the right here," he directs.

Soon there are a few houses and near-empty fields studded with tall longleaf pines and brushy trash trees.

At a T-crossing Hoskins says, "Here you're going to make a left."

Immediately, I see a large commercial truck parked on the gravel shoulder, shaded under a canopy of elm trees. Parked on the opposite side is a white patrol car with a Jefferson Police logo. An officer with his hand over his service revolver is standing toe-to-toe with a larger man who is wearing work overalls, perhaps the driver of the truck. They are not having a polite conversation.

A second officer, young, tall, and densely angular, steps away from his position by the squad car and into the middle of the road holding both hands up, barring us from passing the truck.

"Oops-a-daisy," Hoskins says. "Morning meth run?

Looks like we're going to see how it's done by Jefferson's Finest."

Hoskins pulls out his badge and rolls down the passenger-side window as the second officer begins walking toward us.

Hoskins makes a curt acknowledgment to the approaching officer. "Dallas Police. Need any help?"

My attention is pulled back to the truck when the truck driver gives the confronting officer a shove, and they grapple, the driver looking to put the officer on the ground.

Alarmed, I turn to yell to Hoskins for an assist. The tall officer has reached the passenger side, his own weapon drawn. It's a Smith and Wesson pistol and I think, absurdly, that it's too small a weapon for the size of his hand. The hand comes through the open window, the barrel of the gun moving with too much deliberation and speed toward Hoskins's head. The officer fires.

27

The force of the bullet slams Hoskins sideways and into my right shoulder, slinging blood across the dashboard and onto me before he slumps forward against his seat belt. The gun is now pointed at my head; my hands reflexively come off the steering wheel, my lips ejecting a wet, gasping sound. I'm mindlessly croaking, "Police...police...I'm police..." I can't bring myself to look at Hoskins's face. I know instantly that he's already dead.

Both my hands are up in the air and I don't want to take my attention away from the shooter, but my eyes involuntarily jerk to the left, toward the truck. I'm thinking this is a nightmarish mistake, and the other officer has to come running now, his own hands up to signal horrified intervention. But the cop that was standing by the truck, shorter and thicker across the chest than Hoskins's killer, is now jogging toward my car with his own weapon in hand and pointed in my direction. The driver in overalls slams open the back of his truck, revealing a large, cavernous space within, extracts a wide entry ramp, and angles it to the ground.

The short cop tries to open my door, but it's locked. He raps loudly on the window and says, "Get out." The gun comes up to the level of my forehead and, mindful of the gun from the passenger side, I carefully unlock the door and open it. The short cop immediately grabs me by my jacket and jerks me from the driver's seat.

He disarms me, pulling my gun from its holster and handing it to his partner. All the while I'm reciting, "Wait, wait, I'm Dallas Police...you can't be doing this..."

He yells at me to shut up and then pushes me, facedown, onto the road. He stands over me, one foot on the back of my neck, and orders, "Put your hands behind you."

The fucker is short but really strong.

For an instant I freeze. They are not cops, but they know that I am. This has got to be a drug operation, and my only chance for escape from these guys may come in the first few moments of my seeming to be compliant. I'm not certain they're not going to shoot me in the back of the head anyway.

I slowly begin to put my left hand at the small of my back, leaving my right hand braced against the ground. I turn my head to the side to see that the guy over me has holstered his gun and is reaching for his handcuffs.

They want to take me alive.

The tall cop has quickly gotten into my car and is driving it toward the truck, Hoskins's body still in the passenger seat. He drives it up the ramp, into the containment area. The truck driver is back behind the steering wheel and starts the engine.

The short cop straddles me, then squats down with his

knees on my ass and searches my right pocket. He takes out my work cell and puts it in his jacket. He grabs for my left hand without searching the other pocket, and I realize he doesn't know I have more than one phone. But as soon as my hands are cuffed, he'll continue searching my clothes. I make a whimpering sound to distract him, giving him the cue that I'm afraid and cowed, still in shock.

Now.

I roll explosively to my left, using my bracing right hand for extra thrust, throwing him off balance. I roll with his momentum and then strike up and back sharply with my head, butting his nose and forehead. I feel soft cartilage giving under the impact of my skull, and he screams in pain, but the engine of the truck covers the sound.

He's on his back and I need to get to his gun, but I have to work from a position of strength. I roll away onto my hands and knees, reaching for the weapon the whole while, but his reflexes are too conditioned, and he grabs my wrist and twists. He's mad and in pain, and if he gets the upper hand again, he may kill me after all.

I manage to grind my left elbow into his neck. Still the bastard hangs on to the gun and he fires off a wild shot. I give him hard, successive elbow strikes, but he jabs out with a fist that glances off my cheekbone. Scrabbling away, I kick out as hard as I can, and my boot connects with his jaw like a hammer. He gives a groan but manages to hold on to the gun, even when he rolls onto his side, momentarily stunned, gasping for breath.

The shot had to have been heard above the engine noise. Starting from a crouching position, I sprint away, adrenaline flooding every cell, toward the fields behind the stand of elm trees. The grass is tall, and there are bushes and pine trees clumped together for cover.

The last house I remember seeing was a quarter of a mile from the T-crossing. My left hand reaches into my pocket to grab at my phone. Glancing back, I see the tall cop has jumped from the truck and is running after me.

The loss of attention causes me to stumble and almost fall. I can't run and grapple with a phone. I release the phone back into my pocket and bring up both arms, swing them hard, giving momentum to my legs.

Fifty yards and I look back. The tall cop is closing the distance. The bastard is fast. He's not shooting at me, though, and there's no weapon drawn. They need me alive.

The ground is uneven, and my boots are not made for sustained running, but I will myself to watch the terrain beneath my pounding feet, avoiding holes or rocks or roots that will bring me down. If I can gain enough ground, I can throw myself into some green cover or even climb a damn tree, anything that will give me thirty seconds' grace to put in a call to someone, anyone, before the phone's taken from me.

My breathing is too shallow from fear, my face slick with sweat that streams into my eyes. I focus on a stand of pine trees with low branches another fifty or so yards away. I know he is coming, but I don't look back for ten, twenty, thirty yards. I sense the rushing dense heat of him, the exhalation of spent air pressed through pumping, animal flesh.

Then I do hear him, the crunching sound of dry grass behind me being trampled under a relentless piston. I fire off one last obscenity-laden directive to myself to run faster. And I do for another ten yards before he overtakes me, grabs at my hair, and yanks me backward. My neck pops painfully, a flaring spasm in both shoulders, and I'm flung onto my back. I lie stunned, immobilized, the little air I had remaining knocked from my lungs.

He's on me and I fight, blindly striking out, kicking, gouging, trying to suck in more oxygen, until he punches me once, hard, in the solar plexus. Then he's behind me, one arm around my throat, squeezing, blocking the air from entering my body. A feeling of slow drowning, a last vengeful thought preceding the dark.

28

The training gym is close and hot, rankly smelly from thousands of hours of cadets learning how to stay alive on the streets, the academy instructors trying to compress and intensify decades of real-life scenarios into a few short weeks of police training.

There are more than a dozen of us in loose sweatpants and T-shirts, twelve males and two females, gathering around the blue mats to begin the morning's defensive instruction. The instructor, in his dark, formfitting sweats, NYPD insignia prominent on his chest, stands in the center of the mat, arms crossed, waiting for the talking to cease.

Frank Costello is not overly tall, less than six feet, but with biceps the size of most men's legs and eyes that seem to be everywhere at all times. From Rhode Island, Costello compresses words as though processing them through a wood chipper. *Arm* becomes "ahm." *Hard* becomes "hahd."

He's a sexual predator who relentlessly hits on anything female and who never forgets, or forgives, a rejection.

Especially if that turndown happens to come from an overly confident redheaded cadet.

He tells us that the day's class will be on controlling and subduing an unruly subject. "Many times in your career," he tells us, "you're going to come across some hardheaded hooligan who...will...not...comply."

He motions to one of the cadets, Ed Regan, a guy who flunked out of Marine boot camp within the first few days, to step onto the mat and stand facing him. He's a nice kid but has *stomp on me* written all over him.

Costello says, "In this scenario, the subject is facing you, but he won't let you take his arm or wrist to cuff him. He's not overly belligerent, but he's not eager or willing either." He tells Regan to hold his hands up in a defensive posture.

Costello takes a few steps toward Regan and says to the watching group, "As soon as you're within range, you need to attack the stronger arm first, which is usually the right arm. You step to the subject's right side, taking hold of the arm and pulling downward with your left hand to move him off balance. And watch..."

With a series of smooth, spiral motions Costello secures Regan with a combination monkey grip ending in an effective front wristlock. The motions were practiced, effortless, a thing of beauty to watch. He holds Regan in the wristlock while he tells us, "Now you can cuff the subject or lead him around like a little schoolgirl."

Regan is grimacing with pain, and it's obvious that Costello has been slowly increasing the torque on the cadet's wrist. He then parades Regan around the perimeter of the mat, making sure that everyone can see that he has total control of his subject. There is derisive laughter from the other cadets, but I don't think it's funny, having seen the flash of embarrassment on Regan's face when Costello called him a little schoolgirl.

Costello has noticed my look of disapproval and he releases Regan and points him back off the mat. Regan melds into the group, trying not to shake out his stinging wrist.

"We'll break into pairs and practice this technique, but first," he says, "we'll address a subject who's more combative."

Costello points to me. "Rhyzyk, you're up."

He motions me onto the mat and tells me to turn and face the rear wall, my hands in the Weaver position, knees slightly bent, as though I'm getting ready to fire a gun.

"You will also," he continues, "one day walk in on a subject who is armed and fully prepared to use his weapon. Let's just hope it's not when you're coming out of the john, still pulling up your trousers."

There is more laughter. My back is turned to the group, but I laugh along with them.

"We come upon our subject in the midst of robbing a convenience store or mugging some poor bastard. Our subject in this case is Cadet Rhyzyk." He kicks hard at my right instep, startling me. "Spread your legs wider," he orders.

He's close to my left shoulder and he whispers loudly into my ear, "Only to keep your stance more stable."

He turns and winks to the group and there are a few uncomfortable snickers.

"Cadet Rhyzyk, as we all know, had the best overall PAT scores of any female we've ever had entering this academy. Outstanding aerobic and anaerobic capacity, she ran the mile and a half in less than nine minutes, did fifty sit-ups in sixty seconds, the three-hundred-meter dash in forty-eight seconds. No discernible difference right versus left during the handgun-simulation test. She left a lot of the men in the dust. It was as though she'd been training her whole life for that one day just to teach every last one of us cock-jocks a lesson. Right, Rhyzyk?"

I hadn't joined the academy to make new friends, and I knew full well that being a woman, and a lesbian, would not endear me to my fellow, mostly male cadets. But being a cop was what I wanted, had always wanted, and Costello was damn right about my being prepared. Every workout session, every encounter on a sports field prior to joining the academy was tackled as a way to ensure success through the training period.

"Yes, sir," I say loudly. I'm grinning tightly, saying to myself, *Yeah, that's right, you puffed-up, testosterone-driven meat wagon.*

"The only problem is," he continues, "blazing your way through a physical ability test is not going to do you any good when you're dealing with some guy who's bugged on PCP and who outweighs you by a hundred pounds."

As he's talking, I can feel him moving up behind me, and automatically, I tense, readying my muscles for contact.

"Now," he tells the cadets, "you don't want the subject to know that you're approaching him. So you walk directly up behind him, making sure that he can't see you. Then you step deep under his hips and at the same time drive your right hand under his armpit, achieving a half nelson."

His tree trunk of an arm pins me in the wrestling hold, but his fingers are digging into my neck hard enough to cramp the muscles. My hair is wound into a tight bun, but the short hairs are being ripped out by their follicles.

"At the same time, you want your left hand over the subject's left arm, sliding through at a forty-five-degree angle, achieving a bar arm. Then," he says, forcefully arching my back and spinning me around to face the class, "tightly wedge his back. As fast as possible, bring his left arm behind him. Bend the wrist, turning it into a rear wristlock."

The twist on my hand is excruciating. I can feel the tendons in the wrist straining, the tiny bones threatening to fracture.

"Now's when you cuff your subjcct," Costello finishes. "That hurt much, Rhyzyk?" he asks, smiling to the group, increasing the pressure to where I think the bones in my wrist will just shatter, erupting through the skin like popcorn.

My eyes are streaming, and the blood has drained to my lower extremities, but I manage to keep my face deadpan.

"No," I say.

"And sometimes," he mutters, swiftly bringing his right arm over my head to the front of my neck and squeezing, "you get that asshole who will just...not...comply."

The murmuring, ambient noise of the gym begins to build, from a gentle shoreline rush to a roaring wave, and the swirl of fireflies in front of my eyes spark and then fade to a wash of dark, and I hear Benny's voice inside the roar saying, *If you go down, you'll never want to get back up again.*

My feet begin a desperate jig and then the fluid in my legs catches fire, but I let my knees buckle. Somewhere in my barely conscious brain I register that Costello's grip has relaxed, his head following through with my sagging body. Reversing the momentum, I throw back my head and shoulders and push off the floor hard, catching him off guard, propelling him toward the rear wall. His feet have to shuffle back as well or I will topple him over onto his ass. The quads that I have worked on so torturously at the gym, doing squats by the hundreds, drive us, and he smashes into the wall with such force, the urinal in the bathroom on the other side is knocked down and he fractures his skull.

When I come to, Regan is pulling me up off of an unconscious Costello, and somebody is calling the paramedics.

I feel a tight clamping sensation around my wrists and imagine that it's Regan, still pulling at me to get me off the floor and away from Costello, who is lying motionless beneath me. But then I hear the unmistakable metallic snicking sounds of handcuffs being fastened, and I open my eyes, my lids fluttering against the light.

My boots seem to have become glued to each other, because I can't move my legs apart to stand, and I realize that my ankles have been bound together.

A ripping noise, and something sticky is being pressed with no small amount of pressure over my mouth. I waken fully, panicked and thrashing, as I'm lifted roughly off the ground by two pairs of hands, at my feet and shoulders. My wrists are cuffed in front, and I reach over my head, trying to grab something, a shirt, a handful of hair from my attacker. But before I can connect with anything, I'm thrown roughly into a hard, contained space, the trunk of a car.

I catch a flash of the vehicle—it's the white Jefferson patrol car that must have been driven across the field in pursuit of us—and two male, sweat-stained faces standing over me, the tall cop and the shorter one, still in their patrol uniforms. The trunk door is slammed shut. The darkness is complete, but I can hear the muffled sounds of the two of them talking together.

I begin at once to work at snapping the chain between the cuffs. Depending on the make, restraints can be broken either at the links or at the weld point on the cuffs with enough twisting action, time, and torque applied to them. There is the clacking noise of the moving chain, but I'm hoping the insulation in the trunk will dampen the sound.

A door in the car is opened briefly and shut again. And then the trunk is raised, flooding the space with blinding light. The taller cop is holding a wand with two extended wires at its far end. He jabs me on the thigh, and the volts through my body are like a snake of rotating teeth, liquefying my organs. He jabs me again, and I scream involuntarily through gritted teeth, my feet kicking out at the frame in spasmodic thrusts.

When I've stopped convulsing, he stands with his shoulders hunched over the trunk, bringing the wand within a few inches of my face. The hand holding it is tattooed with bright blue wings and a scarlet sword. My eyes have adjusted to the light and I look up into his face, memorizing the features, the fullness of the mouth, the set of the eyes, the height of the forehead, and the crew-cut hair, a sandy but unmistakable red. He smiles and jabs the electric cattle prod once more into my shoulder.

Afterward, I sense the restraints being released and my arms pulled behind my back. I'm cuffed again, palms facing outward, the metal biting painfully into my wrists, and the trunk is once more slammed shut.

I hear doors opening and closing, and then the patrol car is driven at high speed, bumping hard across the field, knocking my head and knees against metal. The car slows, then angles sharply up an incline—it has to be the ramp to the big truck—and the engine is cut. I can hear the echoing footsteps through the truck cargo area, and the loud banging of the outer truck doors being secured.

There is the deep vibration of the truck's gears being engaged and then forward, tilting movement onto the road.

I'm lying on my left side, my shoulder cramping painfully beneath me, my legs drawn to my chest. I will myself to slow my breathing and start deep inhalations and exhalations through my nose, reassuring my oxygen-starved body that I can, within a few minutes, get enough air through my nostrils alone. I close my eyes, taking stock of what's injured. My cheek where I was hit stings, but, hopefully, no bones are fractured. Neck, back, and thighs all feel strained, but there are no muscles seriously pulled. My biggest discomfort comes from the right deltoid where Hoskins's head struck me after he was shot. Both my car and the patrol car must be in the cargo area of the truck, Hoskins still sitting in the passenger seat, the seat belt holding his stiffening body.

The few moments before his death he was completely relaxed, joking about a possible hillbilly meth run, helpfully pulling out his badge for a fellow police officer. He didn't even have time to register that he was about to be murdered by a man in uniform.

My throat closes; my eyes are filling with tears, and, worse, my nose is filling with snot. *Stop it, just fucking stop it,* I rage to myself. *You'll smother yourself, you stupid bitch.*

I stay focused on how the truck is oriented, trying to gauge distance and turns, but it's hopeless. I can't do anything but keep an awareness of the passage of time, a game that I played with my brother when we were kids. At any point in the day, one of us would turn to the other and ask, "Time?" I was often uncannily correct, guessing the time close to the minute thanks to the internal timekeeper that my mother called the Eve Clock. All women had it, she said, because for most of their lives, females are entrusted with waiting expectantly for loved ones to be born or to die.

But now, in the complete dark of the trunk, it's an impossible task, the adrenaline seeming to squeeze minutes into seconds or string them into hours. The best I can do is stay alert and not lose my nerve wondering what's going to happen when the truck gets to its destination.

I think through my options for escape: I could slip the cuffs, kick out a rear taillight, push through the backseat. But my wrists are too tightly bound and the trunk space is too small to maneuver in. My best hope is to get to the cell phone in my left pocket. If it's still there, and if it hasn't been smashed by my falling on it.

The tall cop with the tattoo and reddish hair must be the same deliveryman that Sergei witnessed as he left El Gitano's head in a box at my door. He's big, and very fast. His eyes, when he looked at me, cattle prod in hand, were calm, almost amused, and I think of Tony Ha saying that Lana's killer was humming as he cut her ears off. That he was a man who enjoyed his work.

The truck stops and starts frequently as it progresses through some nearby small town, perhaps Karnack. But soon, within fifteen minutes, we're driving without perceptible changes in speed, and for quite a distance. Eventually, there are more stops and starts, and then a final stop. But the truck engine stays on for a good while.

I lie on my side, sweating through my clothes, time stretched through the filter of the agonizing deadness in my left arm, straining to hear any approaching footsteps. And then there is the clanging of the cargo-bay doors opening. A heavy sliding noise as the ramp is lowered, and the patrol car engine comes to life. The patrol car is backed down the ramp, its tilt sliding me toward the rear bumper. Afterward, I hear the clatter of the ramp being raised again, and the truck, possibly still containing the car with Hoskins's body inside, drives away.

The patrol car is driven a short distance into a covered space, like a garage. I can hear the engine noises echoing off enclosed walls.

The trunk will open soon.

I can try to squeeze my body around, onto my back, and kick out as strongly as I can with my feet toward my kidnapper's head, but then what? Better to feign unconsciousness while lying on my side, turned away from the opening, and wait for an opportunity to attack.

The trunk opens and a hand presses hard against the side of my face, grinding my head into the frame, and a needle jabs into my right shoulder. A heavy body folds itself over mine, restraining me, smothering me, until I feel a building, undeniable warmth from my intestines to the base of my tongue, and then comes the inevitable toppling off the cliff to nothingness.

29

I'm aware that I'm aware, my alertness turned on like a bank of lights engaged all at once. I'm sitting upright in a hard chair, my head bowed forward, hair falling in a cascade over my eyes. There's a moment of nausea, an unpleasant ringing in the ears, and then those symptoms are gone.

I stare fixedly at my lap and realize that I can't move my hands because I'm in a prisoner's transport restraint, wrists cuffed in front and fastened to a belly strap with a length of chain running to ankle cuffs. I am no longer gagged, and my lips are raw from the tape having been pulled from my mouth.

All of my clothes except for my sleeveless T-shirt and underwear have been removed, boots and socks included. Which means that while I was unconscious, I'd been unbound and stripped. The thin vinyl seat cushion sticks creepily beneath my bare legs, and the cool air causes the skin on the tops of my thighs and arms to gooseflesh.

My neck is stiff and cramped, so I raise my head carefully and see, through squinting eyes, a room bright with diffuse, natural light and painted a soft cream color. It's sparsely furnished: a small couch, a bookcase, one prominent window with sheer, gauzy curtains closed over it. There are no paintings, but there is one large, unadorned cross nailed to the wall with a plaque next to it, the kind of shellacked board that could have been made in a high-school shop class, with the words WELCOME HOME burned into the wood. Underneath the cross is an armchair in which a woman sits.

The woman tilts her head and smiles at me.

The dizziness returns for an instant, and the smile on the woman's face falters. She looks concerned, ready to stand, but she sees my eyes focused on her intently, and instead, she smooths her skirt over her knees and crosses her hands in her lap. There is a patient, untroubled quality to the way she waits, her head now turned toward the light of the window. But I know she is listening, receptive to any move I might make.

I rattle the chains ineffectually and look back up at the woman. She's probably in her sixties, petite, clear-complected, without any distinguishing marks, her hair the color of a West Texas sunset.

As I'm opening my mouth to ask her what the hell she wants with me, she says calmly, "Would you like some water?" She nods to a glass of water with a straw sitting on a small table next to the chair.

Her voice is deeply Southern but soft and sunny, like the paint on the wall.

I hesitate and she picks up the glass and takes a sip, showing me that the water has not been tampered with. I nod my head and she brings me the water. A thought moves sluggishly through my brain: I could stand abruptly, knocking her over. But I can't lean forward. Something has been used to tie the belly strap to the chair. As though reading my intentions, the woman pauses, waiting for me to realize that I'm not going anywhere. She holds the glass close to my mouth as I sip awkwardly from the straw, almost finishing the water.

She then takes a few steps back and continues to study me.

"Where am I?" I ask. My throat is dry and constricted, my voice insubstantial. I sound weak and afraid. "And where the fuck are my clothes?"

"Somewhere between Caddo Lake and Lake of the Pines," she answers lightly, returning to her armchair, and I don't know if she's referring to where we are or the location of my clothes. She sits, patting down a few loose strands of hair with one hand. "Your things are being cleansed."

She said *cleansed,* not *cleaned.*

Her knees and ankles are pressed tightly together, sturdy shoes planted squarely on the floor. Her eyes have lost the drug-rattled stupor and she looks like a respectable grandmother now, but the arch of the brows and the shape of the nose are unmistakable: she's the woman in the mug shot from the Smith County jail that Ryan showed me.

"You're Evangeline Roy," I tell her.

Her smile broadens, as though she's delighted I've figured it out so soon. "And you're Elizabeth Rhyzyk. Detective Rhyzyk," she says coyly. "Had you ever noticed that our initials are the same?"

Her look of pleasure makes my jaw tighten. "You've murdered a decorated police officer. You know what they do to people who kill cops?"

Her blue eyes widen and her mouth turns down sadly, but it's a fake pity. I might as well be talking about dryer lint.

"What's important," she says, "is that you're all right."

"I've just witnessed my partner shot and killed. I've been attacked and k-kidnapped," I stutter. "Fuck you, I'm not all right. What the hell is going on…" My hands clench and unclench, straining wildly against the cuffs.

"Elizabeth," she says, holding up a hand as though I've threatened to strike her. "There's no need for such language. Not between you and I." She winks at me. "You gave my boys quite a struggle, though, didn't you? It threw off their timing."

Her boys. Does that mean her sons, Curtis and Tommy Roy? They'd be in their early thirties if they hadn't actually died in the house fire. About the same age as the fake cops. Or is she just using a Southern cliché, a group of good ol' boys out for a romp?

"Was I raped?" I demand.

One brow comes up, as though she's amused, but she says, "Not that I know."

She points to my legs and my arms and says admiringly, "It's so good to see that you haven't trashed your body with tattoos when so many young females have. It shows that you have respect for your body."

"What do you want with me?" I yell, flecks of spittle flying from my mouth. Something about her unruffled pose enrages and frightens me at the same time.

"What do I want?" she asks. She regards me with something more than warmth. Something closer to hunger. "I want what only you can give me."

I'm trying to imagine what she needs—assistance in eradicating her competition, information, the release of one of her own who's incarcerated in exchange for my free-dom—but she smiles at me in a conspiratorial way that makes the spit in my mouth dry up.

"Why, Elizabeth," she says cheerfully, leaning forward to give her words more weight. "I want grandbabies, of course."

30

Any cop will tell you that some of the most dangerous interactions occur when you're dealing with a calm psychopath. The raging, ranting bug jobs often give a tell before the attack comes, a vocal crescendo or an obscenity-laced preamble, the guy screaming at you about how he's going to bury the ax he's wielding deep in your skull and then have long, satisfying sex with your shattered cranium.

But the serene, reasonable-sounding lunatic, the next-door neighbor who has always been neat and tidy, returning the borrowed hedge trimmer on time, is the one who will end up scooping out your kidneys with a spoon before you can say "Jeffrey Dahmer."

I stare at the woman sitting across from me, blinking for a moment before I begin a frantic, hiccupping laughter. You never tell a crazy person that he or she is crazy, but my unchecked, hysterical cackling says it all.

Her head tilts again, but she's not smiling now.

She takes a deep, steadying breath and tells me, "You're tired, Elizabeth, and you don't yet understand the work you are meant to do. You need to rest and then we'll talk again."

Evangeline stands from the chair and walks to the door, looking not so much pained as disappointed. But her eyes rest briefly on the wall behind me and she regains her composure.

"Where are my clothes? Give me back my goddamned clothes," I demand.

She closes the door behind her, leaving me alone in the room.

"Hey!" I call out, but I hear nothing but her retreating footsteps. Immediately, I rattle and test the chains, but they're heavy and newly bought, and there's no way I can escape them. I need a hairpin or paper clip to try and work the locks, but the room is almost empty, pristine, sterile, like it was staged.

Glancing at the plaque again, I remember James Earle's voice on the phone—how many hours earlier?—warning me that we were in their jungle now. He was an MP, and once a cop, always a cop. He felt intuitively that something was wrong about our being so lost, and he knew that we were only a few miles from Caddo, on our way to Karnack, and that we had been redirected with detour signs. He'll tell Jackie or burn up the phone lines getting someone else to listen to him. They'll start looking for me soon.

With a twisting motion, I squelch around in the vinyl chair to examine what's in back of me, expecting to see another blank and unblemished wall. But when I see what's there, I startle, my neck muscles straining, my eyes wide and disbelieving. On the wall is a large canvas, a painting of Saint Michael slaying the devil, the background of which is daubed with dark and murky colors. The archangel is muscular and pale, his slender arm upraised, poised to bring the blue-metal sword down onto the figure below one sandaled foot, his enemy, a writhing, dark-skinned man with horns. Saint Michael's cape, a deep crimson, swirls in a bright tempest about his wings. His hair, also red, flies up behind him as though the angel has only just landed on the earth, ready for the final battle.

The angel is traditionally androgynous, sinewy, graceful, the pectoral muscles beneath the breastplate molded to a feminine roundness. The painting is a reproduction—it can't be the original one by Reni—but it's a good copy, filled with righteous anger and ritual vengeance. It is, in picture form, the Deuteronomy verse that was written on the note brought to me by Tony Ha.

When I sharpen my flashing sword and my hand grasps it in judgment, I will take vengeance on my adversaries and repay those who hate me.

The door opens then and the tall cop, the one with the blue-winged tattoo, walks into the room. He's not wearing the cop's uniform, though; he's changed into khaki pants and a work shirt.

I steel myself for an assault, a beating, another session with the cattle prod, but his hands are empty, and he unties the rope securing me to the chair. Without looking at my face, he yanks at my elbow, pulling me to my feet. The vinyl pulls wetly at the backs of my legs, and he leads me, shuffling and barefoot, toward the door.

"Where are you taking me?" I ask. He pulls harder at my arm, drags me through the doorway and down a hall. There are several doors on either side of the hall, but they are all closed and the building is completely quiet. It's a house, poorly constructed, with ill-fitting doors and narrow baseboards. It might well be one of the redbrick, work-neglected homes we passed on our way toward Karnack.

At the end of the hallway, he opens the last door into a room the size of a large closet, carpeted and with a twin mattress and box spring on the floor covered with a thin sheet, a near-flat pillow with no pillowcase, and nothing else. There are no windows or closets and the walls are painted a dark, bilious green. The only light source is from an old-fashioned glass-plate light fixture overhead. The one door has a hatch that opens and closes, about face-high and covered with a screen, so they can keep an eye on me.

He begins to shove me into the room, but I tell him, "I need a bathroom."

Kicking at a plastic bedpan next to the door, the kind used in hospitals, he pushes me farther into the room and unlocks and removes the belly strap and ankle restraints, leaving my wrists cuffed but free enough for me to use the bedpan. He backs away from me as if from a dangerous animal and then closes the door. I can hear the lock turning and, after a moment, his heavy footsteps retreating down the hallway.

I sit on the bed and look around the room. To the right of the mattress, about a foot off the floor, is a ringbolt fastened to the wall. I turn my head and see the same kind of bolt secured to the wall to the left of the mattress as well. There is only one reason I can think of why ringbolts would be screwed firmly into a wall: to restrain a prisoner.

My fingers reach for my own Saint Michael's image, but I feel nothing but skin. It's no longer hanging from a chain around my neck. I shake my hair frantically like a dog, thinking that it had gotten caught up in the tangled strands, hoping that the chain will come loose and fall again with a familiar and comforting weight around my neck.

But it's gone, torn loose during the struggle or taken along with my clothes and the phone that was in the left pocket of my jacket. I'm near naked and barefoot in a monk-like cell, my bladder about to burst, and I'm beyond confounded. A best-case hostage situation would mean a relatively short uncomfortable period being held captive before a negotiating team successfully secured my release by giving the kidnappers, at least temporarily, what they wanted. Or before a special tactical team was sent in to red-dot every one of their down-home, country-bred foreheads.

But what Evangeline Roy seems to want from me is so fuck-all weird, so out of the realm of rational thought, that either she's playing with me, trying to unseat my own reason, or she's utterly crazy, in which case all rules of the known universe have been suspended. But she's not so crazy that she hasn't taken on one of the most dangerous cartels and managed to maintain, at least for the time being, the winning hand.

The woman has to know that two police officers disappearing, especially two cops who have worked with the Feds, will bring a battery of state, county, and city officials to beat down and search every scrawny bush behind the Pine Curtain. ATF, DEA, U.S. Marshal Service—they'll all be alerted and on the hunt.

Looking around the room, I take stock of what I have to work with. The possibilities are bleak. I can pull up a corner piece of the carpet, pry loose one of the tack strips, utilize the rows of little nails against a bare neck where the carotid artery lies or on an unprotected pair of eyes. And you never know when a longer nail, a paper clip, even a razor blade used to scrape away old wallpaper, has fallen between the wall and the carpet padding.

I can't concentrate anymore without emptying my bladder and am about to relieve myself over the bedpan when the hatch on the door opens and the tall guy's face is there. I didn't hear him coming up the hallway, which means he's a stealthy, sneaky bastard. Stealthy and clever enough to gain entrance into my locked apartment.

The pressure in my groin is beyond painful. I can wait tensely for him to come into the room, or I can derail his peep show. I put up my middle finger, then turn my back to him, pull down my underwear, and squat over the bedpan. Immediately, the hatch snaps shut and my shoulders sag with relief.

Then the room goes dark.

There must be a light switch on the outside wall. I realize I haven't seen any switches on the inside wall. When I finish, I stand, pull up my underwear, gently ease the bedpan toward the wall with one foot, and then remain motionless until I hear him plodding down the hallway again.

The room is dark but not completely featureless. The cracks around the door let in some ambient light and soon I can make out the white sheet on the mattress. I sit on the edge of the bed and listen for any other sounds, but the house is silent. I scoot to the top of the mattress, lean my back and head against the wall, and wait.

Soon the hours of struggle and the fear all work to numb my waking brain, and I find myself easing into sleep, only to jerk my head back when my chin starts to droop. It keeps drooping, and the thought of leaving my eyes closed, if only for a short while, is suddenly too powerful to fight.

At once, I see Hoskins sitting next to me in the car, his smiling face in profile. He reaches into his pocket to pull out his badge, and next to the passenger-side window appears, not the tall cop, but the young cowboy from Marshall, his hat shadowing his features, the Smith and Wesson pistol pointed at Hoskins's head.

Then comes the inevitable bang, and my eyes open to my prison room, lit again from the overhead bulb. The noise has come from the hatch in the door being opened, and the eyes of Hoskins's killer are watching me. He unlocks and opens the door, holding in his hands the transport strap and chains. Standing behind him in the hallway is the shorter cop—maybe he *is* a cop, as he's still in uniform—wearing a sidearm and holding the cattle prod.

I'm instantly alert, but I have no idea how long I've been asleep. It could have been a few minutes; it could have been hours. There's a thin drizzle of spittle on my chin, so it must have been a deep sleep, however long it was.

The taller one walks into the room and tells me to stand up. Quickly and expertly, he puts the restraints back on. His voice is flat, matter-of-fact, and I'm relieved that he's apparently not in the least aroused by my near nakedness. I may not be his type; I'm tall and muscular, and maybe he likes his women petite and pork-stuffed, but whatever the reason, there is no change in his breathing when he bends down to fasten the cuffs around my ankles, no brushing of fingertips over my calves or thighs, no flaring nostrils that signal carnal thoughts when he cinches the belly strap. There is a blankness about his face, a lack of any emotional engagement. He might as well be trussing a store mannequin.

I flick my eyes to his shorter companion with the cattle prod, and his face tells a different story. He's staring at my underwear at crotch level, and there's clearly plenty of lust-driven thoughts going on between those ears. If I am going to be raped, it will be initiated by him. There was plenty of rage, too, on his face as he was tossing me into the car trunk. I'd more than thrown off his timing. I had fought back, almost broken his nose, and I'd run like hell. Had I gotten away, it would have threatened his very existence.

The fact that I've seen both their faces and could testify in court to all they've done or are about to do—especially when their usual MO is to go masked—is not reassuring.

After the restraints are secured, I'm led back down the hallway into the formerly bright and cheerful room, which is now in shadows, lit by the same overhead light fixture as in my tiny closet, the large window behind the gauzy curtains pitch-black. It's full-on night. I've been missing for hours and there has to be a massive search under way for me and my partner. I just have to stay on my guard and hang on.

The shadows in the painting of Saint Michael are more pronounced, more sinister in their somber hues. Only the crimson burst of his cape and hair and the white reflective highlights on his face and glinting sword shine aggressively. The devil is completely lost in the ocher tones of the earth at the bottom of the scene.

Evangeline perches in her chair, observing me observing the painting. She says, "He's beautiful, isn't he?"

The tall one forces me to sit, and I'm tied again to the vinyl chair. Then he exits the room without a backward glance. The shorter one takes one last look at my breasts, cold nipples prominent beneath the thin fabric of the T-shirt, and smirks at me before leaving.

"Did you have a nice rest, Elizabeth?" Evangeline asks.

"If that's what you want to call passing out in a prison cell," I say. "And the name is Detective Rhyzyk."

"Are you hungry?" she asks.

A sandwich, a bowl of soup, and a glass of milk are arranged on a plastic tray on the table next to the chair. I hadn't experienced any hunger until she pointed out the food, and my stomach rumbles. I don't want to eat, not certain what's been added to the food, but if I don't eat, I can't stay strong.

"After you," I say, and she takes a tiny bite of the sandwich and a spoonful of soup.

"The milk," I prompt her, and she sips at the milk.

She picks up the bowl and the spoon and comes to stand in front of me.

"Are you going to untie me so I can eat?" I ask.

Smiling, she shakes her head, dips the spoon into the soup, and then holds it to my lips. I slurp at the tepid soup and swallow it.

I want to ask her what's going on, if she's aware that the entire Dallas Police Department is probably looking for me, but Evangeline wipes at my chin maternally with a tissue pulled out of her pocket. Her skirt and sweater smell of dry cleaning and some papery eau de toilette. The room is dark, but I can see that her flawless Dolly Parton–esque complexion is actually a thick spackling of makeup covering meth scars. The overdone hair is definitely a wig.

"The painting is from a church in Louisiana," she says. "I took shelter there one night when that was the only place available to me. I was about as far down as a person could possibly be and still be breathing. Many of the details of my addiction you probably already know from my arrest records."

She feeds me more of the soup, which tastes like the watery, canned stuff my mom used to serve with grilled cheese sandwiches.

"The church was abandoned. Burned out, overgrown,

infested with rats, but it still had a kind of dignity to it. I fell asleep under one of the pews and woke to the moon shining through the holes in the roof. It had been raining, but the clouds had cleared, and this shaft of light fell across the floor and onto that very painting. That's when I saw him. And that's when he spoke to me."

As she talks, her attention returns again to the painting. At some point she realizes that I haven't opened my mouth to the spoon, and she catches me eyeing her.

"Oh, yes," she assures me. "He spoke to me. Just like I'm speaking to you now. He appeared to me in the form of a man, a tall redheaded man, but he was the archangel incarnate."

She wipes at my lips again, a little more insistently this time.

"I know it happened, because from that moment on, I was cured of my addiction. It was as though it had never been. Vanished into the air."

She returns the bowl to the table and picks up the plate with the sandwich. There's a thoughtful moment when she faces the black rectangle of the window.

"Do you know what Michael, God's most beloved angel, told me?" she asks quietly, her back to me. "He told me I was to build an army for him. An army of tested, pure-race peoples to bring back the natural order of things. He revealed that Adam was named for the Hebrew word for the red clay of the earth, *aw-dah-mawh*," she pronounces reverently. "The first man who walked the earth had red hair, and also the first woman, as she was made from his body. King David of the Bible had red hair as well. 'For he was but a youth, and ruddy, and of a fair countenance.' It was time for the flame-haired children of God to take pre-eminence once more."

She brings the sandwich to me and presses it lovingly to my lips, as though it is a communion wafer. I take a bite and chew.

"Even the ancient pagans venerated red hair. There were two redheaded giants in the *Iliad*. Menelaus, the great king of Sparta, had red hair—"

I turn my head to the side, refusing another mouthful of chicken salad. "I want my medallion back," I tell her.

"It's in safekeeping," she assures me, and I'm so relieved that it's not lost that I let her ramble on.

"See," she says, gesturing to the painting. "The Archangel Michael, the greatest of his kind, has scarlet hair. But there are so few of us left in the world. We've been subsumed by all the mud people."

I think of the devil, who's portrayed as a swarthy man in the picture, and wonder for how many centuries that piece of propaganda for racial supremacy has been trotted out. The painting Evangeline Roy took from a ruined church in Louisiana is one of many representations of Saint Michael I've seen in many different churches, and in several of them, God's Most Beloved is a blond.

"So, let me get this straight," I say, disbelieving. "You killed my partner and kidnapped me because I have red hair?"

She blinks a few times, as though waking from a stupor. "We need you for our family, Elizabeth. The archangel speaks to me and tells me this is so—"

"It's Detective Rhyzyk," I say forcefully, interrupting her.

I want to scream at her that no one had ever called me Elizabeth, not even my own mother, but I need to back off the verbal bruising. She had said "for our family," not "in our family," as though I were something to be used. The woman is full-blown gonzo, and I should tread carefully. But her wanting me alive is a definite advantage.

She holds up the sandwich, and I take another bite. She strokes my head tentatively with her other hand and tells me, "Your glorious hair was just one of the many signs that you could be one of us."

Like a good girl, I finish the rest of the sandwich, and Evangeline returns the plate to the tray.

"When I saw you on TV," she says excitedly, settling herself into the chair, "after the battle in Weatherford, striding down the halls of the hospital, proud, imperious, reveling in your win, I had hope. And then when I saw the Saint Michael's medal around your neck, I knew that you had been sent to us."

"I'm a cop. It's my job. Saint Michael is the patron saint of police, and the medal was given to me by my mother. It's not a biblical calling."

"Oh, but I think for you it is a calling, and that's why we brought you the head of the Mexican," she says, her eyes shining with pious fervor as though she's referred to the head of John the Baptist. "It was to help you send a message to his people. It was so simple finding him. Frankly, I was surprised with all your resources that you couldn't." She said the last in a mildly scolding manner, as though I'd dropped a ball during a Little League game.

"So you decided you'd just leave the severed head outside my door," I say. "You terrified my girlfriend, my neighbors . . ." I stop and take a breath, ratcheting down the intensity of my voice. "One of your family killed a woman in your ex-husband's house. She was tortured first, her ears cut off, and then her throat was slit from missing ear to missing ear. Was that part of your calling too?"

She tilts her head but says nothing.

"Was the killer one of your sons?" I press. "Are the men posing as the Jefferson cops Curtis and Tommy Roy?"

Mei's voice is now in my head, calmly telling me that Lana's murderer was a destroyer of women.

"The woman was the Mexican's whore," she says.

"As well as your ex-husband's," I add.

Her eyes narrow, her mouth puckering into a lemony, distasteful grimace. She knew the last bit of information, but it still rankles and I want to drive the sword in deeper.

"What did you do with the severed ears, by the way?" I ask. "Save them for stringing on the Christmas tree?"

She sits, hands clasped capably in her lap, the foggy, visionary mantle now gone. Evangeline Roy is all business, the CEO of a growing concern, sitting at the head of a conference table. "They were sent to the Juárez cartel, a warning to stay out of our territory. And, yes, the two men who took you are my sons. They are my sword and my shield. Something needed to be done. I didn't ask them how they planned to accomplish it."

She rearranges her features into a more kindly mask and tells me, "We are only doing what the Mexicans would have done to us. *Will* do to us, if they gain the upper hand. They aren't satisfied polluting their own country. They have to come here, bringing their trash drugs and trash families with them."

As she's talking I'm thinking, *But you're selling meth to the people in your own country, you crazy fucking bitch, destroying lives and whole families.* I could ask her how many hundreds of people were addicted to her meth right here in East Texas, and she'd probably know right down to the exact number and gram weight.

My mouth opens and before I can stop myself, I say, "I'll bet you my red-haired snatch that most of the people buying your meth are good ol' Walmart-shoppin', fried-okra-eatin' white people, some of them pure redneck gingers. How do you justify doing that?"

"Because we give them a choice and a way out," she says, excitement in her voice, as though she's only now getting to the meat of her message. "We only sell to those already deep in the throes of their addiction, and our product is far superior to what the Mexicans are peddling. Cleaner, safer. But we also come with a message of hope. Offer them an escape from their disease. And our family is growing daily with men and women who are given a purpose, a way to jettison their addiction and step up to their rightful place in the world. It takes time. For some it takes a long, long time. But we have money for treatment, and we have guns, so that when the fall happens, and it will come, we'll have a self-sufficient force. Some of our family are in jail now. But some are judges, car mechanics, computer technicians, even police officers. Which is how we enticed you, and how we knew when and where you were coming."

She gestures around the room. "What you see here is just a tiny staging area. A receiving room, if you will. We have manufacturing facilities all over East Texas and Louisiana. Some of them are underground, some of them are on houseboats or in abandoned warehouses. The current downturn in the economy has helped us in numerous ways."

"Saint Michael's army," I tell her.

"Yes," she affirms, her face beaming.

"A syringe in one hand, and a Bible in the other."

The facial wattage dims somewhat. "If you want to put it in that crude way, yes."

"Helter-skelter," I say.

"What?" she asks.

"The end is nigh, the race riots, the fall of civilization, blah-blah-blah...just like the Charlie Manson Family."

"He was a lunatic," she says.

"Oh yeah," I agree. "A manipulative, murdering, crazy little man with a big vision. The most dangerous kind."

She leans heavily against the back of her chair. "Elizabeth," she says sorrowfully. "I was hoping you would see our vision more clearly. I understand it's going to take more time. But time is my gift to you."

"They're looking for me right now."

"Yes," she says. "But they'll look in all the wrong places. They would have to search every house, every barn, every granary in East Texas, and by that time, we'll have what we want."

Right—grandbabies. "Which of your psychopathic sons is to be the happy father?"

"The elder, Tommy."

"Doesn't appear like much of a rooster to me. Seems more interested in playing with knives, if you know what I mean."

"It was Tommy that first brought you to my attention. I chose you because he chose you. It was he that left the offering on your bed. The one you share with the woman. At first I was dismayed that you were living that life. But in a way, it's more fitting. You are technically still a virgin."

"There is no virgin about this girl," I say angrily. "How do you know I haven't worked my way through the Swedish navy as well as the U.S. girls' swim team?"

"You'd like to shock me," she says, wagging one finger at me.

No, I'd like to kill you, I think. But what I say is "You have no possible way of knowing that I can give you what you want."

Evangeline stands, straightening her posture. "Like I told you, Elizabeth, time will be my gift to you. You will *reorient*. And then you will be uplifted with the rest of us. The archangel has promised it."

She said *uplifted*. Something about her tone causes a line of sweat to form across my forehead.

"You'll come to love Tommy, as I do. But in the meanwhile, I hope you will understand that we'll need to take certain measures to keep you close at hand. We can't tie you to the bed every day."

Uplifted. The reverential way she uttered the word makes my heart pound. I recall a room filled with gauzy sunlight, dead people lying stacked in bunk beds, the word *Uplifted* written in orange spray paint on the walls, a squalling infant lying on the floor.

"What did you say?" I croak, my throat closing with fear.

She moves toward me, smiling sympathetically, hands in both pockets of her skirt.

"Tommy has told me that you are a runner. That you're very fast. Almost faster than he is, and he was a track star in college. We can't have you outrunning our Tommy."

She's standing next to the chair and I remember now with startling clarity the crazy man in the Mets jersey chanting, "Ready for uplift," the childishly rendered angels watching over his murdered flock.

Quickly, she pulls out of her pocket a needle and syringe and stabs me in the arm with it. I flinch hard, but the syringe is already emptied.

"I hope that you'll come to understand what we had to do to keep you, to keep us all, safe," she says softly, prayerfully.

"You fucking bitch," I yelp. I look stupidly at my arm

and then at her, the honeyed, familiar warmth rapidly moving up my chest, into my head.

Evangeline has stepped back, watching me closely. "We just can't have you running away. I'm sorry."

The fuzziness begins peripherally, tunneling my vision, matching everything to the blackness on the other side of the window. The futile straining against the chains and straps, the swelling terror against the last two words uttered, the woman staring dutifully at the painting of the beautiful, merciless angel.

31

My eyelids flutter, trying to open against the gummy film gluing my lashes together. I sense the bed beneath me is damp with sweat, or maybe with humidity, like it is at the oceanfront, where the sea air penetrates every porous surface.

Someone sits on the mattress. I feel a weighted depression close to my feet, a hand resting on my leg. It's Jackie. It must be Jackie. I struggle to separate my eyelids again, letting in a bit of light and, in the middle of my line of sight, a shadowy human form. I try raising my head, but I'm just too sleepy, and I let it fall back onto the bed.

I smile, though, so that Jackie can see how comforting it is to have her close. I feel a whispery shifting of a sheet being taken away from my bare legs, feel her gently kneading the muscles in my right leg, the thigh, the knee, the muscle draped over the shinbone. I have a cramping in my calf muscle, as after punishing exercise, and her hand slips around the back of the leg and squeezes the knotted bulk gently.

My mouth is very dry, and I lick my lips, which are as cracked as alligator hide. I want to tell her how good it feels, but my voice is uncooperative. So I keep smiling, nodding my chin once so that she'll keep massaging my leg.

I remember where we are: in Cape May, on the Jersey Shore, our first weekend trip together. Two nights in one of the many curlicued, porticoed Victorian B and Bs, our bedroom decorated with low-end bric-a-brac and faux antiques. A musty room with a pastel floral nightmare of a quilt, but with huge bay windows that open to the Atlantic Ocean breezes, which blow the chintz curtains back into the room like sails before a storm.

We go swimming, Jackie's sunburned shoulders bobbing in the waves in front of me, her face in profile as she turns, taunting me, daring me to follow her into the deeper water. The flash of her delicate feet as she dives under a swell, her ankle bracelet flaring the light like a tiny lighthouse.

I follow her under a wall of water, surprised by the strength of the undertow. I have a momentary, primal fear of drowning below the press of unimaginable weight, then the popped cork feeling of abruptly rising again; I flail my hands until a connection is made with her seal-like skin. She grabs my wrist and pulls me with her to the surface, where we float on our backs, gasping and laughing, undulating together on the waves, my atavistic fear of swimming in the ocean temporarily forgotten.

We flop, rubbery and spent, onto the sand, the bracing wind drying our bodies. And I, with the careful attention of a spymaster at a crowded train station, lean across Jackie pretending to reach for a book but instead lick the salt from her neck.

In our room with the chintz curtains we lie in bed, folded into each other's arms, and I whisper to Jackie that later, when the sun is lower and the temperatures cooler, I'll take an eight-mile jog along the beach. Through the open windows we can hear the inrushing and outgoing waves, sounding like an endless, murmuring conversation.

She moves to sit at my feet and rubs my legs in preparation for the run, smiling at my pleasure in her touch.

She tells me, "You always look surprised whenever I do something nice for you that you didn't ask for."

"Astonished," I say, my eyes closed, feeling her fingers discovering and unteasing every muscle fiber, like an electrician detangling a bundle of metal wires.

"What do you want, Betty?" she asks.

"You," I answer. The pressure of her fingers is increasing, and I inhale slowly to inhibit the contractions against her probing touch.

"I know that," she says, and I hear the laughter in her voice. "I mean what do you want out of life?"

I have a vision of my family, viewed through the heavy haze of smoke from my mother's ever-present cigarettes, sitting at the dinner table in dangerous silence. All of us still, breathless, poised for flight. My brother's tense face pointed in my direction, his eyes a luminous warning beacon. The sound of my father's knife, scraping hard and slow at the bottom of his plate; a fresh beer, his fourth, sitting like an un-pinned hand grenade, close at hand. He's just given me a tongue-lashing for some minor infraction.

Then my brother, without preamble and against all good sense, begins to sing a Madonna song—" 'Papa don't preach, I'm in trouble deep' "—in a high, wavering falsetto. In my naive, girlish voice, I say, "I don't get it." My father's black gaze falls first on me and then on An-

drew, and then the miraculous happens. He drops his knife
onto his plate and begins to laugh; hard, racking belly
laughs. All at once, we're laughing together, the nervous
anxiety forcing our gaiety to a maniacal pitch, and we're
falling out of our chairs in shared, unexpected mirth.

The sun has made me feverish. I feel all at once chilled
and hot, and I begin to shiver.

"Joyful noise," I manage to say, answering her question.
My teeth are clenched painfully, and I try to open my eyes
once more, reaching for the quilt to cover my exposed legs.

Jackie's wearing her turquoise robe, but that can't be
right because she didn't have a turquoise robe at Cape May,
and the pressure of her hands on my leg is now painful,
her fingers pinching forcefully behind my ankle at the midsection of the Achilles tendon. The pinching swells into a
sharp pain, a puncturing sensation not on the surface of my
leg but through it.

I begin to yell, to jerk my limb away from her touch, but
I'm frozen in cement.

You're hurting me, I want to yell, but I can't open my
jaw to utter the words. There is no moving any part of my
body now.

Even so, my last frantic impulse is to run.

32

A cold, wet cloth rests over my forehead, water dripping down my temples and into my hairline. I'm on the single mattress in my prison, staring upward at the glass light fixture overhead. The bulb is on, reflecting muddily off the green walls.

My arms are outstretched, held fast by hospital-type restraining cuffs around my wrists. Turning my head to the right and then to the left, I see that there are ropes tying the cuffs to ringbolts screwed into the opposing walls.

Whatever drug they've given me is still strong in my system, making the room tilt wildly as I move, but by straining every neck muscle, I manage to pull my chin forward off the mattress. At the foot of the bed is a heavyset woman wearing a nurse's uniform: scrub pants and a patterned tunic. The kind worn in a doctor's office. She's quietly talking to Evangeline Roy, and when they sense my movement, they both stop talking and turn to look at me.

"Untie me," I say. My voice is hoarse, as though the vocal cords have been frayed.

Evangeline tells the woman to bring me water and she sits on the bed next to me. As soon as she disturbs the mattress, a shooting pain rockets through my right calf. I try to shift my position, but Evangeline puts a firm hand over my right thigh.

"Don't move," she says, "or you'll injure yourself."

"What?" I croak.

Or you'll injure yourself. I don't remember being hurt, only being tied to a chair, stabbed with a needle. An agitated fear is setting my teeth to chattering. In spite of her warning, I bend my left leg, but I feel nothing wrong. Only in the right leg. The leg that is beginning to throb more urgently.

"Are you in pain?" she asks. "We can give you something for that."

Her facial expression is carefully neutral, but there's a nervous quality about her watchfulness, and I have to close my eyes for a moment, willing myself to breathe through the feeling of being slowly suffocated.

"What have you done?" I demand.

The nurse walks back into the room carrying a glass of water with a bent straw. She hands it to Evangeline, who holds the straw to my pinched lips. I jerk my head away but keep my eyes focused, like a laser guidance system, on the fat nurse.

"I want you to listen carefully to me," Evangeline says. "You were chosen by us for a very special purpose. You don't yet know just how important you are, Elizabeth. You're not aware of the truth of things. You're not right-thinking—"

"You're fucking crazy," I mutter to her, but my eyes are

still on the nurse. The woman's uneasy—whatever she's done to me, she's unsure about it, and scared. "Help me," I say to her. "Help me, please."

"Give her something for the pain," Evangeline tells her, standing up.

The nurse pulls a syringe out of her pocket and moves closer to the bed.

"Stop," I order, and she freezes.

"I'm a police officer," I tell her. "If you help me, I'll make sure that nothing happens to you."

"Brenda," Evangeline barks. "Give her the shot."

"No, no," I say. "Just tell me what's going on."

Evangeline gazes at me through half-closed eyes, the green paint on the walls making her look like a perching lizard.

"All right," I say. "I'll be cooperative, I swear, just don't drug me again."

Evangeline nods and the nurse puts the syringe back in her pocket.

"Go get Tommy," she tells the woman, and the nurse leaves the room.

"Your comfort level will be determined by the degree to which you yield to the truth," she tells me. "And, Elizabeth, I'll know if you're trying to con me or trick me."

Brenda walks back into the room, Tommy following, holding the cattle prod.

"Untie her," Evangeline tells the nurse, and Brenda unbuckles the wrist restraints.

I bring my arms to my chest, rubbing circulation into them.

"Help her sit up," Evangeline tells Brenda.

Brenda looks at her, startled, but positions her hands behind my shoulders, pushes me into a sitting position. My vision first darkens and then clears with a zigzag of crazily shifting, pinpoint lights.

Around the lower part of my right leg, I see a large, bulky bandage with a length of narrow chain emerging from under it and falling off the side of the mattress. Two red blooms, like small poppies, stain both sides of the white gauze. My foot emerges from the bandage, naked and whole.

Tommy moves nearer to the bed, bringing the prod closer to my body.

Evangeline has moved to the foot of the bed and stands with her hands demurely clasped at her waist. "Submission, Elizabeth. Submission is the key to salvation."

She tells Brenda to unwrap the bandage, and I circle both hands tightly at my knee as the binding pressure is released, trying to dull the escalating throbbing sensation at the bottom of the gastrocnemius muscle. I want to tell her to stop, want to turn my head and look away, but instead, I watch more of the length of chain being revealed as the bandage is removed. The last link is attached to a circlet of thin, plastic-coated steel, like a flexible bike cable, which disappears into my flesh behind the outer anklebone, passes through my leg under the Achilles tendon, and emerges on the other side.

I stare at the circle of cable, my mind like a flock of birds smashing into the path of a jetliner, unable in that moment to grasp the idea that it has been threaded through my flesh. But the plastic coating is brown with dried blood, my dried blood, and the reddened, inflamed skin at the straining cuts glistens with some kind of strong-smelling gel.

The far end of the chain is draped off the side of the mattress, and I follow the course of the links gingerly with both hands, careful not to pull on the two incisions in my ankle. I lean dizzily over the edge of the bed, my stomach pushing bile into the back of my throat, and see that the far end of the chain is looped through a hole bored into a large, flat stone. Painted on its surface, in bright yellow letters, is SUBMIT, E 5:21.

"Ephesians," Evangeline says, her voice dimmed through the building roar in my head. "'Submit yourselves one to another in the fear of God.'"

The chain is long, but not as long as I am tall.

"You will be able to move, but only in a limited capacity," she says, and I look up at her, my throat churning to swallow back the acid burning on my tongue. "And only by carrying the stone. In this way will your waywardness be proven unto you."

She smiles at me.

I turn my head slowly to Brenda, who's still holding the bandages in her hands. My thoughts fragment, the broken birds are sucked into an engine of rage and fear, and I begin to retch, both hands covering my mouth. Brenda leans over me, one hand on my shoulder, an absurd yet instinctive response.

"Did you do this to me?" I ask her, whispering muffled through my fingers.

She looks at me in timorous, cow-eyed worry, taken in by my woozy, gentle tone.

I reach out both shaking hands toward her and, before she can react, grab two fistfuls of her hair and bring the bridge of her nose like a missile onto my forehead. A flattening of cartilage, a scream, and I fling her away, onto the floor. I stagger up, lunge for Evangeline standing at the foot of the bed, and my fingers close around her throat, squeezing, but also throttling desperately, trying to separate the cervical vertebrae, to pinch off the nerves to stop any movement, any breath, any more ravings from her, and I know that Tommy Roy is behind me and will jab me with the cattle prod, sending electricity through me and into his mother's carcass as well.

Evangeline's eyes are bulging, and she claws at my hands—she's been caught completely off guard, and that knowledge strengthens me beyond the drug tremors. Her wig begins to slide, exposing a stubbled, pale scalp, and my mouth opens to scream, to bellow, but a pain like a shark's bite breaks my grip, compelling me backward onto the bed. Tommy is holding on to the chain connected to my leg, and he jerks it again, pulling the incisions open further, straining the Achilles tendon at the delicate attachment to the heel, and sending fresh blood streaming over my leg and over the bed.

I rear up again, go at him, the pain a river of fire, and he extends the cattle prod and presses the metal prongs into my stomach, sending me thrashing, helpless, against the mattress.

When the spasms abate, I bare my teeth at him like a rabid badger and say, panting, "I guess in your world…this means we're going steady now."

He makes a feint like he's going to jab me again, but I jeer at him with harsh, derisive laughter.

"Come on," I taunt, kneeling on the bed, the chain rattling around me like wind chimes underwater. "Come see what it's like being kissed by a Polish dyke *kobieta*, you flaccid-dicked motherfucker."

Brenda has pulled herself upright off the floor and is cupping both hands under her bleeding nose, looking wild-eyed and angered. But she backs quickly away from me. The pattern on her nurse's tunic, I now see, is palm trees and dancing monkeys.

Not my circus, not my monkeys, I hear Benny say loud and clear in the throbbing electric mass behind my eyes.

I snarl at her like a dog. "You ready to be kissed by me again, tubby?"

Her brows come down. She's looking at a lunatic.

The door is slammed open, and Curtis Roy walks in, his police uniform without a crease, his pistol pointed at my head. It breaks the surge of adrenaline, and, like a marionette whose strings have been cut, my body goes slack against the wall behind the bed.

"That's just perfect," I say, breathing hard. "The two Roy boys. A redneck double date."

Evangeline has righted her wig. She tugs hard at her sweater, smoothing away all signs of struggle. Her hands shake uncontrollably with fear and a towering rage. The meth scars on her face show behind the troweled-on makeup, like careless heat bubbling up through pancake batter.

"You must be so proud," I croak. I want to keep taunting her, but I have no more breath to speak.

"Tie her up," Evangeline directs, her voice regaining a cold composure.

I'm yanked roughly onto the bed by the Roy brothers, my wrists once more secured to the ropes that are tied to the ringbolts in the walls.

Evangeline tells Brenda to give me the shot of tranquilizer, but before the drug does its work, both Uncle Benny and I tell the red witch, *"Pierdol sie."* Go fuck yourself.

33

It seems as though the woman has been talking forever, reading Bible verses, droning on and on about submission.

"Corinthians, chapter eleven, verse three: 'But I would have you know, that the head of the woman is the man,'" Evangeline says, with a dramatic pause before the next reference. "Corinthians, chapter fourteen, verse thirty-four: 'Let your women keep silence in the churches, for it is not permitted unto them to speak.' ...Genesis, chapter three, verse sixteen: 'Unto the woman he said, I will greatly multiply thy sorrow and thy conception; in sorrow thou shalt bring forth children; and thy desire shall be to thy husband, and he shall rule over thee.'"

In trying to block out Evangeline's harping, I remember the gun-toting crazy man in the building on Norman Avenue in Brooklyn. The place where my first partner had been shot and where I had used the urgent rivalry between the Mets and the Yankees to make a dent in the shooter's psyche.

Somehow, I don't think Evangeline Roy is a baseball fan. And I doubt if she's ever been to Brooklyn. Her reference to being uplifted has got to be a coincidence. To think otherwise unrolls a connected universe of crazies that I can't even begin to wrap my head around. And yet, I wonder—my mind struggling after the scattered details of that day—was the Mets guy's hair sprouting from under his ball cap a light auburn color?

Evangeline's voice is a toxic spill of threatening invective and supernatural punishments.

"How about this," I yell from my bed, unable to bear any more Bronze Age wisdom. "Thou shalt not suffer a witch to live."

My hands are tied, but my mouth is free, and Evangeline springs from her chair like an agitated spaniel, walks to the bed, and stuffs a piece of gauze into my mouth.

As soon as she is seated, I manage to push the gauze out with my tongue and I hoarsely sing at the top of my lungs, " 'Ding-dong, the witch is dead, which ol' witch, the wicked witch…' "

She loudly reads, "Timothy, chapter two, verse eleven: 'Let the woman learn in silence with all subjection.' "

But I'm la-la-la-ing too loudly for her to hear herself think, and so she finally stands and stomps out of the room. She does not slam the door, but I hear her on the other side trying to control her desire to shoot me and have done with it.

I yank futilely at the ropes attached to the wrist cuffs, as I've done a hundred times before, hoping that the screws in the ringbolts will tear out, but there is no give. Lying still and concentrating, I try to count up hours or days since I've been taken. But I have no idea how many of those hours have been spent unconscious; I could have been tied up and on my back for a week. My Eve Clock, the internal clock my mother said all women have, is near to useless next to all the drugs pumped into my system. If I had to guess, I would say that it's been several days since I was taken to the Roy house.

The house is mostly silent. A few creaks of floorboards when someone walks softly down the hall. The quiet closing of a door, the muffled, distant sound of a car driving up and cutting its engine close to my room. I've heard no planes or helicopters. No sounds of any animals or birds. No search dogs.

I hear little conversation, as though everyone outside my room speaks in whispers. No sounds of normal life or life's pursuits.

Meals are brought in, mostly sandwiches, soup, and water, prepared foods that don't require much cooking. I eat only enough to stay alive, but as Evangeline does not now test the food prior to my consumption, I don't know if it's drugged. By the way I have to fight constant drowsiness, though, I suspect that the egg salad swimming in Miracle Whip is loaded with enough tranq to stun an elephant.

I have a new nurse, Connie. Brenda has fled for the hills. Connie is younger, fit, and, judging from her glassy-eyed lack of empathy over my condition as well as her alacrity at doing Evangeline's bidding, she's swallowed the Corinthians Kool-Aid. She changes my bandages and cleans the incisions without answering any of my questions, taunts, or threats. The only reaction I get from her is when I describe in detail the intimate day-to-day love life of the female inmates in Gatesville prison, where she may end up when the Feds bust down the doors to rescue me.

"That's disgusting," she tells me, her mouth twisted in revulsion as she gathers up her empty gauze wrappers and ointments.

"You better acquire a taste for it, Nurse Connie, if you're going to survive doing hard time."

She calls in Tommy to release the restraints. It's been explained to me by Evangeline that daily I'll get three "free" periods to move around the room. Once I've shown "adequate cooperation," I'll be given more privileges, allowed to forgo the restraints altogether.

I watch Connie watching the elder Roy brother as he takes command of the close quarters of the room, undoing the wrist cuffs. It's evident that Nurse Connie has a biblical-size crush on Tommy Boy, something that I might be able to use at some point, as either a deflection or a prod. Maybe I'll tell her exactly how *our Tommy* likes to play with knives around attractive young women.

When I'm released, they both leave and I know I have only a short while to do what I need to do before the door is opened and I'm restrained again.

Careful not to become tangled in or pull on the leg chain, I slowly move to the far side of the bed and sit at the mattress edge, letting the pounding dizziness in my head subside. There's still a thin wrap of gauze, closed with surgical tape, around the ankle, which shows seepage from the incisions, and I gently rub at the tender area around the wounds. The pain is now only moderate when I'm not moving—a deep, dull ache that feels as though the marrow is slowly draining from the bone—but any movement of the leg, specifically a contraction of the calf muscle, sends electric shocks along the nerves from the Achilles tendon to the bottom of my heel. The entire ankle is swollen and warm to the touch, and I'm worried that an infection may be festering.

I take a deep breath and stand up. The leg begins to cramp immediately and I brace myself against the wall, biting down on my lip, trying to control the agonized pumping of my ribs. I relax the calf by lifting the heel off the floor, toe pointing downward, and the painful pressure is relieved. The only way I'm going to be able to walk is by hopping along alternately on my right toes. If I'm unable to stretch the calf muscle, it will very quickly shorten and atrophy. I don't let myself think about the permanent damage that may already have been done to the tendon itself or to the heel attachment that, once torn away, might never fuse perfectly back to the bone.

I've been told by my new nurse that I'll need to start walking so that I don't lose large-muscle strength. But even though I told her to kiss my perfect Yankee ass, I know that I need to build up my strength to make any escape possible.

I bend down carefully and try to pick up the stone. Immediately, I right myself again, my face pressed hard against the wall, rubber-lipped, a black hole threatening to engulf my entire head. When my vision clears, I end up easing myself onto the floor and, by pulling the stone after me, crawl a few feet to the near corner of the room.

The carpet is old and thin, almost curling away from the walls, with cheap quarter-round molding that's chipped and bowed in many sections. The room is dark, even with the light on, and any disturbance of the molding will, hopefully, be hard to spot. I hook my fingers into a space and gently pull. There is a cracking noise and I freeze, but I hear nothing outside the door. I dig in deeper with my nails, and a section of the molding separates and pulls easily from the wall. I set it aside and tug up the corner of the rug and the underpad, exposing the anchoring tack strips. I'm looking for anything, a paper clip, a long nail, anything sharp, but I see nothing other than the carpet tacks. I tug at the tack strip, but it's glued to the floor. I tamp down the padding and the carpet, replace the strip of molding. It gaps noticeably from the wall, so I pull one of the adhesive strips from my gauze bandage, make a loop, sticky-side out, and use it to close the gap. The adhesive may not hold long, but it's the best I can do.

I crawl along the wall to the next corner, passing the floor heating vent. The vent grating is large and old, the metal rusted, but when I tug at it, it doesn't budge. The two screws are not tightly fitted, but I can't unscrew them with just my fingers. So I move on.

The next corner also yields nothing, only the hard kernels of mouse droppings below the carpet and some dust balls. Fortunately, the molding fits tightly back onto the wall.

By my reckoning, fifteen minutes has passed, and I need to work faster if I'm going to examine every corner of the room. I begin to crawl rapidly, only to be pulled up short when the embedded hobble is yanked by the unyielding stone behind me. I'd forgotten to pull the chain along with me. I mouth a silent scream and wait for the pain in my leg to subside.

Stupid, stupid bitch, I think, grinding my teeth in frustration. The drugs are making my mind slow and unclear, but until I find a way to sever the chain, I have to think of the stone as another appendage.

At the fourth corner, the molding breaks off into several fractured pieces, and under the carpet I find one thin, discolored dime. With shaking hands, I drop the dime into my underwear and try to reassemble the pieces against the carpet's edge.

I'm pressing the last piece into place when the door opens. I'm in the corner of the room on the far side of the mattress, my back to the door, my body shielding the damage I've done. I make retching noises as though I'm sick to my stomach, and I hear Tommy yell to Connie to bring in a pan.

Scooting backward onto the bed, careful to pull the stone with me, I gag harder, trying to get Tommy's attention away from the floor and onto me.

"It's the drugs," I say, letting drool leak onto my hand cupped under my mouth. "They're making me really sick."

Connie rushes into the room, bedpan in hand, and shoves it at me.

"Don't you get sick on the mattress," she warns.

I try to will myself to throw up into the pan, but there's not enough in my stomach to comply.

Out of the corner of my eye, I see Tommy turn away from the bed, study the corner of the room where I had been sitting. With the toe of his boot he taps at the carpet, then brushes it along the molding, which crumbles away from the wall like week-old bread. He looks at me and he knows in that moment that I've been up to something.

"What's this?" he asks, pointing to the corner.

I set the bedpan down onto the mattress and meet his gaze. "I'm building a bridge to Babylon," I say. "I was also going to fashion a crossbow, but I ran out of catgut."

There is a narrowing of the eyes, but he leaves the room, only to return a few minutes later with Evangeline. He shows her the molding, and she kicks at the next corner, revealing the surgical tape that had been used to hide the fruits of my probing fingers.

Shaking her head, she says, "Rebellion."

"What? No long-winded Bible verse for bad carpentry?" I ask her, crossing my arms.

They all leave the room, locking the door behind them, but soon both Tommy and Curtis return to the room with Connie following. My arms are pinioned and I'm injected with some kind of narcotic. I remain barely conscious, unable to fight as I'm lifted from the bed by Curtis, Tommy picking up the stone effortlessly and carrying it cradled in his arms.

I'm brought into the room with the Saint Michael's painting and tied into a chair facing it; the stone is settled roughly in my lap. The single, large window is dark behind the gauzy curtains, the overhead light more yellow, and perhaps brighter, than I remember. Or maybe it's that any light outside of my cave seems more luminous now.

Evangeline stands in front of me, the red-haired angel behind her, positioned so that his sword looks to be piercing the top of her head.

I smile at her and say, drunkenly, "Oh, goody, a family reunion. Or is this an East Texas wedding?"

There is an ugly stretch of her lips, but it's not a true smile. She recites, "'Because you did not serve the Lord your God with joyfulness and gladness of heart, because of the abundance of all things, therefore, you shall serve your enemies whom the Lord will send against you, in hunger and thirst, in nakedness, and lacking everything. And he will put a yoke of iron on your neck until he has destroyed you.'"

She pulls something out of the deep pocket in her skirt, the same skirt she wore the last time she jabbed me with a hypodermic needle. It's a pair of scissors, the blades long and pointed.

She directs Curtis to hold my head and brings the blades close to my face. "Hold still now, Elizabeth," she tells me. "You don't want me to put out an eye."

Pulling up a long, thick hank of my hair falling over one shoulder, she nestles the scissors close to my scalp and, with a slow, deliberate snick, cuts the hair, letting it fall onto my lap. It lies over the stone in a continuous, serpentine twist, and I remember seeing the piece of hair hacked from Lana's scalp gently resting in Jackie's hand.

She picks up another hank of hair, waiting until my bulging eyes meet hers. She says, "Elizabeth, the time has come for you to decide."

Another length of hair is cut and falls to the floor next to the chair.

"With your rebellion, you've lost two earthly things that hold great importance for you."

A slow, deliberate closing of the blades, and a longer section is cut free from the crown of my head.

"Your ability to run," she says, "and now your beautiful red hair."

The blades are opening and closing rapidly, and she's recklessly scissoring handfuls of my remaining hair, some of which cling obscenely to the wool of Evangeline's skirt. The air feels colder now, raking across my scalp, the back of my neck.

"Eventually, with time," she tells me, "and with your co-operation, your hair will grow back. And even the hobble can be removed if"—and here she holds the blades close to one eye—"if you obey my rules. If you don't, what you will lose next cannot be replaced. Your family, your friends, your partner, perhaps…"

She leaves the last few words hanging in the air. I want to lunge at her, to hurl the stone at her head so that it'll cave in like a rotten pumpkin, but I'm bound too tightly to the chair. My head lolls forward and I feel myself falling away.

I'm picked up and carried back to my room. The stone is settled next to the bed. The sheet is pulled up over me; the door is closed and locked.

And then the light is extinguished.

34

The street outside the John Oravecz Child Care Center in Greenpoint, Brooklyn, is still rain wet and tropically warm. I run my already grimy hands up and down the vertical iron window guards, which resemble medieval halberds with wicked flared points, keenly aware of the disapproving looks from the nun standing in the main doorway behind me. I'm not sure why the up-and-down movements of my hands are disturbing to her, only that they are, so I continue the stroking motions more rapidly until she hisses at me to get my attention and gives me a warning glare.

When I turn my focus again to the end of Java Street, I see him. He walks toward me like there is no earthly barrier that could delay his progress. As I had hoped, he's wearing his dress uniform, complete with hat, even though it's June and well above eighty degrees, but he promised that he would.

There are few people on the street that afternoon, but

the pedestrians who do pass him smile and say hello, giving him a wider space on the sidewalk. He greets the nun warmly and asks about her mother, and she glows as if the pontiff himself is inquiring. Then he turns his attention to me.

He kneels down so I can throw my arms around his neck, and I take in the heady aroma of tobacco, Old Spice cologne, and, because it's beyond the a.m. of the day, the lingering ghost of Jameson Irish.

He asks me, "Are you ready?"

"Yes," I breathe excitedly, gratefully.

He takes my blackened palm in his, and, after waving good-bye to the nun, we walk together down Java Street to Manhattan Avenue, where we turn south and negotiate the six blocks of low houses, shops, and apartment buildings, their facades covered in dancing graffiti, to Meserole Street and the Ninety-Fourth Precinct station house. He asks me how it feels to be six and if I'm hungry and should we stop into Rizzio's Pizza Parlor to get a slice? I bounce on my toes, nodding dizzily, and he orders the slices, saying, as he always does, "Give us extra cheese and sauce, but hold the attitude."

As we eat our pizza, first folding the dough vertically in half and draining the river of grease onto a napkin, I haltingly read to Benny the day's date and headline from the *New York Times* someone left on a neighboring table—"June twenty-eighth, 1984. Jack...son says Cuba offers to free twenty-six de...tained as pol...i...ti...cal prisoners"—showing him how well I'm progressing at summer reading camp.

The man behind the counter does not take money from my uncle when we leave, saying it's his birthday gift to Sergeant Rhyzyk's favorite niece. And Benny smiles at me as we leave the shop, knowing the man would never take money from him anyway.

We pass kids sitting on stoops, wearing tight pants, with wild, rainbow-dyed hair who are playing music loudly from a boom box.

I shriek delightedly, telling Benny, "It's the Police. Get it? The band is called the Police."

When we get to the Ninety-Fourth, Benny pauses outside for dramatic effect. It's the first time I've been allowed into the station house. We walk through the double doors and the two police officers at the big receiving desk wave and call out, *"Sto lat,"* the traditional Polish birthday greeting meaning "one hundred years."

The gray-green walls, the warren of booking and interview rooms, the messy, barely contained chaos of the other officers' desks, my uncle's office with his big desk levered impossibly into the tiny space, all fill me with something akin to religious awe. The exhilaration of Dorothy stepping from drabness into the stridently colored and surreal world of Oz. There are two photos on my uncle's desk: one of me and my brother and one of his wife, dead for four years.

Officers stick their heads in to talk to their sergeant, congratulating him on his arrest of the man responsible for the shooting of two women and eight children last spring and discussing the progress, or lack thereof, of the Mets. My hair is ruffled, I'm called Annie, which I loathe, and asked if I've seen the new summer movies, like *Police Academy*. Officer Fitzgerald, a giant bear of a man feared by every truant kid in the borough, brings in sweets from the Rzeszowska Bakery. He pinches my cheek hard enough to draw tears and wishes me a happy birthday.

Not one officer asks after my father, who also works the Ninety-Fourth. They don't have to tell me that he's been suspended from the force pending an investigation of the savage beating and subsequent death of a robbery suspect he arrested. My father is at home now, biding his time, but confident that he'll soon be reinstated, for not a single brother officer in his department has stepped forward to give anything other than a sterling account of his behavior during the incident. These same officers come by our house late at night and cloister themselves in my father's study, looks of wary self-preservation stamped onto their sweaty, worried faces, but that's a world apart from the easy, trusting camaraderie they share with my uncle here.

Benny tells me he has one more important surprise for me before he takes me home.

We pass through the station doors and walk to the nearby YMCA, where I wonder if my uncle has another grand scheme planned, like a surprise party inside. But he stops at a pay phone and tells me to hold out my hand. He places into my damp palm a dime and tells me that this one thin coin is the most powerful connector on the planet.

"It's true," he assures me, smiling at my puzzled face. "With a dime, a soldier at Christmastime, his arms full of presents, can call his family in the Bronx and tell them he's just arrived at Penn Station and is about to get on the subway. A man can call his wife to ask her what kind of bread he was supposed to buy at the market. A kid can call his mom to ask her if he can hang out just ten more minutes with his hooligan friends.

"All over this country, people can stand in one place and speak to someone else who's miles away. Hear their voice and the sounds that surround them *in that moment.* A snitch can drop a dime on someone—call the station house from Lower Manhattan, ask for me, and give me information I need to catch a very bad criminal. We can take the bad

guy off the streets and put him in jail, making Franklin or
Greenpoint Avenue a whole lot safer to walk on at night.

"But tomorrow," he says, bending down so that he's eye
level with me, "that all changes." He pulls a quarter out of
his pocket. "Tomorrow, Friday, June twenty-ninth, you'll
need one of these to call your mom."

Benny's not smiling now. His brown eyes have a wistful,
sad quality to them, and I want to assure him that it's not
so bad. That there are quarters enough to make all the calls
in the world. But somehow his explanation has imbued the
dime with a whole history that I know nothing about, can
never know, because it's all passing away.

As if reading my thoughts, he says, "It just doesn't
sound the same to say 'drop a quarter' on someone,
does it?"

I shake my head, wanting to throw my arms around his
neck or make a silly face to get him to smile again. He
stands, pulling away from me slightly, and the gulf between
us is more than just feet and inches; it's years of experienc-
ing loss and disappointments. And the thought of adding to
his disappointments is unbearable and so when he asks me
if I want to make one last dime call, I grin and nod with
absurd enthusiasm, and he lifts me up so that I can take the
heavy receiver in one hand and drop the dime into the slot
with the other. He sets me down and starts pressing the key-
pad numbers. It seems as though the sequence of numbers
is very long, and they beep in my ear like robotic insects,
but when he's finished, I hear the distant ringing of a phone.

It rings for a long time and when I turn to look quizzically at Benny, to ask him who I'm calling, there's no one
standing behind me. I wheel around to scan the street in the
opposite direction, the receiver still in hand with its thick
umbilical cable anchoring me to the box, thinking that he

had seen a friend or fellow officer and moved away to talk to him. But he's not on the sidewalk in either direction or in the street behind me or on the stoops of the town houses next to the Y. In fact, there's no one on the streets. No pedestrians, no cyclists, no pigeons pecking the ground at my feet.

That's when I notice that there are no cars parked on the street either; it's as though I've wandered onto an abandoned movie set, a staged copy of a Brooklyn neighborhood.

The ringing in my ear has stopped, and a voice at the other end says, "Betty?"

"Uncle Benny?" I wail fearfully, my heart thrashing against my ribs.

"Betty," he says, "we have only a few minutes before the operator comes on to disconnect us. Are you listening?"

"Yes," I say, my mouth an open cave of distress.

"You know how I got that guy to admit to killing those women and children?" he asks.

"No," I answer, my eyes scanning the streets for any shadows moving across the pavement. I look down and see that I'm bare-legged, standing with no shoes on the glass-strewn, filthy streets of Brooklyn.

"I got him to think I cared about him," he tells me.

Even though it's summer, I'm feeling chilled, and, with a rush of shame, I realize that I'm wearing only a T-shirt and underwear. I wrap one arm across my chest in an agony of embarrassment, but I can't let the connection with Benny go.

"You got him to sympathize with you?" I offer, surprised at the deep tone of my voice.

"No, no," Benny says impatiently. "He didn't give a damn about me. It's not about eliciting sympathy *from* her. It's about getting her to believe that you feel empathy *for* her."

Her—why is Benny saying "her" when it was a guy who was the murderer?

"I don't—" I start.

"Just listen," he says impatiently. "You're taking the wrong tack with her. You can't outlast her or buy time being a hard-ass. Be the apologetic, obedient daughter she's looking for. Make her your mother."

"My what?"

A cheery female voice comes onto the line. "You have thirty seconds before the call is disconnected. Please deposit another ten cents."

"Betty," Benny says, his voice vibrating as though he's standing in front of a large oscillating fan. "Do you understand what I'm telling you? She's full-blown gonzo, but she's a mother. Make her think you care. Get her to let down her guard, then make your move."

I'm desperately searching the ground for loose change, another dime to slide into the slot, but there's nothing, not even a wad of gum on the concrete.

"Don't get stuck in the abyss of your own morass," he reminds me.

I'm unashamedly crying now, gripping the receiver hard, jamming it against my ear to catch the last of his receding voice.

"And, Betty," he says from far away, laughter playing on the edge of his breath, "dimes arc also good on slightly loose screws..."

"I'm sorry. Your time is up," the female voice intones, and the line goes dead.

35

My sub-mission. Not *submission,* the act of yielding to a superior force as the message on the stone commands, but rather an underground, covert plotting to redirect the flow of events. A basement insurrection, where the long knives of vengeance are sharpened quietly, patiently in darkened corners while Evangeline spins out her Old Testament revelations, verbal tapestries of such monstrous proportions that they would make even sleeping infants cry and feral dogs slink away in terror.

Evangeline has spent several days—or what I think are several days, based on the sporadic periods of eating, fitful sleeping, and staggering painfully around my windowless prison room carrying a large, smooth rock in my arms—reading the Bible to me at mealtimes. None of this "Forgive thine enemy" New Testament stuff either but Bronze Age, patriarchal, split-your-skull-open threats to the little, nonbelieving peoples of the earth. The righteous slaughter of babes in arms, the crushing of whole tribes, and natural disasters to drown the world are all served up by my hostess along with breakfast, lunch, and dinner. Her enthusiasm for Armageddon is endless. And standing behind her as she sits in a chair and reads to me is Curtis in his police uniform, holding the cattle prod.

He can't be a true, active-duty cop, as he appears at her beck and call morning and night, but the uniformed presence must come in handy in helping her to tear down the material world—as in ambushing and kidnapping real-life law enforcement officers.

Tommy has disappeared from the house, and the only clue I have to his whereabouts is a fragment of conversation caught when Evangeline walked into my room with Curtis following behind, saying, "…finishes his run over to Shreveport."

She held up a cautioning hand to silence him, but I pretended not to hear. Lately I've been hanging my head in slack-jawed, passive apathy, a defeated slumping of my shoulders, my hands over my eyes.

Sub-mission.

I've taken Benny's dream warnings to heart and listened patiently to the pattern of Evangeline's ranting, rarely speaking, not moving in a confrontational way, embodying a blank, receptive canvas for her to paint upon. I'm lying in wait for an opening to pretend an attentiveness or sympathy for her psychotic beliefs and then thrust in the proverbial sword of the infidel. As with the instructor at the police academy, I want her to think that I am weakening, am down for the count, before seizing my chance and, hopefully, strangling every ounce of life out of her with my leg chain.

Don't get stuck in the abyss of your own morass, Benny

had reminded me. *Pretend* to be defeated, just don't *actually* be.

But there's a new urgency now in trying to escape. The leg wound has become infected. The incisions are two seeping, red gashes behind my ankle, swollen and painful to the touch. The slightest tug on the embedded hobble is like a burning torch being plunged into the tendons. My entire lower leg is warm, and I've got a low-grade fever. The nurse, Connie, has started me on what she says are antibiotics, but there's been no lessening of the infection. Walking is becoming increasingly more difficult because of leg cramps, spasms so severe that they send me flailing onto the ground, clutching at my calf muscles with clawlike fingers, grinding my teeth to keep from agonized screaming. When I don't move, the cramps subside. But if I don't move, I'll truly weaken and won't be able to walk at all.

In the past few days I've discovered that the house is not where Evangeline sleeps. My ears have become attuned to the subtle sounds of doors opening and closing—the main door heavier, with more heft than the inside doors—of car engines advancing and retreating, of voices appearing and disappearing. Connie and Evangeline take shifts. Within a few hours of Evangeline leaving, Connie is there to check on me. The one constant in the house seems to be Curtis.

"'When he raises himself up,'" Evangeline reads on, "'the mighty fear; because of the crashing, they are bewildered...'"

Without looking directly at Curtis, I know for certain that he's staring at me. Tommy may have shown no interest as yet in his future bride, but little brother is another thing altogether.

Curtis wants what's intended for another. I've encountered men like him before. It's the shackles that give him the hard-on, not the woman. For a guy like that, dominance is the key to bliss. If I'm not able to con Evangeline quickly enough, then maybe I can manipulate her younger son.

And as subtly as I can, I'm giving him a glimpse of paradise. As I sit in bed with my back against the wall, the sheet fallen away from my legs, I let my T-shirt fall down over one shoulder, exposing the top of one breast; my nipples through the thin fabric are hard as two inverted upholstery tacks. My legs are bent, drawn toward my chest, and I spread my knees slightly, as though too weary to keep them together, giving him a straight shot at the V in my underwear.

I sigh and groan, and Evangeline asks me what's wrong. I tell her in my most pathetic voice that I'm ready for something for the pain. Any entreaties to see a doctor or be taken to the hospital I know will be denied.

Until now, I've refused narcotics by mouth, but I want them to think I'm on a downward spiral. For the briefest instant my eyes meet Curtis's gaze, and I look away, like a frightened deer, as though terrified. If today goes the way of yesterday, Evangeline will finish her reading, leave my room, and whisper some last-minute instructions to her son. Then the door to the outside world will open and close again. The heavy rumbling of a large vehicle, an SUV or truck, will start up and drive away.

And I'll be left alone in the house with Curtis until the nurse returns for the pre-dinner checkup. In the afternoon hours I'm supposed to limp around the bed "exercising," hours that will be interrupted by the hatch in the door opening at odd intervals so that Curtis can spy on me.

Today will be different, though. I feel it. I can almost smell the animal intent coming off him in waves, the son who covets his older brother's baby incubator.

Evangeline leaves the room and then returns and hands me a pill and a glass of water. I sit up, letting both knees fall open for Curtis's benefit. I take the pill and down it. A little hydrocodone won't incapacitate me and will allow me to endure the pain of having to move decisively. I'm going to need a buffer for whatever pain in whatever form is going to be inflicted on me.

I whisper something unintelligible, clear my throat, and say to her, "Thank you for your kindness. I'm sorry I've been so much trouble."

Be the apologetic, obedient daughter, Benny told me.

I raise my beseeching gaze to her, my eyes opened wide and vulnerable, lower lip trembling. Evangeline lays a hand briefly on the top of my head and smiles radiantly, benignly. The Madonna of Rock Crystal Meth. Our Lady of Loony Tunes.

She covers me efficiently with the sheet, and I catch a glimpse of Curtis's head following the movement of my pale and vulnerable thighs.

I glance at him, my face conveying *Please don't hurt me.* But the gray matter behind my eyes is screaming, *Come on, fuckface. Come and get you some of this. I have something for you.*

Evangeline continues reading, " 'The sword that reaches him cannot avail, nor the spear, the dart or the javelin. He regards iron as straw, bronze as rotten wood. The arrow cannot make him flee.' " She closes her Bible.

"Finish your lunch, Elizabeth," she tells me. "It will build up your strength. Then rest. Connie will give you more medicine later for your leg." She stands at the foot of the bed, smiling with expectant pleasure. "Tommy will be back tonight. He'll want to spend some time with you."

I bet he will, I think, but I duck my head modestly, as though I'm actually shy about the prospect of being raped. Twice, if Curtis has his way.

"I'll have Connie help you get cleaned up," she says, and I give her a barely perceptible nod. "You know, Elizabeth, with your continued cooperation, you'll get a bigger room. A warm shower. A better blanket. Even a place to walk outside. Do you understand?"

An intake of air, another nod from me. *Such a good girl.*

"Do you want the restraints on?" Curtis asks her.

Evangeline regards me for a moment, taking in my pathetic form, weighing and assessing my demeanor. "No," she tells him. "I think we can leave them off for a time. I believe Elizabeth is gaining some acceptance."

When she leaves the room, Curtis follows after her, but he catches my eye and grins at me, the tight, mirthless stretching of lips of the SS officer who's taking a cigarette break before continuing the torture.

My heart rate has accelerated enough to make me feel light-headed, the first welcome, spreading warmth of the pain meds radiating from my gut to my arms and legs, exaggerating the effect. I slow my breathing, willing my shoulders to relax, acutely aware that, although the room is cool, a scrim of oily sweat has erupted on my forehead and chest.

She didn't put on the restraints. My hands and arms are free.

I check to make sure the hatch in the door is shut and then reach down under the elastic band of my underwear. My fingers close around the dime I had found under the carpet. One slender little coin. That powerful connector that Benny spoke of in my dream. His reminder that dimes could be used on slightly loose screws had confused me;

at first it seemed a random spark in an otherwise cohesive imagining, but then I recalled, like a nail gun to the head, the metal grate covering the heating vent. The rusted grate secured with two long screws. Screws that I couldn't budge with my fingers alone but that I did manage to remove earlier this morning using the edge of the dime. It gave me just enough torque to begin the rusty unwinding. The dime is now pitted and slightly bent, but it did the job.

Below the grate was a shallow well space angling down to the heating ductwork. And into this space had been swept, in preparation for the carpet to be laid, I assumed, floor debris. Some small, bent nails, dust bunnies, and the remnants of a shattered overhead light cover. Long, wicked shards of frosted glass.

I had gathered up several of the thickest, pointiest pieces and slipped them between the mattress and the box spring. Then I quickly put the grate back over the well and refitted the screws.

Curtis, I know, will be returning and I want to be ready for him. I pull the shards of glass out from under the mattress and slide them under the pillow for easier access. Soon there is the rattling of the door being unlocked and Curtis slips into the room, cattle prod in hand.

He stands watching me for a few moments, then tosses me one of the wrist restraints, still attached by rope to the ringbolt.

"Put this one on," he tells me.

My throat closes, and I struggle to keep my face neutral.

"You won't need those," I say. "I'm not going to fight you."

He shakes his head. "I know you're not. Put that on."

I need my hands free to reach for the glass shards.

"I won't...I won't resist," I plead, pulling the sheet

away to expose my legs, willing him to believe that he can take me without a struggle.

But he raises the prod and I know that more begging will not sway him. I'll have to wait for another opportunity.

I buckle on the right cuff and he moves to my left side to restrain the other wrist.

He sits on the mattress as he secures the restraint.

"If you kick me," he tells me, "I'll use the prod on you till your heart stops."

Curtis then stands next to the mattress and begins to un-button his shirt. "If you bite me, I'll hurt you in ways you'll never forget."

When he gets all the buttons undone, he reaches down to pinch one of my nipples hard. The sensation is a sharp ladder of pain from breast to temples, flooding my eyes with tears.

"You can scream all you want, though," he tells me, grinning.

A knock at the door startles him, and he straightens almost comically.

"Who is it?" he yells.

Another knock. "Goddamn it," he swears, feverishly buttoning his shirt again. "Just a minute," he calls out impatiently.

When all the buttons are fastened, he walks briskly to the door, opens it, steps outside, and closes it behind him. There is the sound of a female voice, and the door opens again.

"Nurse is coming," Curtis tells me. But it's not Connie, it's Brenda, her two eyes blackened from the broken nose I gave her. She comes into the room carrying a large basin of water and a washcloth and towel folded over one arm.

"You're here early," he says to Brenda, arms crossed over his chest.

"I'm here to clean you up," she tells me, ignoring Curtis. She looks surly, still angry over my attack on her. Her movements bristle with resentment.

Brenda thumps the basin down on the floor next to the mattress, hard enough to spill water over the edge.

"Where's Connie?" Curtis asks.

"You think I know?" Brenda snaps. "She's not here and I am." She begins dipping the washcloth into the basin and wringing out the excess water.

"It'll help if you undo these straps," she tells Curtis, her voice strident. "I'm not washin' the nasty bits. She's got to do that."

"That's not going to happen," he says.

Brenda is running the washcloth roughly down my right leg, the water barely tepid. She points to the incision behind my ankle. "That looks bad. I'm going to need some ice for the swelling."

When he doesn't move to leave she raises her head in annoyance. "Would you please just go get me some ice in a bag? There's some in the big meat freezers in the far car park."

Curtis looks at her for a moment like he's going to challenge her, but then she says the magic words. "Evangeline is not going to be happy if this leg gets any worse."

With an exasperated breath, he leaves, taking the prod and closing the door behind him.

Brenda immediately drops the washcloth and crosses rapidly to the door, puts an ear to the wood and listens for an instant. The skin below her eyes is puffy, a purplish gray, forehead shiny with sweat, her nose grossly swollen. Her hair looks greasy and uncombed, her naked, frowning mouth like an unhappy baby's. But there is a barely suppressed tension to her movements, and her breathing's rapid. She turns to look at me, reaches into a pocket of her nurse's tunic, and pulls out a small pistol. The barrel points at me like a black, accusing finger.

I jerk away defensively, a sudden demented vision of my body being shoved into one of the large freezers—where El Gitano's headless body was kept?—but she sits next to me on the mattress, setting the gun, like an offering, on the bed. Then she begins to undo one of the wrist restraints.

"I didn't do that to your leg," she tells me, wiping at her forehead with the back of one hand. She's not crying but her eyes are veined with red. "Evangeline did it. I just gave you the deep sedation. I didn't know they were going to do that to you."

She stands and moves to the other side of the mattress, releases the other restraint with shaking hands.

"This has gone too far," she says. "Too many people have been hurt."

I sit up quickly, grabbing the gun. The pistol grip feels like a warm handshake.

"Give me your phone," I say, holding out my hand.

She shakes her head. "There's a guard posted twenty-four/seven at the front gate, down the road about a half a mile away. He takes all our cell phones while we're at the house. They use portable radios. That's how they talk to one another.

"I want you to kill Curtis Roy," she tells me. Her eyes, narrowed to two slits, meet mine. "If he's arrested, she'll just get him out again. He raped me, just like he will you. He deserves to die. I just can't do it myself."

I want to ask her what the plan is after I kill Curtis, but I hear the outer door to the house opening and then closing again, hard. Curtis will be back in the room in a few moments. My mouth is dry and rancid, like the bottom of a birdcage, my head filled with loose grains of sand. The leg chain rattles as I reposition myself.

Brenda stands up, throws herself back against the far wall. She looks at me, terrified. "Just don't forget that I was the one who helped you," she whispers.

The door opens and Curtis comes fully into the room before his brain registers that I'm out of the restraints, on my knees on the bed, pointing a pistol at his head.

"Get down!" I yell. "Or I split your skull wide open."

He looks from me to Brenda. He drops the bag of ice to the floor. Then he charges me. I squeeze the trigger, and no explosion. There is no round in the chamber, and before I can rack it, he's tackled me. He's over me, a grain thresher of churning hands and arms. I flail desperately against him, but one of his fists connects with the side of my head. The gun is twisted viciously out of my hands and into his. The butt of the gun is smashed into my cheekbone and the tiny, dim galaxy of the overhead light doubles, then doubles again.

I can hear Brenda screaming. Curtis extends an arm toward her. He's saying something, but I can't understand the words. My hands are plunging under the pillow. A searing pain as a piece of glass slices open one searching palm. The pistol fires again and again, at least half a dozen times, followed by a minute gap of silence. Curtis watches Brenda collapsing to the floor, her hands over her bleeding chest. His shirt is pulled away from his pants, exposing belly above the belt line. Both of my hands come out from beneath the pillow, each with a fistful of glass. The first hand engages in a downward arc with enough power to jam the longest deadly icicle into the tender flesh, the tip gliding into the taut muscles like a knife into a Christmas ham, stopping only when the killing tip bucks against his pelvic bone. I twist the glass and it breaks off inside him.

Curtis doubles over, screaming in pain. A sideways sweep and I deflect his gun hand, follow that with a hard, rapid palm strike up under his nose, my arm seeking to drive the cartilage into his brain. His head snaps back, but instantly he brings his head at me again, nose leaking blood, lips curled in furious pain. His eyes are open only to the promise of my slow, painful death, his chin careening toward me like a hatchet. I raise the remaining winking shard straight up, bracing it against one split and bleeding palm, and with his own forward momentum, he impales the unguarded, pulsing hollow of his throat on the glass.

Gurgling noises erupt from his mouth and he throws himself off the bed, swinging the gun frantically in the air. He lands on the floor, firing the pistol wildly, emptying the magazine into the ceiling; glass and wood chips fall like rain over my head. Within ten seconds he is lying completely still.

I'm still on my back, my breath a sharp keening wind squeezed in and out of my lungs. *Get up, get up, get up,* some unrecognizable inner voice chants, and I wipe the sweat from my face, feeling the blood from one palm coating my forehead like a mask.

I crawl off the bed, forgetting the weighted leg chain, and am brought up short with a painful tug. Panting, I crawl to Brenda, dragging the stone behind me. She's not breathing; her bruised eyes are open and vacant.

A quick check of Curtis's unmoving body proves he's gone to meet his Maker as well, blood still leaking from his neck wound onto the floor. His own gun is not on him, so it has to be elsewhere in the house. Like Brenda, he has no cell phone.

The sword that reaches him cannot avail, nor the spear, the dart or the javelin, I reflect with cold irony. But a shard of glass...

"Slings and arrows, motherfucker," I tell Curtis as I crawl past him, dragging the stone to the door.

The door is unlocked and I crack it open, listen for any sounds. Hearing nothing, I heave up the stone and stagger out into the hallway. I need to find Curtis's gun or some kind of weapon. The cattle prod is propped up against the wall so I grab it in one hand, cradling the heavy stone precariously in the other arm. My right palm where the glass has pierced is seeping blood, making my grip on the prod slippery, and it almost falls from my grasp as I shuffle to the right, toward the room where I've been taken several times to meet with Evangeline. The one with the painting of Saint Michael. I know there's a window in the room and I need to get my bearings.

I don't even try to mask the noise of my progress, the clumping rattling of the chain, the sound of the prod banging against the walls, my labored breathing and groaning like a wounded animal. Had there been anyone else in the house, he or she would have heard Brenda screaming, and shots would have been fired well before I left my prison cell.

The door to the Saint Michael's room has been left ajar, the area bright from slanting sunlight coming in through the picture window. The light makes me squint; it seems to be late afternoon. I lose my balance and fall awkwardly against the wall. The large painting of Saint Michael looms next to me. I turn toward it, the image having its own force of gravity, the swirling colors pulling me in like water down a drain, and, dropping the cattle prod, I plant a balancing hand against the canvas to steady myself. Saint

Michael gazes down at the eternal foe pinned beneath his feet, his sword held in his right hand poised to strike, the fires of hell behind him, and I see what I've never seen before. In his left hand, he's holding a chain, the length of which stretches over the back of the devil, the near end disappearing behind the angel's right leg, at ankle level.

A nerve in my calf explodes, and the muscles in my arm quiver from holding on to the stone. I close my eyes for a moment, the narcotics talking to me, telling me to sit in Evangeline's comfortable chair and wait for the End Times to come, putting a stop to the pain. When I open my streaming eyes again, the angel is looking at me, admonishing me, scolding me as only a medieval unrelenting Catholic icon can do. And I'm certain to the core of my being that if he could talk, he would be telling me, as Benny would, that there's no crying in roller derby and that winning comes only from a hard ass sliding down a long track.

When I pull my hand away from the canvas, I leave a wet, bloody palm print over the demon's balding pate.

I pick the prod up off the floor and am halfway to the window when I hear the distant rumbling sound of a large truck engine approaching. There are hedges outside the window so I have no clear view. But the truck is nearing the house. I turn back into the hallway, a clumsy careening behemoth, the weight of the stone threatening to pull me over. I limp and stagger to the other end of the hall, the muscles in my right leg knotting up. There are doors to the right and to the left, and I open each one quickly and find a kitchen, a near-empty dining room, and, finally, an interior door that opens onto a foyer fronted with a heavier wooden door with little frosted windowpanes set into the top half of it. The roaring engine is coming from that direction.

I go down the hall to the left and find another door that

opens onto a mudroom with a washer and dryer and a patio exit door made of glass. Sneakers and work boots are scattered on the floor. Coats hang on a wall rack. I jam my feet into a pair of too-big men's sneakers, grab the longest, warmest jacket and throw it over my shoulder, and open the back door.

The air is only cool, but in my weakened condition it might as well be freezing outside. My eyes are nearly shut against the light, and I hobble blindly across a tiny cement patio to a narrow lawn, limping grotesquely toward an adjacent stand of trees and shrubby brush. To the left of the house are several open carports and one enclosed metal hut, a garage or work shed, and I hide myself from view by crouching behind the trunk of a large pine tree. I crane my head around in time to see an oversize pickup truck pull into one of the carports. The engine is cut and two men get out of the cab, one of them Tommy Roy.

They open the back of the truck and begin unloading boxes and carrying them into the storage building. The bed of the truck is full, and it will take them a while to complete the unloading. I can only hope they will finish before Tommy decides to go inside. Behind me is a narrow dirt road running parallel to the house. On the far side of the road is a thick growth of trees. The beginning of a pine forest.

My lungs are burning, my thighs look fish-belly white, pimpled with chill, but I need to keep moving through the forested area to find a house or a busier paved road to get help.

I set the stone and the prod down and quickly pull on and zipper the heavy jacket. Then I tuck the prod under one arm, pick up the stone in both hands, and, bent low, creep across the road and into the trees.

36

The towering pines are spaced wide apart, but the ground is choked with shriveled pine needles, ferns, and vine runners. Tall, fibrous reeds scratch my bare ankles as I walk, catching at the links of the chain on my right leg, tugging painfully at the embedded hobble that is exposed like a dangling subway strap outside the thin bandage.

To my own ears, the crunching noises beneath my feet sound like a dinner bell for wolves. After I walk for five minutes, the ground, which had been hard-packed at first, becomes spongy from the rotted vegetable matter holding in rainwater, and the mud sucks at my feet, threatening to pull off the loosely fitting sneakers. The muscles of my back quiver as the stone becomes heavier by the yard.

The trees soon grow closer together, separated by only a few feet. There is no clear path; it is wild, undeveloped land without even a deer track to follow. I'm vaguely aware of the sun just beginning to set behind me, a reddish tinge marking the bark of the tops of the trees.

I step hard into a deep depression hidden under rotting ferns, and I lose my balance. Releasing the stone, I fall forward, trying to catch myself with my hands. The rock misses crushing my feet, but I land on top of the rock, bruising my chest against it, getting the breath knocked out of me with a groaning cry. I raise myself up with both arms, the painted yellow letter *E* for Ephesians on the stone winking beneath me, and a boiling pain erupts out of my right leg. Teeth gnashing, breath rapid and shallow, I ease back into a sitting position and pull my left leg and then my right leg from the slimy depression.

The gauze has been ripped from the ankle; the incisions tore open in the fall and are bleeding freely. I wipe away, as best I can, the rotted vegetation from the wounds, and I fish out the sneaker that was pulled free from my foot and put it on. My brain skitters around the thought that if I were to examine the incision more closely, I'd be able to see light coming through from the other side. At this I lean over and vomit up everything that is left in my stomach.

Using a slender tree trunk, I pull myself, hand over hand, to my feet. I yank on the chain to bring the stone closer to me and stand for a moment, clenching my jaw, willing myself not to faint. I use the tree for balance as I pick up the stone, and then I keep moving.

Every few steps, I lean against another tree, and then another, pausing a moment and then lurching forward again. Like a demented pinball, I think. A Pine Curtain pinball.

My face, neck, and chest are slippery with sweat, as are my palms—one of them still seeping blood—which makes holding on to the stone more difficult. At one point, I lean against a massively tall pine; a loblolly, I recall from some shrouded recess in my brain. I'm grateful that at least there are no exposed roots to trip me up.

Then I realize that I've lost the cattle prod. I must have dropped it when I fell into the muddy depression.

I think how good it would be to slide down to the earth and rest with my eyes closed, my head braced against the fragrant bark, the stone settled on the ground where it belongs. It's getting darker, and I consider sleeping all night in the woods. I'd be hidden, I'd gather my strength, and then I'd press on in the morning. But simply being still for a few moments has brought on the fever chills. One night in the woods and I'd die from either thirst and exposure or the infection in my leg. I'd be found in the woods tomorrow as stiff and imposing as a Polish war memorial.

In the distance, there is a new sound, a bass rumbling. It recedes and then advances again, like a dark wave. It's Tommy Roy's truck on the move.

I glance down and see a dark, wet puddle next to my right leg. Blood from the wound has overflowed the sneaker and is pooling in the dirt. I push away from the loblolly and shuffle-walk, bending forward like an ancient crone in order to rest my elbows against my hips. My biceps feel like they've been shredded, and I can't rely on the muscles to keep the stone up against my chest anymore.

Shuffling in syncopated rhythm, the longer beat on the left foot, the right foot barely a resting break in my stride, I continue forward. If I could just get rid of the fucking stone, I think, I'd make it. It's the stone weighing me down, suffocating me, tearing at the muscles and tendons in my arms and legs. I think of how much ground I'd have eaten up only a few days ago running freely, my body whole and strong. I could run all night at an easy pace and probably be back in Dallas by morning.

The tip of a fallen branch catches at the hobble, bringing me up short again. Exasperated, I hurl the stone onto the ground, and like a miniature meteor, it throws up a shallow collar of dust. With both hands I pull at the chain in opposite directions, the metal cutting into my palms, trying to separate the links. I find a fist-size rock, place the chain over another larger stone, and pound the links with whatever strength I have remaining in my right arm. I pound until the shrill whistling noise in my throat makes me stop. There were sparks off the metal, but I can't break the chain; the rock I'm holding is not heavy enough and the ground underneath the other one is too soft.

The low rumbling of the truck vibrates through the forest from the other direction this time, as though the driver has circled back around. They're still far away, but they're looking for me, and at some point they will get out of their truck and begin to search in the trees. I've left enough signs for a blind person to track me.

Get up, you fucking baby, the internal voice screams. I need to pull myself up and keep moving forward, but the thought of even standing is too much to bear.

Get the fuck up and keep moving. Sitting here whining like a little girl. Boo-hoo-hoo, poor pitiful you. Start walking before I kick your ass so hard the Roys won't have anything left to kick.

I think of the damage done to my body. Of the reptilian, sanctimonious countenance of Evangeline Roy. The near rape by her son. The murder of Lana by her other son. Tommy Roy standing over Jackie's bed as she slept.

With a sickening jolt I realize that it's the first time in days that I've allowed myself to think of Jackie. More horrifying than any outrage, though, is the realization that, for the briefest instant, the time in which it would have taken an atom to break apart, I couldn't recollect her name. But now the name has summoned forth a flood of memories:

her body sleek and buoyant in water, her scent, the excruciating welcome of her smile.

No, no, no, no, no crying now. There's no crying in roller derby. Just get up. And walk.

On my hands and knees, I raise my head to find and grab hold of the nearest tree, and in the distance, about fifty yards in front of me, I see a dark green wall. I hoist myself up, hug the stone to my chest, and begin moving toward it.

Within twenty yards, I can make out that the green wall is a high, chain-link fence covered over and nearly obscured by choking vines and ivy. It must be a privacy fence to a residence. I've made it to a house.

I stagger down the length of it. The fence is too vast to belong to just one modest house. Behind it is either a large estate or, better yet, a residential community. Soon, I can see the tip of a tall, steeple-like structure, as on a church, looming over the top of the fence.

There is no break in the fence that I can see, and I open my mouth to call out for help. I'm dehydrated, my mouth parched, and in the time it takes to summon my voice, I look again at the church steeple. A church means a church community. Evangeline has a church community. All of those good souls she's saved through her ministry of the coming Apocalypse.

I close my eyes for a moment and listen for any sounds coming from the other side of the fence. I hear nothing, not even Tommy Roy's truck. After gasping along for another twenty yards, I find a break in the vines that reveals a gate with a length of chain holding it closed. There is a rusted lock through the links, but no one has thought to secure it. I put my eye to an opening between the gate and a fence post.

On the other side of the fence, looking like a movie set for a Western, is a small compound of old-fashioned one-

and two-story buildings with wooden porches and a few log cabins, lined up on either side of a narrow dirt road that's rutted deep with what looks to be wagon tracks. It's a pioneer reenactment village, I realize, something that's popular all over Texas, harking back to a simpler time when men were men and their women knew to keep their bonnets on and their mouths shut.

The compound, at least for now, is deserted, the storefronts neat and tidy. A large banner suspended from two poles and hanging across the main street reads KING JUBILEE HERITAGE AND HISTORICAL VILLAGE, JUNE 1 THROUGH AUGUST 31, 2013. FUN FOR THE WHOLE FAMILY!

The lock is easy to remove, but the gate squeals when I open it, causing me to freeze, my heart racing in my chest. There is no answering noise, so I ease through the gate, close it behind me, and head for the nearest building, which is the church, a boxy, whitewashed structure with a tall steeple that screams Protestant self-denial. Through one of the front-facing windows I can see a few uncomfortable-looking wooden pews and one ornate, dilapidated organ. There are neat stacks of hymnals on a table and a simple, unadorned cross affixed to the wall. But unless I wanted to hurl the enormously oversize Bible resting on the pulpit at my pursuers, there is nothing inside I can use for my protection.

The thing that ultimately keeps me from entering the church is the painted letters over the double doors, which chill me to the bone and echo the wooden plaque in Evangeline's sitting room: WELCOME HOME.

Next to the church is the one-room schoolhouse, and I can't imagine it contains anything to improve my chances of escaping the Family either. A pencil for jabbing, a ruler for the slapping of wrists. I erupt in choking, hiccupping laughter that brings on a fit of coughing, the bubbling up of terror and exhaustion. A wave of dizziness narrows my vision, and my knees begin to buckle. I struggle to stand in the middle of the narrow dirt road, the stone in my arms a monstrously weighted thing that wills me to set it down and then lower myself to the ground as well and rest awhile. I drop the rock and lie curled up on my side, using the stone as a pillow.

I hear the vibrating sound of a large vehicle somewhere beyond the pines, but I don't care. Closing my eyes, I think of my brother and how he must have felt letting the water of the Atlantic Ocean cover him. Releasing himself finally into the abyss.

"He got sucked down into the abyss of his own morass," Benny is telling me. "But you're not going to allow that to happen. I won't let you."

My brother's death has incapacitated me, has broken me. I am a raging hole of despair and anger. I have taken to my bed, stopped talking, stopped eating. I had started at the police academy, but I am done with that too.

Uncle Benny is at the door to my bedroom. I've never seen him so angry.

"Get up," he orders, yanking the blanket off my bed, the blanket I have used to cover myself for days on end.

"I've never been disappointed in you until this moment," he tells me.

The tears for my brother have dried, but now there are new tears, not of loss, but of shame. Benny looks down at me, enraged, but below his anger is the fear that he will lose me as well. I sense this as surely as I sense his untiring love for me. He reaches out his hand, and I let him pull me up from my bed.

My eyes snap open. Dust and grime cloud my vision,

but I can see, directly across the street, a wooden shack with a sign that says BLACKSMITH FORGE over the door. A blacksmith forge with metal tools. I push myself to sitting, then to standing, and when I'm certain I won't pass out, I heave up the stone and slowly, agonizingly, cross the road.

The front-door handle is merely a latch; it opens easily, and I stumble into the room, wilt into a cane chair against one wall, and allow the stone to crash to the floor. All my limbs shake uncontrollably from the collapse of my internal adrenaline pump and from fever, but the room is warm and still, and I look for the thing that will free me.

Most of the implements and iron bits resting on worktables and against the walls are archaic-looking, their functions a mystery to me. There are a few sharp pikes and one large crowbar, which might be of use. And at the far side of the room is a small anvil on a low platform, the hammer still resting on it.

Taking a steadying breath, I will myself to stand again and drag the stone by its chain to the platform. The anvil is small with a long narrow horn at one end, but the blacksmith's hammer is massive, strong enough to bend metal bars. I heave the stone onto the platform and with both arms bring my quivering right leg up so that my foot can rest on the body of the anvil, near the horn. I slip off the filthy sneaker and see that my foot is black with dried blood. After I make the high step up, all the muscles in my leg begin to cramp as though fire ants were stinging every nerve. The flesh around the gaping incisions at my ankle is swollen, a brilliant, unhealthy scarlet. I have to lower the leg for a few seconds, massaging the flesh, waiting for the cramps to subside. Grimacing in pain, I reposition my foot again on the anvil.

I press one link of the leg chain over the tip of the horn,

like slipping a ring onto a finger, and reach for the hammer. There will still be a length of chain running from the hobble, but at least the punishing, heavy end will be gone.

I grasp the hammer in one hand and try to lift it, but the weight of it coming off the anvil almost pulls me backward. I have to grab it with both hands to wield it, and the first strike, even though it hits the link, doesn't have enough power to break the chain. I exhale forcefully a few times, lift the hammer again, and strike the metal.

Nothing.

Stinging sweat pours into my eyes and into my palms and I have to wipe my hands on the jacket to dry them. I grab the handle once more. A stronger swing, a strike, and the link breaks like a cheap piece of plastic.

I remove the broken length of chain and ease my leg back down again. I allow myself exactly thirty seconds of blubbering, my head hanging over the anvil, hot tears falling and splattering on the metal like liquid mercury, the relief of ridding myself of the stone as exhilarating as stepping away from a plunging chasm.

Using one of the long iron pikes resting against the wall as a cane, I grab the crowbar and make my way cautiously back onto the street, the remaining length of chain clattering behind me.

The next building on my side of the street is the apothecary shop. I find the front door locked. It has two large plate-glass windows, one on either side of the door, but a break-in would be obvious to anyone approaching the building from the main street. I limp around to the back and find another door. It too is locked, but I jam the crowbar into the frame and within minutes I'm inside.

The exhilaration of freedom has given way to a desperate thirst, but a quick glance around the re-created nineteenth-century drugstore reveals nothing but shelves of ornate, and empty, physicians' bottles and jars, their labels for tincture of iodine and potassium bromide faded and curling. Vials of cocaine tooth drops and opium-drenched sleep remedies rest inside the large glass druggist's case. *What I wouldn't give for some laudanum drops right now,* I think. I'm tempted, for the briefest moment, to take one of the vials out of the case, but then I come to my senses. Even if there remained a trace of the drug inside one of the bottles, it would have lost its efficacy a hundred years ago.

Next to a velvet-upholstered surgical chair, a Victorian torture machine of levers and restraints, is a basin with some muslin strips, cut and folded for bandages. They're dusty, but I shake them out and wrap several of the strips tightly around my ankle. The sensation at first is almost unbearable, but soon the compression helps to dull the pain of the brutalized tendon. I tie the remaining cloth around the cut in my hand.

The next building is the printing press, front door locked. It also has a rear entrance, but long nails have been driven into the frame, securing the door. It would be futile to try and force the door open. But at the far corner of the press is a large rain barrel three-quarters full of water, a few pine needles floating at the surface. The water looks fairly clean, but I have no idea how many mosquito larvae may be floating in it, suspended until they can hatch in some warm host body. I plunge both hands into the barrel and drink from my cupped palms until I think my belly will explode. If I survive, I'll be on massive doses of antibiotics for my leg. If I don't make it, it won't matter anyway.

Wiping my dripping mouth with one sleeve, I feel the faintest vibration beneath my feet. It's a low-level throbbing that soon crescendos to a mechanical roar. The vehicle making the sound is fast approaching from the opposite end of the compound, where the main entrance lies, obscured by another vine-covered gate.

Crouching, I crane my head around the front of the building, peering down to the far end of the street, and soon hear the idling engine of a large truck on the other side of the fence. There is the slamming of truck doors and the rattling of chains against the gate.

A moving, disembodied voice, not Tommy Roy's, yells, "I'm going to check the far side. See if the gate is open at that end."

The truck's engine is turned off, and the silence allows me to hear the progress of the running man crashing along the fence as he circles it to the gate that I passed through fifteen minutes ago.

I don't know if Tommy Roy, waiting on the other side of the main entrance to the compound, has a key or a bolt cutter or just a gun to blast apart the lock, but if the other man discovers that I'm inside the enclosure, Tommy will be coming through that gate.

The next building has a shingle over the door that reads JUSTICE OF THE PEACE. I move as rapidly as I can across the narrow porch and try the door, and it opens. Once inside, I pull the latch bolt, locking the door. It's a large room containing an old rolltop desk, several small chairs, and one long coffin standing on end, open and empty. Inside it is nailed a sign reading HORSE THIEF. Next to the coffin, tacked to the wall, is a hangman's rope. A narrow staircase with a velvet rope across it leads to a shallow second-story landing, but if there were any doors there originally, they've been walled over. There is one narrow door, vented in three successive half-moon shapes, that opens to a water closet with a wooden commode fitted snugly into the space.

On the desk is an old manual typewriter and a large nineteenth-century revolver. Throwing aside the crowbar, I grab the revolver and check the cylinder, foolishly hoping to find at least one cartridge loaded, but it's empty. My brain fires off ridiculous, random scenarios: pitching the typewriter down from the landing onto my pursuer's head, bluffing my way to freedom with the empty revolver.

I hear a male voice roaring from the end of the street where the forge is. "The gate's open. I'm searching the buildings."

A moment later, I hear half a dozen gunshots twanging off metal and I know that Tommy Roy has found the solution to the locked front gate. Both men are now inside the compound.

I kneel in front of a window and watch Tommy, his pistol drawn, shoulder his way into the first building—a general store—at the opposite side of the street.

The second man calls out, "Tommy, she's been in the forge. I'm going into the apothecary's."

They're working their way down both sides of the street now, coming from opposite directions. After the apothecary store on my side of the street is the printing press, which is nailed up tight. And then the JP's.

I decide to sneak out the back of the building and stagger for the entrance as rapidly and quietly as I possibly can, hoping that Tommy has left his keys in the truck. I pick up the dragging chain, begin hobbling my way to the back exit, and see, above the door, a brace of old muskets hanging on the wall. One of the muskets has a bayonet.

I drag a chair over and haul myself up to stand on it. With a forceful tug, I free the rifle from its brackets. The bayonet is rusted but sharp, more like a narrow sword than a pike, and firmly fastened to the end of the rifle. I stumble down from the chair and risk a peek out the window again in time to see Tommy walking into one of the little log cabins across the street. He comes out right away and walks toward the neighboring cabin. I catch the faintest strain of a melody coming from him, a bitter cadenced sound, and I realize that he's loudly, and angrily, humming.

Tony Ha had heard him humming as he butchered Lana Yu. Like a man happy at his work, Tony had told me. Lana had been only a job for him, a means to get information. I've just killed his brother, and, for the first time, I begin to think that I should take precautions to end my own life rather than fall into his hands again. I look at the hangman's noose and then up at the railing across the second-story landing.

The other man is rattling hard at the doors to the printing press, and then there is the sound of his boots slamming across the porch, moving in this direction. He's coming for the front door.

There is only one place to hide. I close the water-closet door behind me just as the front door is muscled open, the broken lock splintering the frame. I hear the heavy footsteps of the man as he moves about the room. Then the sound of him mounting the stairs, even though there is nowhere for anyone to hide on the landing. His footsteps rattle down the stairs again, and I grip the rifle hard in both hands, ready to strike with the bayonet once the door flies open. But chances are he'll shoot me before I can attack.

His footsteps creak past the closet toward the back door. I can see his moving form through the half-moon vents.

A pause in the footsteps. He turns back to stand in front of the closet door, his bulk blocking the light. It's dark inside the closet, but he puts an eye against the topmost vent.

He leans his bulk against the door and says, "Gotcha."

The third vent is chest level, and, with every ounce of strength, I jam the bayonet through the half-moon opening, just below his sternum. And then, twisting the blade, I aerate his lungs.

He makes high-pitched keening noises of surprise and pain and when I finally pull the blade from his chest he collapses in front of the closet door. He's thrashing, kicking against the floorboards, trying to summon air with which to scream for help, but the vital gas leaks from his lungs and he soon stops moving.

I push against the door, but his body is blocking it. Panicked, I brace my feet against the commode, my back against the door, and, with successive tries, I get the door open just wide enough for me to squeeze through.

My breathing is loud and wheezing. I'm close to collapse, and I let myself sink to my hands and knees, panting, with black at the edges of my vision. I hear a distant voice. It's Tommy Roy calling out to his companion.

He hollers, "Checking the schoolhouse!"

And after the school, he'll search the church, and if he doesn't hear from his partner soon, he'll know something's wrong.

I pat down the dead man for his weapon, but find no gun. Not in his hand or in his belt or on the floor nearby where he might have dropped it. Ever more frantically I search the room, thinking it could have gone sliding under a piece of furniture, but find nothing.

"What kind of Texan doesn't carry a gun?" I rail at the body. "Thought you wouldn't need it hunting down a girl, didn't you?"

I stand up, kicking him in the ribs for good measure.

My only chance now is to get to the truck and hope that the keys are in the ignition. Or pray that he'll be true to his redneck nature and have several loaded hunting rifles inside the cab. Tommy is about a hundred yards away, maybe a little more than a football field's distance. Once he gets traction, he can get to me in about twelve seconds. The justice of the peace office where I'm hiding is the closest building to the main entrance. Given my injuries, it will take me half a minute, at best—if I don't stagger and fall—to make it to the gate. Another fifteen seconds to reach the truck.

I wait for him to walk out of the schoolhouse and enter the church. I throw open the door and shuffle-walk toward the gate, my feet kicking up dust like twin tornadoes. With the remaining length of leg chain in one hand, rifle in the other, I press forward, the pain a dragon with its teeth in my calf, its burning scales of acid and flint razoring the flesh from my bones.

I'm a few feet from the gate when I hear a noise far behind me. A guttural cry of discovery. I don't stop; I move faster. But the truck is too far away. The gun too heavy. A bayonet against his pistol too absurd even to contemplate.

The cry again, ragged, bounding, closer this time. He'll be on me in a few seconds. I don't want him to shoot me in the back, so I turn, alarmed to see the solid form of Tommy Roy running, looming, not with a gun in his hand but with his knife outstretched.

This is right, this is proper, that I face my attacker. My right arm is raised, the bayonet poised to slash downward like a stabbing sword, the chain held hard in my left hand, like a balancing counterweight against the storm. One savage, wounding jab from me before he severs my windpipe.

Saint Michael, protect me, I pray.

He kicks up dust with his own churning feet, and through the scrim of red Texas dirt behind him I see the shimmer of forms in motion. Figures like the ghosts of Jubilee's past.

His knife's edge is a lover's reach away, but there is an explosion, like the cracking of mighty wood, and he pulls up short, and falls facedown at my feet.

The moving figures behind him are two. Not ghosts. Not angels. But men. With guns.

I look down at Tommy Roy, unmoving on the ground.

I place one foot on his flame-colored head and grind it into the dirt.

Then I close my eyes. And I fall with him.

37

It's like the scene from *The Wizard of Oz* when Dorothy wakes up from her dream of being over the rainbow and finds, standing around her bed, the real-life versions of the Tin Man, the Cowardly Lion, and the Scarecrow. Except in this case, standing around my hospital bed are Seth Dutton, Tom Craddock, and Kevin Ryan, allowed into my room only after the nurse had given me a bump in my pain meds.

I think only to blink my eyes, but when I open them again, the three men have changed their positions in the room. The morphine is playing with my perception of time, telescoping minutes into seconds, scrubbing whole hours into a pit of amnesia.

The doctor saw me earlier in the day and gave me the sum total of the damage done to my body while in Evangeline's care: a fractured cheekbone, a badly bruised sternum, severe dehydration, multiple scratches and bruises, a deep cut in my palm requiring half a dozen stitches, and a torn

Achilles tendon that will require surgery. He saved the best for last, assuring me that they will do all they can to repair the damage. But there's no guarantee that I will ever be able to run again.

Jackie stood on one side of the bed, holding my hand, trying to look professionally detached as the doctor droned on but with a grip on my fingers that was more painful than the collection of hurts that seemed to radiate from every part of my body, converging together behind my left cheekbone, cracked like a brittle mirror by the butt of a gun.

James Earle stood on the other side of the bed glaring at the doctor, chin down, brow furrowed, as though the doctor himself were responsible for the bad news.

Jackie had not left my side through the whole of the night, sitting perched in a chair, alert to any movement I might make, hovering over the nurses like a vengeful Valkyrie, refusing even to eat until I insisted that James take her to the cafeteria. I had murmured in Jackie's ear that if I was going to be a breeding ground for emerging mosquitoes, the least she could do for me was ingest some relatively benign bacteria.

My colleagues had filed in just as Jackie and James were leaving, offering sympathetic, encouraging pats on the shoulder for Jackie, respectful handshakes and nods of professional recognition for James, the somber you're-one-of-us inclusive head bobs that one cop will give another after a particularly difficult job.

Now the four of us just stare at one another, awkward in the silence. I'm conscious enough to be aware of their sidelong gazes of pity as they take in my shorn head and bruised face, my ruined leg swathed in bandages and elevated on a pillow. Their expressions chill the room like a sudden blast of Freon. Easier to take would have been looks of disapproval that I'd been overtaken by a bunch of deranged meth dealers or disappointment that I'd not seen the threat sooner. Or even looks partially blaming me for Hoskins's death. They all know I was held prisoner, brutalized physically. But for them, the question that hangs most heavily in the air, that rests most troublingly on their faces, is, Was she sexually violated? Because no matter how closely we worked together, no matter the years, no matter the circumstances, the widest gulf in understanding for male officers to overcome would be the rape of a fellow female officer.

"You know you guys look like the Tin Man, the Cowardly Lion, and the Scarecrow, right?" I tell them, my words slurring.

They smile and relax.

Craddock points to Ryan. "He's definitely the one with the brains."

Ryan's face reddens and he grins; Seth nods in agreement and then there's oppressive quiet again.

Seth leans over the bed, his forearms resting on the handrail. "The drugs good here?"

"The best," I assure him. I smile and wince from the pain in my cheek, go to cross my arms, dangling blood pressure cuff and IV lines, over my bruised chest and wince again. I blink and when I open my eyes, the three have shifted once more, this time toward the door.

"Okay," I call out. "I give. How'd you find me? And why the fuck did it take you so long?"

I know the date—Monday, September 30—by looking at the nurses' whiteboard on the wall facing my bed. I'd left for Uncertain the Monday before, September 23. An entire week in hell.

They shuffle back into the room.

Seth stands nearest the bed. He tells me, "The Harrison County Sheriff's Office contacted us within twenty minutes of your not showing up at Caddo Lake. We couldn't reach you either but figured it was bad cell phone reception. But it was really James Earle that set the fire to the pan. He called Jackie right after talking to you on the phone, and she called us. The old man knew something wasn't right."

I struggle to stay alert while they, as briefly as possible, run down the timeline to my rescue. The sheriff's men had started searching for us as soon as they heard that we were headed toward Karnack instead of taking the more direct route to the lake. The highway patrol soon found some detour signs near the town that had not been set up by road maintenance and, on the shoulder at a country-road intersection, a place where large trucks rarely went, deep impressions of a commercial truck. Two crushed cell phones—work phones, mine and Hoskins's—were found roadside.

Ryan and Craddock drove out to the location, bringing one of the sweatshirts I'd left in my desk for the local K-9 unit. The dogs followed my scent to the field where I had run and discovered my second, personal cell phone. The phone that must have bounced out of my pocket when I was tackled by Tommy Roy.

In my befuddled mind, a question about Hoskins tries to present itself, but it swims away before I can collect it, and I sip at some ice water to stay focused.

As I had asked him to do, Ryan had followed up on the drawing of the winged tattoo and discovered close head-shot matches of two brothers the same ages as the Roys and with bright red hair attending Chowan College in Murfreesboro. One of the brothers was a track phenom.

The brothers' names were Thomas and Curt King; mother's name, Angela.

Ryan shrugs and says, "*Roi* is French for 'king.' I figured it had to be them."

"See, high-school French is not completely useless," I mutter.

Ryan had tracked the King family, two brothers and their mother, from North Carolina back to Texas. Then the trail got weak. There were several businesses in East Texas incorporated under the Angela King name, but most of them were shell companies with employees who never admitted to having seen any of the King family in person.

The image of the banner at the compound snakes across my memory: THE KING JUBILEE HERITAGE VILLAGE.

Seth reaches down and pats me on the arm. "We kept searching for you, Riz, but we were pretty certain you were gone."

He looks at Craddock as though waiting for approval to continue.

Craddock says, "It was Bob who brought us to you."

"I don't understand," I say, the drug stupor diminishing at Craddock's alarming words, the elusive question I had about Hoskins trying to resurface.

"Before he died, he was able to make a call," Seth tells me.

"That's not possible," I say, shaking my head emphatically. "He got shot in the head."

The recollection of Bob's body being slammed against mine, his blood spattering on the dashboard, makes the room tilt sickeningly.

"We know," Craddock says. "We found his body. The bastards had left it in the car, hidden in the woods, close to a junkyard. Don's Auto Parts near Lake of the Pines. In the yard were several large commercial trucks. When we searched the car, we retrieved his cell phone, pushed under the front seat."

That was the question I had wanted to ask. The whereabouts of Bob's second, personal phone.

"The phone was covered in blood," Seth continues. "His fingerprints on it. We figure...he didn't die right away; he must have been stunned at first by the shot. At some point he regained consciousness long enough to pull his phone out of his pocket and press one auto-dial button for help. The person he dialed answered the call. She knew the call was from him, but she couldn't hear anything but breathing."

"What number did he dial?" I ask.

Craddock looks down at his hands. "His daughter's."

I lick my lips and glance away, swallowing back tears that, once started, will be impossible to stop.

Seth clears his throat gently and continues. "He must have then shoved the phone under the seat. It allowed us to track his location. It didn't look good for you being alive, but since we didn't have a body yet, we bided our time."

We didn't have a body yet, Seth had said, and I realize that he was talking of looking for me, my lifeless corpse. Bob, stunned and probably terrified, almost dead, had made one last, herculean effort to reach out to the living.

Seth is looking at me, concerned. I give him a nod to continue.

"We tapped the junker's phone and knew right away he was in touch with the Roys. And we knew from conversations they were holding a female cop. We watched him for days before he finally led us to the Roy house. The hardest thing I've ever had to do in my years of law enforcement was leave Bob's body in that car."

I feel the drug trying to drag me into sleep, but when Seth tells me they'll come back tomorrow with the rest of the story I take hold of his arm and croak, "The hell you will. Finish it."

A battery of local officers, Texas Rangers and four federal agents, followed the junker to a gate at a dirt road leading to the house, where a brief exchange of fire took place with two armed guards. The three of them, the junker and the two guards, were killed almost immediately by the Ranger snipers and the house at the end of the road was breached.

Seth says, "I don't have to tell you what we found in the house. A woman and Curtis Roy dead. And that's a story we all want to hear when you're stronger."

"How did you know to find me at the village?"

Craddock smiles sadly and says, "Well, it wasn't hard. You bled like a wounded water buffalo through the whole house, across the yard, and into the woods."

Ryan says, "Craddock and I followed your tracks through the trees while the rest of the force drove the length of the dirt road behind the house, hoping to find you on the far side of the property. We heard several shots fired, and we took off running in that direction. And for ten minutes we ran. I had a hell of a time keeping up with Daniel Boone here."

"Daniel Boone, my ass," Craddock says. "It was Ryan who took out Tommy Roy with his service pistol. That shot was close to fifty yards."

"Just proves fat men can run when they need to," Seth says, and we all laugh.

I study Ryan, his baby face not quite as babyish as when we'd raided the St. Borromeo students' party. Killing someone will do that to a person.

Ryan is looking at me, his lips slightly parted, brow furrowed. "When I dropped him, you were in the middle of the road, fending him off with a bayonet. You had to know he was going to kill you, but you stood your ground."

"Yeah, well, I wouldn't have stood for long. Lucky for me you scored so high in marksmanship, Kevin," I tell him, and his smile widens. "I bet the sergeant has a plan to give you a commendation for that."

Ryan's smile falters and he looks at Craddock, who looks at Seth.

"What?" I ask, but they grind their hands in their pockets and their eyes all go in different directions. Seth tells them to wait outside, that he'll join them in a minute.

When they've left, Seth squeezes my arm. "Sergeant Taylor had a heart attack a few days after you went missing. He was taken right away to the hospital but was dead on arrival."

I close my eyes, unable to cope with the swelling of grief, and let myself be carried under by the dark wave this time. As soon as the burning tears begin to leak from behind my closed eyelids, Seth leaves too.

I don't bother calling out to him to ask after Evangeline Roy. If they had found her, they would have told me. There are still too many unanswered questions about where she came from and how she managed to pull herself, in a relatively short time, to the top of the heap of the drug game in East Texas. If she's not dead, she's already regrouping, waiting for new followers. Waiting for uplift.

38

A week before Thanksgiving, Jackie and I move into our new home. It's a small two-bedroom house with a tiny yard—a starter house, I believe it's called—but the fixtures are new, the roof is solid, and the foundation is, as yet, uncracked. The neighbors seem unfazed by the appearance of lesbians on their tranquil, suburban shores.

A few days after my rescue from the Roys I had surgery to repair the ruptured Achilles tendon and spent the entire month of October clomping around in a cast and then a boot, watching too much television with my leg elevated on the couch, trying to keep my temper in check. I started rehab six weeks after surgery, but it was slow going. And I had the distinction of scaring away more physical therapists in seven days than any other patient in the history of the facility. Time will tell if I'll be able to walk without a limp, let alone run.

Thanksgiving Day, we invite everyone: all of Jackie's

family, including her truculent grandparents; Seth; Nadia, our Russian neighbor, and her two sons; even the general from Weatherford, sans Civil War uniform, who we discovered had been rendered homeless, reduced to living in his car. We sit at three different tables, somehow making conversation with one another, all of us gravitating to our most suitable dinner partners. Nadia and Rodean, Jackie's grandmother, exchange recipes, finding in common a love of all things made with root vegetables. Anne insists on serving Seth personally, pressing on him second and third helpings of everything, smothering him with motherly attention.

Jackie had asked me in my fever dream, the dream of being on the beach at Cape May, what I wanted out of life. "Joyful noise" is what I remember telling her.

She now pulls me aside between the soup and the turkey courses to tell me how happy she is. She hands me a gift-wrapped box and says, "Happy anniversary, Betty. Nine years ago today, I met a ferocious woman who changed my life. I can't imagine being in this world without you."

Inside the box is a new Saint Michael's medallion with a long silver chain. I smile and kiss her, then slip the chain around my neck. I will wear it every day, and I will go to my grave without admitting to her that the gift has made me profoundly sad. It's as though the new Saint Michael medal forever supplants the old, erasing all of the memories attached to it and affirming that the Saint Michael given to me by my mother and worn by three generations of Rhyzyk women is gone forever.

After dinner, I find James Earle and the general sitting in chairs in the backyard, talking about their war experiences, James in Vietnam, the general in Korea, and passing a flask amiably back and forth. Sergei and Jackie's nephew

Lonny volunteer to walk Rita the rescued poodle around the neighborhood, and they return an hour later, both wearing a light fog of marijuana.

After the orgy of pumpkin and pecan pies, the muted sounds of the football game—Green Bay being destroyed by Detroit—accompany the inevitable snores from men lapsing into sugar comas. I wander through the house like an invading spirit, searching for something to quell a sudden restlessness. I look at all of the people brought together by birth and by unlikely circumstance and remember the toast that James Earle had made outside of Babcock's Barbecue, calling us the unclaimed. For most people, that's true at least part of the time. For the rest of us, it's true most of the time.

Seth catches my eye and asks me if I knew that most Thanksgiving dinners take eighteen hours to prepare but are consumed in only twelve minutes. Halftimes at football games are twelve minutes, he reminds me. He tells me with a drowsy smile that he doesn't think that's at all a coincidence. I laugh and agree with him.

For a moment I think I'll flop down next to him on the couch, share with him the beer I've just opened, and confide to him that I might have been wrong about the answer I gave him to the question he posed to me that night at Slugger Anne's. He'd asked me what I had given up to be a great cop. My response, coming from a place of pride and more than a little defensiveness, had been that I had given up nothing.

My answer now might be very different. Or then again, it might not. To speak of it out loud would just be so much whining. I hand him the bottle and tell him I hate his guts for beating me back to work.

I walk to the front door, slip on a light jacket, and step

out onto the front porch for some air. It's late afternoon, the street empty and all too quiet. Benny's voice has been silent since my dream of the pay phone on the deserted Brooklyn street. I'm worried that I won't hear him until I'm able to run again.

My hand in my jacket pocket finds my car keys, and after sending a quick text to Jackie, I get in my car and drive off much too quickly, burning rubber in a way that will probably bring concerned neighbors out onto their front yards to look for hooligan teenagers.

I drive down to Riverfront Street and turn into the parking lot fronted by the two large cylindrical tanks, the bronze buffalo, the oil derrick, and the old-fashioned phone booth—the Fuel City truck stop, taco stand, and car wash, which I haven't visited since that day two years ago when I delivered my defiant message to the Dallas skyline. There are, even at this fading, twilight hour, a few cars and pickup trucks parked in the lot. Fuel City's doors are open 24/7, even on holidays, and half a dozen people are lined up at the brightly lit takeout windows to pick up their Thanksgiving tacos.

I limp to the back of the building and lean against the metal pen holding the small group of longhorns huddled together. The temperature is dropping, close to freezing, and the bars where my hands are resting are uncomfortably cold. I'm wearing only a thin leather jacket with no hat or gloves, and I've begun to shiver.

I look for and find the liver-spotted steer with the largest sweeping horns, the left one now broken at the tip. The cement wall at the back, the one painted with colorful balloons and the optimistic message WHERE DREAMS COME TRUE, has started to fade and crumble. It's pocked with small holes, and I wonder if maybe the old renegade got fed up with the hollowness of the sentiment and took a few runs at the wall.

The longhorn regards me dully until I climb through an opening between the poles and start walking slowly toward him. I look once over my shoulder, but no one seems to notice the tall, too-thin woman with shaggy red hair and a limp approaching the half-ton animal cautiously, like a wounded matador. The steer lowers his head defensively but there is no menacing shaking of horns. Just a few slow blinks and one long exhaled breath to let me know he has me in his sights.

I ease closer, within a few feet of his massive head, ready to stumble away should he commit to charging, and we eye each other for a while until he decides I'm not a threat. He lifts his head again, nostrils wide and open to the air, and I reach out one tentative finger and connect with the stiff hide, encrusted with Trinity River bottom dirt and smelling of diesel fumes.

I know that, when I'm ready, I'll have to face what I went through with the Family, to, in Uncle Benny's words, "reap some grim," to sick up all of the rage and frustration over being violated, ridding myself of their poison. To come to terms with the violence I inflicted on others. With Evangeline's slipping away.

In normal times, that would have meant pushing myself to run twelve miles when I was only prepared for seven.

I have another month and a half before I go back to work, on limited duty. It'll be strange walking into the station and not seeing Sergeant Taylor at his desk, his vital, get-it-done energy gone.

His replacement has already set up shop in his office. Another get-it-done cop who spent five years in Narcotics before being transferred to a different division. An ambitious man who then spent five years in Homicide. I'm speaking, of course, of Marshall Maclin.

The reflections of the lowering sun have begun firing off the glass buildings to the east; the electric lights blink on at the Reunion Tower, the tiny red Pegasus rotating in its slow and stately flight over the office buildings and the expensive high-rise apartment dwellings.

I turn and watch all the neon come on and I decide that, after all, it is a fucking beautiful skyline.

ACKNOWLEDGMENTS

This book would never have been written without David Hale Smith, editor of the *Dallas Noir* anthology, who challenged me to write a contemporary crime story for the collection, which was the foundation for *The Dime*. For that I am so very grateful.

My deepest gratitude also goes to my wonderful agent, Julie Barer, who encouraged me to explore new directions, and to my editor, Joshua Kendall, who enthusiastically embraced this project, guiding the manuscript with a keen editorial eye and a wicked sense of humor.

I am indebted to the following people for their generosity in sharing their time and expertise, assisting in the research for this book. Whatever I got wrong is totally on me: Det. Brantley Hickman of the Plano Police Department; Det. Marilyn Hay (ret.) and Det. Paul Park, both of the Dallas Police Department; Dr. Jeanne Joglar; Deana Kalley; and Dana and Julie Moon. Many thanks to Theo and Lorin Theodosiou for their spirited conversations and unstinting support.

My heartfelt thanks for all the incredible support from Mulholland Books and Little, Brown: Michael Pietsch, Reagan Arthur, Heather Fain, Nicole Dewey, Sabrina Callahan, and Pamela Brown. I now know that my life is charmed, because once more I got to work with the best copyeditors on the planet, Pamela Marshall and Tracy Roe.

And to all my family and friends who have supported and cheered me on, I will be forever grateful.

ABOUT THE AUTHOR

Kathleen Kent is the author of three bestselling historical novels, *The Heretic's Daughter, The Traitor's Wife,* and *The Outcasts*. She is also the author of the short story "Coincidences Can Kill You," published in *Dallas Noir,* which was the inspiration for *The Dime,* her first work of crime fiction. Kent lives in Dallas.